THE SIGN OF THE CAT

LYNNE JONELL

with illustrations by the author

SQUARE FISH

HENRY HOLT AND COMPANY ∾ NEW YORK

For Bill, with all my love

An imprint of Macmillan Publishing Group, LLC
175 Fifth Avenue
New York, NY 10010
mackids.com

Our books may be purchased in bulk for promotional, educational, or business use.
Please contact your local bookseller or the Macmillan Corporate and Premium
Sales Department at (800) 221-7945 ext. 5442 or by e-mail
at MacmillanSpecialMarkets@macmillan.com.

Library of Congress Cataloging-in-Publication Data

Jonell, Lynne.
The sign of the cat / Lynne Jonell.
pages cm
Summary: Duncan, eleven, is very smart with the rare ability to speak Cat, but his
mother has always insisted he appear only average, and when a perfect test score
draws attention to him, he not only discovers the wisdom of his mother's rules,
he finds himself crossing the seas on a quest for his true identity.
ISBN 978-1-250-07981-7 (paperback) — ISBN 978-0-8050-9684-2 (e-book)
[1. Identity—Fiction.   2. Cats—Fiction.   3. Adventure and adventurers—Fiction.
4. Ability—Fiction.   5. Mothers and sons—Fiction.   6. Fantasy.]   I. Title.

PZ7.J675Sig 2015
[Fic]—dc23

2015000787

Originally published in the United States by Christy Ottaviano Books/
Henry Holt and Company
First Square Fish Edition: 2016
Book designed by Véronique Lefèvre Sweet
Square Fish logo designed by Filomena Tuosto

1 3 5 7 9 10 8 6 4 2

AR: 5.4 / LEXILE: 770L

A ship in harbor is safe—
but that is not what ships are built for.

—John A. Shedd, *Salt from My Attic*, 1928

Contents

CHAPTER 1   *The Cat Speaker*   1

CHAPTER 2   *A Strange Sail*   12

CHAPTER 3   *Up the Drainpipe*   23

CHAPTER 4   *Not-So-Good News*   36

CHAPTER 5   *Graveyard Council*   52

CHAPTER 6   *A Visitor in the Night*   63

CHAPTER 7   *A Noble Summons*   80

CHAPTER 8   *Hero of the Nation*   91

CHAPTER 9   *A Glass of Cherry Punch*   107

CHAPTER 10   *Dangerous Duty*   114

CHAPTER 11   *The Bloodstained Jacket*   128

CHAPTER 12   *Squisher and Grinder*   139

CHAPTER 13   *The Unknown Enemy*   154

CHAPTER 14   *Overboard*   166

CHAPTER 15   *Lost at Sea*   178

CHAPTER 16   *The Sea Cave*   190

CHAPTER 17   *The Princess Lydia*   205

CHAPTER 18   *Traitor Island*   215

CHAPTER 19   *Building the Raft*   227

CHAPTER 20   *Shadow Fight*   241

CHAPTER 21   *Duke's Island*   250

CHAPTER 22   *Captured!*   260

CHAPTER 23   *In the Cage*   272

CHAPTER 24   *The Rusty Lock*   286

CHAPTER 25   *Army of Cats*   303

CHAPTER 26   *The Young Duke*   312

CHAPTER 27   *Cat Justice*   327

CHAPTER 28   *Kittens' Revenge*   341

BONUS MATERIALS   360

Island
of Dulle

Capital
City

Duke's
Island

The
Arvidian
Sea

The Kingdom of
ARVIDIA

CHAPTER 1

The Cat Speaker

DUNCAN WAS A BOY WHO COULD SPEAK CAT.

He had known cat language since he was small, because the cat who lived at his house took the trouble to teach him. It wasn't until he was a little older that he realized this was highly unusual.

Of course, all humans would be able to speak Cat if they were taught at the right age. But as most cats can't be bothered, the right age goes by for nine hundred and ninety-nine out of one thousand, and the chance is lost forever.

Duncan McKay was one in a thousand. Maybe even one in a million. Not that it was helpful to him now. He fingered the report card in his pocket nervously as he sat on the second-floor landing, watching through the window for his mother to appear on the crooked street below their house. He had gotten too many As this term, and she would be upset.

"Why me?" he asked Grizel, who was a very old cat by this time. "Why did you teach me to speak Cat?"

Grizel did not answer. She was crouched halfway down the stairs, watching a mouse hole. There had never been a mouse there, not once, but she was not a cat to neglect her duty.

Duncan kicked a heel against the old black sea chest that served as a window seat, and gazed out over the island cliffs to the sea. He hated not getting answers to perfectly reasonable questions. He was eleven and big for his age, and he was tired of being treated like a little boy. "Why me?" he asked again, a little louder.

"Why not?" Grizel snapped. She was testy about the subject; the other cats made fun of her because of it, and she had regretted teaching him more than once. Still, she was not a bad-tempered cat. She wouldn't have snapped at him if she hadn't been cranky from hunger and disappointed about the mouse.

She turned away from the mouse hole and looked up at the boy who sat on the second-floor landing. His face was shaded, but the afternoon sun streamed through the stairwell window and brightened his rough gray pants with their twice-patched knees.

A cat will hardly ever apologize for being rude. It usually doesn't see the point. But Duncan's lap looked warm and full of sun, and Grizel's spot on the stairs had fallen into shadow.

She butted her head against Duncan's leg, blinked, and opened her eyes wide, with a tiny upward twist between her brows. This was Cat Trick #9: Melting Kitty Eyes. She had not been a kitten for a long time, but she could still act adorable when necessary.

Duncan took her on his lap and began to stroke her behind the ears.

Grizel kneaded his stomach with her paws. "I taught you to speak Cat because I felt sorry for you when your father died," she said. "All in all, I think I did a good thing. I've been able to explain why fresh tuna is better than the stuff in a can, for instance. And you have quite a knack for purring."

"That's nice if you're a cat," Duncan said, watching out the stairwell window for his mother. "Only, I'm a boy."

"You can't help that," said Grizel. "I've never held it against you."

Duncan didn't answer; he was trying to remember when his father had died. Had there been a funeral? He had been very small. There had been a forest of black-trousered legs around him, and someone smelling of pipe tobacco had picked him up and whispered gruffly in his ear. "You'll be the man of the house now," the voice had said. "You'll have to take good care of your mother."

Duncan had tried. While he was still too young for school, he tied an old shirt around his neck for a cape and practiced fighting evil villains. When he was a little older, he gave his mother all the copper pennies he found in the street. And when he was older still, he began to do small jobs at the houses where his mother taught music lessons. He gave her the coins he earned—at first the common five- and tenpenny pieces, later the larger brass barons and, on occasion, a silver-edged earl—and he tried hard to obey her rules, even the strange ones.

But some of her rules were very strange indeed.

Duncan unfolded his report card and looked at his grades with a sigh. He had made sure to get five questions wrong on his last history test, but it hadn't been enough.

Grizel tapped at the report card with her paw. "You could tell her that A means 'Average.' Or 'Actually Not That Good.'"

Duncan snorted.

"It could also mean 'Annoying,' or 'Atrocious,' or 'Abominable'—"

"What are you, a dictionary?"

"Or you could change the As to Bs," Grizel suggested. "Just draw a line along the bottom. And smudge over the pointy top."

"That never works." Duncan knew this because he had tried it before. "I could make it an A minus, maybe, but that's about all."

Grizel yawned, showing delicately pointed teeth and a small pink tongue. "Why don't you just get a few more wrong? There's nothing so hard in that."

"I hate getting things wrong," Duncan muttered.

"Other boys," Grizel observed, "would be pleased to have a mother who didn't push them to get good grades. Other boys would be *grateful*."

Duncan did not particularly care how grateful other boys might be and made this point under his breath.

Grizel flicked her tail and went on as if she hadn't heard. "A good son might have a little faith in his own mother. A clever boy might understand that she had a *reason*—"

"For what?" The report card crinkled in Duncan's hand. "For telling me never to get a gold star, or earn a medal, or win a prize? For telling me I should never stand out?"

"For keeping you hidden," Grizel said sharply. "And safe."

Something cold patted quietly inside Duncan's chest. "Am I in danger?"

"Did I say that?" Grizel closed her eyes until they were slits in her furry golden face. "I don't recall using that word."

"You said 'safe.' And 'hidden.' So there's got to be something she's keeping me hidden from, right?"

Grizel sank her shoulders more deeply into the round curve of her body. She seemed to grow more solid. A faint snore escaped her.

Exasperated, Duncan bounced his knees up and down. The cat held on with her claws, her eyes tightly shut.

"There's no danger," said Duncan. "You made that up. This is the safest, most boring island in all Arvidia. It's even named Dulle, which should tell you something."

The snoring grew louder.

"Fine. Be that way." Duncan detached Grizel's claws from his leg one by one, set her on the floor, and looked through the window again. His mother wasn't on the street that led to their house, and he couldn't see her walking up the steep cliffside road.

Instead, he saw a striped tabby cat rounding the corner. Its head was up, its tail well back, and altogether it had the purposeful look of a cat with business to accomplish.

It stopped beneath their window and looked up, meowing.

Grizel put her forepaws on the windowsill. Duncan opened the window and leaned out. "What?" he meowed back.

Grizel nudged Duncan aside with her head. "It's for me," she hissed. And to the cat in the street below she meowed, "What news?"

"Cat Council tonight," called the tabby. "At moonrise. In the graveyard."

"What for?" Grizel asked. "What's on the agenda?"

"Kitten examinations," said the tabby. "Territory disputes. Dog-taunting assignments. Old Tom warning about impending disaster. The usual."

Duncan grinned. He loved kitten examinations.

"Can't stay to talk—lots more cats to notify," said the tabby, turning away.

"I'll be there," called Grizel to the cat's retreating back, and its tail swished once in acknowledgment.

"I'm going, too," said Duncan.

Grizel leaped onto his lap. "If you do, the other cats will make fun of me again. They'll say, 'Can't she go anywhere without that red-haired *master*?'"

Duncan rubbed the top of her head gently with his knuckles. "I'm not your master, and they know it. And my hair isn't red anymore. It got darker this year—it's practically brown. Especially on a cloudy day."

Grizel settled herself more comfortably, curling her tail around her flanks. "You shouldn't go. Your mother wouldn't like it if she knew you were sneaking out at night."

Duncan was silent. Of course his mother wouldn't like it. But it wasn't as if he was doing anything *bad*.

"If I don't tell her," he pointed out, "she won't need to worry."

Grizel looked at him through half-shut eyes. "A mother's rules are for her kitten's own good."

"I'm not breaking any rules," Duncan said firmly. "My mother never said, 'No going to cat councils in graveyards.' Not once."

Grizel made a small huffing noise. "She may not have said that *exactly*—"

"See? You even agree with me." Duncan curled his fingers around the cat's bony jaw and began to scratch her under the chin. "Good kitty, *nice* kitty." He let his fingers pause. "Promise you'll wake me up in time to go?"

Grizel tipped her head and squeezed her eyes almost shut. "Scratch a little more to the side, and I will . . . yes, right *there*." A rumbling vibration began in her chest as she subsided into a contented purring.

Duncan did not want to be a bad son. But there was no way his mother would understand about the cat council, and he would rather not mention the graveyard. She always got a worried look on her face when he visited the grave she had told him was his father's.

He scanned the cliffside road again. Maybe his mother was teaching an extra piano lesson today. He should probably set the table for supper. And maybe tonight he could offer to play their old game of Noble Manners. It was getting boring for him (what use was it to learn all the customs and dances and courtesies of nobles—barons and earls and dukes—when he would never be one?), but it seemed to please his mother. With any luck, she would forget to ask for his report card.

Grizel gave a little mew of protest. Duncan, who had forgotten to keep his fingers moving, began to scratch again, this time behind the cat's ears.

Petting a cat was not the most exciting thing in the world. Still, it was pleasant, sitting in his favorite spot on the stairs. The small window overlooked the bay far below, curved and shining in the late-afternoon light, and he could see the fishing boats coming in from the sea, floating like curled-up leaves on the water. Halfway up the hill, the rooftops of his monastery school flashed orange and gold in the sun.

Duncan and his mother lived in the cliffside part of the

island of Dulle, where the sun scorched them in summer and the sea wind scoured them in winter. It was a long walk down to the bay, and they did not often have the money to pay for the freshest fish. But Duncan loved the little house that was tucked under the overhanging cliffs. He loved being up high where he could see everything spread out beneath him, as if he were a king looking out over his realm. And sometimes at night, if there was no mist, he could even make out the glittering lights of Capital City on the far curving edge of the sea.

Someday he would sail there to make his fortune. And then he would be able to take care of his mother so she wouldn't be afraid anymore. He didn't know what Sylvia McKay was afraid of, exactly, but he was sure that when he was a man, he would be able to protect her from whatever it was.

Something moved at the edge of Duncan's vision. He snapped his gaze to the street below and saw a tiny white kitten.

It looked like Fia, a kitten he had seen roaming the monastery school. He had given her treats once or twice. But what was she doing out alone?

The kitten blinked up at his window. Even from this height, Duncan could see the startling difference in her eyes—one blue and one green. It was Fia, all right.

He slid Grizel gently off his lap and thumped down the stairs in his socks. He undid the double lock that his mother

9

had installed—*snick, snick*—and he was out on the cobbled street, paved with stones as smooth as the Arvidian Sea could make them.

"What is it, Fia?" He sat down on the doorstep, its rough edges warm beneath his hands. "Are you lost?"

"Not me!" Fia swiped a tiny paw at Duncan's knee. "Only *baby* cats get lost!"

"Ah," said Duncan.

Grizel slipped through the open door and gave the kitten a disapproving look. "Where's your mother? You shouldn't be out on the street by yourself."

Fia switched her tail. "I'm just as big as my littermates— well, almost—and *they* can go out by themselves. Anyway, I have a message."

Grizel shook her head. "You can't be a messenger cat. You haven't even passed your kitten examinations yet."

"I'm *going* to pass them," said Fia with dignity. "And I'm *practicing* to be a messenger cat. And I have news for Dunc—"

Fia stopped midword and swallowed hard. She tensed as if to dart away, but she was too slow for the cream-colored cat who streaked from behind a flowerpot and bowled her over with the force of a small, four-legged truck.

The white kitten squirmed under the pressure of two firm paws.

"*I* have news for *you*," said Fia's mother. "You do *not* leave the monastery grounds unless I am with you. Do I make myself clear?"

"But I want to tell Duncan something!"

The cream-colored cat stiffened her whiskers. "Are you a cat or a postmaster?" she demanded. "We cats do not concern ourselves with human affairs. We have enough to do with our own. And I certainly have enough to do with looking after one harum-scarum little kitten who can't seem to obey the rules."

Grizel coughed behind one paw. "Human affairs aren't *completely* without interest, Mabel. You have to admit that you usually wander down to the bay when the boats come in. And you're not too proud to beg for a fish head or two."

Mabel drew herself up with dignity. "Of course I don't expect you to understand," she said frostily. "You've never been a mother—you haven't a mother's feelings. But I, who must provide for my litters—"

"One every year," Grizel murmured to Duncan.

"—must get proper nourishment. Come along, Fia. We needn't waste any more time." She picked Fia up by the scruff of the neck and stalked away.

"But what about my message?" Duncan meowed after them. "What's your news, Fia?"

Fia's small voice came floating back. "Your mother is—"

Fia's words were cut short by a fierce shake, and Mabel, with the kitten dangling from her mouth, disappeared around the corner.

CHAPTER 2
A Strange Sail

D UNCAN KNEW WHAT HE WAS SUPPOSED TO DO if his mother was working late—do his homework, make himself something to eat. But today had been the day when they took the national tests at the monastery school, and Friar Gregory, his teacher, had assigned no homework.

Grizel butted his leg with her head. "What about supper?"

At the word, Duncan's stomach sent up a small grumbling sound of discontent. He opened the icebox and saw what he had expected to see: a little bread, a little cheese, a couple of wilted carrots. Enough for one person, perhaps, but certainly not for two.

Duncan chewed on a fingernail. If he ate it all, his mother would come home to nothing. She would say she wasn't hungry, of course—or she would say that they had fed her supper at her last music lesson. It might even be true.

He closed the icebox slowly. Probably his mother was fine. Probably she had something to eat. And whatever Fia had wanted to tell him about his mother, it was probably something that only a kitten would think was important.

"Try the sea chest," suggested Grizel, who had seen what was in the icebox and had not been impressed. "I've seen her take money out of it, in an emergency."

Duncan glanced up the stairway to the landing. The old black sea chest with its brass bindings had been there as long as he could remember, but his mother kept it locked, and he had never once seen inside. "This isn't exactly an emergency," said Duncan.

"Of *course* it's an emergency." Grizel's meow was insistent. "There's no *fish*."

"There's no money, anyway. If there were, she would have bought some food." Duncan shrugged, trying not to care that the icebox was nearly empty. He pursed his lips in a whistle and pounded up the stairs to the window again. Maybe his mother was coming up the road by now. Maybe she was late because someone had paid her early and she had stopped to buy groceries.

The cliffside road was still empty, but in the bay below there was plenty of motion. The fishing boats were closer now, inside the sweep of beach that curled around the bay like a cat's tail. People, so small from this distance they looked like moving black dots, gathered at the shore, waiting to buy fresh fish for their suppers.

But there was something else moving. A scrap of white, out at sea. Duncan leaned out the open window and shaded his eyes, squinting. A sail, but on what boat? The fishing boats were almost in. And the big supply ship from Capital City had already come yesterday and gone again.

He licked his finger and tested the breeze. The boat at sea had her sail out full—she was running before the wind, heading straight for the island of Dulle. She might enter the bay in a half hour.

Grizel brushed up against his side and gave an inquisitive meow.

"There's a new boat coming in," said Duncan. He stepped over Grizel and hurried down the stairs.

"And where do you think you're going?" The cat followed him, her whiskers stiff.

"Down to the wharf. There might be mail. There might be news." Duncan yanked on his boots and promptly broke a bootlace. He grunted his impatience and tied a reef knot to join the broken ends. Hanging around sailors was useful— he'd learned all his knots from them years ago.

"There might be trouble from your mother if you go down to the docks." Grizel planted herself in front of the door and fluffed out her fur to make herself seem bigger. "You know she doesn't allow you to go there when the ship from Capital City comes in."

Duncan pushed the end of his bootlace carefully through the eyelets. "She doesn't allow me to go when the *supply* ship comes in. That's because it's big and uses dangerous equipment for unloading. But this is only a sailboat, and it looks pretty small to me." He knotted his laces tightly. A boy who was clever and quick on his feet stood a good chance of making some extra money if he got to the wharf when a boat first docked. The skipper might need an errand run or a message delivered.

"But your mother will worry!"

"She won't know I've gone until I get back safely. And she'll like it if I bring some fish for supper." Duncan stood up.

Grizel's ears pricked forward with sudden interest. "Or eels?"

Duncan reached for the door. "You won't get anything if you don't move out of my way."

Grizel hesitated. "Put on your cap, then. You told your mother you would. And I'm coming with you."

Duncan rolled his eyes. The leather cap his mother insisted he wear when he went outside was a little much, in his opinion. With the earflaps down, it covered every bit of his dark red hair, and it even buckled under the chin. It was a good cap to have when the sea wind turned cold—the other boys had caps like it, too—but it was stupid to wear it on a sunny afternoon. Still, Grizel was right. He had promised.

"You'd better fasten the chin straps," said Grizel, but Duncan ignored her. Only little boys buckled their caps.

Duncan galloped down the cobblestone streets, his chin straps flapping. The narrow lanes were shadowed in the late afternoon, but the flower boxes were full of bright color, and the scent of freesias filled the air. *Clatter, clatter* went Duncan's boots, and the noise echoed off the houses, built from gray island stone so long ago that moss had crept up almost to the windows. The doors were painted blue, or green, or red, and windows were hung with curtains of the thick white lace that island women tatted, sitting in the sun. Duncan had seen them at their work, elderly women with knobby fingers, and he knew their cats.

"Slow down!" cried Grizel. "I'm not a young cat anymore!"

Duncan looked back at the small moving patch of fur a full block behind and felt a pang. Grizel *was* an old cat—he hadn't realized how old. But if he went much slower, he might not be at the wharf when the boat docked, and someone else would get whatever jobs were going.

"I'll wait up at the bookstore," he called back, seeing the familiar green awning ahead. It wouldn't hurt to wait one minute, and he wanted to see if the bookseller had turned the page.

He skidded to a stop and pressed his nose against the bookstore window. The book he'd looked at every day for three weeks was still on display, but the page hadn't been turned since yesterday.

"*A Recent History of Arvidia*," he murmured hurriedly to

16

himself, saying the title aloud for the pleasure of it. *"Being the True Tale of Kings and Queens, True Loves and Vile Hates, Clashes at Sea and on Land, Together with an Account of Great Ships and Their Builders."* A sign next to the book said, INCLUDES MAJOR EVENTS OF THE PAST TEN YEARS!

Duncan looked hungrily at the picture, which showed a three-masted ship being built, and wished that he could see the illustration on the next page. Maybe it would show directions for building a smaller boat. The fishermen had taught him how to mend a boat, but he had never built one from scratch.

"You could go *in* the bookshop," said Grizel, arriving slightly out of breath. "Then you could open any book you like."

"No money," said Duncan briefly. "Let's go."

"It doesn't cost anything to look." Grizel gazed wistfully at the bookshop. The owner was generous with kitty treats, in her experience, and she wanted one.

Duncan scuffed the toe of his boot over a loose pebble. He never liked to go into any shop unless he had coins in his pocket. Then, if he didn't buy anything, it would be because he didn't *choose* to, not because he couldn't.

Grizel stared at him with her yellow eyes. "You have too much pride," she said. "You have the pride of a Mc—" She coughed delicately and spit up a furball.

Duncan kicked up the loose gray pebble and dropped it into his pocket. He glanced down the long, narrow street, already crowded with people hurrying home from work or shopping. "Let's go. Do you want me to carry you?"

Grizel's whiskers twitched as she looked around. "Other cats might see."

"Now who's too proud?" Duncan grinned. "Keep up if you can. I'll meet you at the docks if you get that far."

He stepped over Grizel's furball, dodged a woman with a market basket, and took off at a cheerful trot. Today might be his lucky day. Maybe the sailboat was owned by a rich person—a noble, say—who would pay extra because Duncan was so quick and polite. Maybe Duncan would earn enough to buy food *and* the history book in the display window. He loved history the most of all his subjects; it just about killed him to get poor grades in it.

He hadn't gotten a poor grade today, though, on the national tests—he was almost sure of it. Best of all, his mother would never find out.

The cobblestones rounded under Duncan's feet as he ran, and his legs gave an exuberant spring. Snatches of sound came and went in his ears—the clatter of pans, a burst of conversation, a barking dog. Narrow houses loomed overhead, breathing cold from their mossy foundations, and his boots made an echo like the footsteps of a giant. He turned a corner without slowing, and a gathering of seagulls exploded suddenly in a flurry of feather and noise.

He jerked back instinctively and looked over his shoulder.

Had anyone heard the commotion? Had he drawn attention to himself?

Duncan winced and shook his head. That was his mother's fear, not his. It was his mother who told him to keep quiet, to stay in the background. It was his mother who worried if his grades were too good, or if he came close to winning a race.

A single clear note rang in the air: the monastery bell, ringing the quarter hour. The shadowed lane was cool, and Duncan shivered lightly as the sweat dried on his skin.

He did not like to think that something was wrong with his mother. But no other mother he knew wanted her child to be second-best.

At the end of the long row of tall houses, a blue rectangle of sky grew steadily larger. He was almost to the lower cliff road, and that was halfway down to the wharf. If Grizel was behind him, Duncan couldn't see her. Perhaps she had gotten tired and gone home.

He emerged onto the hot, bright limestone track, with the monastery school a stone's throw away and the bay shimmering cool beyond. Big blocks of squared stone edged the roadway, and Duncan climbed onto one to get a better view, shading his eyes against the reflected sparkles of the sea. The white scrap of sail had grown larger. He had been right; it was not a very big boat, certainly not big enough to be called a ship. It had only a mainsail and a jib. Still, it looked fast and well handled—but unbelievably, the boat was still sailing on a broad reach. Couldn't the skipper see the rocks on the point? If he wanted to enter the bay, he would have to tack in a hurry. There was no reason to cut the point that close, no reason in the world . . .

Unless the boat wasn't going to enter the bay at all.

Duncan scrambled off the stone blocks, ran uphill to a headland that extended beyond the road, and forced his way through a mass of junipers to get to the opposite side. He turned his back on the bay and looked to the west, where the sea crashed heavily against the stark cliffs. There was no bay to speak of on this side of the island, no sheltered spot where a boat could anchor in safety. The sailboat was going to pass the island by.

His stomach growled, complaining. Duncan bent over to ease the empty feeling in his middle and picked up a smooth white rock he saw at his feet. It was warm from the sun, and he held it tightly.

The sailboat was close enough now for him to see a jaunty blue pennant streaming from the mast. It made a tempting target. Duncan tossed the stone up and down in his hand— but he didn't throw it. It wasn't the sailboat's fault that he was hungry and needed to earn money. He dropped the rock in his pocket to keep the gray pebble company and turned back to the road.

Grizel, limping slightly, emerged from the shadowed street, stalked to the road's edge, and stared out to sea with narrowed

eyes. Her head moved slowly, following the course of the triangular sail.

On the hillside below, rooftops shone like copper in the
last rays of the sun. Beneath them, in the spacious bayside
houses, children were sitting down to suppers of roast chicken
and potatoes and greens. They were being told to clean their
plates or they wouldn't get dessert. Some of them were pouting.

Duncan knew this because he had been in their large and
beautiful homes. At one time or another, his mother had
taught music to most of the island's children, and he had gone
with her. It was only in the past year that she had allowed him
to stay on his own while she taught music lessons after school.
But he hadn't forgotten what he had seen and heard while
playing quietly in the corner or reading a borrowed book behind the potted palms.

Grizel curled her tail around his knee. "We can still go
down to the beach. There might be fish heads to eat."

Hands jammed deeper into his pockets, Duncan scanned
the waterfront. The fishermen had already pulled their boats
up onto the beach opposite the wharf where larger boats
docked. Fishermen mostly did their own work, but sometimes
he had helped them splice ropes or repair nets. If he was helpful enough, he might be given a leftover fish. It would be one
from the day before, one that wasn't quite fresh.

"Or," Grizel continued, butting her blunt head against his
shin, "we could go down to the baron's manor house. They

have a new cat living there, I'm told. I hear he gets a lot of extra kitty treats."

"That's nice for you," said Duncan. "I can't say *I* like them."

"Robert usually has a tin of something to eat in his room," Grizel pointed out.

Duncan gave this some thought. Robert was the baron's son, and Robert's little sister, Betsy, took piano lessons from Sylvia McKay. Last year, Robert and Duncan had played at sword fighting together, whacking each other with sticks all up and down the green lawn of the baron's estate. Robert would undoubtedly have something to eat stashed in his room, and he would almost certainly share with Duncan, if he were asked. But Duncan hated the thought of going down there to beg for food.

"And you could walk your mother home," Grizel suggested. "She's teaching a piano lesson there right now."

Duncan was startled. "How do you know?"

Grizel rolled her eyes. "I shall never cease to be amazed at the inadequacy of the human ear. Honestly, can't you hear your mother's voice? She's counting out the rhythm to 'King's March.'" Grizel cocked her head to one side, her ears pricked forward. "Young Betsy doesn't seem to have mastered the concept of six-eight time, I'm sorry to say."

CHAPTER 3
Up the Drainpipe

DUNCAN STOOD ON THE DAMP GRASS at the back of the baron's manor house. Above him, on the broad window ledge, a large smoke-colored Persian was napping in the slanting rays of the afternoon sun. The tip of his silvery tail hung over the edge.

"Go on, ask him!" Grizel hissed.

The tail twitched slightly.

"Mrraow?" Duncan gave the mild, inquisitive meow that informed a cat he had no aggressive intentions. Lacking a tail to indicate his attitude, he tilted his head in a friendly gesture.

The smoky gray cat rose, stretched his massive body, and looked down with the permanently irritated expression of all Persian cats. "Name?" he inquired. "Territory?"

"Duncan McKay, of cliffside." Duncan waved his hand in Grizel's direction. "And Grizel."

"Business?"

Duncan glanced at Grizel, who examined her paw with apparent deep interest. "We just wanted to say welcome to the island, and make sure you got the invitation to the cat council tonight."

"*Kitty treats*," coughed Grizel behind her paw.

Duncan ignored her. "Oh, and have you seen my mother? I think she's teaching a music lesson."

The Persian's flat, squashed face underwent a contortion that Duncan realized was meant for a smile. "Ah, yes—Mrs. McKay. She plays a lovely violin. By the way, since when do boys speak Cat?"

Duncan ignored this last question. "You must mean she plays the piano. She doesn't play the violin."

The Persian's smile disappeared. "I suppose next you're going to tell me that I haven't sat by her feet and listened? Her playing is lovely, lovely. . . . It makes me think of tender, plump little mice. . . ."

"It makes me think of delicate little songbirds," Grizel interjected dreamily.

Duncan stared at her. "You've heard her play the violin?"

Grizel jumped back a little, her ears alert. "No, no, I was just *imagining*. Because she's such a lovely woman, see? *If* she played the violin, I think it would sound very sweet indeed." She turned to the smoky Persian with a decided change of subject. "And you are?" she inquired. "I don't believe I caught your name, sir."

The Persian frowned again. "You can call me—"

"Mr. Fluffers!" The high-pitched call came from the room behind the cat. The Persian made a sudden motion, as if to dart away, but his bulk kept him from moving quickly enough. A little girl's hands grasped him beneath the shoulders and picked him up. He dangled there as Betsy rubbed her face against his fluffy neck, his expression one of long-suffering resignation.

"There you are, Mr. Fluffers! I've been looking all over for you! Naughty kitty, to run away and hide during my piano lesson!"

Mr. *Fluffers*? Duncan did not exactly laugh, but it was a near thing. Down by his ankles, Grizel pretended to cough.

The Persian gazed down at them from his helpless position, haunches swaying as Betsy rocked him. "I prefer," he said in a strained meow, "to be called Spike."

Duncan felt his face undergo a spasm. It was a terrible thing to laugh at cats—they never forgot the affront to their dignity. But if he didn't laugh soon, he thought he might burst from the strain. He made a massive effort and kept his expression serious.

Betsy leaned out the window and grinned at him. "Robert's stuck in his room," she said cheerfully. "In disgrace. The rest of us have to go to dinner. And your mother is in the music room. She said she has to arrange some music for me, so the cook sent up a supper tray to her."

Duncan grinned right back. He had forgotten how much

he liked Robert's little sister. She had told him everything he needed to know, without fuss and without his even asking. Still, for Grizel's sake, he had one more question. "Are you taking Mr. Fluf—um—the cat to the dining room with you?"

Betsy shook her head, and her pigtails whipped back and forth. "He goes to the kitchen, where his bowl is." She looked down at Grizel, who was gazing at her earnestly. "Your cat can come to the kitchen door if she wants. I'll put out some extra sardines and kitty treats for her. Mr. Fluffers is already too fat, anyway. Aren't you, Fluffy Wuffy?"

The Persian shut his eyes as if in pain. "If any particular cat," he remarked, "cares to join me for dinner, I simply beg that she will remember my preferred title—"

He choked a little as Betsy pulled him back inside.

"I'd be delighted to join you, Mr. Fluf—I mean—Spike!" meowed Grizel, and she moved with alacrity along the shrubbery, disappearing around the corner of the house.

Betsy poked her head out the window one last time. "Robert could probably use someone to cheer him up while the rest of us are having dinner. You can still climb the drainpipe, can't you?"

Of course he could; Duncan swarmed up the familiar drainpipe as quickly as a cat. The metal brackets rattled under his weight, and his boots scraped on the rough brick, but if the family was at dinner, no one would hear him—the dining room was at the far end of the manor. And any of the baron's guards, standing their usual watch in the corner tower, would be looking out to sea for incoming ships. Maybe they, too, had seen the sailboat with its jaunty blue streamer. Maybe they were also wondering why it had come so close to the island if it was just going to pass by. It wasn't as if it could have anchored on the rugged west side; there was nothing there but steep cliffs and a few goat paths.

Gripping the second-story ledge, Duncan got an elbow up, and then a knee. Robert's room was the third window on the left. It had been a long time since Duncan had visited the manor house; once he'd stopped accompanying his mother to her music lessons, there had been no reason, really. Robert had a tutor and a club where he went with the other island children who had the money to join, and their paths just hadn't crossed.

With a mighty effort, Duncan heaved himself onto the broad stone shelf that ran around the manor beneath the windows. He couldn't avoid a clatter as his foot banged against the drainpipe.

Whoosh! The sash of Robert's window flew up. A head poked out, the hair brown and curly. Robert caught sight of Duncan, and his mouth opened in astonishment.

Duncan put a finger to his lips.

"What's that racket out there?" The voice coming from inside the room was a little loud, a little annoyed, and clearly accustomed to command.

Robert gave Duncan a wink and pulled his head back into the room. "Maybe it was a squirrel climbing the drainpipe?"

The baron grumbled some more but, to Duncan's intense

relief, did not put his head out to look. The last time Duncan had paid a visit, he had accidentally stampeded the sheep that the baron kept around to crop his grass—if *stampede* was the right word for the bunching, stupid way they all scattered at the least little thing—and the baron had not been happy.

Duncan pressed himself against the outside wall and breathed quietly in and out. Inside the room, the baron still talked, and his voice floated clearly through the open window.

". . . and no son of mine is going to fail to get into the Academy. Is that clear?"

Robert's reply was an unhappy mumble.

"Of course you want to go!" The baron's voice took on a piercing note. "You've been on the list since you were born. You're a noble's son. You're going to be properly educated, and that means you're going to the Academy in Capital City."

Duncan felt a sudden constriction in his chest like a fist gripping. Although Robert might have trouble getting into the Academy, there was no question that his family had the money to send him. Robert's passage would be paid on the finest ship, his trunks would be packed with new clothes, he would have all the books and pocket money he wanted. . . .

Then, someday, Robert would come back and be the baron, and Duncan would take off his cap to him.

Duncan swallowed the bitter taste in his mouth. He tried to remember that Robert was his friend.

The baron was still rumbling away in tones of deep displeasure. His voice had lowered, but Duncan heard enough to understand that Robert, too, had taken the national tests that day. Being the baron's son, with a private tutor, his test had been graded immediately. And Robert had failed.

Duncan's breath quickened. He had beaten Robert—he was almost sure of it. Robert would never know, of course.

Duncan's mother would never know, either. Scores for the national tests were not put on report cards. They were not published in the paper. And last year, when the test results were handed out, Duncan had forgotten to show them to his mother.

She had never missed them. That was when Duncan had decided to study hard, all year, for the next national test. Because just once, he wanted to do his very best. Just once, he wanted to see how he really measured up against everyone else.

He had taken that test today. And soon, maybe in a week or so when the tests were scored, he would know how he had done.

The baron's voice, which had been rising and falling all this while, rose one more time: "—expect you to study an extra three hours each day. You'll take the makeup test at the end of the month, and you had better pass it, my boy."

There was a sound of a door being forcefully closed, and then Robert's head popped out again. "Quick! Get in!"

Duncan swung his legs through the window and dropped to the floor. Robert grinned, sizing him up. "You're bigger than the last time I saw you. Want to have a sword fight? I got real sabers for my birthday!"

Two crossed sabers hung on the wall. Their edges were

blunted with thin rubber, naturally, but they looked beautifully dangerous all the same. Duncan took one down and curled his fingers around the grip. The steel was cool to his hand, and perfectly balanced. He swished it through the air.

Robert ducked.

"Sorry," said Duncan. "Couldn't resist."

But Robert already had the other saber in his hand. "Fight! Fight!"

Duncan shook his head. "There isn't enough room in here for a real sword fight."

"Let's go outside," Robert begged.

"I thought you had to study." Duncan trailed his finger along the edge of Robert's bookshelf. It was jammed with books.

Robert shrugged. "I have a whole month to do that. My father wants me to practice swordsmanship, too, because he wants me to make the fencing team at the Academy. And my tutor thinks they'll probably let me in on academic probation. I only missed a passing grade by three questions."

"Don't you have to eat dinner now?" Duncan's hollow stomach twisted painfully.

Robert rolled his eyes. "I'm supposed to go without dinner tonight because of my score on the test. I don't care, though— I've got emergency supplies." He pulled out a dictionary, a math book, and a volume of Arvidian history, and reached behind them. He retrieved a shallow metal box and opened it to reveal a stack of chocolate bars wrapped in silver foil.

The creamy scent of chocolate rose from the tin, and

Duncan's mouth filled with water. He swallowed painfully and turned his eyes to the history book. "Hey, this is the new one that includes current events! I saw it in the bookstore window—it just came out last month."

Robert shrugged. "My father thinks that if he gets me more books, I'll get better grades." He held out the metal tin. "You can have as much chocolate as you want, if you give me a bout with the sabers."

Duncan picked up the book with a casual air. "Can I borrow this, too?"

Robert grinned. "Keep it. Just give me my saber battle."

Duncan didn't take long to decide. "All right. I'll just let my mother know I'm here, so she doesn't leave without me." He tucked two bars of chocolate into his pockets, took a bite of a third, and opened the door to the hall. He knew the way to the music room. He had sat there often enough in years past, kicking his heels and looking at all the different instruments in their cases, ready for guests who wanted to play.

The chocolate melted slowly on Duncan's tongue. His footsteps were muffled on the ornately patterned rug that ran the length of the hallway, and above him, portraits of Robert's ancestors, going back hundreds of years, stared down from the walls.

Lucky Robert. Anytime he wanted to know what his great-great-great-grandfather looked like, or any other relative, he could just walk up to a painting.

Duncan would settle for a picture of his father. He had never seen one, although his mother said that all he had to do was look in the mirror to get a good idea. He supposed that meant his father had a long nose and gray eyes and dark red hair, nearly brown. Still, it was only a boy's face that looked back at him from the mirror, not a man's.

He stepped into the fore-chamber of the music room. This was a little alcove where someone could wait, listening, without disturbing the musicians until the song ended. The velvet curtain in the archway was hanging straight down. He was reaching out to pull it back, when suddenly a sweet, muted vibration filled the air. He cocked his head, listening. A violin? It was being played so softly that he hadn't heard it out in the hall. He didn't know it was possible to play a violin that softly—or that sweetly.

The tune was simple; the notes were long and slow, not flashy or difficult at all. Even so, there was something about the tone that seemed to fill his heart almost to bursting. He pulled back the curtain an inch and looked through the gap. Sylvia McKay's back was to him; he saw a side view of her in one of the mirrors that lined the room. He took in his breath, startled.

She had tossed off the ugly green scarf that she wore everywhere and shaken out her wavy brown hair. Her shoulders, usually stooped, were thrown back, and in the curve of her bow arm, there was a sense of sureness and mastery that he had never seen before. Her eyes were closed and her thin face was strangely beautiful, absorbed, fully given to the music pouring from the strings.

Was this really his mother? And if she could play like this, what was she doing giving piano lessons to children who couldn't count the beat?

Something furry brushed against his leg: the baron's cat, looking up at him smugly. "Ha! I *told* you she could play the violin."

"It's not polite," said Grizel, behind him, "to say 'I told you so.'"

Spike flicked an ear. "But it's so very *satisfying*."

Grizel did not answer. She had just eaten half of Spike's sardines and seven of his kitty treats, and she was at a moral disadvantage. She lifted her tail high; she walked straight through the gap in the curtains into the music room and rubbed against Sylvia McKay's leg.

The music stopped. The curtains flew back with a jangle of brass rings. Duncan's mother stood in the archway, her cheeks pale, still gripping the velvet curtain with one slim hand.

"I'm just visiting Robert," Duncan said. He made a vague gesture toward the music room behind her. "I didn't know you played the violin."

The worry line etched itself deeper between his mother's brows. "Oh, I don't *really* play . . . it was just the simplest tune. . . ." She snatched her green scarf from her pocket.

Duncan watched as she tied her hair up like a washer-woman's and rounded her shoulders into their usual stoop. She looked older suddenly, and not nearly so pretty.

"I thought you were good," he said quietly.

"Don't say that," she said. "And don't tell *anyone* that I play the violin."

Duncan frowned. Here was one more thing he had to keep hidden. Didn't his mother have any confidence at all?

Maybe she just needed some encouragement. "You could be in the island chamber orchestra, I bet," he said. "If you just practiced—"

Sylvia McKay's mouth relaxed slightly at the corners.

"You have a better sound than the concertmaster," Duncan persisted. "I heard him once, when he came to our school."

His mother shook her head. "I haven't played for a long time. Didn't you hear how softly I was playing?" She smiled at him. "I didn't want anyone to hear my mistakes."

Duncan looked away. He didn't want to call his mother a liar. But he had heard violin students practicing at the monastery school, and it took most of them years before Duncan stopped wanting to cover his ears every time they lifted the bow.

"I think you're *good*," he said stubbornly. "You just don't know it." He smacked his hands together with a sudden idea. "I bet you could get into the Capital City Orchestra, even! I hear that pays really well. We could move to Capital City! And I could go to the Academy!" He caught a glimpse of his mother's expression and forged ahead. "I could get a job cleaning classrooms, maybe, to help pay for it—"

"Stop, Duncan!" His mother's hands gripped his shoulders. "You must forget you heard me play, and never bring this up

34

again to *anyone*." She gave his shoulders a little shake. "I can't tell you why, not now. You just have to trust me. This is important, son."

Duncan's silence verged on the sullen. Maybe she didn't want to go to Capital City, but she could still get more money if she taught violin lessons as well as piano. And concertmaster for the small orchestra on their own island was a paid position. Why wouldn't she even try? Any normal person who played the violin that well would *want* people to know about it.

"Promise me, Duncan?"

Duncan felt the trembling of his mother's hands on his shoulders. He looked up at her haunted, anxious eyes and winced.

So maybe she was a little crazy. She was still his mother, and he had to take care of her. Right now he guessed that meant making another dumb promise. He nodded without enthusiasm, then changed the subject to something more cheerful. "Robert wants to practice his fencing with me," Duncan said. "He got new sabers for his birthday."

The worry line between his mother's brows eased. "Be careful," she said. "And when you're through, we can walk home together. I've almost finished arranging Betsy's music."

Duncan watched her thoughtfully as she turned back into the music room. He wondered how many mothers would tense up when a son gave a compliment—but relax when the same son announced he was going to fight with sharpened steel. Not many, he guessed.

CHAPTER 4

Not-So-Good News

D UNCAN'S SABER FLASHED IN THE SUNLIGHT as he
advanced. Robert was pretty good—he had a private
fencing lesson once a week—but the fencing master came to
the monastery school, too, and Duncan had been practicing
hard for years.

He felt savage enough for a real battle. He made his salute,
he rapped Robert's sword with a quick beat—he advanced, he
feinted, he counterattacked, all with an increasing sense of
resentment.

His mother had a skill that could earn them money. They
didn't need to starve or live in a house that was falling down.
But she refused to use it. Why?

The cats were on the sidelines, turning their heads from side to side as they watched the back-and-forth.

"I'd bet on your boy with the cap," Duncan heard the baron's cat say. "His balance would be better if he had a tail, of course, but he's really quite good."

"He'll lose," said Grizel morosely. "He always does."

But Robert was on the retreat, and Duncan followed, attacking without mercy. No one was watching—and just this once, he wanted to win. With reckless abandon, he parried an attack and lunged forward, scoring a touch on Robert's shoulder. Robert stopped, looking surprised.

Duncan grinned. "Didn't see it coming, did you?"

"You're getting better," said Robert.

A scraping sound came from the manor house as the dining room windows were flung open, and the baron and baroness leaned out to watch the match.

Duncan swept off his cap with one automatic motion. He made the correct bow, his dark red hair glinting in the last rays of the setting sun. As he straightened, his upturned eyes caught sight of his mother, one floor up. Her hand flew to her mouth as if to stifle a cry. Duncan felt a pang like an arrow striking.

"Come on," said Robert. "One more time? I want some revenge."

Duncan nodded. But this time, he slipped his guard and gave Robert the opening he needed. Duncan passed backward, faltered, dropped to one knee—as long as he was going to lose, he might as well make it dramatic—and flailed upward in a riposte, a return thrust that went deliberately wild. Robert scored decisively. From the dining room window came the sound of two proud parents clapping.

Duncan and his mother walked in silence up the bayside road. Duncan had not enjoyed losing to Robert.

When he was younger, it had felt like a game to make sure he never seemed like the smartest in the class, or the fastest in a race, or the best at anything. But he wasn't small anymore, and he was tired of never coming in first. Sometime soon he would bring it up once more—sometime soon he would demand yet again to know why. But not today. Today he had something else to ask her.

Grizel, trotting at his heels, began to meow. "Why don't you tell your mother about the sailboat you saw today, the one with the long blue streamer? Your mother would like to hear about that. Tell her about how it didn't come into the bay, and the long blue flag, why don't you?"

Duncan cocked an eyebrow at the cat. What was this—some weird cat obsession with flapping cloth?

Grizel meowed again, as insistent as if she were begging for fish, but Duncan did not answer. It was hard to conduct a conversation in Cat with his mother present.

Of course, he could always speak human to Grizel. Cats understood human language; they just couldn't speak it. Still, it was awkward when someone else was listening. If he meowed, he sounded like a little boy pretending to be a cat. If he spoke human, people around him assumed he was speaking to *them*—and either way, he ended up sounding strange, like someone who heard voices that weren't there.

So he had learned to be careful. He switched from human to Cat, depending on the circumstances, and no one was the wiser. Grizel had made him promise to keep his Cat-speaking ability a secret from all humans, and he didn't mind. He had to keep so many secrets for his mother's sake that it was nice to have a secret of his own for a change.

Grizel was still meowing about the sailboat with the blue flag, but Duncan was thinking of something else. "My birthday is coming up soon," he said.

Duncan's mother smiled. "One of the best days of my life." She gave his shoulder an affectionate pat.

Duncan plowed ahead. "I was wondering if you'd decided what you were going to tell me about my father this year. In fact, I was thinking that maybe this year you could tell me more than one thing. You always say to wait until I'm older, but I'm going to be twelve, and that's older than I've ever been."

They turned onto the cliff road, and the mown grass of the bayside hills gave way to straggling weeds. Small insects buzzed and rose, whirring, in the air as Duncan and his mother passed.

"I'll tell you one new thing," said Sylvia McKay with a note of false cheer, "just like always. Only, let's wait until your birthday comes, shall we?"

Duncan didn't argue. He would bring it up again later, after she was done being upset about the As on his report card. Every year he was getting older; pretty soon she wouldn't be able to avoid telling him everything he wanted to know.

Sylvia McKay asked him about school, and he told her that Charlie Stewart had gotten sick and thrown up right in the middle of a test. Duncan asked his mother how music lessons had gone, and she said that Annabelle Parker still couldn't keep the beat to save her life. Just to keep Grizel happy, Duncan told his mother about the sailboat with the blue streamer and how it had sailed close to the island but never docked.

"Oh, really?" His mother's step hesitated briefly. "With a long blue pennant, you said?" She stopped at the edge of the road to gaze out at the sea. "You didn't go to the dock, of course."

"No," said Duncan.

The sun had fallen below the curving rim of the sea, but an afterglow lit the bottoms of clouds in bright tangerine, lined with gold. The breeze had died down to a whisper. The waters of the bay were flat and still, and far out at sea a ship sat becalmed, her many sails limp.

Duncan's heart beat a little faster. Two strange sails in one day! He squinted, but he could not see the ship clearly without a telescope. It might be a schooner.

"Because you know you must never go to the wharf when a strange boat comes in," his mother continued, "no matter how small."

Duncan frowned. "I thought it was just the big supply ship

you were worried about. Don't you know I can earn money at the wharf? You always used to let me go down and help the fishermen with their nets and things. And sometimes even skippers of small boats need an errand run."

"Yes, but now you must not go down anymore. I've told you that this year is different."

Duncan could feel his frown deepening. He said nothing.

They were on the monastery road. On cliffside terraces, children were out after supper to play, shooting marbles and jumping rope to a chant Duncan had heard hundreds of times. "Charles, Charles, Duke of Arvidia, went to sea with the Princess Lydia," the children sang. Duncan's mother did not like him to sing that song. It was one more of her silly rules.

Duncan pursed his lips and whistled along, loud and cheerfully. She had never said he couldn't whistle it. She couldn't stop him from doing everything.

"Son," said his mother.

Duncan braced himself for a lecture.

But his mother seemed to have something else on her mind. She put a hand on his shoulder and spoke with quiet intensity. "I'll tell you one thing about your father right now. He was brave and honorable. Never forget that, Duncan."

"I won't," said Duncan, startled.

"And don't go down to the dock for any reason until I tell you it's all right. And don't speak to any strangers, and when you're outdoors, keep your cap on at all times. Do you hear me, now?"

The look Duncan dreaded most was back on her face, and her eyes were bleak. He glanced away and saw that they were at the monastery already.

The monastery was a collection of ancient stone buildings and curving pathways, edged with gardens and surrounded by a mossy stone wall. The long, low building with a series of arched windows was where Duncan went to school.

"Mrs. McKay!" Friar Gregory, his black robes flapping, came puffing through the monastery gates. "I'm so glad I caught you! Can you come in for a short conference, do you think?"

Sylvia McKay put a hand to her throat. "About Duncan?"

"Don't look so worried!" Friar Gregory smiled broadly, his cheeks puffed out like a chipmunk's. "This is good news. Come in! I'll just run ahead and clear off a chair for you. I'm afraid I stack my papers on every available surface. . . ."

Duncan avoided his mother's eye as she passed him, her heels rapping on the flagstone path. This had to be about his report card. Too many As—what a tragedy.

Grizel rubbed against Duncan's leg to say good-bye. "I don't much care for the monastery cats—especially Mabel— but I know some cats across the road who are generous with their kitty treats. Don't wait up," she added, flipping her tail as she padded away. "I might be late."

"Mew!" The cry was tiny but fierce, and a small white bit of fluff leaped out from behind the stone wall to pounce on Duncan's foot.

Duncan glanced down and sighed. "Watch the claws, Fia."

"It was a good pounce, though, wasn't it? If you were a mouse, you'd have been scared, right?" Fia looked up at him anxiously with her blue and green gaze.

"Terrified," Duncan said. He saw a flicker of brown as his mother's skirts whisked through a stone archway into Friar Gregory's office.

Fia waved her tail in triumph. "I knew it. I'm going to pass my kitten examinations tonight, no matter what they say." She gave a flick of her ears in the direction of the courtyard gardens, where three pairs of kitten eyes glimmered in the shadows. "And I was a good messenger cat today, too, wasn't I?" Then she added grumpily, "Until my mother interrupted."

"What *was* the message?" Duncan had forgotten about it until now. He squatted down to speak to the kitten at her level. "Something about my mother, was it?"

Fia gave a little spring of delight. "I get to tell you the whole message now! Just wait—I have to do this right." She placed her front paws together on the ground in the formal manner, lifted her chin, and stiffened her whiskers. "Your mother," she intoned, "is going to be so *proud* of you!"

Duncan waited for more. "That's it?"

Fia unstiffened. "That's all," she admitted. "I heard Friar Gregory say it to the headmaster. He said it twice."

"But proud of what? Didn't Friar Gregory say?"

Fia's kitten shoulders went up in a shrug. "I didn't

understand, exactly . . . something about a ship, a Skerl ship. But I told you the most important part. If *I* did something to make my mother proud, I'd want to know!"

Duncan frowned. A Skerl ship? What was that? Fia must have gotten it wrong—this had to be about the report card. Unless it was about his map project. He had done well on that, putting in all the large islands of Arvidia, and all the smaller ones that were known—perhaps a hundred in all. He had drawn little ships on the major supply routes, and he had even drawn ships exploring the uncharted waters to the south and west. Maybe he shouldn't have worked so hard on it, but once he got started, he kept thinking of ways to make it better.

Still, it didn't seem like something to have a special conference about.

Fia pranced around his heels. "You'll find out more if you listen at the door," she said. "I always do."

Duncan had been taught not to listen at doors. Still, that didn't mean he couldn't walk past slowly, just in case he heard something interesting.

Friar Gregory's voice was loud and exuberant, and it echoed down the stone walkway with a fine and ringing resonance. "I knew there was more to Duncan than his grades showed. He listened in class, he asked good questions, and he seemed to understand the material. But when it came to tests, or handing in work to be graded, he was never much above average."

Sylvia McKay's voice was quieter, but it carried beautifully through the open door. "Not everyone can be a straight-A student. I don't expect it of him."

"But we *should* expect it!" There was a crackling sound, as if a paper was being waved in the air. "This proves that we should!"

Duncan edged closer to the office door. With a sinking heart, he recognized the paper clutched in Friar Gregory's fist. It was his answer sheet from the national test.

"I began grading this afternoon," boomed the friar, "and when I saw how Duncan had performed on the first section, I set aside everything else to grade his entire test. Do you know how many people in Arvidia have gotten a perfect score on the nationals? Two, that's how many! Two, in twenty years—and now, with Duncan's test, *three*!"

The triumphant word rang out. Duncan felt as if it echoed in some vast and breathless space within him. A perfect score! He was the best! No one in the whole nation could have possibly beaten him!

Friar Gregory paced the room in his excitement. "The Academy at Capital City offers two scholarships a year to the best students in the nation. There's no question in my mind that your son will get one."

"See?" mewed Fia at Duncan's ankles. "I told you it was about a Skerl ship! That's good, right?"

Friar Gregory turned at the meow and caught sight of Duncan hovering in the hall. "Come in, my boy! How would you like to go to the Academy in Capital City this fall?"

Duncan could not trust himself to speak. He managed a nod.

Friar Gregory had not stopped smiling in his delight, and now he clapped Duncan on the back. "Excellent. You must get serious about school, though; no more slacking. They'll expect your best at the Academy."

Sylvia McKay's fingers gripped the chair arm. "There must be some mistake."

Friar Gregory's cheeks flattened, as if the air had leaked out of him. "It's true this is the first time Duncan has shown this sort of ability on a test," he admitted. "But never fear"—he was smiling again now—"there is a makeup test in a month's time, and Duncan's score on that will prove there was no mistake."

Sylvia McKay's hands relaxed. "Another test? He can take another test and get a lower score?"

Friar Gregory nodded. "In cases like this, where a startling result comes out of the blue, it's usual to require a second test to make sure there was no cheating." He smiled at Duncan. "But I've known you for years, Duncan. I'm quite sure you didn't cheat."

Sylvia McKay set Duncan's plate before him on the rickety wooden table. He stared at the old bread and cheese, the two wilted carrots, without seeing them. He could not believe what his mother had just said.

"You want me to *fail*," Duncan cried. "You want me to *lie*."

Sylvia McKay toyed with the shriveled carrot on her plate. "I'm not asking you to lie—"

"You ask me to lie every time you tell me to pretend I'm less than I am. Don't you understand," Duncan added bitterly, "that Friar Gregory will think I cheated?"

His mother's face paled. "*You* will know that you are honorable," she said with an effort. "What does it matter what other people think, if you know the truth?"

"It matters," Duncan said through his teeth. "You know it matters." He stood up and his chair fell over with a crash. He was trembling.

His mother clasped her hands before her, lacing her fingers together tightly. She gazed up at him, her eyes swimming. "Aren't you going to eat your supper?"

Duncan looked at his plate. His mother had given him everything in the icebox and kept just one small carrot for herself.

There was an odd sliding sensation in Duncan's chest, as if something tender within him had hardened, or been encased in stiff leather. "I'm not hungry," he said, and ran up the stairs.

It was dark, but the moon had not yet shown itself. A small breeze rose with the coming of night, and a smell of the sea wafted through Duncan's bedroom window along with the monotonous rasping of crickets.

Duncan lay rigid in his bed, his jaw jutting toward the ceiling. He had never been so furious in his life, nor so

47

bewildered. He hardly heard the meowing in the street below or the sound of his mother opening the door to let Grizel in from her wanderings. And when the cat came into his room and jumped onto the bed, he did not speak or move.

"Well?" Grizel said. "Aren't you going to scratch me behind the ears? Or stroke my fur? Or be polite in any way?"

"No," said Duncan. He flung an arm over his eyes.

Grizel's tail flicked slightly. "You know, a little catlike courtesy wouldn't be amiss, especially if you want to come along to the cat council in the graveyard tonight."

Duncan turned his head away.

Grizel padded over to his head and brushed his chin with her whiskers. "You seem upset. Did you have an encounter with a dog?"

Duncan spoke into his pillow. "My mother won't let me go. She says I have to fail the next test."

"Won't let you go? Go where?"

Duncan choked out the explanation in a few short sentences. "She says not to worry, that I'll understand it all someday," he finished. "But I can't wait for someday! This is the year everyone enters the Academy, if they're going. If I don't go this year, next year she'll say I'm too old to start."

Grizel patted his ear softly with her paw. "You won't be too old to start at the Academy next year. Trust me."

"Well then, she'll think of another reason I can't go. And she won't even tell me why! Grizel," he said, sitting up suddenly, "do you think she's crazy?"

"Shh!" Grizel's ears pricked to the alert. "She's coming."

Duncan pulled the covers to his chin and closed his eyes. He did not want to talk with his mother anymore. And he hoped she would not kiss him good night.

He heard his mother stop in the doorway. After a while he heard her footsteps again, fading away down the hall to her room.

Good. All he had to do now was wait for her to fall asleep. Moonrise wasn't for another hour yet. He had time before he had to leave for the graveyard. . . .

He was dreaming. He knew he was dreaming, for he struggled to wake, but the dream held him as it had so many times before. Everything was the same—the damp, slippery rock, the sound of the sea, a cat's whisker of a moon riding over all. And behind him, a lighted window high in the dark. That was all— the window in the night, and salt spray on his neck, and a sense of longing so powerful that when he woke, he felt dampness on his cheek, like tears.

It was not tears. It was Grizel's rough, wet tongue, and she was licking his face. "Wake up, if you're coming."

Duncan scrambled into his clothes. The stones he had picked up that day were still in his pocket, and they knocked gently against each other as he bent to find his boots.

"Make it snappy." Grizel switched her tail in irritation. "If you make me late, I'm going to regret waking you up. It's almost moonrise."

Boots in hand, Duncan slipped down the passageway,

avoiding the creaky floorboard in the middle. He made it to the second-floor landing without a sound and stepped carefully past the sea chest to the window. At sea, the ship that had been becalmed seemed to have found some wind at last. The moon shone upon her filled sails, and Duncan could see that she was a two-masted schooner, moving slowly into the bay.

He squinted. Were those *square* sails near the top of the mainmast? Square sails were for ships that sailed far, not just between local islands.

Grizel hissed a warning. Duncan heard his mother's door creak open.

He melted into the shadowed corner behind the sea chest and stood perfectly still. What excuse could he give for being up at this hour, fully dressed, with his boots in hand? Maybe he could convince his mother that he was sleepwalking. Or maybe he could say that he was going to fill the cat's water bowl and was carrying his boots because . . . he had a sudden urge to polish them?

No. He would tell his mother he was going to visit his father's grave because he was so upset about the Academy. With any luck, that would make *her* feel guilty. And it was even true—the cat council was in the graveyard, after all.

Quiet footsteps approached. Duncan opened his mouth, ready to explain.

But Duncan's mother never turned her head to look for what might be in the shadowed corner. She walked across the second-floor landing and started down the steps. As she passed, Duncan saw that she carried her shoes in her hand.

Click. Click. Sylvia McKay unlocked the door. She slipped on her shoes, tied a scarf on her head, and stepped outside. *Click. Click.* She locked it again.

She glanced down the street in both directions and pulled her scarf forward, as if to hide her face. Then, with a swing to her legs that had nothing hesitant about it, she walked briskly over the cobblestones toward the cliffside road. By the time Duncan gathered his wits and ran after her, she had disappeared.

CHAPTER 5

Graveyard Council

T HE SEA WAS SILVER AND BLACK beneath the rising moon, and the clifftop grasses were dry, springy underfoot, and curled like sheep's wool. Duncan sat beside his father's grave with his arms wrapped around his knees, and shivered lightly. He wished he had thought to bring a jacket. Even in summer, the sea breeze cooled the windswept top of the island. In winter, the wind was a razor, cutting straight to the bone.

It had been winter the first time he'd seen his father's grave. He had been very young then, but he had asked so many questions that at last his mother had taken him to the cemetery by way of an answer. He had shivered small in his thin coat, but as he traced his father's initials on the cold tombstone with a pudgy finger, something in him had understood that his father was not just gone but was never coming back. Now, years later, when Duncan was allowed to roam about the island on his own, he came back to the grave every so often to talk things over with himself and whatever part of his father might still be listening.

He ran his long fingers over the carved initials: CDM. The *M* was for McKay, of course, but his mother had refused to tell him what the other letters stood for. He liked to think that the *D* was for Duncan.

Somewhere in the dark, crickets chirped steadily with a soft *creak creak*. In the hollow on the edge of the cemetery, cats were gathering. They appeared over the rim, pointed ears first, followed by the lithe moving shadow of their bodies, edged with brightness where the moon tipped the fur. As each tail disappeared into the dark cup of the hollow, a pair of shining eyes joined the rows of waiting cats.

All cats' eyes shine in the dark, but not always with the same color they have in the day. Duncan watched as a wavering line of kittens was ushered in by their nervous mothers, but he could not see which one was Fia. He scooted closer. Grizel preferred that he keep his distance at council meetings—he wasn't a cat, as she had frequently explained—but if he lay on his stomach behind the large gravestone and propped his chin on his forearms, he could see everything without being in the way.

The cat known as Old Tom was pacing back and forth near

Duncan. "No sense at all!" he grumbled, his tail agitated. "I came on the supply ship yesterday with urgent news from Capital City, and do they put me first on the agenda? No! They start with kitten examinations!"

"They always test the kittens before any other business," Duncan meowed, "because it's so hard for them to wait."

The tomcat pricked his ears forward. "Ah, you're the boy who speaks Cat. It's rare to find a human so intelligent, so cultured."

Duncan grinned in the dark. Cats were incredible snobs. They could understand human language perfectly well, but they acted as if they couldn't. They preferred to be addressed in Cat—the most civilized of all tongues, in their opinion.

Old Tom sniffed. "Maybe you're bright enough to listen to my warnings. The felines on this island never seem to."

A pair of Siamese cats strolled past Tom, flicking their whiskers. "Maybe it's because there are so *many* warnings," said one. "Like the droopy-ear syndrome. Or the tail mange that was supposed to make our rumps bald."

Tom's whiskers bristled. "Those were real dangers! There could have been an epidemic!"

"Or the dangers of catnip for kittens," said the other, snorting, "when everyone knows that kittens don't even like it."

Tom scowled. "That wasn't catnip; it was *kitnip*. A completely different thing."

Duncan remembered the catnip-versus-kitnip discussion. Catnip was a kind of mint leaf that could make cats almost crazy. No one worried about its effect on kittens because kittens didn't even seem to notice it. But according to Tom, a different variety of leaf had been found on one of the islands; it didn't attract grown-up cats, but kittens would crawl from their mother's sides to get hold of it. The cat council, curling their tails with impatience, had suggested that Tom bring a sample—if he could find one. Tom never had.

The first Siamese cat winked at the other. "Do you remember the meeting where he warned us to lower our stress levels or we'd get Twitchy-Tail?"

Hissing with laughter, the Siamese cats moved on, leaving Old Tom sputtering. "It's easy to laugh," he said with indignation, "but I was just doing my duty! That's why I travel to the other islands on the supply ship—to discover the latest news. And this about the missing kittens is very serious, very serious indeed. I've been hearing about it on almost every island. . . ."

Duncan had stopped listening. The kittens were being tested on their mousing skills. The moon, high enough to fling its beams through the fork of an old ash tree, dappled the testing ground with silver light.

A small rubber mouse, tied to a string that was looped over a tree branch, was pulled jerkily along the ground. The line of kittens watched it alertly, every small head turning as the mouse went past.

The first kitten in line pounced, caught the mouse neatly between its paws, and was given an approving *meow-woww* from the judging cats. The second kitten did the same. Then a white kitten stepped forward, small and pale in the moonlight.

The mouse stopped, jerked ahead, and stopped again. The kitten hesitated—pounced—and landed on her nose as the rubber mouse was yanked up and away.

"Fia kitten, excused from further testing," intoned the voice of the cat who held the string, and the white kitten stumbled away, swerving to avoid her mother.

"Perhaps I can assist in this matter," said Old Tom, moving forward. "I've been known to be a comfort to the youngsters, in my day."

Fia sidled around a shrub as Old Tom drew near, and fled to the shadows of the graveyard. Her mismatched eyes shone in the dark. They disappeared as she blinked, then shone again, like two tiny lamps.

Duncan understood why she avoided Tom. Fia had her pride; she didn't want some old cat making a big fuss over her failure. So when she came closer, seeking refuge behind the gravestone, Duncan pretended she wasn't there.

The kittens were practicing their hiss-and-arch. Two more kittens were excused for substandard hissing.

"I know how to do the hiss-and-arch perfectly," said a small, lonely voice at Duncan's elbow. "I can sproing my claws, too. And I would have caught the mouse, but a stupid cricket jumped, and I caught it instead."

Duncan made a sympathetic noise. "You'll pass next time."

"But I wanted my Explorer's permit tonight." Fia scraped her claws on a fallen branch. "I'm tired of tagging after my mother all the time. It's *boring*."

The kittens finished their final test—scampering—and those who had passed were announced. Fia narrowed her eyes and began to groom herself. "Tibby, Tabby, and Tuff—it would be," she muttered, licking behind her right foreleg. "Now they're going to think they're better at mousing, too."

"What else do they think they're better at?" Duncan was curious.

Fia's blue eye shone amber and her green eye golden as she turned her gaze on Duncan. "*Their* eyes all *match*." She twisted her head to reach a spot on her shoulder and licked it savagely.

Old Tom was speaking now. His elderly voice came in fits and starts as he turned his head from side to side: "—a disturbing new trend—kittens—seem to be disappearing in record numbers—no indication where they have gone—"

There was a commanding meow from the edge of the cemetery, and the shadow of an adult cat loomed beyond the last gravestone.

Fia's head went up and she scampered off. From a distance, Duncan could hear the mother cat's scolding.

"How many times do I have to tell you, Fia? Don't go running off by yourself; it can be dangerous. Weren't you listening to Old Tom?"

The cemetery road curled around the top of the island like a lock of hair cut off for remembrance. Duncan scuffed down the limestone track, idly kicking at the weeds that grew along the center. Some distance ahead, Grizel crouched, alert, then disappeared into a patch of wild grass. Below him was the sea, stretching out endlessly and full of unknown mysteries.

He wasn't afraid of being out in the dark. Of course he wasn't supposed to leave the house after bedtime, but Duncan had long ago decided that while human rules were fine for the day, cat rules were what counted at night. Although he wasn't a cat, as Grizel never tired of pointing out, Duncan figured that a boy who could *speak* Cat should be able to prowl after dark once in a while. Besides, he learned a lot at the cat councils—at least when he could hear what they were saying.

"Mrrrow?" Duncan called, and Grizel emerged from the weeds with an unlucky mouse dangling from her mouth.

"What did Old Tom say?" Duncan asked. "I couldn't pick up most of it."

Grizel dropped the mouse and held it under one paw to answer. "He was making a big hiss about nothing. Apparently, on several islands, kittens have wandered off, and their mothers can't find them. You know kittens—they're always going on some little adventure or the other."

Duncan frowned slightly. "But if the kittens aren't finding their way back—"

"Then they've probably left home for good." Grizel gave a

small, impatient hiss. "Some mothers are overprotective, if you ask me."

Duncan's thoughts flew to his own overprotective mother. Where had she been going so late at night? He was no closer to the answer, but he intended to find out. "Let's go, Grizel."

"I want to eat my mouse," Grizel objected. "And I need a rest. My pads are sore from walking all over the whole island today."

"We'll stop at the stone throne," Duncan said. "We're almost there."

He had discovered the throne last year. It was an outcropping of rock thrust from the western cliffs, shaped like an oversized chair. It was Duncan's favorite spot on the whole island. By day, he could drop pebbles over the side into the water of a narrow cove far below and count how long they took to make a splash. By night, he could look out and see the glow of Capital City just over the horizon.

The goat path was not one he cared to descend in the dark, but the throne was at the first turn. Duncan scrambled up and settled against the rock with his legs dangling. Grizel stayed on the path, taking advantage of the pause to eat her mouse. There was a quiet sound of crunching. Far below, there was a faint tinkle, as if the breeze was blowing through hollow reeds or setting the lightest of wind chimes in motion.

He gazed out at the dark sea and the long, shimmering track of the moon. He loved being out at night; he felt that he could take deeper breaths somehow. He was free at night—he was king of the island. Here on the stone throne, he never had to come in second.

Duncan's fingers curled around a small lump of rock, still warm from the day's sun. The lights of Capital City glowed enchantingly on the distant edge of the sea. The Academy was there, somewhere.

His hand tightened on the bit of rock until the edges cut into his palm. Sylvia McKay couldn't force him to write the wrong answers on the makeup exam. But even if he earned a scholarship, she could still keep him from going to the Academy. There would be papers to sign. There would be things to arrange. He was only eleven—he couldn't go without her permission.

The rock broke off in his hand. The breeze blew lightly, drying his cheeks and bringing the faint wind-chime sound to his ears once more. It wasn't wind chimes, and it wasn't hollow reeds, but it was familiar somehow. . . .

Grizel was halfway through her mouse. She was making a contented noise as she ate—*rawr rawr rawr*—and Duncan smiled a little. He could eat, too; he still had a chocolate bar in his pocket.

He had given the two he hadn't eaten to his mother, but she had handed one back, insisting that he keep it for himself. If he knew her, she would eat only a quarter of hers and give him the rest another day.

He put the broken rock in his pocket, took out the candy

bar, and unwrapped it. One bite, two bites, three bites . . . he held the chocolate on his tongue and let it slowly melt, flooding his mouth with a taste he wished could last forever. He tipped back his head to look at the stars, great swaths of them flung across the sky like a fishing net.

It was hard to be mad at someone who loved him so much she would go without food for his sake. But he needed more than love from his mother.

A swift, whirling gust blew up from the cliffs and brought the tinkling sound with it, louder and clearer than before. Duncan leaned over the throne's broad ledge. Of course! The sound was the wind singing thinly through taut wires, the faint tinkling rattle of metal shackles in a sailboat's rigging. Below him, in a cove so narrow that he hadn't thought of it as a bay at all, was a boat with a single mast. The sails were furled, but the moon's light caught at mast, hull, and shrouds, and sketched the boat in lines of silver. It was the sailboat he had seen earlier that day, the one he'd thought had passed the island by.

Grizel's crunching suddenly stopped. There was a muffled sound of voices on the path below, and a gleam of light from a shaded lantern.

"Thank you," came the voice of Duncan's mother. "It's not so steep here—I can get home without your light."

Duncan slid back into the shadows.

A low, gruff voice said, "I might not return for some time. I think I've been watched lately. And the money—I know it's not enough—"

"What you bring is very helpful," said Sylvia McKay.

She was saying something else that Duncan could not hear. He listened with every nerve strained, but the fitful breeze spiraled up again from the cliffs with a sound of rustling bushes and rattling rigging, and the noise of voices mixed with the murmur of the sea. Then the breeze died down, and in the lull the voices came clear again.

"—like to see the lad before I go."

There was silence for a heartbeat. The sea crashed and hissed on the rocks far below.

"Come quietly, then," said Duncan's mother, and the dark shape of a bush changed as she turned and brushed past it. "Just for a moment, no more. You can look in while he's sleeping."

CHAPTER 6
A Visitor in the Night

D UNCAN HELD PERFECTLY STILL. He heard the bushes rustle on the goat path, then the crunch of limestone as his mother and the strange man reached the cliff road.

He waited for the footsteps to fade. "Come on," he said to Grizel. "We can still beat them if we skip the road and take the cat's way home."

Grizel followed him up the goat path, complaining. "I'm an old cat, remember? I can't run that fast."

Duncan scooped her up in his arms and trotted across the limestone road. "I'll carry you—*ooof!*" His foot landed on something that rolled, and he staggered.

"Your night vision isn't good enough for running," Grizel warned.

"But yours is." Duncan held her so she could see the ground ahead. "Warn me if something is in my way."

He cut through the scrub beyond the road, prime cat-hunting ground with low junipers and plenty of cover for mice. Between the moon's light and Grizel's night vision, he managed to avoid running into anything too solid. At the lip of a small bluff overlooking his neighborhood, he slid down on his heels, half squatting, one hand sliding along the steep ground for balance. When he reached the street, he had dirt in his socks and a rip in his pants. It didn't matter; he could see his house ahead, and the street was clear. He had made it.

Duncan galloped to his front door, fumbled in his pocket for the key, and pulled it out in a hurry. The key went flying. He heard the tinkle of metal against stone.

He patted the cobblestones frantically in the dark.

"Better hurry up," meowed Grizel. "I hear footsteps."

"I can't find the *key*!"

Grizel gave a hissing sigh. "Hold me up to the door, then. I can pick the lock."

Duncan stared. "You can?" He lifted Grizel and watched in astonishment as she put her claw in the keyhole and delicately twisted it right, then left.

Click. Click. The door opened, and Duncan locked it quickly behind him.

"I never knew you could pick locks!" He tore up the stairs, leaped into bed, and pulled the covers over his clothes.

"I have many skills that you don't know about," Grizel

said. "Most cats can do far more than humans realize. For instance, Cat Trick #32."

"What's that?" Duncan was still breathing hard from his run.

"I just told you. Lock picking. And speaking of tricks, you'll never convince your mother that you're sleeping if you pant like a dog. Breathe like a cat. Take air in delicately. Keep the whiskers still."

Duncan didn't have whiskers, but he didn't argue the point. He took in a deep draft of air and tried to calm his pounding heart, but his breath was still loud and ragged when he heard his mother's key in the lock.

Grizel waved her tail. "No matter. I will delay them on the stairs with Cat Trick #17: Getting in the Way. I am particularly good at that."

This turned out to be true. Duncan heard stumbling on the stairs, a loud irate *mrrrraaaoww!*, and then low, soothing, apologetic voices.

It was enough time to get his breath under control. By the time his mother was at his bedroom door with the strange man—Duncan saw their silhouettes in the doorway through his lashes—he was breathing deeply, as if he had been asleep for hours.

"Stand in the shadows," came his mother's voice in a whisper.

There was a soft scraping of metal as a slide opened in a dark lantern and a ray of light speared out. The reddish glow through Duncan's eyelids told him when the light touched his face.

From the shadowed corner of the room came a low intake of breath. Duncan felt the floorboards tremble beneath the bed as someone moved silently closer. There was a fragrant, oddly familiar smell of salt, pipe tobacco, and dried sweat, and then a low, rough whisper—"He looks more like his father than ever. I would have known him anywhere."

The metal slide scraped and the lantern went dark. "He looks *far* too much like his father," said Duncan's mother. "Especially this year."

"You could color his hair," the man said slowly. "But of course you'd have to keep on doing it. All the hair dyes I've seen fade with time, and hair keeps growing out."

"It costs too much," Duncan's mother whispered with an edge of exasperation. "Shall I pay for dye and have no money to buy his food? And what could I give for the reason? He already has too many questions about things I dare not explain. Come away, now, you'll wake him."

The man didn't move. "He knows nothing yet?"

"Come away!" The whisper was urgent.

Duncan had an overpowering desire to open his eyes. He rolled his head to one side, as if in sleep, and stole a glance from beneath his lashes. He could see the middle third of the man, silhouetted in the light from the window—a thick pair of breeches, a frayed shirtsleeve, a gnarled set of knuckles.

There was silence for a full minute after Duncan moved.

Then the man spoke again, very low. "He should know there's danger, or he can't protect himself."

"*I* protect him!" said Duncan's mother. "If he keeps to my rules, the danger is small."

"But when are you going to tell him?"

She whispered something under her breath. Duncan thought the word was "never." Then she said, "Not for years, anyway. I want to keep him safe and free of this—this burden— for as long as I can."

Duncan's thoughts tumbled over each other like angry cats. Years? He couldn't wait years! Should he sit up this minute and demand to know everything? He had a right to know. But he was still in his clothes; his mother would know he had sneaked out of the house in the night. He might find out more if he kept silent.

Duncan lay tense and alert; his whole body strained to listen. He could still see the dark bulk of the man just outside the bedroom door.

The hall floorboards creaked under the man's shifting weight. "You want to keep him safe, my lady? A ship in harbor is safe, but that's not what a ship is made for."

Duncan stared up at the cracked plaster ceiling while the voices murmured indistinctly in the hall.

All this had something to do with his father. Over the years, his mother had told him a few things. Did they add up to any sort of clue?

His father had owned a boat. Duncan's mother had told

him that on his seventh birthday. The following year, Duncan had spent a lot of time around the local fishing boats, learning to mend nets and spear fish in the shallows. Grizel had been very pleased with the fish heads that had come her way.

The next year, Sylvia McKay told him that his father had not been a fisherman. That was the year Duncan decided his father had been a sailor. He was not allowed to go to the wharf when a strange ship docked, but there were plenty of small craft that sailed the bay and around the island, and their owners often needed an extra pair of hands on a windy day. Duncan had learned to tie reef knots and bowlines, to trim a sail and to steer, and generally to make himself useful.

Then there had been the year when she told him his father was an excellent swordsman. Duncan had worked very hard at his fencing after that.

Could his father have been in the Island Patrol? They carried swords. They were like the King's Guard, only on ships, and they went from island to island as needed, to keep order and bring lawbreakers to Capital City for justice. There wasn't much crime on the island of Dulle (the worst thing Duncan could remember was when old Angus had had too much to drink at the wharf bar and stole three eggs from a henhouse), so the Island Patrol didn't come around very often. Of course, there was always the possibility of danger from strange ships. Maybe his father had made an enemy on another island.

The voices outside his door had stopped. Duncan flung back the covers and sat up, listening hard.

A faint mutter of conversation came floating up the stairs from the kitchen below. Suddenly he heard his mother saying sharply, "*No*. I'm not going to tell him yet."

The front door closed. The double lock clicked twice. Through Duncan's open window came the quick tap of footsteps in the street, rapidly fading away.

Duncan awoke to a thin crack of sun, piercing through a gap in the curtains. He had been dreaming again, that same dream of the bright window high in the dark. This time, though, something had been chasing him. He got up abruptly and pushed the hair out of his eyes. The dream was already fading, leaving nothing but a faint memory of dread.

Downstairs, Grizel was happily crunching something in her bowl—sardines, by the smell—and there were rolls and fresh fruit on the table, along with a note. It said that his mother had gone to her first music lesson of the day, but she'd packed Duncan a lunch and hoped he would have a good day at school and remember to buckle his cap.

Duncan stared at the food. Fresh fish, rolls from the bayside bakery, fruit from the wharfside grocers—his mother must have gotten up very early indeed, if she had walked all the way down to the wharf and back up the long hill.

He sat down to eat and studied the note again. There was nothing about where she had gotten the money for food. Nothing about the strange visitor of the night before. He checked his lunch bag to see if, perhaps, there was another note in there, but there were only sandwiches and a chocolate bar that he recognized.

Duncan felt his heart twist under his ribs. What was he supposed to do with a mother like this? She wouldn't let him take a scholarship he had earned, she wouldn't tell him anything he wanted to know, she held him back at every turn—but at the same time, she'd gotten up hours before the sun rose just so he could have the freshest rolls for his breakfast, and she hadn't even taken one bite of Robert's chocolate. She had been hungry, too, he knew. Yet she had saved it for him.

Duncan shoved his chair back with a loud scrape. He went out to look for the key he had dropped the night before and found it behind the downspout. He washed his breakfast dishes and hung the towel to dry. Then he opened the new book that Robert had given him and walked slowly up the stairs to the sea chest by the window, where the light was better. He laid the book on the brass-bound chest and turned the thick, creamy pages with something like a return to happiness. Here was the picture of the ship being built that he had seen in the bookshop. He turned the next leaf with a careful hand and looked eagerly at the colored bookplate. It showed the ship at anchor, two men with bright uniforms and swords, and a small girl with a slim silver crown.

Duncan gave a grunt of satisfaction. It was the story of the Bad Duke and the Lost Princess. Everyone knew what had happened, but it was still a recent enough tale that it wasn't in the older history books. Here was the princess, only seven years old, her long dark hair in a single braid beneath her little crown. In the picture, she was just about to begin her royal tour of the islands of Arvidia so the people could see their future queen. The two men going with her were the king's most trusted advisers: Charles, Duke of Arvidia, in the tall, pointed hat with the plume, and the Earl of Merrick, wearing a shorter, rounded hat with a wide brim.

If the princess had lived, she would be almost fourteen by now. The king, her father, still had hope, but almost everyone else had given her up for dead.

Here was a picture of that strange animal, the tiger, that had been sent as a present to the king from a far land. And here was a whole page about the tragic hero, the Earl of Merrick. . . .

Duncan's hand curled around the book, and his thumb smoothed the corner of the page. The earl was shown in bright, vivid colors, his sword half drawn, his noble face wearing a look of surprise and fury mixed. Behind him, leaping from a rock, was the dark and twisted figure of Duke Charles, sword already slashing at the earl's unprotected head. In the background huddled the little princess and her serving woman, clasping each other, while bodies of various duke's and earl's men lay at their feet.

The artist had put in a lot of blood. Duncan gazed at the earl's head wound, just beginning to spout red. Suddenly, the picture was crumpled by two furry paws, then a leaping cat body.

"Hey!" Duncan glared at Grizel. "What did you do that for? Now you've torn it!"

Grizel flipped another page, as if to cover her mistake, and curled up in the sun. She blinked her golden eyes at Duncan. "Don't you have to go to school?"

Duncan put on his cap without enthusiasm. His feet lagged on the road to the monastery; they turned down the goat path to the stone throne instead. He lay on his stomach across the arm of stone, still cool from the night, and stared down at the dark indigo water in the shadow of the cliff. The cove was empty. The sailboat and the man who had come to visit his mother were gone.

The morning was clear, and the sky was a bowl of blue with ribbons of cloud. In the distance, the monastery bell rang, three tones that hung and shivered in the still air. Duncan gathered up his books slowly. He had never been late before, not once.

The wrought-iron gate was shut and locked; it rattled when Duncan pushed on it. Latecomers were supposed to ring the small bell that hung from the gatehouse. Then they had to go see the headmaster.

Duncan did not want to see the headmaster. He did not want to go to school at all. There wasn't much point if all his mother wanted him to do was fail.

A cream-colored cat brushed through a gap in the gate's iron scrolls, her whiskers held at a disapproving angle. It was

Fia's mother, Mabel, and her meows were sharp as she questioned him.

Duncan shook his head. "I haven't seen Fia anywhere." He thought that Fia was probably too embarrassed to show her face after failing her kitten examinations, but he didn't mention that to Mabel. "Isn't she with the other kittens?"

Mabel hissed her annoyance. "I can't find them, either. They'd better not be getting into mischief." She stalked off, her claws clicking on the flagstone.

Duncan looked after her thoughtfully. He hoped the other kittens weren't picking on Fia.

He walked along the outside of the monastery wall. There was a stone missing where he could wedge his foot, and a tree branch just low enough to swing up on. He could see a lot from the top of the wall, and maybe he would see Fia. He was already late for school; a little later wouldn't hurt.

Duncan scrambled onto the stone wall. There was a friar cutting herbs in the monastery garden and another walking to chapel, but there was no white kitten anywhere.

He had a good view of the cliff road and the harbor below. The schooner he had seen last evening, becalmed, was now at the wharf. He could see the harbor crane swinging, as small as a toy from this height, and the dockworkers, like tiny ants, scurrying to unload the ship.

The wharf was a popular spot with cats. Could Fia have gone that far?

Duncan balanced on the wall. If he went down to the wharf, he would be more than a little late. And his mother had strictly forbidden it.

On the other hand, the monastery gates would be open for noon recess. Friar Gregory would probably excuse Duncan this once, after his score on the national test. And he hadn't actually promised his mother to stay away from the wharf.

The wharf was a cat's paradise, as far as Duncan could see. Fishing folk were cleaning their catch, and fish heads and entrails lay free for any cat to take. Seagulls screamed for their share, and as Duncan watched, one snatched a morsel of fish out from under a wharf cat's nose and flew, triumphant, to perch on a piling.

He took a deep, satisfied breath. The wharf smelled like no other place on the island. There was clean salt air gusting in from the ocean, intermingled with tar and hemp and the sweat of workingmen, and over all was the pervasive stink of seaweed and fish. The wharf cats were meowing about the usual things—how to litter-train kittens, the best way to hack up a furball, and the latest gossip about the stupid beagle at the corner. Duncan rarely found cat conversations interesting.

But the schooner fascinated him. He could see the rigging perfectly now. There were the usual triangular sails, easy to raise and quick to shift, good for fast sailing among the islands of Arvidia. Atop the mainmast, though, were two square sails in a bunt. Square sails were for long voyages, when the trade winds blew steady—so this must be a top-rigged schooner, good for both kinds of sailing. Duncan had only seen such a ship in books, and he gazed at it with hungry eyes. Ships meant for long voyages hardly ever stopped at the insignificant island of Dulle, but this schooner might even sail to distant kingdoms beyond their own.

The ship loomed above the scurrying people on the docks, its side like a wall. Duncan looked with longing at the gangplank, a slanting ramp that led from the dock to the ship. Someday he would walk up a gangplank just like that. He would stand at the railing as they sailed and watch Capital City grow closer, and at night he would not need to squint to see its lights.

"Get out of the way, boy!" a dockworker shouted. Duncan backed into a piling, one of the massive wooden posts wrapped in thick rope that anchored the dock to the seafloor. He wedged his foot in a coil of rope and hoisted himself up until he could see.

Sailors were working, swaggering, shouting. Stevedores swore horrible oaths as they rolled some barrels off the ship and lowered others over the side. A crane swung heavy crates out of the hold and onto the dock, and its machinery made a clanking that drowned out almost everything else. Over all was the constant slap and suck of water against the pier, the creaking of the ship, and the incessant cry of seagulls as they swooped and dove. Duncan ducked as one came too close and snatched at his dangling chin strap.

He held on to his cap, lowering his head, and saw a cat that he recognized. Old Tom was on the boardwalk, pacing back and forth.

Duncan climbed down. "Have you seen Fia anywhere?" he meowed. "The little white kitten with one blue eye and one green?"

The tufts over Tom's eyes rose in alarm. "Another missing kitten?"

"You, boy!" A harsh, grating voice came from the ship.

Duncan whipped up his head and saw two men at the ship's railing. One was big-shouldered, like a bull, and completely bald. The other was tall but thinner, with a long, sharp nose and a bandage showing beneath his wide-brimmed hat. He looked strangely familiar.

The big bald man called again. "Does this island have a daily paper, boy?"

"Yes, sir!" Duncan stood up straight.

"Here's a ten-copper coin. Buy a paper, run it back in five minutes, and you can have another copper for yourself." The man's shoulder bunched as he tossed the coin across the watery gap.

Duncan's hand shot out to catch it, and in the next moment, he was pelting toward the nearest newspaper stand, almost a block away. As he ran, he peeked at the coin with a furtive joy.

The wharf was where the jobs were. Even the old women came down to the ships to sell the lace they spent hours making with their clicking needles. They didn't sell much, their cats told Duncan, but a little bit was better than nothing.

And there weren't just ships at the wharf. There were horses and donkeys harnessed to carriages and carts. Another day, maybe Duncan could help out the drivers and earn even more coins.

He was standing in line at the newspaper stand, shifting impatiently from one foot to the other, when a sudden thought stilled him.

Could he earn enough to pay his passage to Capital City?

Someone tapped his shoulder. "Are you buying a paper or not?"

Duncan mumbled an apology and paid for the newspaper with an odd flutter in his middle. He ran back to the ship, thinking hard. Two days ago, he wouldn't have even considered leaving his mother. But a lot had happened since then.

The gangplank bounced under his feet as he trotted up with the newspaper. He came to a halt before the two men and bowed.

The bald man had a heavy forehead sloping down to a nose that looked as if it had been broken in a fight. He snapped the newspaper against his thigh, as if shaking dirt off it, and handed it to the tall man in the well-cut coat.

Duncan eyed the thin man curiously. Close up, he could see that the bandage showing under the hat was old and yellowed, with a small brown stain. The man's face was pale and thinly handsome, with brows like ravens' wings and dark eyes beneath. He gazed at Duncan with a faint frown.

"Here's your copper." The bald man slapped the coin into Duncan's hand. "Run along now. Don't hang about. You've been paid."

Duncan narrowed his eyes. "I thank you, sir," he said with cold courtesy. He walked down the gangplank, his back straight as a ship's mast. The bald man with the pulpy nose thought he was just some dirty wharf brat, but the bald man was wrong.

Old Tom was waiting on the boardwalk, rumpled and upset. "I warned them kittens would go missing!" he meowed. "But would they listen to me? Nooooo."

Duncan didn't want to get Tom started again. "I'm sure Fia will turn up soon. Are you planning to sail on this ship?"

The tufts over Tom's eyes came down toward his nose. "That," he said, "is not a cat-friendly ship."

"Really?" Duncan looked up again at the men standing at the railing. The big-shouldered man had turned to watch the unloading, but the tall man with the dark eyes was still looking in Duncan's direction. "How do you know they don't like cats?"

"I've never seen a cat get off that ship," said Tom, "no matter what port I've seen it in. It's my opinion that the earl hates cats."

"The earl?" Duncan stared at the tomcat. An earl was a very high noble indeed—higher than a baron, certainly. The only noble higher than an earl was a duke—not including the king or his family, of course. "What earl?"

"The Earl of Merrick, naturally." Old Tom sniffed. "He sails all over, says he's looking for signs of the lost princess (when everyone but the king knows she must be dead), but he won't ship a cat to keep the rats down. I call it unnatural."

Duncan took in a breath. Of course! Now he knew why the tall, dark man looked familiar. That face had stared at him from Robert's history book only this morning. That man had been wounded and almost died in his battle with the treacherous duke Charles. And to this day, it was said, the earl wore a bandage over his forehead to remind him of his failure to protect the princess.

Duncan's throat was choked with glory. He held the gaze of the Earl of Merrick—the hero of the *nation*—for a breathless, frozen moment in time. With a rush of blood to his cheeks, he remembered his manners.

He tore off his cap with a sudden sweep of his arm and bowed. The morning sun blazed down and turned his hair to dark red flame. And then, like a spear leaping, Duncan whirled, jamming his cap back on as he ran. He had news to tell at school!

CHAPTER 7

A Noble Summons

D UNCAN DID NOT GET IN MUCH TROUBLE for being
late. When Friar Gregory heard who Duncan had seen
at the wharf, he pulled open the large map at the front of the
room and launched into a history lesson. The teacher showed
the path that Princess Lydia had taken on her royal tour
through the Arvidian Islands, and where the ship had battled
a terrible storm at the edge of the Great Rift.

Duncan had heard of the Great Rift—a strange, uncharted
band of sea with fogs and storms, waterspouts that could de-
stroy a ship, and whirlpools that would suck boats down,
never to be seen again. No one had ever crossed it until that
great storm of seven years ago. The royal ship had anchored
near an unknown island. It was little more than a big rock

with high cliffs on every side, the remotest island ever discovered in Arvidia. Suddenly the lookout had pointed to four people in the water, two of them very shaggy, clinging to the remains of a wrecked boat.

Two of them were miners, men who said they came from the land of Fahr, on the other side of the Rift. The other two were not people at all, but their tigers—animals that had scarcely been heard of in Arvidia.

Duncan knew that one of the tigers had been sent to the king, as a royal gift. If Duncan ever got to Capital City, he would visit it at the zoo. . . .

Friar Gregory walked up and down the aisles. "Now, the ship stayed at anchor for some time. But what happened the day the princess was kidnapped? Can anyone begin?"

Duncan's hand shot up. He had read about it just this morning. "The Bad Duke—"

"Call him by his proper title, please," said Friar Gregory. "This is a lesson, not a character assassination."

Duncan shoved his hands in his pockets. Duke Charles *was* a bad duke—the worst that had ever been, and no matter how fair Friar Gregory tried to be, nothing would change that. "Yes, sir. That duke told the princess she should set her foot on the farthest island and give it a name. But there was only one narrow bit, on the opposite side, that she could stand on—all the rest was cliffs that no one could climb. So they decided to go to that spot with a small group from the ship."

Friar Gregory nodded. "Thank you, Duncan. Gavin, what happened next?"

"When they got to the island—" the boy began, but he was interrupted.

"How did they get to the island?" the friar asked. "Was there a harbor deep enough for the royal ship to dock?"

Gavin looked puzzled for a moment. "There couldn't have been a wharf, sir. The island was uninhabited."

"Correct." Friar Gregory stroked his chin. "So, who knows how they got from the ship to the beach? Alison, your hand was up first."

"They took two ship's boats, sir."

"And what are ship's boats? I thought the ship *was* a boat."

"If it's big enough, we don't call it a boat—we call it a ship," Alison answered gravely. "And a ship always carries at least one boat, and sometimes more small boats, like rowboats or little sailboats. The sailors lower them into the water, and they go back and forth between the ship and the shore, like a sort of water taxi."

"Excellent. Duncan, can you finish the story?"

Duncan nodded. "They sailed around the island and landed on the other side. Once they were out of sight of the ship, the duke and his men attacked the earl, kidnapped the Princess Lydia, and sailed away into the Rift. The earl's men tried to follow in the second boat, but they were too late. In the distance, they thought they saw a whirlpool take hold of the duke's boat. Afterward they found a broken bit of the boat with its name painted on."

"A sad tale," said Friar Gregory. "How can we be sure it is true?"

"Because there were witnesses!" cried Duncan. "The earl's men saw what happened, and the earl himself was wounded, almost to death. He wouldn't have done that to himself."

"Witnesses can be bribed," said the friar, "and the earl's men might be loyal to him, no matter what he'd done. Is there any other way we can know the truth of the tale?"

Duncan's ears grew warm, and his fingers did a quick double tap on his thigh. Friar Gregory almost sounded as if he were calling the earl a liar. "There *were* other witnesses, sir," he said. "A whole shipful of them."

The teacher inclined his head. "How could people see what happened from the ship, when the fighting was on the far side of the island?"

"May I draw a map, sir?" The book Duncan had read this morning had made it clear. He went up to the board and took a piece of chalk.

"See, here's how the island curved around the flat bit. But here, past the sandy part, the flat ledge extended out into the sea a long way, like a point, barely above water. It stuck out so far into the sea that if you walked to the very end, you could be seen from the ship."

"Go on." Friar Gregory clasped his hands, smiling.

"The duke and the earl were there, together with the princess. They were clearly seen, silhouetted against the setting sun. All at once, the duke pulled out his sword, struck the earl a cowardly blow, and pushed him off the ledge. Then Duke Charles threw the princess over his shoulder and ran out of sight, back to the beach and his small boat. By the time the ship managed to raise anchor and work its way around the island, the duke had sailed off into the Rift. The earl's men tried to follow in their small boat, but first they had to pull the earl out of the rocks where he had fallen. They were wounded, too."

"Excellent," Friar Gregory said. "Full marks. Now, for extra credit, who can tell me why the duke would do such a thing? He had lands and power already. What good would it do him to kidnap the princess?"

Duncan gazed out the window. Who cared why the duke had done it? He was just plain bad, through and through.

Suddenly there came a clatter of hooves and a snorting of horses. A gleaming black carriage stopped at the monastery gates.

The bell at the gate tinged sharply. The gatekeeper shuffled out with the key. Every student's neck craned as gray trousers emerged from the cab, then muscular shoulders and a bald head. A disappointed sigh moved across the classroom like a breeze over a field of dry stalks. "That's not the earl," someone said as the man strode toward the monastery office.

Duncan's chair clattered to the floor. He was on his feet, staring. "It's the earl's man! The one who paid me!"

How the cheering started Duncan didn't know, but Friar Gregory was pounding on the desk to restore order when the door to the classroom opened and the headmaster's assistant poked his head in.

"Duncan McKay? You're wanted in the headmaster's office. Now."

Duncan hesitated at the half-open office door. He didn't want to interrupt when the headmaster was talking.

". . . the only son of a widowed mother. Yes, we're very proud of the lad—and although it hasn't yet been announced, I think I can tell you that his score on the national test couldn't possibly be better!"

Duncan flushed. He could see the headmaster's profile as he sat at his desk, and the legs of the man sitting in the chair opposite, crossed at the knee. The gray trousers had ridden up on the crossed leg, and a wedge of hairy calf showed above the stockings. Duncan reached out a hand to knock.

"Come in, my boy!" Father Andrew was beaming. Duncan stepped forward and gave a quick bow, aimed halfway between Father Andrew and the stranger.

"Sit down, Duncan. I was just telling Mr. Bertram, here, a few things about you. You seem to have caught the earl's interest! The Earl of *Merrick*, Duncan!"

Duncan found it suddenly very hard to breathe. In the pause, a cream-colored cat wound her way into the office and settled under Father Andrew's desk. Her green eyes stared at

Duncan from the shadows. *Meeoow?* she questioned. *Mrrraow-wow?*

Duncan shook his head slightly. No, he hadn't found Fia; but didn't Mabel have any more sense than to interrupt? He couldn't exactly meow about her missing kitten, not now.

Mr. Bertram cleared his throat. "You ran off too quickly, young man." His tone was friendlier than it had been on the dock. "The earl wanted to speak with you."

"Me?" Duncan's voice squeaked with astonishment. He tried again, lower down. "Me, sir?"

"You interested him. He said, 'That's not a common boy,' and told me to follow and give you this"—the man held out a silver coin—"as a reward for your unusual quickness and courtesy."

Duncan stared at the glinting coin on the man's palm. A silver piece! It was more money than he had ever earned at once.

Mabel crept out from under the headmaster's desk. "We can't find *any* of the monastery kittens," the cat told him in a quick, insistent series of meows. "Have you seen Old Tom? I want to ask him some questions!"

Duncan didn't dare meow back. "At the wharf," he said under his breath, still staring at the coin.

"Yes, yes, the earl saw you at the wharf," said Mr. Bertram, sounding impatient. "Take it, boy, can't you?"

"And what do you say to the gentleman?" prompted the headmaster.

Duncan gave his head a small jerk to clear it. It was confusing to have two conversations going at once, and it was making him look like a fool.

"Thank you, sir," he said, taking the coin with another small bow. He felt with delight the weight of silver in his hand—heavier than the coppers he was used to—and tried valiantly to ignore the cat who was still attempting to get his attention.

Mr. Bertram uncrossed his legs. "By the way," he said, "if the boy could be excused from school this afternoon, I'd be happy to give him a tour of the schooner, and present him to the earl, too. The earl was very impressed with Duncan . . . McKay, was it?" He smiled. "I am sure the boy reflects great credit on your school. Perhaps he could tell the earl about the superior education he has received at this fine monastery. The Earl of Merrick is a very great supporter of education, you know. A very great *financial* supporter."

He reached to shake the headmaster's hand, but Mabel crouched in front of him, meowing desperately up at Duncan. "Old Tom *tried* to tell us that kittens were going missing. If only I had listened more *carefully—mrrrroooooww yow yow yow yowwwww!*"

Mr. Bertram took his foot off Mabel's tail. "I'm sorry. I seem to have stepped on a cat."

"Oh, dear!" Father Andrew watched in concern as Mabel streaked out of the room. "I hope there was no damage done."

"No," said Mr. Bertram, inspecting the top of his shoe. "She didn't scratch the leather at all."

There was a little silence.

"Oh, damage to the *cat*, you meant!" said Mr. Bertram, smiling.

Duncan bounced a little on the cab's leather seat and looked out in delight as the landscape jolted past. This was much faster than walking. In fact, his whole life seemed to be speeding up suddenly; he felt a little dizzy. He could not get over the feeling that he was dreaming, somehow.

But the intoxicating smell of leather and sweet oil, the brisk *clip-clop* of the horses' hooves, and the jouncing he got as they bumped along the cobblestone streets had never been a part of any dream he had had.

Mr. Bertram was asking the usual questions that grown-ups asked children. How old was he? What did he like about school? Where did he live? What did his mother do? Was she home in the afternoons, or did he let himself in with a key?

That last question wasn't usual. But Mr. Bertram had a special fondness for keys, he said; it was a hobby of sorts, and he liked to see all the different kinds. Duncan handed over the house key that he kept in a buttoned pocket. He was glad Mr. Bertram was quiet as he examined the key. It was more fun to watch the rapidly moving landscape than to answer questions.

It wasn't until the cab had passed the third cluster of cats that Duncan realized something unusual was going on. He opened the window and hung his head out so far that the straps of his cap fluttered in the breeze, but he couldn't hear anything distinctly—just a jumble of agitated meows.

The stevedores were still loading the schooner. A large crate was rolled out of a shed, bound with ropes and fitted with a padlock. As Duncan followed Bertram up the gangplank to the schooner, the harbor crane's iron hook swayed down on its chain and was attached to the ropes. Duncan watched from the deck as the crate was slowly raised, bit by bit, from its pallet on the dock. He took a step closer and then another step. There was a faint noise—something he could barely hear.

"I'll go and find the earl," said Mr. Bertram, behind him.

"Yes, sir," said Duncan, never taking his eyes from the crane. "Oh, I forgot—may I have my key back, please?"

"Certainly, certainly—it's right here," said the man, fumbling in his pocket. A moment later Duncan heard a tiny *ping*.

"Oh, how unfortunate! I seem to have dropped it into the deck vent," said Mr. Bertram. "Don't worry. It will be below somewhere. I'll be right back."

Now the crane's great arm was swinging the crate over the deck of the ship toward the large square hole in the deck—the cargo hatch. A man on deck had a long hooked pole to guide the crate in its slow journey.

Duncan wondered if he was hearing things. There it was again—a thin, pitiful crying, barely audible amid the shouts of men and the grinding of machinery. It sounded almost like a kitten, crying for its mother—no, more than one kitten. It sounded like a whole *crate* full of kittens, swinging overhead. . . .

Choking with horror, Duncan looked up as the crate's shadow passed across the wooden deck. It was almost to the cargo hatch—they were going to lower it into the hold—

"NO!" he shouted. He waved his arms at the crane operator; he ran at the man with the long pole, grabbed his arm, and yanked hard.

Confusion. Yelling. The crane operator turned, startled, and the boom swung partway back. A man let go of his rope. Another pulled his too hard. The pulley block shifted, the load tilted crazily, and the hook unhitched. The crate hurtled down, crashed onto the deck, and splintered into pieces. Kittens of every color poured out, crying, scampering for the gangplank. One white kitten lay motionless on the deck.

CHAPTER 8
Hero of the Nation

DUNCAN RAN TO THE KITTEN AND LIFTED HER with careful hands. Fia stirred weakly.

"Are you all right?" Duncan whispered. "Say something, Fia!"

Fia's tiny chest moved as she breathed in and out. "Mommy?" She opened first the blue eye, then the green, and blinked at him.

"Is anything broken?" Duncan asked anxiously.

Fia waved all four paws, one after another, then her tail. She wiggled her ears, scrunched her nose, and sneezed. The sudden motion didn't seem to cause her any pain.

Relieved, Duncan tucked the little cat into his shirt, where she could feel his heartbeat. "You're safe now; just be still and rest. I'll take you to your mother soon." He buttoned his shirt up tight so she could feel secure and protected.

Duncan rose to his feet and turned around, bracing for trouble. Bertram was on deck again, and behind him was the earl.

Bertram's eyes darted from the wreckage of the crate to the earl to the escaping kittens, his mouth open as if he had been given a problem too difficult to solve. The earl spoke sternly. "What is the meaning of this, Bertram?" he demanded. "Who had that crate delivered to my ship? Is this someone's idea of a joke?"

Bertram blinked.

The earl's voice was loud enough to be heard by everyone on deck. "I allow my ship to carry other people's freight from time to time, but a crate of kittens is going too far. This must be reported to the island police."

Bertram adjusted his face. His expression became both serious and shocked. "Yes, my lord."

The Earl of Merrick glanced at Duncan. "And here is the lad who was clever enough to smash the crate. But why did you do it? Did you know it held kittens?"

"I heard them meowing," Duncan said. He didn't add that they had all been crying for their mothers.

The earl shot Duncan a keen look from under his bandage. "Smart lad. Bertram told me about your score on the national tests, too. You're a credit to Arvidia."

Duncan ducked his head, flushing. Then suddenly he remembered his mother's game of Noble Manners. "That's kind, sir, but it is *you* who are the credit to Arvidia."

The earl chuckled. "Perhaps we should congratulate your mother for raising such a fine scholar. I believe I'll send her flowers! Give Bertram your address, and he'll see to it . . . after he reports to the Dulle police, of course."

Bertram pulled out a notepad and pencil. "Come, boy, the address," he said in his rasping voice. "Don't you think your mother would like flowers?"

Duncan hesitated. His mother would love flowers, but she would hate getting attention from a stranger, even if he *was* the hero of the nation. Still, he could hardly say no to the Earl of Merrick. He slowly recited his address.

The earl smiled a charming, crooked smile. "Come, I'll show you around the schooner while Bertram is gone. Would you like to see the ship?"

"I would like that very much, my lord!"

Bertram snapped his notebook shut. "Perhaps the lad would like refreshments, as well."

"An excellent idea," said the earl. "Speak to Cook about it, will you? Oh, and Bertram . . . a word in private . . ."

The two men stepped away, the earl speaking in low, stern tones. Duncan caught the words "crate" and "kittens" and nodded to himself. The earl would find out who had done such a terrible thing and see that it never happened again.

Duncan peeked inside his shirt to check on Fia. The kitten was sleeping. He really should get Fia back to her mother—Mabel was probably frantic by now—but it wouldn't take much time to see the ship, and he would never get a chance like this again.

The earl was coming back. Off to one side, Duncan saw Bertram exchanging a few words with a large man in a dirty apron. Then Bertram jerked his head at a strong-looking sailor and strode down the gangplank. The sailor hitched up his pants and followed Bertram to a waiting black carriage and its stamping horses.

"And what would you like to see first?" said the Earl of Merrick.

A half hour later, Duncan had climbed the rigging, peered into the hold, looked at the tween deck, where the crew slept, patted the figurehead (it was a wolf), and pretended to fire the two bow chasers, long brass guns like cannons that were mounted on low wooden carriages painted with the names *Belcher* and *Bulldog*. The earl had seemed interested in him the whole time, too. Somehow, without quite knowing how it had happened, Duncan found himself telling the earl all about himself and his mother—not just the usual things, but how his mother made him wear a cap all the time, and didn't want him to come in first in anything, and wouldn't let him go to the Academy.

Perhaps, Duncan thought uneasily, he had told the earl too much. But if the king and the whole nation of Arvidia trusted the Earl of Merrick, certainly Duncan could trust him, too.

And now the earl was showing him the great cabin.

It was the largest one, placed at the rear of the ship. The *stern*, Duncan corrected himself. You never talked about the back of a ship—that made you sound like a landsman. You always called it the stern. And the front was the bow. But he had only been on small boats, never a ship, and so he had never seen a cabin like this, with a wall of square windows that stretched from side to side, filling the room with light.

A long, curving bench ran under the windows, with lockers beneath for storage. Duncan knelt on the bench and gazed out at the bay and the shimmering sea beyond. Surprisingly, there was a little walkway just outside. He found the door and stepped over a high threshold onto a narrow balcony. The fresh breeze from the bay brushed his cheeks. Below him, seagulls skimmed the surface of the water, screaming their high, piercing cries as they searched for small fish to devour.

"Do you like the gallery?" asked the earl, behind him. "Not many ships have them, but I enjoy a private walkway behind my cabin."

Duncan was confused. "I thought that was the name for the ship's kitchen."

The earl stood beside him at the railing, looking down at the dimpled water that sucked and splashed against the ship's hull. "Not quite. A ship's kitchen is called a *galley*. This little balcony at the back is the *gallery*."

Duncan repeated the two words in his head so he would be sure to get them right.

"And the quarterdeck is just above us," said the earl, pointing.

Duncan moved an inch or two away from the earl, who was standing very close. Then he tipped his head back to look at the underside of the deck above. It made a nice canopy of shade on a hot day.

The gulls screeched. One had caught a fish with its sharp beak and beat its wings strongly as it bore its prize away. Two other gulls mobbed it, attacking with outstretched claws, trying to get the fish for themselves.

"That's hardly fair," said Duncan.

"The attacking gulls," said the earl, "think it's unfair the first gull has the fish."

Duncan had never thought of it like that.

"It's all in your point of view, you see. Now, your mother's point of view is different from yours. You want a good education and a future, but she wants you to stay close by her side. Who is right, I wonder? The one who is nervous and fearful, or the one who isn't afraid to grasp opportunity when it comes knocking?"

Duncan was silent. He knew his mother was nervous and fearful, but it felt disloyal to say so out loud. "My mother would do anything for me," he said at last. "She gives me her share of food when we don't have enough."

The earl leaned on the railing, gazing out at the far

horizon. "A mother can be very noble, certainly, but if you had a father, he would advise you to strike out, to have ambition. Alas, you have not been so fortunate."

Duncan turned his head so sharply that a dangling chin strap hit his neck. "How do you know I don't have a father?"

The earl seemed momentarily disconcerted. "Bertram told me. He heard it somewhere. At your school, perhaps?" He stretched out his hands before him on the railing. They were pale, long-fingered, elegant hands, and they moved gracefully as he spoke. "I was poor and fatherless myself."

"You?" said Duncan. "But you're an earl, sir!"

"Nobility does not necessarily mean wealth. If, for example, a grandfather mismanaged things, and a father gambled away what was left and then inconveniently died, it might be difficult for a mother to scrape together the money to send her son to the Academy. A boy like that might have to scrub in the kitchen and clean up other students' dirt to pay his fees, when *they* should have been working for *him*."

The gulls came screaming down once again. A streak of blood showed red on the breast of the one with the fish, and it dropped its prey into the oily water.

The Earl of Merrick wove his thin fingers together on the railing. "You told me that your mother teaches music lessons. What kind of instrument? The violin?"

"She teaches piano," Duncan said quickly.

"Ah. My mistake." The earl lowered his voice as if confiding a secret. "I have a *very* special fondness for the violin. I'm a trustee for the Capital City Orchestra, you know, and I'm always looking for good musicians to recommend."

Duncan's eyes widened. This could be his mother's chance! If the earl listened to her play and said she was good, she'd *have* to believe it. She wouldn't be afraid to audition anymore; then Duncan could go to the Academy after all! Of course, he had promised never to tell, but surely the Earl of Merrick was safe?

The earl gazed keenly into Duncan's eyes. "So she *does* play? I can see it in your face—she does!"

Duncan was relieved. If the earl had already guessed, it wouldn't be breaking a promise to tell him more. "My mother is better than anyone I've ever heard," he whispered, "but she won't play in front of people."

"Oh?" The earl tipped his head to one side. "Perhaps you can encourage her to be less timid. *You* were certainly bold, the way you smashed that crate of kittens. You might make a good ship's boy."

"I would like that," Duncan said shyly, "but my mother would never let me."

The earl chuckled. "A mother wants to keep her baby boy safe. But there comes a time when he must break away and become a man." He gazed at Duncan thoughtfully. "Of course, most boys are too timid to leave their mothers until they are almost full-grown. But there are a few boys—a very few—who are brave enough to leave home much sooner."

Duncan looked past the gallery railing to the sea, bright in the sun's glare. He raised a hand to shade his eyes, and his fingers brushed the leather of his cap.

He had forgotten to remove his cap in the presence of the earl! Duncan stammered an apology, reaching up to take it off, but the earl forestalled him with a hand on his wrist.

"Please, keep your cap on. You should buckle it, too." The earl glanced aside at the crowded wharf. "We must indulge your mother in her little whims. It's a very fine cap, you know, leather lined with sheep's wool. Poor boys generally wear a canvas cap, made of sailcloth. . . . I wore a canvas cap myself when I was a boy," he said, his mouth twisting into a smile.

It was true that Duncan's cap was a fine one. He slowly buckled it.

"Does your mother get money from somewhere else, I wonder, to buy such a cap? From someone besides a piano student, perhaps?"

Duncan took a step back. The earl was asking a lot of personal questions. No matter how trustworthy he was, still there was no need to tell him everything. Last night, the man who had visited his bedroom had seemed to think there was need for secrecy, too. Duncan had almost forgotten that, in the excitement of meeting the nation's hero.

"But perhaps I'm being too personal," the earl said at once. "I do beg your pardon. Please come into the cabin. I see that Cook has brought us his famous cherry punch."

The cook was a big man, with hairy arms and thick powerful hands that made the tray he was carrying look like a toy. "Shall I pour, my lord?" He set down the pitcher and goblets, wiped his hands on his stained apron, and stretched his lips in a smile, showing teeth that were strangely gray. "Is the boy sitting here?"

Duncan watched him, half fascinated, half repelled.

"Yes, pour a glass for Duncan," said the earl. "And help me with the deadlights—I want to show the boy. He'll find them interesting."

The cook smiled even more broadly. "They lock up tight!"

Deadlights were stout wooden panels, like shutters, that covered the windows. Two long bars fit over the deadlights to keep them in place, and were locked with a brass key. The cabin grew dim, but light still filtered in through two small round portholes on the sides.

"We fit the deadlights when there's a storm raging," said the earl. "It keeps water from crashing in when the seas are high." He began to pour a glass of the cherry punch for himself, then stopped with the pitcher in midair as if struck with a sudden thought. "How is your penmanship?"

Duncan would have won a prize for penmanship at school if he hadn't blotted the paper on purpose. "Not bad," he said.

The earl reached past a typewriter on his desk, took paper from a drawer, and uncapped a bottle of ink. He handed Duncan a pen with a metal nib. "Sit down and write your name in cursive. Here, at the bottom." He looked around him. "You don't mind if the deadlights are up, do you? Often at sea you have to write without much light, you know."

Duncan dipped the pen in the ink, tapped it against the bottle so it wouldn't blot, and signed his name with a flourish. It looked perfect.

The earl looked admiringly at what Duncan had written. "I'll have to show this to Bertram," he said. "He thinks his nephew would be a good ship's boy, but I need a clever lad. Bertram's nephew can barely print." He folded the paper and tucked it in his pocket, smiling. "Now, I wonder . . . ," he said softly.

Duncan waited a moment. "You wonder what, sir?"

The earl lifted a shoulder. "You *seem* like a fine, adventurous lad, but are you bold enough to take action?"

Duncan's heart was beating a rapid patter. "What kind of action, sir?" He moved restlessly and bumped the table.

The earl reached out to steady Duncan's glass of cherry punch. "I think I'm going to do a short sail, just to Capital City and back. Two days, no more. I've been looking for a good ship's boy, and I might be willing to try you out. I'd pay, of course. A brass baron a day."

Duncan's mouth opened slightly.

"I plan to visit the Academy while I'm there," the earl went on, casually picking at his fingernails. "I don't see why you couldn't come along. You could see the place and meet the headmaster. He'll be impressed at your test scores, I imagine."

There was something swelling in Duncan's throat that made it hard to speak. "You mean," he said breathlessly, "I could go with you *now*?"

"There's no time to ask permission," warned the earl. "We're sailing with the ebb tide as soon as the loading is done."

Duncan could not make the decision sitting still. He stood abruptly and paced to the porthole.

The breeze had freshened, and he could feel the tide tugging at the ship. Judging by the marks on the pilings, high tide was hours past. It was true that there was no time for him to ask permission. Even if he knew where his mother was teaching at the moment—and he didn't—he would not be able to get there and back before the ship sailed, much less take the time to explain anything to her. There was an hour, no more, before slack water, and then the tide would turn.

It was an incredible honor to be invited to sail with the Earl of Merrick. The other boys would give almost anything for a chance like this. And it had all happened because he had skipped class and run to the wharf!

That daring action had brought him a silver coin, and his first ride in a carriage, and a meeting with the nation's hero. It had given him the tour of a real ship and the offer of a job that would make Robert stare. What wonderful things might happen if Duncan took another daring action?

It was the sort of chance that might never come again. He had to take it. He *would* take it. And when he returned, safe and sound, his mother would see she had been wrong to worry. He smiled out the porthole at the island he would soon be leaving.

The wharf was crowded with an unusual number of cats. There were cats lined up along the boardwalk, cats perched on top of every piling, and more were arriving every moment. What were they all meowing about? It was impossible to understand any one of them when they were all making so much noise. He would have asked Fia if she could make any of it out, except she was still peacefully sleeping inside his shirt.

Then he heard an anguished meow from the dock, louder and more piercing than any other cat's. "Fia! Fia! FIIIIII-AAAAAA!"

It had to be Mabel. The high, dreadful yowling of a mother cat who had lost her kitten went on and on, and Duncan wanted to put his hands over his ears. He knew mothers worried, but he didn't know they felt like *this*.

He leaned his forehead against the brass porthole collar and stared out, unseeing. This was how *his* mother would feel. For two whole days, she would believe he was dead, or kidnapped, or trapped somewhere, calling for help and needing her. She would not be able to sleep. She would not know what to do. She would never think that her son had left her on purpose, without even a note to say good-bye. . . .

Duncan shut his eyes. Suddenly it didn't seem brave, or bold, or daring to sneak away on the earl's ship. It seemed dishonorable and mean.

"I can't do it, sir. I'm sorry." Duncan got the words out somehow.

The earl stood at once. "A pity. I thought you might have been plucky enough to take the risk, but I see I was wrong."

Something crumpled in Duncan's chest. He stared up at the earl, dumbly miserable. There came a tap at the door.

"Ah, here's Bertram at last."

Duncan started to follow the earl out the door but was waved back.

"Please," said the earl, "sit down and drink that punch before you go. Cook made it especially for you—he'll be insulted if you don't have at least one glass."

Bertram winked from the passageway. "Have two," he said, and closed the door.

It was quiet in the dim cabin. Inside Duncan's shirt, the kitten breathed lightly against his chest. Through the open porthole, the cries of gulls mingled with the stamp of men's feet and a mechanical clanking. Duncan caught a glimpse of the dock crane; they had fixed its ropes and tied someone's sea chest—black with brass fittings, like the one at home—to the hook.

Duncan's grief was like a stone inside him, cold and heavy. He had come so close to his dream. His mother would never know what he had given up for her sake, and he could never tell her.

He rubbed the back of his sleeve across his eyes and sniffled. Maybe he would stay on the ship just a few moments longer. He caught sight of a small telescope hanging from a hook, and put it to his eye.

The cats on the wharf were still raising a ruckus. He caught a few words; he was pretty sure one was "kittens." The spyglass brought them so close that he could see their individual mouths meowing, but the sounds were too confused to hear clearly.

Fia stirred inside Duncan's shirt. Her tiny claws pricked his skin as she stretched. "It's stuffy in here," she complained, and Duncan undid the top button.

"Are you feeling all right?" he asked. "After your fall?"

Fia's pointed face peered up at him from inside his shirt. "I'm all right *now*."

"How did you end up in that crate?" Duncan squinted through the spyglass again. There was Old Tom—he had climbed up on a pier. He was meowing something that Duncan couldn't quite make out.

"I can't remember exactly," Fia said. "There was something—something good—in the street. I smelled it. And then I came out, and it was only this little pile of leaves, but it was wonderful! You could smell it, and taste it, and *roll* in it." Fia shut her eyes, purring in remembered ecstasy.

"And then?" Duncan prompted.

Fia curled up against his chest. "Next thing I knew, I was stuffed in a smelly bag with a lot of kittens. We were put in a crate and then it crashed and you found me."

Suddenly there was a lull in the meowing, and Duncan could hear Old Tom's yowl clearly above all the rest. "Kitnip! Kitnip found in the streets! Keep your kittens with you at all times!"

So Old Tom had been right all along.

Fia's head lifted sharply, as if she had heard a trumpet call. "Mommy?" she mewed.

Duncan hung the telescope up, ashamed. It was time to get Fia back to her mother; he had delayed too long. . . .

It took a minute before Duncan understood why the cabin door wasn't opening. Someone had locked him in.

He banged on the door's heavy panels, but no one came. All at once there seemed to be a lot more noise on the ship—a thunderous stamping, a metallic clanking, a creaking of timbers. The deck tilted under his feet. He looked out the porthole, where the line of cats grew suddenly smaller.

They were sailing away.

CHAPTER 9
A Glass of Cherry Punch

"HEY! HEY!" DUNCAN BANGED on the cabin's low ceiling. Then he yelped out the round porthole, twisting his head so that his voice might be heard on the deck above. "I'm still here! Take me back to the docks!"

Above him a powerful voice struck up a sea chanty—"From Isle of Dulle we're bound away"—and a thunder of male voices joined in with "Away, lads, heave away!" Duncan's cries were drowned out by loud, tuneless singing and the slap of canvas as the sails billowed out to catch the sea breeze.

If only the deadlights hadn't been in place! Duncan rattled at the bars, but the pins were locked and the earl had taken the key. He ran to the porthole again and tried to push one shoulder out, with no success.

Fia wriggled against his chest. "You're squishing me!"

"Sorry." Duncan stared out the porthole. If a fishing boat came by, he would wave and call for help.

Fia clambered up to his shoulder. "Are we prisoners?"

In a way they were. But accidental prisoners? Or had Bertram locked them in on purpose? There was no reason Duncan could think of why *anyone* would lock him up.

He blinked at the circle of tossing water and tilting sky. The waves crested and curled and subsided, foaming in hypnotic curving lines that were always changing and yet always the same; he watched them as if the answer were contained somewhere in their endless motion.

But Fia's small mews were worried—too worried for a baby cat. Duncan tried to cheer her up despite the hollow feeling at his core. "Maybe you'll get to stay and be a shipboard cat. You said you wanted to explore, right?"

Fia sniffed. "Not on a ship where they put kittens in dark crates."

Duncan put the telescope to his eye. He could still see the line of cats, but they were tiny specks, for the ship had passed the mouth of the bay.

All at once he lurched, caught off balance. There was a hesitation in the ship's forward motion, as if the schooner had paused to catch her breath, and then the deck tilted under him the other way. The ship had come about. A glance out the porthole told him that the ship had cleared the point and was now sailing along the west side of the island.

He braced his feet for the new slant and looked keenly through the spyglass up at the familiar cliffs. He knew the landmarks from the sea. The narrow entrance to the cove must be coming up, and above it, the stone throne where he loved to sit. This would be his last glimpse of his home for two days, he knew, for even if the earl discovered in the next minute that Duncan had been locked in, there was no way the ship would be turned back for the sake of one stowaway. The earl would have lost his tide; once docked, the ship would not be able to leave for another twelve hours. Duncan wasn't important enough to cause that sort of delay.

A small glee unfurled in Duncan's middle. He was going to be a ship's boy after all—and with no blame to him, for hadn't he turned down the earl? His mother would be upset, of course, but there was nothing he could do about it now. In two days, when he returned from Capital City, she would be so happy that it would make up for all the worry.

Fia curled around his neck and patted the telescope curiously with her paw. Duncan showed her how to put her small eye to the lens.

"Can you see the stone throne?" he asked. "That big boulder that looks like a chair for a giant?"

Fia pressed against the eyepiece. Her tail went up like a flag. "Why is Grizel on the cliff?"

Duncan nudged Fia aside. He scanned—it *was* Grizel! Why had she run all the way to the cliff? She was waving her tail . . . no, lashing it. . . .

Duncan took in his breath sharply. She was signaling. She was not signaling in semaphore, holding flags in different positions, the way human sailors did. She was signaling with her tail in Cataphore, the language of seagoing cats. Unlike the subtle motions of whiskers and ears that cats used face-to-face, Cataphore could be seen at long distances. Grizel had tried to teach him once, but since he didn't have a tail, he hadn't paid much attention.

"Let me see!" Fia's whiskers tickled as she butted her head against Duncan's jaw.

Duncan stared intently through the telescope at the small moving figure on the clifftop. Grizel arched her back, clawed the air, put her tail straight up—no, now it was sideways—and now it was at an angle.

Duncan clicked his tongue with impatience. He couldn't understand any of her signals.

"Have you learned Cataphore yet?" he asked Fia as he yielded the telescope. "Tell me what she's saying."

Fia hesitated. "Cataphore's kind of advanced. I haven't even passed my kitten examinations."

"Try anyway," urged Duncan. "You're a cat. It might come naturally to you."

Fia shrugged her tiny shoulders. "That looks like 'keep your back up,'" she meowed. "And maybe 'keep your claws out.' Then . . . let's see . . . she's making the number seven."

Duncan chewed on a fingernail. "Cat tricks go by number," he said abruptly. "Number seven—that's Perky Ears, right?"

Fia hesitated. "Now she's making letters with her tail, but I'm not very good at spelling yet."

Duncan fought the urge to grab the telescope away and see for himself. "Just do the best you can. Say the letters out loud to me." He fumbled with his free hand for the pen and pulled a fresh sheet of paper out of the drawer. He wrote "Back up, claws out," as fast as he could, and waited, pen poised, for more.

"*W* . . . *A* . . . ," said Fia. "*C* . . . *H* . . . *O* . . . *W* . . . *T* . . . *F* . . . *O* . . . *R*."

Duncan looked at what he had written. Wachowtfor. It didn't make any sense. He mouthed the syllables aloud, slowly, and the sound created meaning in his brain. "Watch out for!" he said, excited. "She's telling us to watch out for something—what? What else is she spelling?"

But Fia said nothing. One eye had become distracted by the reflection of light on the water that played across the cabin wall. Now she was swaying on her hind feet, her paws outstretched to catch the dancing bits of light.

"Hey!" Duncan dropped the pen. "Pay attention! Tell me the next letters!"

Fia glanced carelessly through the telescope. "*E*," she said.

"*E?* What's the rest of it?" cried Duncan. "Come *on*, Fia!"

"*E, L, S*," Fia rattled off, and pulled her eye away again, entranced by the darting flecks of light.

"Eels? Watch out for *eels*? Are you sure?"

"They're moving!" cried Fia, pawing the air. "I can catch one, I know I can!"

Duncan stifled a groan as he put his eye to the telescope. He should have known better than to trust such an important job to a kitten. By the time he managed to focus on Grizel once more, she was so small he could barely see her lashing tail.

"When she whips her tail back and forth, what does that mean?" he demanded.

Fia had given up on the dancing sparkles and was investigating the swinging cot, but she answered promptly. "Danger," she said. "If it's three long lashes and one short. Or maybe—" She twined her paws together uncertainly. "Maybe it's three short lashes and one long. And if it's two long and two short, I think it means 'you have a wood tick.' Or maybe 'your mother has fleas.' It's something bad, anyway, I'm pretty sure."

Duncan doubted his cat had run all the way to the cliff just to tell him about wood ticks or fleas. Somehow Grizel must have known he was on the schooner and had tried to warn him of danger. But what kind of danger? He was supposed to worry about *eels*?

He watched with a strange catch at his heart as Grizel's form blended into the cliffside and disappeared. The island of Dulle was faded and misty in the distance when at last he took the telescope from his eye.

Duncan spread out his paper on the polished wooden table and puzzled over the words. Back up. Claws out. Perky Ears. Watch out for eels. They made sense individually, but not together.

He was thirsty. He picked up his glass of cherry punch and took a sip. It tasted strong, but not unpleasant. He jumped when Fia poked her head out from behind a curtain that hung to the deck.

"I'm exploring the earl's closet," she announced. "There's a place behind the walls and under the deck where I can squeeze through. And there's a smell of rat!"

"Watch out," said Duncan. He yawned widely, suddenly sleepy. "You're not much bigger than a rat yourself."

"I hope there *is* a rat," said Fia. "I can practice my pouncing skills!"

She popped out of sight. A scrabbling sound came from behind the closet curtain, then faded into the rest of the ship's noises and was gone. Duncan yawned again and hoped Fia had the sense to run away if she met a rat bigger than herself.

He looked at the drink in his hand. If he was going to be on the ship for a while, he had better not insult the cook. He lifted the glass to his lips and drank deeply.

It was odd how tired he was all of a sudden. He leaned his head against the bulkhead wall. In a minute, he would look at the paper again and try to figure out what Grizel had been trying to tell him. It was something important, he was sure. He would just close his eyes for a little while. . . .

The glass of punch slipped from his hand and shattered on the wooden planks. Duncan's knees buckled, and he slumped to the deck.

CHAPTER 10
Dangerous Duty

DUNCAN WOKE WITH A FOUL TASTE in his mouth and a head that felt as if it had been hit by a hammer. To complicate things, he was swinging back and forth, his hair was sopping wet, and he had to throw up.

He gripped the ropes of the hammock and struggled to sit upright. Immediately he felt worse. He groaned, collapsed on the rough wooden deck, and hit something that felt like a bucket.

It *was* a bucket. He crawled after it as it rolled away, and grabbed it with a desperate hand. He put his head over it in the nick of time.

Afterward the taste in his mouth was worse. He wiped his face with his sleeve and looked around. A shaft of dim light illumined low wooden beams overhead and what seemed to be a space full of hammocks, all swinging gently.

He hauled himself back into his hammock. He didn't know where he was or why, but he felt too horrible to care.

"Meow?" Fia's inquiring voice came from the beams overhead. "What were you doing with your head in that bucket?"

"None of your business," Duncan muttered.

Fia's high meow pierced his head like a skewer. "I've been exploring all the between-places, but humans keep *chasing* me—"

If he shut his eyes, Duncan wondered, would the room stop going round and round?

Fia dropped down onto Duncan's chest with a jarring thump and rapped his chin with her paw. "Get up, will you? Come on!"

Duncan covered his ears.

Bang! A hatch flew open. A shaft of light filtered down, illuminating the dust floating in the air. Heavy boots clumped down a ladder, and a loud voice called, "Heeere, kitty, kitty, kitty!"

In an instant, Fia was wriggling her way inside Duncan's shirt, poking his skin with her sharp little claws.

"You, boy! Have you seen a kitten?"

Duncan's shoulder was roughly shaken, and he struggled to sit up. He could feel Fia trembling inside his shirt. "It's too dark in here to see anything. What do you want a kitten for?"

"What for?" the sailor repeated, grinning. "You're new on this ship, aren't you?"

The deck swooped beneath Duncan so violently that he clutched for the bucket. He didn't have the strength to ask what the sailor meant. He bent his head over the bucket one more time, heaving, and the sailor chuckled.

"Rough waters, mate," he said. "You'll feel better once you get your sea legs."

"When will that happen?" gasped Duncan.

"Two or three days. Buck up, lad—they'll put you to work soon enough, and that will take your mind off your stomach."

"I can't stay here even one day." Duncan fell back with a moan. "My mother doesn't know where I am. I've got to get home—or at least get a message to her."

The sailor shook his head, his loose, stringy hair flying back and forth against the shaft of light. "Take my advice and forget about her. Little nancy boys who whine for their mamas don't last long on this ship, see?"

Duncan was determined not to be the sort of boy who whined for his mother, though he thought of her often enough in the miserable night that followed. He lay curled in his hammock, weary and ill, swaying with the roll and plunge of the ship, trying to sleep while the ship's crew snored in hammocks all around him. Their bodies were so close that if he put out a hand, he could touch one, yet he had never felt so alone.

He did not know why he had been locked in and drugged, but it seemed clear that he had. Bertram was the most likely culprit—with the cook a close second. Duncan thought back to the way Bertram had first suggested refreshments, then spoken privately to the cook. When the earl had left Duncan in the great cabin, Bertram had been the one who shut the door—and locked it behind the earl's back, no doubt.

The next morning, as soon as he could stagger on deck, Duncan asked to see the earl.

The earl was not quite so friendly as he had been. He ran his eyes over Duncan and did not ask him to sit down. And when Duncan told him of his suspicions, the lines in the man's face deepened, and his brows snapped together.

The Earl of Merrick drummed his long fingers against the armrest of his chair. "I was prepared to give you a chance; you seemed a likely lad. But now I am not so pleased with you. First off, Bertram has been my faithful servant since boyhood. He would *never* do such a thing."

"But—" Duncan protested.

"And I will get exceedingly angry if you continue to make unfounded accusations. For one thing, that cherry punch was meant for me as well. Would Bertram try to drug *me*? To what end?"

"I don't know," said Duncan stubbornly, "but the cook was in on it, too."

The earl laughed. "All the cook did was add rum to the punch, as always. Here on board ship, we drink a great deal of rum, man and boy both—it is the sailor's drink. Clearly you liked it, for the pitcher was drained when I returned to the cabin, and you were passed out, drunk, on the floor."

Duncan gaped at him. *Drunk?*

"I was not impressed," said the earl with a downward flick of his raven-wing eyebrows.

"I wasn't drunk—I was drugged," Duncan said hotly. "And I didn't drink the whole pitcher, and I was *locked in*."

The earl's mouth curled in sardonic amusement. "Are you entirely sure that your memory is accurate? A boy who had his first taste of rum might easily overdo it. Here is what I think happened: You got drunk with rum, you fumbled with the door latch and imagined that you were locked in, you fell and hit your head and were knocked out. That's enough to fuddle anyone's brain."

Duncan shook his head. It had not happened that way—he was sure of it. But he could see how the earl might think so.

"Drunkenness on board is a punishable offense. You will have extra duties for two weeks." The earl pulled a piece of paper toward him and made a note.

"Two *weeks*?" Duncan cried.

"Would you prefer a flogging? That can be arranged." The earl tapped his pen.

Duncan's mouth was open, but his voice did not seem to be working. At last he squeaked, "I thought you were going to sail for two *days*, to Capital City and back to Dulle!"

"Plans change," said the earl, waving a dismissive hand. "You were still lolling about in your hammock yesterday when we stopped at Capital City. I got new information that makes it imperative to sail south."

"But—you *promised*—"

The earl's long fingers strayed to his bandage, toying with the frayed edge. "Perhaps you don't understand honor and duty. Perhaps you think I have nothing better to do than to ferry a penniless boy back to his dull, tame, fearful life."

Duncan flushed. More than ever, he wished he had not confided in the earl.

"Some people get drunk because they try to find courage in a bottle." The earl's lip curled slightly. "You were afraid to come on as a ship's boy. Perhaps you drank the whole pitcher to give you the bravery to stay."

Duncan's cheeks burned as if he had been slapped. "I'm not a coward!"

The earl smiled thinly. "You'll have the chance to prove it. If you don't back down from any duty, however dangerous, you will—in time—earn my trust."

❧

The mast surged and swayed under Duncan like a living thing. He gripped it tightly and pressed his cheek against the weather-beaten wood. He was in the crosstrees, the open platform high on the mainmast, and far below was the ship, looking small and impossibly narrow on the wide, wide sea.

Looking down gave Duncan a hollow, scooping sensation behind his ribs. He was used to heights—he had climbed the cliffs at home often enough—but he wasn't used to heights that *moved*. The ship's mast didn't just bob up and down; it swung forward, back, and side to side, and Duncan, clinging near its top, felt as if he were a pen writing great curving loops on the sky.

If he lost his grip, he would plunge straight into the sea. Or he might fall onto the deck and break his back. Or maybe he would bounce off the rigging, hit the railing, and *then* fall into the water. Would the ship come about in time before he drowned?

It was better not to think about it. And it was definitely better not to look down. Duncan twined his legs around the crosstrees, pulled a spyglass from his pocket, and scanned the far-off line where sea met darkening sky. If he saw a sail or land, he was supposed to give a shout to the crew on deck. That was the lookout's job.

A small grin spread over his face as he adjusted the telescope's focus. If someone had told him a month ago that he would have lookout duty on the Earl of Merrick's ship, he would never have believed it. But it was true! And he did more besides—scrubbed the deck and spliced rope and went aloft in all weathers, learning to set sail, take in a reef, and steer by sun and stars, and the thousand and one things a ship's boy could learn if he was bright and attentive. He was busy, but not too busy to think—or to watch Bertram.

Clearly Bertram was the earl's trusted right-hand man. Bertram was sent on errands to the small islands they stopped at; Bertram gave directions to the sailing master; it was Bertram who was with the earl most often, poring over charts of Arvidia and the surrounding sea.

Duncan was being careful. He had never taken another drink of cherry punch (or rum, for that matter) or eaten any food that he hadn't seen another sailor eating first. No one was keeping him safe anymore, so he would have to do it himself.

All the same, he'd had more close calls in the past month than seemed natural. He'd almost gone overboard twice; he'd nearly fallen off the foresail yard when the footrope broke; and when a backstay parted and a heavy wooden block came swinging at his head, it was pure chance that he'd happened to duck in time.

Bertram had been standing at the taffrail, a silent, hulking presence, watching each time that Duncan had nearly lost his life. But Duncan didn't see how Bertram could possibly have caused all those accidents.

Still, Duncan made sure he was never alone with the big-shouldered man, or standing too near. And he was always watching for Bertram to make some mistake—to say or do something that would convince the earl that the man should not be trusted.

For Bertram's crimes were not just drugging Duncan and locking him in. They also included stealing a crate full of kittens. Duncan didn't know why Bertram was interested in kittens, but he intended to find out. He felt certain that Bertram had not reported the kitten incident to the police back on Dulle when he went off in the carriage with Duncan's key.

Duncan went hot and cold each time he thought of how stupid he had been to give Bertram his house key—and his address. Sure, the earl may have wanted to send Sylvia McKay flowers, but Bertram could have taken advantage of that to harm Duncan's mother. The one thing that saved Duncan from tormenting himself was the fact that he *knew* she had been gone, teaching piano lessons, the whole time.

He missed his mother most dreadfully. During the day, of course, he was too busy for more than a brief snatch of memory or a piercing sense of loss. And most evenings he rolled into his hammock so exhausted that he was asleep within thirty seconds. But when the bell *ting*ed to mark the middle watch and he woke in the night, it was different. There, in the slow-breathing dark, with men swaying in their hammocks all around him, thoughts of his mother, Grizel, and home hollowed out Duncan's middle and left a stone on his chest.

Then the bell rang, the sun leaped up, the day's duties started, and Duncan would run up the rigging with a gasp of laughter as the wind blew through his hair. He had never felt so alive. He didn't bother to wear his cap; his hair was stiff and harsh with salt. His hands were growing calluses, and he was having the adventure of his life.

Of course, the sailors were a little rough and teased him more than he liked—but at least they never teased him about having red hair, for which he was grateful. Fia had gone into hiding so she wouldn't be chased, but there were plenty of spaces where she could curl up in comfort, as she told Duncan at night, and she was learning the passageways between. And though Bertram was an ever-present worry, Mr. Corbie, the sailing master, was friendly.

The master was an old salt with stumpy legs, curly gray hair, and bright blue eyes in a weather-beaten face, full of interesting information about the ship and how to sail her. He was teaching Duncan how to steer by the stars. Duncan knew the major constellations, of course—the Cat and Kitten, the Huntress, the Dog, the Crown—but he had not known that a line drawn from the Kitten's tail, crossed with a line from the Cat's right ear, would lead him home.

Now, high in the crosstrees, the breeze grew cool as the sun dipped below the horizon, and the first stars shone in the east, tiny pale fish swimming out of deep indigo blue. Duncan lowered the spyglass and gazed across the wide sweep of darkening sky. Soon he would not be able to see at all.

If he never got to go to the Academy, it wouldn't be so bad to just stay on a ship. He would love to keep sailing on and on, exploring all the different islands. There were more than he had ever dreamed, many more than there were on Friar Gregory's classroom map. Duncan had only to shut his eyes to see the map's carefully drawn islands, penned in brown ink, scattered across the sea like pebbles tossed from the hand of a giant. In school, he had been taught that the islands were all one nation, but he had not realized how very wide Arvidia was from one end to the other or how long it took to sail between islands. And he had not known that there were many, *many* more islands, small, rocky, and uncharted, that weren't on any maps at all.

There was a sudden shout from below and a blast of laughter. Duncan looked down to be sure that no one was calling for him, then snapped the brass telescope to his eye once again. He couldn't get so lost in his thoughts that he forgot his duty. He wanted the sailing master—and the earl—to think he was reliable.

The shouts from below grew louder, and there was a sound of stamping feet. A thin, high meow pierced through a momentary lull in the noise, and then a streak of white leaped for the mainmast and went up it like a rocket.

"*Meow meow meow meooooow!*" shrilled Fia. "Help me help me help me—"

Duncan held out his hands as the kitten clawed her way through the crosstrees. But Fia, in her unreasoning terror, dodged his grasp and ran out to the very end of the topsail yardarm.

"Great," muttered Duncan. He looked down at the knot of laughing, shouting men at the base of the mast. If Fia had only jumped into his arms, the men might have thought she was hidden somewhere among the rigging or in a bunt of sail, and he could have kept her safe. But now the white kitten was trembling at the very tip of the horizontal yard, clearly visible against the darker sky, and every eye was on her.

"Fia," Duncan said, his voice low and calm. "Walk back to me. Come on."

The kitten's fur was on end, ruffling in the wind. "I can't!" she mewed desperately.

"Sure you can. You got out there by yourself, didn't you? Just put one paw in front of the other."

Fia's eyes were wide and panicked. She dug her claws more deeply into the wooden yardarm. "You mean—let go?"

"Just lift one paw at a time," coaxed Duncan. "But don't look down, whatever you do—no, I said *don't* look down! Look up! Look at me!"

It was too late. Fia stared at the waves far below, clearly paralyzed with fear.

"Catch the cat, boy!" came a shout from below. "Crawl out on the yard and grab it!"

A sudden silence, and then the earl's voice, pitched loud enough for Duncan to hear: "If he's not brave enough, I'll send someone else to do it."

Duncan scowled. Of course he was brave enough to rescue Fia. But if he brought her down, what would the crew do to her? Old Tom had said this was not a ship for cats—and he had been right.

Duncan eyed the topsail yard, a pole like a long, thick branch extending at right angles to the mast. It had footropes. It had a jackstay to hang on to. It was just the same as the foresail yardarm—only higher, of course. And thinner. And of course there was more wind, and more sway, and farther to fall if he lost hold. . . .

Duncan swallowed hard and stretched one leg out to the footrope.

"Noooo!" came a howl from below. "Get on the *windward* side!"

Duncan pulled his leg back. He had almost done a very

stupid thing. Of course no one should ever climb out on the leeward side of a yard—any little jolt or gust and the wind could push him right off. But if he were on the windward side, the wind would be pushing him flat against the wooden yardarm, helping him hang on.

He slid onto the footropes. There was no one on the other side of the mast for balance, and he felt a sudden lurch as the topsail yard sagged under his weight.

His hands tightened on the jackstay until his knuckles went bloodless. But Fia was mewing pitifully, and below him, a shaking of the rigging told him someone else was climbing up. He had to get to the kitten first.

With the stout wooden yard pressed hard against his stomach, and the wind blowing firmly against his back, Duncan inched out. He kept his eyes on the far horizon—no looking down for him—and he was almost all the way out to Fia when he realized that he had been looking at a dark mass for some time.

"LAND HO!" he cried. "Two points off the starboard bow!"

Below him, the shouts and laughter ceased at once. Duncan didn't have to glance down to know that every eye was turned to the southwest and that everyone who had a telescope was looking through it attentively.

Now was the time. He took two more long sliding steps and reached. His hand slipped behind Fia's forelegs and tucked her inside his jacket with one smooth motion.

"I was so scared!" Fia's triangular face turned up to his, and her tiny pink mouth opened in distress.

Her whiskers tickled the underside of Duncan's chin. "Shh!" he said.

"Hey!" The sailor on the rigging below pointed to the yardarm. "Where's the cat? Didn't you catch it?"

Duncan called, "I was looking out at the island, and when I looked back, she was gone. Did you see her fall?"

The sailor shook his head. "She's probably already drowned."

Duncan squeezed out a short laugh. "Too bad for her."

The sailor grunted as he made his way down the ratlines. "Too bad for you. There's a reward if you catch 'em fresh."

Duncan didn't know what the sailor was talking about. He climbed back to the crosstrees and took his spyglass from his pocket. The island ahead was small, with a huddle of buildings beside a bay.

A small head bumped his chest, and a white paw poked up to pat his throat.

"Would you *please* stay hidden?" Duncan whispered, exasperated. If Fia wouldn't stay quiet and still, he was never going to be able to protect her.

"But I have to *show* you something." Fia's meow was urgent. "It's in the very bottom of the ship, and if you sniff it, it smells just like—"

"Show me later," said Duncan, and he buttoned his jacket to the top.

CHAPTER 11

The Bloodstained Jacket

I T WAS EARLY IN THE MIDDLE WATCH when Duncan woke with a start. Something had brushed his face. He lay perfectly still in his hammock, and it came again—a furry paw patting his cheek, and with it, the tiniest of meows in his ear.

"Now?" Fia's whiskers tickled his neck. "Can I show you *now*?"

Duncan sighed deeply and swung his legs to the deck. He didn't bother to put on his shirt—it was getting too small for him anyway. Bare-chested, he slipped past the hammocks that held the sleeping, snoring crew, and snatched up a candle, a dark lantern to put it in, and some matches. He shut the metal slide so that only a thin line of light showed, and ducked through the hatch that led to the hold. His feet found the smooth wooden slats of the ladder, and he went down, down, all the way to the bottom.

He yawned widely as he set the kitten on the rough wooden planks and rubbed the sleep from his eyes. The air was thick and musty; it smelled of bilgewater. Huge hanks of rope hung between bales and boxes, and all around him, Duncan could hear the gentle, incessant creak of a ship at anchor.

He felt stupid. What was he doing, following a kitten when he should be sleeping? He put his foot wrong in the dark, stumbled, and nearly fell. He stood up, breathing hard. If he had dropped the lantern, he might have started a fire. And a fire in a wooden ship was no laughing matter.

"Hurry up, Fia," he said. "Show me whatever it is, and let's get out of here."

"There! There!" Fia cried. "Take a sniff!" Her ears pointed at a row of large boxes, black, brown, and faded gray. They were the crew's sea chests, tucked against a forward bulkhead.

Duncan stared at her in disbelief. "You want me to sniff a sea chest? Are you out of your little kitty *mind*?"

"Just this one." Fia leaped onto a black, brass-bound chest and put her nose down to the lid. "See? It smells like *Grizel*!"

Duncan lifted the lantern. He didn't have a cat's sensitive nose—he wouldn't have been able to smell Grizel's scent in a hundred years. But he had eyes. In front of him was the very chest that had stood at the top of their stairs at home for as long as he could remember. He knew every nick, every dent, every scratch.

So Bertram had used Duncan's house key, after all. No wonder he had taken a burly sailor with him. Duncan's breath came harshly through his nose as he imagined the two men breaking into his house, frightening Grizel away, clomping down the stairs with his father's sea chest between them. Duncan's mind held an image of the door left swinging open and his mother coming home to find the marks of muddy boots, the sea chest gone, and Duncan nowhere to be found.

He wrenched his mind away from the unbearable thought. In its place came a fierce realization—this was proof of Bertram's evil deeds. The earl would have to believe Duncan now.

Fia unsheathed a claw. "Do you want me to pick the lock?" she asked.

Duncan stared at the chest. His mother had kept it locked and never told him what was inside. "Isn't that an advanced skill for a kitten your age?" he whispered.

"Yes," Fia admitted, "but I've been hiding down here for days, and I've been practicing."

The big brass lock didn't need to be picked after all. Someone had forced it already. At Duncan's first touch, it fell open and hung from its hinge, dangling.

There was a squeak from behind a coil of rope, and the sound of a tiny scuffle, but Duncan hardly noticed the rats fighting in the shadows. With hands that shook slightly, he hung the lantern from a nail in the bulkhead and opened the metal slide all the way. A wide shaft of light streamed out, making the chest's brass bindings gleam and tinting the white kitten's fur with gold as she leaped off the chest.

Duncan put his hands on the chest lid and pushed up. The hinges creaked. The lid swung back. His heartbeat quickened as he leaned over the edge to look inside.

The first thing he saw was an old white shirt. He touched the familiar frayed cuffs, the small monogram on the collar—*McK*, within an embroidered square with points on top. It was the shirt he had once used as a cape, pretending to fight evildoers. He put it on and buttoned it to the neck. It was too big for him, but it felt warm and comforting, almost like a father's arms, and his other shirt was getting so small he had burst a shoulder seam. He rolled up the cuffs and looked in the trunk again.

It wasn't very full. There was a long wooden tube, the sort that held rolled-up ship's charts, empty. There was a jumble of clothing and a glint of gold lace at the bottom, and a belt of fine leather with two straps and a loop. And something else shone with reflected light—something long, thin, and ever so slightly curved.

He drew in a breath and reached inside. His hand curled around the hilt. His father's sword. It had to be his father's sword.

Duncan sat back on his heels. He set the blade across his thighs, and its thin, wicked edge flashed silver as it caught the light. It was too heavy for him now, but someday it wouldn't be. . . . With an interior bubble of delight, Duncan examined it more closely.

There was gold on the hilt. Duncan did not see the insignia of the Island Patrol, or the King's Guard. Instead he found a stamp of the letters *McK*, inside a double square with points on top like a crown—just the same as the monogram on the shirt. There were three lines, like rays of light, angling out from either side. It wasn't a symbol that he recognized, though it seemed vaguely familiar. Maybe it was the emblem of some kind of special forces.

Hardly breathing, Duncan set the sword aside and reached into the chest again. He saw a swordbelt of fine leather. He lifted out a jacket of deep blue broadcloth, with brass buttons in a double row and something gold pinned on the collar. It was a kind of uniform, Duncan knew. He was sure he had seen it somewhere before. It was slashed under one arm, with a large brownish stain, crusty with—

"Blood!" Fia sniffed at the fabric in alarm. She leaped away to the next chest over, then to the box stacked on top of that.

Duncan did not want to think about whose blood it was. With an effort, he returned the jacket to the sea chest, and as he did, he saw the gold on the collar more clearly. It looked almost like a wave, or wings.

He blinked. It was the Gannet Medal—two arched wings of the seabird that haunted every island in Arvidia. Not many won the Gannet.

Duncan frowned. Maybe this wasn't his father's uniform after all. Someone who was decorated with the Gannet Medal would be *known*. But Duncan couldn't remember ever hearing of a famous McKay.

He scrabbled in the bottom of the chest, but there was only a sort of folder, flat and wide, made of soft leather. He dropped it when he heard a panicked meow from somewhere above his head.

"I smell something!" Fia's meow was as close to a shriek as a kitten could produce.

Duncan snatched the lantern and lifted it, training the light on the bulkhead (as all walls in a ship were called). Like most bulkheads, this one had a space of a few inches at the top for ventilation, and it was on this ledge that Fia was crouched. She was looking over into the area behind—the cable tier, perhaps, where the great anchor ropes were coiled, twenty inches around, as thick as a man's thigh.

"You're always smelling something," Duncan said. "Anyway, that's just the anchor cable in there. It's not a giant snake or anything."

Fia shook her head. "I'm not scared of any old rope. But there's a smell of kittens—kittens *afraid*. . . ."

"Are there any kittens in there now?"

Fia sniffed the air delicately and shook her head. "The scent is old. But there were kittens. And they were scared."

There was no door in the bulkhead, but the stacked chests and boxes had been lashed in place and made a good stair.

Duncan found them easy to climb, even with a lantern in one hand, and when he got to the top, he lay on his stomach and put his eye to the gap.

There were no thick coils of rope stacked high. There was one hanging rope that looked as if it might come from a hatchway above, but the bit Duncan could see was not even as thick as his wrist.

He moved the lantern in an attempt to see more of the room. Now he could see the top part of a machine with a handle that looked like a giant grinder. But if the cook wanted to grind something, wouldn't he do it two decks up, in the galley?

"I can smell your scent in there," Fia said suddenly.

Duncan rolled his eyes privately. "You're just smelling me right here, you goof."

"I don't think so." Fia dug her claws into the wood and poked her head through the gap. "There's an old scent of you down there. Were you ever in that room?"

"Not that I know of." Duncan stifled a yawn. He was finding it hard to worry about a room where kittens might have been scared long ago. Besides, he was feeling good. He liked thinking of his father with a uniform and a sword and a medal from the king. And he could hardly wait to tell the earl what Bertram had done.

"Where are you going?" demanded Fia. "Let's find out what's in that room!"

"Later," said Duncan. He climbed backward down the

stacked boxes, feeling blindly with his feet, and landed on a heaped sailcloth. He tripped and almost fell on the leather folder that he had dropped.

Fia followed him, still meowing in frustration. As Duncan reached for the leather folder, a newspaper clipping fell out.

He held it to the lantern, reading eagerly at first and then with growing disappointment. It was just some old column about the Capital City Orchestra. They had played a special concert to celebrate the fourth birthday of the Princess Lydia. A lot of nobles were there. . . . Duncan skipped over the names. There had been a beautiful violin solo, blah blah blah. . . . Everyone was entranced, blah blah. . . .

This wasn't any help. Maybe his father had been a music lover, but that didn't explain what Duncan most wanted to know.

He opened the leather folder and saw some papers and a photograph. The photo showed a man and a woman, smiling, holding a baby between them. In the background was part of a stone building that looked familiar somehow. And the woman and the man looked almost like people he knew—or had known once.

Duncan brought the photograph closer to the lantern. With a skip of his heart, he recognized his mother. Younger, happier, with her hair loose on her shoulders and no covering scarf at all.

Then, the baby she was holding must be himself. And the tall man with the strong nose and the military hat had to be—

Hissst! Fia leaped onto his knee. "Do you hear footsteps?"

Duncan shook his head. He kept his eyes on the photograph. It was hard to see in such dim light, and his vision was blurring.

"Someone's coming!" Fia's meow was urgent. Now heavy footsteps could be heard over the gentle creaking of the ship, and the hatch above was filled with a lantern's swinging light.

Fia tried to close the dark-lantern's slide with her paws. There was a smell of singed hair. "I think I burned a toe," she said in a faint meow.

"Close your eyes—they shine in the dark," Duncan whispered. He stuffed the photograph and papers into the folder, threw a corner of sailcloth over the lantern, and closed the sea chest hurriedly. He stifled a yelp as the heavy lid pinched a finger on one hand. He sucked on his sore finger and crouched behind the sea chest in the shadows.

Large feet descended the ladder. The face of the night watchman came into view, peering down into the hold. "Rats again," said the man in a tone of deep disgust, and turned back.

Duncan waited a minute to be sure he was gone, then opened the folder in a small circle of dim lantern light. The papers crackled, their yellowed edges crumbling in his hand. He bent closer, squinting. There were names, dates. . . . He read them, but it was like trying to read through water. The meaning shimmered and would not come clear.

The air in the hold was fetid; it smelled of rat droppings and old cheese. Duncan felt strangely dizzy. He did not want to look at the papers again. He did not want to try to make sense of them. There was a dread pressing upon his shoulders; there was a truth lurking in the shadows that he did not want to see.

Fia had curled up on his thigh and gone to sleep. Duncan stroked her soft fur, feeling the tiny heartbeat beneath his fingers. There was something wonderfully comforting about a cat, however small. He picked up the papers once more and forced himself to read them carefully.

He had not understood the news clippings and other papers at first. They seemed to have nothing to do with him or his parents. For one thing, the violinist for the royal court, the famous "Sweet Bow of Arvidia," was called Elizabeth, not Sylvia. The name on the birth certificate was not Duncan McKay, but Duncan McKinnon. McKinnon was an old and noble name, a name storied in the history of Arvidia, nothing to do with him.

Duncan brought the birth certificate closer to his eyes. The birth date was his own. The mother's maiden name was spelled out in full: Elizabeth Sylvia Lachlan. And the father's name was there, too: Charles David McKinnon, with his full title beneath. . . .

Duncan shut his eyes. Instinctive denial came rushing in—it couldn't be, it *couldn't* be—but it was too late to unread the papers. It was too late to stop the pieces from coming together in his mind.

A slow tide of shame washed over him, a sick, hot flood

rising up into his throat and choking him with dismay. His father was not the hero Duncan had imagined. He wasn't even an ordinary, decent man with a family and a job.

His father was hated. His father was despised. His father had betrayed king and country, and to this day, his name was mocked in the streets by chanting schoolchildren.

His father was Charles, Duke of Arvidia.

CHAPTER 12

Squisher and Grinder

D UNCAN LAY AWAKE IN HIS HAMMOCK. The air smelled of unwashed bodies and foul, fetid breath. The lumpy shapes of sleeping men, swinging gently like bundles tied up in string, were beginning to show in the faint gray light coming through the hatch. It was almost dawn.

He would not go to the earl and tell him that Bertram had stolen the sea chest. Duncan didn't want to draw the earl's attention to the sea chest in any way. The papers, the uniform, the sword—all would only show the earl that Duncan was the son of the man who had tried to kill him seven years ago.

Bertram must know already. Maybe he'd suspected the truth from the moment he first saw Duncan on the wharf or running up the gangplank to hand him a newspaper. Perhaps he'd had a good idea when he talked Duncan into giving up his key. It was certain he would have had no doubts at all once he'd rummaged through the sea chest.

Had Bertram told the earl what he knew? Or was he saving the information to use against Duncan at a future time? There must be some reason Bertram wanted Duncan in his power, or he wouldn't have locked him in the earl's cabin.

Duncan wished he could talk things over with Grizel. He wished he could tell his mother that he understood, now, why she told him not to stand out or get noticed, why she insisted he wear his cap all the time. She had wanted to save him the shame of being known as his father's son. She had not wanted him to get spit on in the streets.

He swung his legs out of his hammock and tiptoed between the sleeping men to his duffel bag, hung on a bulkhead peg. There was something he had to find, and he only hoped he hadn't thrown it away.

The stout canvas bag had been handed to him on the third day he was aboard, and was filled with a pick and mallet for caulking deck seams, a sewing kit for keeping his clothes in repair, and foul-weather gear from the slop chest. But it was not for any of those items that Duncan was looking as he rummaged deep in the bag with increasing haste.

In the shadowed gloom of the tween deck, he dumped out the duffel bag and found it at last—his cap. He jammed it on his head, tucked in every stray lock of hair, and buckled the straps tightly.

Once Duncan had thought it would be wonderful to be a noble—but no more. For one thing, his father the duke's lands and estate had been forfeit to the king when his treachery was discovered, and so Duncan was as penniless as he had always been.

He didn't care. He didn't want anything of his father's—not his lands, not his money, not his uniform or his sword or his name. It was bad enough that Duncan had his father's face and distinctive dark red hair; he couldn't get rid of *them*. The minute he was old enough to grow a beard and disguise himself, he would.

He looked down with disgust at his father's shirt. He would wear it, but only until he could get another shirt that fit him.

The bell rang for breakfast. The sailors thundered up the ladder, but Duncan stayed behind and took off the shirt. Then he folded the collar to cover the monogram, stitched it down, and did the same on the other side so it wouldn't look unequal. Duncan's stitches were not as neat as a real seaman's yet, but they were good enough to keep his father's initials from showing, and that was all he cared about.

"ALL HANDS!" roared the master. "ALL HANDS ON DECK!"

Duncan stumbled up the ladder after the other sailors. As soon as his head cleared the hatch, he felt the wind like a slap. It was going to storm; the sails had to be furled. He climbed the rigging to his duty station, then glanced downward to see Bertram by the taffrail, looking up. Beside him was the earl.

Duncan frowned. Bertram was a liar, a thief, and a kidnapper—and the earl's most trusted right-hand man. It seemed a dangerous friendship.

The schooner heeled in a sudden gust. Duncan's foot slipped, his fingers lost their grip, and he doubled himself over the foresail yard, hanging on by his armpits. For a moment, he clung there, bewildered, as the wind in the rigging took on the pitch of a scream. He had a sudden image of falling into the storm-tossed waters. No one would ever find him. His mother would not even have a grave to visit. . . .

His mouth twisted as if he had eaten something bitter. She could always pick some random grave with the right initials and call it his. That's what she had done with his father. All these years, Duncan had been visiting the grave of a total stranger.

Duncan wrenched his mind back to the job at hand. The squall was gusting strongly, land was in sight, and the topsail had to be reefed. He forced his bleeding fingers to wrestle with the reef point until it came free. Then came the order "Haul out to leeward!" and he pulled hard with the other sailors until the foresail was furled in a second bunt.

Rain slipped down the neck of his jersey and trickled along his back. He had forgotten to put on his oilskins when he went aloft—it had not been raining then—and now, miserable and bone-chilled, he knotted his reef point securely and slid down to the deck. But it wasn't until the tacks, sheets, and halyards were coiled away that the starboard watch was finally dismissed and he could go below.

"Hey, lad, run on up to the galley and beg Cook for a pot of coffee!"

Duncan nodded wearily and turned back to the ladder. Wet, cold, tired, it didn't matter—the ship's boy was the one to run errands. He trudged forward through the rain to the galley, tucked under the forecastle. He stood under the overhanging ledge and knocked at the half door.

Hssss!

Duncan looked up, startled.

Fia's blue and green eyes stared down at him accusingly from her perch on a corner brace. "So, are we going to investig—instigavess—I mean, are we going to sniff out that room? You know, where somebody scared kittens?"

Fia's meow was barely loud enough to be heard above the noise of the rain, but it still made Duncan nervous. "Shh!" he said. "Talk to me later!"

Duncan jumped as the galley door opened and Cook's round face peered out. When he saw Duncan, his smile broadened greasily and his teeth gleamed like polished metal. "What do you want?"

"The starboard watch wants a pot of coffee," said Duncan. "If you please."

The cook had thick, powerful arms with black hair running down past his wrists to his knuckles. He balanced easily on the sloping deck as he poured a gallon of boiling water into an enamel pot, threw in four handfuls of ground coffee, and stirred it with a long spoon. Then he wiped his hands on his dirty apron and turned around quickly. He caught Duncan gazing at a pan full of ship's biscuit.

"Want an extra biscuit, do you?"

Duncan's stomach growled in spite of himself. "No, thank you—" he began, but a grating voice behind him interrupted.

"Not hungry?" Bertram's bulky shoulders filled the doorway. "You must be working too little. Boys are always hungry unless they're slacking. Better put him to work, Cook."

Duncan was cold, wet, and exhausted from his labors in the driving rain. But his mother had taught him to control his expression; it was part of her game of Noble Manners. He knew his face showed only a distant, polite interest as he asked, "Would you like my help, Cook? I'd be glad to offer it."

He had the satisfaction of seeing Bertram's eyes narrow and his lips compress. "Think you're better than the rest of us, eh, boy? Think you're like the earl, who doesn't want to get his hands dirty. . . ."

Bertram had clearly never practiced Noble Manners—his resentment was showing all too clearly. Duncan almost smiled. He had thought his mother's teachings on manners were just a frivolous sort of thing—a way of being pleasant at a king's court. He had never before realized what an advantage it gave him, to be able to control his emotions. He had a power that Bertram did not have.

Duncan made his tone even more courteous, lifting his eyebrows the barest degree. "I beg your pardon; I believe I *did* just offer to dirty my hands in the service of the cook. But quite possibly I am mistaken."

A dull red crept up Bertram's neck to his cheeks, and his shoulders bunched as his thick fingers curled in on themselves. But he, too, seemed to be making an effort to control himself. All he said was, "It's a long voyage, lad . . . plenty of time for something to happen, without anyone getting his hands dirty at all."

Duncan sat on a bench under a row of hanging pots, with a bushel of potatoes on one side and a bucket of salt water on the other. A lantern swung above, giving just enough light for him to use his knife. He was used to peeling potatoes—he had done it often enough at home—so he had lots of chances to glance around. Somewhere below was the mysterious room that Fia wanted to investigate, but the galley itself was commonplace. Rows of jars on barred shelves, barrels full of meal and salted beef, ladles and knives hanging above the stove— none of it was very interesting to a spy.

There was, however, a door to an inner storeroom, and Duncan watched under lowered lashes as the cook went in and out.

A cloaked figure stepped into the galley, shedding water from his hat brim.

"Peeling potatoes?" said the Earl of Merrick. "Isn't it your watch below, boy?"

"He offered to help me," said the cook.

"I see. How very noble of him."

Duncan glanced up quickly. Was there something in the earl's tone that was almost—mocking?

Perhaps he had imagined it; the earl's expression was perfectly serious as he took off his wide-brimmed hat and dried it on a towel. His bandage had become disarranged, and he pushed it up with long, elegant fingers.

Cook reached for one of the potato peelings and held it up. "Look here!" He smiled, showing his dirty teeth. "I thought he might be a gentleman's son who'd run away from home, with his manners and all, but only a poor man's son knows how to cut peelings this thin. Doesn't want to waste any food, this lad!"

Duncan ducked his head to avoid the gaze of the two men. He watched from the corners of his eyes as the earl dug two hairpins out of his vest pocket, adjusted the bandage across his forehead, and pinned it in place on either side.

A peeling curled from Duncan's knife, and he dropped the finished potato into the water with a plop. It suddenly struck him that it was a little weird to wear a bandage for seven years.

The earl put his hat back on. "I'll be going ashore in my gig as soon as we anchor at this island; I'll have a late supper in my cabin. But a good supper, mind you, Cook," he added, smiling from beneath his bandage. "None of your leftovers."

"Aye, aye, sir! I will make you a *very* special supper to-night, sir, if you let me go ashore. I need fresh herbs and some . . . other ingredients."

"Very well. You can ask for the jolly boat and two sailors to row you."

"All hands! All hands to weigh anchor!" The cry pierced the door of the galley, and a rush of clattering feet followed. The slope of the deck changed; the sound of wind grew suddenly less. Duncan guessed they were gliding into the protected bay of the latest island. Duncan stood up—he was one of the hands with a job to do—but the earl turned to him.

"It doesn't matter if you're a poor man's son. I want someone who is smart and quick on the job." He gave Duncan a half smile. "I've been watching you, and I think you've earned this." The earl fished inside his cloak, found the pocket he was looking for, and handed Duncan a small piece of thickened cloth.

Duncan turned it over in his hand. Staring up at him was the earl's badge—a wolf's paw, claws extended, on a dark green shield edged with gold.

"Sew it on your cap," said the earl, "and wear it as long as you are in my service."

Duncan took his sewing kit above deck, where the light was better, and was surprised at how black and dirty his cap was inside. It smelled funny, too. Sailors didn't do much washing, of course, but after a whole month, he guessed it was time to wash his hair. It had never felt stiff and coarse like this at home.

The rain had dwindled to a fine mist by the time the earl's gig, a small boat stowed on the schooner's deck, was lowered into the waters of the bay. Duncan watched at the railing as the earl climbed down the ladder at the side of the ship, timed his jump, landed in the gig, and was rowed off to shore.

Duncan fingered the badge on his cap. He should be thrilled to have such a badge from the nation's hero, brave and honorable.

The words called up an echo in his mind. He could see his mother's face, gray and bleak. They had just passed children, jumping rope to a mocking chant: *Charles, Charles, Duke of Arvidia. . . .*

His mother had said then that his father had been both brave and honorable. "Never forget that, Duncan," she had begged, and he had promised.

But *both* men couldn't be honorable. One of them had to be the darkest villain. And a whole ship full of witnesses had sworn that the villain was his father.

Duncan had gone back to finish the potatoes when the cook gathered up two gunnysacks to use as shopping bags and left to go ashore.

"The hairy man is gone! Now we can spy out that room underneath the food place!" Fia leaped down from a crossbeam onto Duncan's shoulder, and her pointed claws dug through his shirt by way of emphasis.

"Ouch!" Duncan's knife made a jagged cut in the potato

148

he was peeling. "Pull in your claws, will you? And just because Cook is ashore doesn't mean I can run around spying with you. I have to finish these first, and then put them on to boil—"

Fia butted his left ear with her blunt, furry forehead, accenting her words with each thump. "I've *waited*, and now it's *time*. Come *on!*" She jumped lightly to the bench and glared up at Duncan. "Kitten business is more important than potato business."

Duncan suppressed a grin. When Fia scrunched up her face in that sour and disapproving way, she looked just like her mother, Mabel. "Have you grown?" he asked. He hadn't seen Fia much lately, but she seemed longer in the legs and thinner in the face.

"I've been battling rats," said Fia. "That would make anyone grow. Hurry *up*." She led the way to the storeroom door, her tail held like a flag.

Duncan tried the knob. "It's locked."

Fia's blue and green eyes rolled ever so slightly. "Of *course* it's locked," she said. "Lift me *up*."

Duncan did not enjoy being ordered around by a kitten, but he obeyed. Fia put out a claw and probed the brass keyhole. There was a quiet *click*.

"You're getting good at this," Duncan said, and creaked open the door.

The galley storeroom was crowded to bursting. There

were barrels on the deck and dried sausages hanging from the beams. There were boxes and bags, casks and bottles, shelves full of tins and a folder stuffed with what looked like recipes.

In one corner was a square open hatch. A luff tackle, three pulleys set in blocks, was attached to the beam above it, and a rope nearly as thick as Duncan's wrist dangled straight down into darkness.

"There! Over there!" Fia shrieked. She rushed to the edge of the hatch and put her head over. Her pink nose quivered.

Duncan took a lantern and leaned over the hatch. "It must go all the way to the hold. Are you *sure* you smelled kittens down in that room?"

Fia's pink nose quivered. "I was sure *then*."

Duncan knelt at the lip of the hatch and put his head over the vacant space. A dank, slightly decayed smell curled faintly in his nostrils.

He sat back on his heels, calculating how long it would it take Cook to shop for supplies and get rowed back to the ship. They'd have to hurry.

He loosened the rope's end from the cleat on the wall and pulled. The pulleys creaked, and the dangling rope straightened, swinging as it rose. Up through the hole came a large iron hook with a sling attached. Duncan passed the rope's end around his body, under his arms, and took a good grip. Then he set his foot in the sling, hung the lantern from the iron hook, and slowly, carefully, lowered himself and the kitten down through the decks. Unlike every other hatch Duncan had seen, this one did not open onto the deck spaces around it. They were in some kind of narrow shaft. Duncan looked up as the square patch of dim light above grew faint and far away.

Thunk. Duncan's feet hit bottom unexpectedly, and he fell to his knees. His grip slackened on the rope, and the heavy iron hook dropped. The lantern's light went out.

"Ow!" Duncan gripped his shoulder where the hook had struck him a glancing blow. Fia's eyes were two points of light, glowing amber and golden in the dark, and when she blinked, he could see nothing at all.

"Light a match, and then you can see," Fia suggested.

"I was just going to," muttered Duncan, fumbling in his pocket. The match flared with a small spurting sound, and it gave him enough light to find the lantern and set it upright. A second match lit the candle within, and when the flame was steady, he stood up and looked around by its glow.

The curve of the hull told Duncan that he was on the port side, below the waterline. He was in a small room, and a strange-looking machine was before him. Made of green-painted iron, it stood on six legs like some metallic monster. At the top was a large, square funnel, or hopper; to the left was a sort of wide spigot, with a basin beneath. In the center were two blocks that came together like a press for stamping out flat sheets of metal, and on the right was a wooden handle, worn from long use, that turned like a crank. A tub, a drainage board, and a scarred wooden counter filled the rest of the space; Duncan scarcely had room to take two steps in any direction.

Fia's small body pressed against his ankle, trembling.

Duncan bent down to pet her. "What's wrong?"

"Kittens were very afraid," whispered Fia. "Right there."
She pointed with a paw that wasn't quite steady.

Duncan lifted the lantern to look more closely at the big
machine. At shoulder height was a handle like a lever, sticking
out of a long vertical slot—it looked as though it was meant to
move back and forth. There were letters painted on the metal.
"G—R—I," he read aloud, but the long handle cast a black
shadow across the rest, sharp-edged like a knife.

Duncan moved the lantern to read the rest of the word.
GRINDER.

He squatted down to read the word on the lower end of the
slot. SQUISHER.

Duncan felt suddenly cold.

"I smell your scent here." Fia had left the safety of his ankle
and prowled a little distance away. "Here, by the tub." She pawed
at an empty jar that rolled along the floor. "What does this spell?
J—E—T—B—L—A—C—K—S—H—O—E—P—O— I can't tell
what the next letters are. There's something dark smeared on
them."

Duncan picked up the small jar of shoe polish. It was
empty. Who had been polishing shoes down here? He turned
abruptly. "I've never been in this room before in my life. And
if you're wrong about smelling my scent, maybe you're wrong
about smelling kittens, too."

There was a thump. Duncan cocked his head.

"What?" Fia poked her nose in the air again.

Duncan could hear the slap of waves on the hull, and the ship's timbers creaking. Somewhere behind the bulkhead, a rat squeaked. But he had heard something else.

It was time to get out of there. Duncan leaped for the dangling rope and jammed his foot into the sling again. "Hang on, Fia."

With a luff tackle, Duncan could pull himself up hand over hand, inches at a time. It seemed to take forever, but it was only a few minutes before his head cleared the hatch of the galley storeroom.

The door was still shut. With a last heave, Duncan lifted himself enough to get a foot onto solid wood. One hand still clung to the rope; with less weight on the sling, the hook shot up and Duncan lurched. His other arm flailed madly for balance. His fingers brushed a shelf, and a folder of papers fell to the deck.

Duncan was sweating. He cleated the rope with two quick turns, gathered up the papers any which way, and crammed them back into the folder. If he moved fast enough, he could be peeling potatoes by the time Cook walked in.

He shoved the folder back on the shelf, but a sheet came loose and fluttered to the deck. Duncan reached for it in one swift motion—and stopped.

He straightened slowly, staring at the paper in his hand.

It was a recipe for Kitten Pie.

CHAPTER 13
The Unknown Enemy

KITTEN PIE. CAT TAIL STEW. DEEP FRIED PAWS. Cat-aroni and Cheese. In one horrified moment, Duncan's eyes swept the contents of the folder. He felt ill.

"What does it say?" asked Fia, on his shoulder. "Kittens can't read all those big words."

Duncan had just come to the recipe for Kitty Jelly 'n' Jam. He swallowed hard and closed the folder. "It's just some old recipes. Pretty boring."

Fia blinked at him. "Then why do you smell afraid all of a sudden?"

Duncan shoved the folder back on the shelf with more force than was needed. "I'm afraid Cook will come back and find me in the storeroom. Let's get out of here."

"But why did they keep kittens down in that room?" Fia's voice was unrelenting in his ear. "And what was that big machine *for*?"

Duncan winced. Fia was just a kitten; she shouldn't have to know these things. He locked the storeroom door behind him and breathed more easily; he had not been caught. He picked up his potato knife and started peeling once more.

Cook must have discovered kitnip when he was hunting for kitchen herbs. As they stopped at different islands, he would go out in the night and use it to entice kittens away from their mothers. Old Tom had picked up the news and tried to pass it on at the cat council, but he had been laughed at. Duncan suspected that the cats on the island of Dulle weren't laughing now.

Fia tapped him on the side of her neck with an insistent paw. "You're not answering my questions."

Duncan made up an answer that wouldn't give Fia nightmares. "Someone is probably stealing kittens to sell them to pet shops on other islands. They keep the kittens in that room, and naturally the kittens are afraid in the dark without their mothers."

Fia's eyes grew wide, and her paw trembled. "That's *bad*! What are you going to do about it?" she demanded.

It was a question Duncan asked himself. But he was only the ship's boy. Who would believe him, if he told what he suspected? He had no proof. People would think that the kitten recipes were someone's idea of a joke. They would say that the squisher-grinder was for ordinary food preparation.

"I can't stop it all by myself," Duncan said to Fia. "But maybe I can prove who the kitten stealers are." He dropped a potato into the water and reached for another. "Cook is one of them, for sure. And Bertram."

"And the earl," said Fia.

Duncan glanced at her, startled. The earl might be a little weird about his bandage, and he might be blind to Bertram's true character, but Duncan doubted he would stoop to harming kittens. "I don't think the earl knows what's happening. He was angry when the crate burst on the deck and he saw what was in it. He even sent Bertram to report it to the island police. Bertram might not have actually reported it," Duncan added hastily, "but it wasn't the earl's fault that somebody stole kittens and tried to load them onto his ship."

Fia jumped to the bench and paced back and forth. "Maybe it *was* his fault. He doesn't smell right to me."

Duncan laughed. Fia's nose wasn't always accurate. "You said you smelled *me* down in that room below the galley, and I'd never seen it in my life."

Fia's ears went back. Her blue eye was brighter than her green in the dim light of the galley, but both looked accusing. "I did smell you," she insisted.

"Fine, then," Duncan said. "If you're so sure the earl's bad, why don't you spy on him? Bring me back some proof. After all, you're the one who told me there are hidden passages all over the ship, for a kitten your size. There's one that goes right to the earl's closet, remember?"

"I've been scared of the earl," said Fia in a small voice.

"Why? Has he ever done anything to you?"

Fia shook her head.

Duncan shrugged. "Until you have proof, you're just a kitten with—" He stopped and pressed his lips together. He didn't want to actually hurt Fia's feelings.

"With what?" Fia leaped from the bench to the deck and looked up at him with whiskers bristling. "What were you going to say?"

"Nothing."

"Yes, you were," said Fia bitterly. "You were going to say I'm just a kitten with eyes that *don't match*. Weren't you?"

"No! I was going to say that you're a kitten with—"

Fia turned her back and disappeared down a rathole.

"An overactive nose," Duncan said to the empty room.

Duncan stood at the railing amidships, taking deep breaths of clean salt air. The storm had blown itself out, and the misting rain had almost stopped. To his relief, he saw that the jolly boat was still on the beach, beside the earl's gig.

He took off his cap to scratch his head. Maybe now would be a good time to wash his hair. He would have to do it in salt water, with a bucket drawn from the pump, unless Cook would let him have fresh. Somehow he doubted it.

Mr. Corbie, the sailing master, was standing with his legs

apart and his hands behind his back. Now and then, he would put a telescope to his eye and scan the shore. His right foot tapped, as if impatient to be pacing.

Duncan moved a little closer. He was impatient, too—eager to get home to his mother, anxious to get Fia off this ship that was so dangerous to cats. "Sir," he said, "when are we going back to Capital City?"

The master grunted. "I wish I knew, lad. The islands are getting fewer and farther between, and there's nothing at all where we're headed."

Duncan scratched his head again. The master glanced at him sharply. "Do you have nits in your hair, lad? Come here."

Duncan ducked his head for Mr. Corbie's inspection. The sailing master gave a surprised grunt. "Whyever did you dye your hair?"

"I didn't!"

"Go look in a mirror, then. It's coming in a fine strong red at the roots." Mr. Corbie winked at him. "There's nothing to be ashamed of, having hair the color of fire. Time you're getting a bit older, you'll see that the girls like it that way."

Duncan put on his cap silently.

The sailing master snapped open his telescope and handed it to Duncan. "Here, I need to check some charts. Call me the moment the earl's gig leaves the beach."

Fishing boats on the sand, screeching gulls, a cat perched on a piling, all sprang closer as Duncan put the spyglass obediently to his eye. He scarcely saw them. He was seeing, instead, the shaving mirror hanging in the small closet sailors used as a lavatory. His hair had always looked dark in that mirror, darker than usual and not at all red—but the light was so dim there, he'd never given it a second thought.

And now he remembered the small empty jar of black shoe polish in the mysterious room, two decks below the galley, and Fia's sensitive nose that had picked up his old scent.

There was a luff tackle there, and a sling with a hook. It would have been easy for someone to have lowered Duncan down, dyed his hair with shoe polish in the deep tub, and brought him back up.

Duncan gripped the brass telescope, his hand clenching. He could imagine easily enough how it had gone. Bertram and the cook would have carried his unconscious body out of the cabin, joking to anyone passing by that the boy had taken too much rum and that they were going to wake him up with hot coffee. Once in the galley, they would have shut the door and done their business. Then they would have dumped him in a hammock to sleep it off.

Bertram had known who he was, all right; he'd had plenty of opportunity to study Duncan's face at the monastery school, in the headmaster's office; but Bertram had made sure that no one on the ship would recognize him. And after that, there had been a surprising number of accidents that could have easily killed Duncan—or anyone else who got in the way.

Duncan swept the telescope slowly across the beach, watching carefully now. Bertram had gone to the island along with the others, so Duncan was safe enough for the moment. Shadows played across the gray cliffs behind the beach, so like the cliffs at home. Perhaps Grizel was on the stone throne now, looking out to sea, watching for him to return. Maybe his mother was there, too.

Bertram was the unknown enemy that his mother had feared so. The earl might have been too noble to threaten a woman and a small boy, but Bertram—Duncan could easily believe that Bertram would. The earl's right-hand man would have been there on the day Duke Charles kidnapped the princess and wounded the earl. . . . Bertram might have tried to fight the duke himself, and lost, and watched in pain and helpless rage as the earl, his master, had been given a wound that almost killed him. Bertram might have vowed, that day, to take his revenge on any family the duke had left.

And who knows? Maybe he had thought to gain the duke's title for his master. Or maybe he had thought that he could get some kind of money or treasure from the duke's widow. Perhaps that was why Bertram had stolen the sea chest. . . .

There was a bustle near the ship's boats; Bertram was boarding the jolly boat, followed closely by Cook. The cook tossed one burlap bag to a waiting sailor, but the other one he held carefully closed at the top.

Duncan held the spyglass with hands that shook slightly. Was the bag *moving*?

The glass fogged up. He rubbed the lens with his shirt and put the telescope back to his eye. The oarsmen were rowing with steady strokes. Cook, though, seemed to be struggling with the bag in his lap. He jumped suddenly, as if he had been poked—or clawed—and a moment later, his roar of pain came faintly across the water.

Duncan held his breath. Bertram had taken the bag—he was swinging it around—

He smacked the bag against the thwart.

Duncan's hands gripped the spyglass so tightly that the curved brass edge cut into his palm. He watched, unbelieving, as Bertram sat down on the bag, hard. The jolly boat rocked with the sudden shift of weight and the roar of sailors' laughter.

Something thick and hot rose in Duncan's throat. He struggled to swallow down the sickness. Had there been *kittens* in that bag?

"Hey, boy!" A sailor loomed at Duncan's side. "I thought you were supposed to be watching for the earl. Isn't that his boat shoving off?"

Duncan got a grip on himself and looked through the glass. Yes, there was the gig—he could see the earl's bandaged head as he took his place in the bow. On either side, three men gripped the gunwales and ran the boat out through the surf. As he watched, they leaped aboard and fell to their oars.

"Thanks," he managed to say, and then ran to knock on the master's door. But after he passed on his news, he found a dark corner of the tween deck and leaned there, trembling. He hoped that Grizel and Fia would never find out that he had watched a whole bag of kittens be squished and had done nothing to stop it.

"ALL HANDS TO WEIGH ANCHOR!" The cry echoed down the hatch. The thunder of feet was followed by a creak and shudder as the capstan was turned and the anchor dragged free from the sea bed.

Duncan climbed the rigging with the others and let out the sails. But he did not go down with them when the supper bell rang. He didn't think he could stomach anything that Cook had made, ever again.

It was breezy in the maintop, and a little chilly, but the sailbags around the edge gave some protection from the wind. Duncan sat huddled with his knees to his chin and gazed at the small island as it sank into the horizon. The storm front was moving off, and the low shelf of cloud had lifted just enough to reveal a bleared sunset, dull orange and sullen purple, like a bruise on the sky.

The maintop was a good place to be alone. When the ship was sailing steadily and no one needed to take sails in or shake them out, the high platform was a spot where Duncan could sit and think. But his thoughts were not happy ones.

He had already tried to warn the earl about Bertram, only the earl wouldn't believe anything bad about the man unless he was presented with proof. The poor kittens were probably all eaten by now. The only real proof Duncan had was the sea chest, and his dyed hair with the thin edge of red at the scalp.

But if the earl looked in the sea chest and at Duncan's hair, he would realize that Duncan was the son of his greatest enemy.

Duncan felt a shiver go up his spine at the thought. Still, if he didn't tell the earl, the earl would not get rid of Bertram, and Duncan would be in danger. . . . *Fia* would be in danger.

Night fell, and a thin rain began to drizzle. The rigging was coarse under Duncan's hands as he slid down, but in the month he had been at sea, he had developed thicker calluses. He dropped lightly to the deck and skipped down the ladder beneath the raised stern deck.

He knocked quietly at the door of the great cabin. The latch on the door needed fixing, or had not completely shut, for the door swung open slightly. Duncan poked his head in. "Sir?"

The great cabin was empty. The wide sweep of windows glassily reflected a shimmer of light from the passageway behind him. Duncan could see the door to the balcony—or the gallery, he had to remember to call it that—and the curving row of lockers beneath the bench, the solid table with its carved chairs, and a wooden crate that looked as if it had once held fruit.

There was a creak on the companionway, and Duncan glanced up to see feet descending the ladder. They were shod not in the earl's polished boots but in the canvas shoes of a sailor.

Duncan ducked inside the door to the earl's cabin. He did not want to explain to anyone why he was waiting for the earl; he would step out as soon as the man had passed by.

The cabin door swung open and shut with the pitch and roll of the ship, letting in a shaft of light that grew wide and then narrow. The footsteps came closer, and now there was a sound of clinking. When the door gaped open a third time, Duncan caught sight of a broad, hairy arm and a stained and dirty apron.

Quick as thought and twice as silent, Duncan ducked behind the curtain that hung before the earl's closet. He pushed between the earl's hanging clothes and pressed his back against the bulkhead.

Cook bumped the door open with his wide posterior and shuffled in with a covered tray and small lantern. There was a clatter of cutlery and the ring of a crystal wineglass, and then the hanging lantern was lit; Duncan could see its warm glow at the edge of the closet, where the curtain didn't quite meet the bulkhead wall. He shifted position, bracing himself so that he would not stumble at the ship's motion, and put his eye to the half-inch gap.

There was a bump at the door—here was the earl at last. He strode into the cabin, boots glistening with spray, his cloak swirling. The earl's hands undid the clasp at his throat and let the cloak fall. A hairy arm caught it before it hit the deck.

"Should I hang this up in the closet, my lord?" Cook asked.

Duncan stopped breathing.

"No, spread it over that crate to dry first," came the earl's voice. "And open a window. It's stuffy in here."

Duncan breathed again, slowly, soundlessly. He watched, willing the cook to go away.

Footsteps. The cook's cheeks bunching in a smile. The clink of silverware and the sound of a cover being lifted off. Then the cook stepped back, and Duncan could see.

There was a deep pie plate, with a golden crust on top. Something long and fuzzy curled around one side. Two pointed triangles stuck out above the golden crust, just the size of . . . of cat ears.

"Ah!" said the earl. "Kitty Pot Pie! My favorite!"

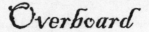

CHAPTER 14

Overboard

DUNCAN'S KNEES FELT STRANGELY WEAK. He sank to the floor of the closet, numb with shock. The Earl of Merrick ate *kittens*?

The atmosphere behind the curtain was stifling—he felt as if he couldn't breathe—but Duncan didn't dare stir. The earl would know he had been spying.

And what would the earl do then?

Duncan sat in dull misery as the earl finished his supper. The horrible sound of jaws steadily chewing was almost more than he could bear. He bent his forehead to his knees and tried to think of something else, something happy. He failed.

Someone knocked at the cabin door; a voice spoke. The

earl dabbed his lips with a napkin and laid it over his plate, covering up the tail and ears garnish. "Come in."

Through the crack, Duncan could see a blue-trousered leg and a man's hand holding a long roll of paper.

Something soft and furry touched Duncan's ankle, and his heart nearly bolted through his chest. Was it a rat? Fia had once found a rathole in this closet. . . .

It wasn't a rat. The eyes were larger than a rat's, and they glowed different colors. Fia nestled against his ankle, her tail curled around her. She started to meow a soft question, but Duncan shook his head and touched her muzzle with his fore-finger.

She climbed lightly up his sleeve and pushed her mouth against his ear. Her meow was so soft he could barely hear it.

"I've come to spy on the earl, like you told me to," she said.

Duncan flinched. It was his fault Fia had put herself in this danger. He gave her his most serious, earnest look. "Shhhh," he whispered in her soft, pointed ear.

The voice of the sailing master boomed out suddenly. "I need to know where we're going, in order to set a course. North, my lord? Back toward civilization? Here's the chart."

Duncan put his eye to the gap between the curtain and bulkhead once more. There was a sound of rustling as the paper was unrolled. The earl set his dinner tray down on the deck to make room. The napkin had slipped a little, showing one fuzzy ear, and the earl twitched the napkin back in place to cover it. The master had not bothered to look at the supper tray. He leaned on the table, both hands on the chart.

"No," said the earl, and his fingernail tapped on the paper. "Here's where I want to go. It's not far. We'll pick up the Arvidian Current soon, and it will take us there."

"To the Great Rift?" Mr. Corbie blew his breath out forcibly. "You can't be serious. There's nothing there but danger—and death if you get too close."

The Earl of Merrick laughed, high and sharp, and the hair on Duncan's skin lifted. "Death for someone, perhaps," he said, "but not for me."

"My lord," said the master, his voice strained, "it's not a laughing matter. Look here." A stout finger jabbed on the table with a thump. "That's where the warm Arvidian Current curves and begins to go north—and meets the cold Rift Current that flows in the other direction. When they meet, they brew up all sorts of weather. The farther we go toward the Rift, the more we'll run into fog and wind and storm. There are hidden reefs, rocks to break a ship upon, and that's a bad thing in a fog—or anytime, my lord. There are whirlpools, too, great wide ones and small treacherous ones. I've heard that, at times, the Rift boils like a cauldron; one of those whirlpools could suck your ship down before you knew what was happening. Then there are waterspouts—whirling tornados that pick you up and put you down in pieces—and if that isn't enough, we don't know how wide it is. Nor do we know what's on the other side. And there's no reason to go there. None at all, my lord."

"I have my own reasons," said the Earl of Merrick. "And I have a chart."

"A chart, my lord? For the *Rift*?"

"A new chart," said the earl, his voice suddenly cold. "Drawn by someone who crossed it and returned. Successfully. As I shall do."

"Sir! If you're still looking for the princess, all Arvidia knows that you've done your best. You won't find any trace of her in the Rift—not even a scrap of her petticoat or a beaded shoe!"

The earl did not answer. His gaze swept the room and stopped at the closet. No, at the bottom of the closet curtain, where it nearly touched the deck. . . .

The skin on Duncan's arms grew cold. Was something showing? His feet were well inside the curtain, as were his hands. Fia was tucked out of sight next to his ankle, and her tail—

Her tail. Back and forth, Fia flicked the tip in and out beneath the hanging curtain. A keen eye might have caught the movement.

Duncan's hand stole down and covered Fia's tail, stopping the telltale motion.

The earl's chair scraped, as if he had made an impatient movement. "You agreed to be my sailing master, Corbie. You agreed to take this ship where I want it to go."

"I didn't agree to suicide, my lord," said the master. "Begging your pardon, but that's what it will be if we go into the Rift."

"Not into it. Just to the very edge. There's an island I know of where we can take our bearings."

"You mean we're going to the island where—" The master's voice wavered.

"Where Duke Charles betrayed king and country?" The earl smiled. "Just near enough to take a bearing. There's no sense going to the island itself—it's just a barren rock. Then we'll explore the edge of the Rift, making plans for the real expedition, when I become the—"

The earl coughed, took a drink of water, cleared his throat. "I mean to say, at some future time, I will hire a new sailing master—one *not* too timid to brave the Rift—and he will be well rewarded."

The master cleared his throat. "Beg pardon, my lord. It's just that when it comes to danger for the ship—"

"I quite understand," said the earl. "Now, set that course."

There was a low murmur as the sailing master mumbled calculations to himself. Then came a rustle as the chart was rolled up, a quick stamp and stride, and Earl and Master were out of the cabin. In a moment, Duncan heard their feet on the ladder.

"All hands to tack ship!" The cry echoed down the hatch and was immediately followed by the usual thunder of rushing feet.

Duncan had no desire to be seen coming out of the earl's cabin. At last, cautiously, he pushed aside the curtain that hung over the closet door.

The ship heeled suddenly as, above decks, the sails were sheeted home and caught the breeze. Duncan staggered on the slanted deck and tripped over the wooden fruit crate, falling to his knees. He reached for Fia, but she was already sliding halfway across the wooden planks. She banged against the earl's supper tray with a clatter of crockery, clawing at the napkin.

Duncan got across the deck quickly, but he was too late. Fia was staring at the remains of the earl's dinner in horror. Her wide eyes caught the lantern's light in amber and gold. She looked uncanny, like a ghost cat haunting the ship, but her meow was the simple, wailing cry of a frightened kitten for her mother.

"Shh, it's all right, I'm here!" Duncan reached for her, but his sudden motion startled the terrified kitten. She leaped past him and skittered around the fruit crate. A gust of wind swirled through the half-open window, and the candle in the big hanging lantern flickered wildly. The door blew open to the gallery outside, and the candle went out.

"Fia! Where are you?"

A thin meow came faintly to Duncan's ears. In the dark cabin, the starlit sky shone through the windows in repeated squares. Had she run outside, onto the gallery?

Duncan felt his way along the window bench, scraping his

shin. The open balcony at the stern of the ship might seem like a safer place, to a cat. . . .

The cloud shelf had blown away, leaving only ragged wisps to trail across the face of a gibbous moon. The stars were bright, and the sea creamed behind the ship in a gleaming silver wake.

"Fia!" Duncan called softly. He stepped high over the coaming and through the door, out onto the narrow walkway.

The ship took a sudden lurch, rising to a rogue wave. Duncan's knees buckled, and he grabbed the railing. There was spray in his face, and he turned, crouching, in the dark. The rushing sound of water and the thrumming tune of the wind in the rigging were loud out in the open. Duncan strained his ears, but he could not hear Fia's meow.

All at once, the windows behind him glowed with golden light. A shadow moved across the railing, and Duncan could see someone's hand lighting candles.

He raised his head another inch, enough to see the ragged tail of a bandage and a shadow looming large. In the next instant, the shadow pounced on something Duncan could not see, then held up a tiny, struggling shadow to the light.

"Here's a fresh kitty, just the size I like best!"

Duncan was through the door and into the cabin in a heartbeat. He bashed his shin on the crate but barely felt it. "Don't eat her!" he cried.

The earl held Fia by the scruff of her neck. The white kitten hung there, writhing and twisting, but the earl only tightened his grip, smiling. "Eat her? Why would you say such a thing?"

"I saw you! I saw your kitty pie—" Duncan choked on the words. He flung back his head, defiant. He couldn't hope to beat the earl in a fight, but maybe he could make the earl loosen his grip long enough for Fia to leap away and hide.

And what would the earl do to him then? Duncan told himself that it didn't matter—his world was shattered already. His father was the nation's most despised traitor. And the nation's hero was a monster who ate kittens.

Fia's meows were furious. Her claws slashed the air while she hissed out all the cat insults she knew.

"She's a feisty little kitty, isn't she? But her eyes are different colors," mused the earl. He swung her gently back and forth, her tail dangling. "I wonder if that affects the taste."

"Please. Don't eat her. *Please*, my lord." Duncan was desperate enough to beg. It didn't matter about his pride.

The earl's smile turned crooked. "Fine. I promise I won't eat her."

Duncan's fists, which had been clenched by his side, did not relax. How could he believe the earl's promise about anything? Duncan would distract the earl with questions. Maybe the man's grip would loosen and Fia could escape. "Why do you eat cats, sir? I mean, you, of all people . . ." Duncan swallowed painfully.

"I have my reasons." The earl's eyes glinted with amusement in the candlelight. "Maybe I want nine lives, like a cat. Maybe if I eat enough cats, I can get a few extra lives for myself!"

The earl couldn't be serious. "But that isn't really true, sir. It's just an old saying."

Fia mewed, "A *stupid* saying! Made up by bad dogs! By *stupid* sons of *bad* dogs!" She swiped at his wrist with her paw and missed.

"You don't believe the nine lives?" The earl chuckled. "All right, then. Maybe I just like the taste."

Duncan felt slightly sick. He looked away.

"I can't say I enjoy grown cats," the earl went on. "Too stringy. But kittens, now. Kittens are tasty. Tender, too."

Fia's mews were taking on a hysterical note.

Duncan forced himself to keep the earl talking. "But why did you start to eat them in the first place? Was it something stupid, like a dare?"

The earl's face took on a strange intensity. "I eat cats for the noblest of reasons. I eat cats for the sake of my country. But you wouldn't understand; you're just a boy." He reached for his hat with his free hand, glancing slyly at Duncan. Then he clapped it on his head and strode over the coaming, out to the gallery and the night air.

Duncan followed. He couldn't leave Fia in the earl's hands, but he didn't know how to get her back.

The Earl of Merrick stood at the railing, his head lifted. He seemed to be making a speech to the stars. "Arvidia has an old, sick king and no princess waiting to take the throne. I, the Earl of Merrick, must stand ready to help my country in her hour of need! And eating cats—" He turned to Duncan, grinning crazily. "Eating cats is going to be very useful one of these days. I know the secret, you see."

"What secret?" Duncan shifted his weight uneasily. The earl was deranged, completely nuts.

"And do you not know?" The earl's eyes were bright. "You seem to feel very strongly about this cat, for example. Is she your *friend*? Do you feel you *understand* her in some special way?"

There was some trap here; Duncan could feel it. Would it be better, or worse, to admit the truth? As he stared at the earl, Grizel came suddenly to mind. She had made him promise never to tell anyone that he spoke Cat. She had told him it was important.

Duncan had been a little careless about promises to his mother. He had found excuses, ways around them. . . .

He would keep his promise to Grizel.

"She's just my pet," Duncan said. "And what I understand is that she's *scared*—anyone could see that. Won't you please let her go? Now that you've promised not to eat her?"

Fia had stopped meowing, but she looked at Duncan with pleading, terrified eyes.

"Of course, my boy! The Earl of Merrick is a true nobleman, and a nobleman *always* keeps his promises!" He flung out his hand in a heroic gesture. Fia went flying into the night in a high, soaring arc. There was a tiny splash.

Duncan pressed against the railing in shock. *"Fia!"*

"Oh, too bad," said the earl. "But I hope you notice I kept my promise not to eat her."

Duncan dashed into the earl's cabin, seized the wooden crate, and ran back out to the railing. "Fia! Swim! Swim to the crate!" He threw it with all his might into the frothing wake of the ship. He could see Fia's tiny form struggling on the surface of the water. The light caught her desperate eyes in pinpoints of amber and gold.

"Bring the ship about!" Duncan cried. In his anguish, he found himself shaking the earl by the arms. "Turn it around!"

The earl shrugged. "It's only a cat." His smile glittered as he gazed at Duncan. "Of course, when a *person* goes overboard, we *always* go to the rescue."

Duncan took in a fierce and ragged breath. He climbed up onto the railing and clung there for a moment. "All right, then. You can bring the ship about for *me*," he said, and leaped.

The water was cold, and salt, and very wet. Duncan plunged beneath the surface, kicked violently, and popped up, gasping. He struck out toward the small scrap of kitten, just barely visible as she struggled to reach the floating crate.

Through some miracle, Fia hadn't drowned yet. Duncan reached the crate first and pulled Fia in close to his chest, warming her with his breath.

The sea was not as calm as it had looked from the ship. Duncan heaved up and down with the swell, his arm hooked through the slats in the crate. Strangely, he had not heard the shout for all hands on deck; the orders to bring the ship about must have happened while he was underwater.

But the ship did not seem to be turning around.

"Hey!" Duncan's voice sounded thin and small across the increasing gap of water. He lifted an arm, waving. "Over here! HEY!"

The Earl of Merrick, silhouetted by the light from the cabin, stood perfectly still on the gallery. Then Duncan saw the low, wide-brimmed hat change shape as the earl turned and went inside.

Now the earl would give the alarm. Duncan was watching so intently that he forgot to time his breathing to the waves. He caught a mouthful of salt water and spit it out, coughing. He shook the water from his eyes.

By the time he looked up, he would see the sails shifting, would see the ship's broad side turning toward him, would see the crew hanging over the railings, lowering a boat to pick him up. . . .

Duncan stared, floating, waiting.

The windows of the great cabin shone gold in the night. The luminous squares dwindled in size as the ship sailed steadily away.

"He's leaving me," Duncan said in disbelief. "He's leaving me all alone out here!"

The dark blot of the ship faded in the distance. The lights winked out.

"Not *all* alone," said Fia, and she licked his cheek with her sandpapery tongue.

CHAPTER 15

Lost at Sea

THE MOON SHONE COLD AND DISTANT on the wide, dark sea. The heaving swell moved up and down as if some huge, watery animal were breathing in and out. Small and almost invisible on its vast surface floated a wooden crate, and clinging to that crate was a boy. On the boy's head was a kitten.

Duncan wedged his hands more firmly between the slats of the rough wooden crate. His scalp hurt. Fia's claws were hooked into his cap, but she couldn't seem to help digging her claws in deeper when an unexpected wave smacked into her. Still, the top of Duncan's head was a better place for her than the half-sunken crate. At least his head was out of the water most of the time.

The air at the water's surface was warmer than it had been at the height of the maintop—and after the first shocking plunge, the water seemed even warmer than the air. But all the same, by the time the moon set, Duncan was chilled and shivering.

The sea was inky black. Duncan wondered what sea creatures were below him and if any of them had teeth. He had a sudden image of something large, dark, and hungry swimming toward his legs, mouth gaping wide.

He wrenched his mind forcibly from this thought and looked up. At least the clouds had blown away; he could see the stars, crushed across the heavens like tiny bits of broken glass. They were beautiful, but they were very far off, and somehow they made him feel even more lost. The world was a bigger and more heartless place than he had ever imagined. And he could not understand why the earl had left him to drown.

It was a long and miserable night. Duncan did not dare to shut his eyes—what if his grip relaxed and he let go of the crate?—but he was very tired. Finally he thought of his belt. Carefully, he took it off and laced the end through the slats of the fruit crate. Then he worked the loop around his body and under both arms, so that when he buckled the belt again, he hung in a sort of sling. At last he closed his eyes, worn out from effort and cold and loss. He slept.

He woke with a cramp in his arm, an empty feeling in his stomach, and a sensation of warmth on his cheek. He blinked. In the east the sun was rising in a blaze of pink and gold. He turned his stiff neck, scanning the horizon. Surely somewhere was an island he could swim toward.

He squinted in all directions; he could see nothing but water. East, south, west, and north, the sea was an endless circle with him at its center. And though the warmth of the sun was welcome after his cold and shivering night, before long he wished it was not quite so warm.

The day wore on in heat and blinding sun. Fia climbed down from his cap and into the front of his shirt, where the seawater cooled her and the cloth protected her sensitive ears and nose from sunburn. After a while Duncan took off his pants and carefully arranged them around his head like some strange, wet turban, draping the trouser legs over his cheeks and the back of his neck. He needed protection from the sun, and he could swim better in just his shorts, anyway. His shoes had fallen off long ago.

Were he and Fia getting somewhere? Or just bobbing up and down? Duncan couldn't tell. His eyebrows were crusted with salt, and his eyes hurt from the reflected light, yet he had to keep a sharp lookout for anything that might be an island. They were at the very southwest edge of the mapped sea, which of course meant that islands were few and far between. But he didn't say this to Fia. He told her that the Arvidian Sea was full of islands.

"Jammed with them," he said. "There are so many, no one's ever counted them all. So of course we're bound to run into one sooner or later."

"Will it have water?" asked Fia faintly. "And food?"

Duncan's stomach growled at the thought. He had missed meals before, but never two in a row, and his stomach was letting him know it. Still, water was what he wanted more than anything. He swallowed the dryness in his throat to answer Fia's question. "There will be mice, maybe, and birds for sure. How good are you at catching birds?"

"I only ever practiced on mice," said Fia a little nervously. "Birds are advanced."

"You'll figure it out." Duncan hoped so. He would be happy to eat a roasted bird—a mouse, not so much. Of course, first they had to find an island.

The sun was more than halfway down on its journey to the west. Duncan's thirst grew until it dominated his every thought. If only the water all around him were fresh! But the briny sea was full of salt, and he spit it out every time he happened to get a mouthful. He was not tempted to swallow, because he knew what happened to becalmed sailors who drank seawater. They went crazy.

Fia had to be just as thirsty, if not more so. When Duncan listened, he could hear the tiny wheezing whimper that came out with each breath, as if her misery couldn't quite be contained in her small body.

He tried to distract her. "You know a lot of bad words, for a kitten," he said.

"What?" Fia lifted her small, weary face to his.

"All those cat insults you meowed at the earl! I didn't know there were so many ways to call someone a stupid, scabby, stinking, slobbering dog. Did you have to learn them for your kitten examinations?"

"Not . . . really. I just made them up for when Tibby, Tabby, and Tuff were mean." Fia's meow was hoarse, and she made an obvious effort to swallow. "They were fun to use on the dog at the corner, too."

Duncan looked fondly at the kitten. No cat was attractive when wet, and Fia was perhaps the most limp, bedraggled-looking kitten he had ever seen. Her fur, where it wasn't plastered to her skin, stuck out in random tufts, and her blue and green eyes looked bigger than ever atop her skinny, unfluffed body. But she still had plenty of spark, though it was a little subdued after almost a whole day afloat.

"It's amazing," Duncan said, "how much you know for how young you are."

Fia said, "Kittens learn much faster than human babies. Human babies don't even take their first *steps* until they're maybe a whole year old, but we kittens are running around in weeks. We learn faster, we grow faster, our hearts beat faster—"

This was true, Duncan thought as Fia rattled on; but cats died faster, too. He thought of Grizel with a pang. She was not much older than he was, in human years, but she was very old for a cat. He hoped she was helping his mother feel less lonely.

The thought of his mother was like a knife beneath his skin. He rocked endlessly up and down in the dreamy blue waves, knowing that she would be thinking of him, crying for him. She would be blaming herself for not keeping him safe.

If only she had told him who his father was, as she surely had meant to do one day, he would have been more careful. But if she *had* told him, Duncan would have scarcely been able to hold his head up for shame.

The earl must know who he was. Why else would the earl have left him to drown? Duncan remembered that Bertram had said it would be a long voyage, with plenty of time for something to happen. It had seemed like a threat, somehow, though Duncan had not understood it.

He understood it now. The earl had wanted to get rid of him but hadn't wanted to get his elegant hands dirty with the stain of outright murder. Bertram and the earl had been in no hurry—they knew that on a long sea voyage, there were many opportunities for accidents to happen, without any questions being asked. They would not have wanted the sailors to suspect anything. If Duncan hadn't helped things along by jumping off the ship himself, no doubt he would have had an accident soon—near the Rift, perhaps.

The earl was vicious indeed, if he wanted to kill Duncan just because he was the son of his old enemy. But then, Duncan already knew he was a kitten eater, and that was pretty low.

Duncan stroked Fia gently behind the ears, and she closed her eyes in pleasure. A quiet purr, like the rumble of a tiny engine, vibrated against his chest, and he smoothed down the wild, damp tufts of Fia's salt-encrusted coat. The earl must be crazy. He seemed to think that eating kittens would give him some kind of power—something to do with running the country. It didn't make any sense.

Meow! Meow!

Fia's paw was pointing. "A sail! A sail!"

Duncan gulped. He had been so busy thinking he had forgotten to scan the horizon. There, perhaps two miles away, was a ship.

His breath came quicker. He narrowed his eyes, squinting to see better. A ship was as distinctly different as a person and would be recognizable from this far away to anyone with a telescope.

Duncan pressed his thumbs and forefingers together so that there was a tiny space in the center he could look through. He had learned this trick on the island of Dulle, when he used to sit on the stone throne and look out to sea. Narrowing his field of vision had the effect of sharpening it. It took him a few moments to get the ship in view, but at last he was able to take a good, long look.

He swallowed his cruel disappointment. Number of masts, type of sails, her lines—he would have recognized her at an even greater distance. "It's the earl's schooner," he said, his voice flat. "Even if a lookout saw us, and the sailing master came about just to pick us up, the earl would only try to get rid of us again."

Fia's face showed uncertainty. "Maybe we'd get a drink first." She licked the salty edges of her mouth.

"They can't even see us," said Duncan.

"But we can see them," Fia protested.

"That's because it's a whole ship—it's huge. But us? We're small. We don't have any flares to set off, either. If we got closer, there might be a chance, but they're going away from us. Look where the sun is. They've caught the Arvidian Current, I bet. It will take them right up next to the Rift."

Duncan remembered, with a pang, the map of Arvidia marked with its currents. The Arvidian Current ran west now, but then it would curve northward and back east . . . back home. How he longed to be there himself.

He watched as the ship sailed sweetly on a broad reach, the wind belling her sails like some perfect picture of what a ship should be. She looked beautiful, though very far away, and he watched her until she was out of sight.

It was growing darker. A breath of coolness blew across the surface of the water. Soon, Duncan knew, he would be shivering again. Would his thirst be less in the night? Or would it just get worse and worse until he died? He closed his eyes as if to shut out the thought. He was not dying, not yet. He would think about something else.

An image of a tall, brimming glass of water floated into his mind.

No. He would think about home, where the earl's schooner would go in the end. By now, his mother would have guessed he was with the earl. Friar Gregory or Father Andrew would have told her Duncan had gone to the ship.

It came to Duncan that since his mother had been a

duchess, she would have met the earl already, many years ago. Maybe the earl had gone to one of her concerts. What had she thought when the earl came back from the royal tour telling everyone that her husband had kidnapped the princess?

She must have believed that the earl was lying, or she never would have told Duncan that his father was good and honorable and brave. She must have thought Duncan was in danger from the earl, as well, or she wouldn't have told him never to talk with strangers or go to the wharf when strange ships docked.

But Sylvia McKay—no, Sylvia McKinnon—had no proof that the earl was lying, had she? Maybe she had just refused to believe that her husband was a traitor.

Duncan wanted to believe right along with her. But there had been all those witnesses. Even Friar Gregory, trying so hard to be fair in the classroom so long ago, had agreed that a whole shipful of witnesses couldn't be wrong.

A gust out of nowhere blew Duncan's eyes open and dashed cold spray in his face. The sky had grown very much darker, and a black cloud—where had that come from?— extended all the way down to the surface of the water and was moving in fast.

It was a black squall. He had heard about these sudden storms at sea.

"Hang on!" he shouted to Fia, above a quickly rising wind. "Here it comes!"

The water churned around them, and the endless rocking

turned into a violent bucking motion, as if the sea wanted to throw them off its back. Duncan checked the belt that was tied to the crate, gripped the wood with both arms, and hardly noticed Fia's claws as she dug into his chest.

The rain poured down as if someone were dumping a bucket the size of the sky. Duncan and Fia held their heads up, mouths open, but they couldn't get much that way.

This was stupid! Feverishly, Duncan unknotted his pants and held them up in the downpour. He wrung them out, held them up, and wrung them out again. When the water tasted almost fresh, he squeezed it into his mouth.

"Fia! Suck on the cloth!"

His fingers fumbled with the buckle of his cap; it would hold much more. He rinsed it, squeezed it, rinsed again, until the accumulated salt of hours was washed away. The first capful he drank had an odd chemical taste and was still a little briny—he couldn't help getting some spray into it—but it tasted better than anything he had ever drunk in his life. He filled another capful, and another—and then the squall was gone, racing away to the northwest as fast as it had come. He buckled on his cap again over his wet hair. At least it had gotten a washing.

The sun gleamed out from behind clouds, turning them deep orange and gold. The sea was purple, shining like metal. And there, hidden by the squall until this moment, was an island.

Duncan stared for one paralyzed instant. He rubbed his eyes. And then he started to swim. He pushed the crate ahead of him and kicked his legs as hard as he could. He aimed to the right of the island, for if he didn't point himself in the correct direction, the current might carry him past the land.

Fia, now gripping the top of the crate with her claws, stood like some sort of feline figurehead, her ears pricked rigidly forward and her tail lashing. She urged him on, mewing, "Kick! Kick!" with every stroke, but Duncan didn't have the breath to tell her she was irritating him. He was already swimming with every ounce of strength he had.

Now that they were closer to the island, he could see breakers, white lines of surf where the sea crashed into a reef. If he didn't find a gap in the breakers, he and Fia would be dashed to pieces.

"Watch out!" cried Fia. "Rocks ahead!"

Duncan was too busy kicking to answer. His face was in the water half the time, his leg muscles were on fire, and he had to breathe. He flung his head up to check his position and gasped in dismay, choking as he sucked in seawater. The offshore current was strong, going fast. Three or four miles an hour, perhaps? Too fast—he wasn't going to be able to get to the island no matter how he tried—

His legs felt like wisps of green straw. He kicked with feeble desperation against the inexorable current, hanging on to the crate with only one arm and using the other to windmill through the water. Maybe the current would curve around the island; maybe the tide was high and would push him right up past the rocks onto some quiet beach. . . . He lifted his head and saw that the island was already behind him.

Duncan let his legs dangle limp and useless. He watched the island grow smaller until at last it disappeared.

"It had trees," said Fia, in a tiny meow.

"It must have had water, then," Duncan said dully.

The sun slipped under the horizon. Duncan leaned his arms on the crate and put his head on them. He noticed that the crate was a little lower in the waves than before. It still buoyed them up, but for how long?

He found he was too tired to care. And in spite of hunger and thirst, in spite of fear and longing and despair, he was weary, so weary. He closed his eyes.

Duncan dreamed that he was at the still center of a world that heaved up and down. He opened his eyes, confused. Water was lapping at his feet, but there was sand on his cheek and warmth on his back.

He blinked. In his low field of vision, he could see something that looked like a dirty white rag—Fia, half dead with exhaustion, splayed out beside him. Beyond her was the edge of a battered wooden crate. And farther away, across a stretch of pale sand, were two huge, furry paws.

He sat up and shaded his eyes. The paws belonged to something that looked like a striped tabby cat—only ten times as large. It was an animal Duncan had seen only in pictures, but it was bigger and more fierce than he had imagined. It stared at him with head lowered and tail lashing from side to side.

"Prepare to *die*," growled the tiger.

CHAPTER 16

The Sea Cave

THE TIGER'S GROWL WAS LOWER and more rumbly than a meow, but it was still recognizably Cat. Even if Duncan had not understood the tiger's words, the whipping tail and bared fangs sent a message that was impossible to mistake.

A tremor raced up Duncan's spine, and his hands felt cold. His eyes darted in all directions, searching for escape. The cliffs surrounding the narrow beach were sheer and high as a castle wall, great slabs of rock impossible to climb. There was an opening in the rock face behind the tiger—its den, obviously—but that was all. The cliffs curved around the tiny beach, enclosing it in arms of stone ending in long, rocky points, and beyond the rock was the sea.

At his feet, Fia stirred, and Duncan wondered miserably if the tiger would eat her. She wouldn't be much more than a mouthful.

The tiger's ears flattened. He moved into a half crouch, rumbling in his chest.

Fia got unsteadily to her feet. She stared at the tiger, her eyes wide.

Duncan cast a quick glance around. There were no stones nearby to throw; there was only the crate. He wrenched at the slats with his fingers, trying to tear off a piece to use as a weapon. If only he had taken his father's sword when he had the chance!

The tiger moved slowly forward, his shoulder bones rising and falling in hypnotic rhythm. His intent golden gaze never left Duncan's head.

Fia's meow splintered the air. "He's going to pounce!"

Fear gave Duncan's hands a sudden, desperate strength, and a jagged piece of wood broke off at last. With unconscious reflex, he fell into his fencing stance: one foot back, his body balanced, and the wooden slat raised like a sword. The words he had been taught to say before every fencing match emerged without thought.

"In the name of the king!" he cried as the tiger leaped.

Everything slowed down strangely. Duncan saw it all in one vivid moment: the clear morning light, the dark cliff, the sharp-edged shadows lying blue on rock and sand; the body of the tiger in midair, white, black, and tawny, every hair tipped with brightness. Then—much too close—open mouth and gleaming fangs, and in the next instant, the tiger rammed into Duncan with the power of a crashing wave. The wooden slat was brushed aside as if it didn't exist, and Duncan went over on his back, hard. Heavy paws pressed down on his chest. The tiger's breath was hot and rank on Duncan's face.

He couldn't move. He couldn't even breathe. Duncan suddenly knew that he did not want his last sight on earth to be the slavering jaws of a tiger. Pinned, helpless, he flicked his eyes to the sky beyond, to a blue so pure it made his heart ache. He waited for the end to come, his heart beating like the wings of a moth.

But the end didn't seem to be coming. Instead there was a lot of high, furious meowing and low, anxious growling.

"I'm *sorry*, already! I wouldn't have knocked him over if I'd known he was a king's man!" The tiger's rough tongue licked up one side of Duncan's face all the way to his eyebrows, depositing a fair amount of saliva. "Is he dead? Why isn't he saying anything?"

"Get OFF him!" shrieked Fia. "You must weigh a TON—look at him, he can't even BREATHE!"

"Oh, all right," grumbled the tiger. "Calm down. You don't have to be so piercing. I have sensitive ears."

The relief was incredible. Duncan rolled onto his side, his cheek damp from tiger drool, trying to breathe again. The animal must have put over a hundred pounds of pressure on his chest.

"You have sensitive *ears*?" Fia's meow scaled up even higher. "You probably just broke all his *ribs*, you overgrown tomcat!"

The tiger made a chuffing sound of exasperation. "How was I supposed to know he came in the name of the king? I was already pouncing before he said anything!"

"Did it ever occur to you to ask?" Fia demanded. "Or are you stupid? Did someone drop you on the head when you were a kitten?"

Duncan would have laughed if he had had the air in his lungs to do it. Kittens weren't known for their scolding abilities, but Fia had learned from the best—her mother, Mabel—and had developed a fine cutting edge to her meows.

"I wasn't a kitten; I was a cub." The tiger's voice was turning sullen. "I said I was sorry. You don't have to insult me."

Duncan lay still, taking shallow, wheezing breaths, in and out in a careful rhythm. Clear water slipped across the pale sand, frothing a little at the edges, and slid back to sea. He watched as the next wave lapped at his outstretched fingers. The tide was coming in.

He pushed himself up with his elbow, groaning only twice, and took a good look at the sheer rock wall that enclosed the beach. It stretched high above him, gleaming a lighter gray in the sun's glare, but there was a wide, dark band along the base, marked at its top with a white rim of crusted salt. It was the high-tide mark, and it was over his head. In a few hours, the beach would disappear beneath ten feet of water. And the opening to the cave would fill with water, too. Where had the tiger come from?

Duncan gazed at the animal. The tiger's tawny coat seemed to almost glow in the sun, and the black stripes were strongly marked. A salt breeze ruffled the white fur at his throat. He looked magnificent, if somewhat apologetic.

The tiger cleared his throat politely. "Welcome to my island."

Fia groomed herself behind a foreleg. "Some welcome," she muttered.

The tiger ignored her loftily. "I am honored to greet a king's man, sir." He bowed his head with stately courtesy.

Duncan blinked. Of course, the tiger was only following the usual rule for cats. If a cat did something embarrassing, it always pretended nothing had happened. But given that the tiger had been about to kill him only two minutes ago, it was a little strange.

Fia gave the tiger a withering glare. "Who says it's your island, anyway, you big bully?"

The tiger looked suddenly uncertain. "I'm not a bully. I was just doing my job."

"Like what?" Fia lifted her eyebrow tufts. "Pounce first, ask questions later?"

"Go easy, Fia," said Duncan. "Listen, tiger—" He paused. "What's your name, anyway?"

"Brig," said the tiger, "at your service. Short for Brigadier."

Duncan scratched under the edge of his cap. "That's a military title," he said, mystified.

The tiger sat back on his haunches, stiffened his neck, and pressed the edge of one paw to his forehead. It took Duncan a moment to realize he was trying to salute.

Duncan felt a sudden spasm of inner mirth, and he bent over at once, hiding his expression. He didn't dare laugh. He mustn't. He smoothed down Fia's bristling fur and got his face under control. If Brig was saluting him, he had better act like a superior officer and return the salute.

"All right, Brig," he said, "at ease. Right now we need water, and food, and a way off this beach before the tide comes in and drowns us all."

"Of course, sir," said the tiger. "Follow me." He gazed over Fia's head as if she were beneath his notice, turned on his massive paws, and paced with injured dignity across the damp sand to the cave.

Duncan stepped through the rocky opening. It was cooler out of the sun's glare, but his eyes were not used to the dim light. He walked cautiously forward, feeling his way, one hand trailing against the slimy wall. This was no tiger's den, as he had first supposed. This was a sea cave, dry only at low tide, and its walls were damp with algae.

The sand under his feet was packed hard in little ridges, and the cave grew steadily darker as he walked. The small hairs lifted on Duncan's arms in the chilly draft, and he looked back at the entrance, now only a faint triangle of light in the distance. He shivered lightly. Where was the tiger taking them? He started to ask, but his throat, dry and salty, scratched on the first word. Now that he wasn't in immediate danger of drowning, or of being eaten by a tiger, he remembered how terribly thirsty he was.

Duncan cleared his throat and tried again. "Where are we going?" He couldn't see the tiger at all, but he could hear a snuffling sound ahead. Two golden eyes blinked like small, round lamps as the tiger turned.

"Come along, sir, *if* you please." Brig's low rumble echoed hollowly in the cave.

Duncan took one blind step toward the tiger, then another. Suddenly his feet splashed in something wet.

"*Don't* chase away the fish, sir." Brig's reproachful voice came at him out of the darkness. "Why don't you wait on the stone ledge with the Fia kitten?"

"I can't see in the dark," Duncan said, exasperated. "I'm not a cat, in case you hadn't noticed."

Water swirled against Duncan's ankles, and there was a sense of something large approaching. Brig's eyes blinked out of the darkness. "Don't worry, sir. The others have the same problem. I suggest you catch hold of my tail."

The others? How many tigers were on this island? Duncan grasped the thick, ropelike tail that swished into his hand, and he was led to one side. His feet left water and found a ledge of smooth, flat stone. It was covered with algae, like the walls, and was as slick as ice. Duncan managed three careful steps before he stumbled and fell to his knees.

"Ow!" Duncan touched one knee with a cautious finger. It felt damp and slimy, but with blood or seaweed? Suppressing a groan, he sat up. He stretched his legs over the rock's edge, and his feet sank into water. There must be a pool here, in the inner cave, filled with seawater left over from the last high tide. He splashed a little up onto his knees and then licked his finger, just to be sure. Salty.

"We need water," he croaked to Brig.

"*Please*, sir! A tiger in the act of catching dinner must *not* be distracted!"

Fia whispered, "I don't like it here. This cave smells like eels."

Duncan drew his feet out of the water and rested them on a little knob of rock. Eels had teeth.

His eyes were growing used to the light. High above, from some crack or flaw in the rock, a thin sunbeam came filtering down, hanging in the air like a straight golden thread. By its light, Duncan could just make out the bulky form of the tiger as he stood in the pool, staring intently at its surface with one paw lifted. Then, so fast that Duncan hardly saw it, the great paw flashed down. With a scooping motion, Brig pulled up a small fish, neatly hooked on his claws, and tossed it into Duncan's lap. Duncan tried to grasp it, but it was all slippery scales, wet and firm and flipping back and forth.

"Use your *claws*," said Fia. "Like this." She pounced on the wildly flopping fish, hooked her claws neatly behind its gills, and bit through its spine. Then she dragged the fish off his lap and began to devour the head with smacking sounds and small kitten growls.

Duncan wiped his scaly hands on his shirt. "Brig, how about water?"

"Soon, sir," said Brig. "I have to catch dinner for five."

For *five*? Duncan frowned. There must be other tigers on the island. But where? The cave seemed to end at the pool; he could just make out the rear wall, shiny with algae. Maybe back on the beach there was a way up the cliffs—for tigers. If it involved leaping twice his height, he had a feeling he wasn't going to make it.

He had to get himself and Fia to safety before the tide came in and drowned them in the cave. The tiger seemed to be a military sort; maybe he would take orders.

"Brigadier!" Duncan said in his most commanding voice. "Attention!"

The tiger reared up out of the pool. "Sir! Yes, sir!"

"We need to get to a safe place—away from the tide—and we need water to drink. Now, Brig!"

"Impossible, sir. I have my orders to catch dinner before I go back."

"Well, I'm giving you *new* orders," said Duncan.

Brig shook his shaggy head. "She outranks you," he said, "and her orders came first. Sorry, sir. Now, excuse me. I have a job to do." The tiger took up his fishing position.

She? Duncan grabbed his hair in frustration. This tiger

was driving him mad. "Tell me where the safe place is, then, and I'll go there myself!"

"That will not work, sir." The tiger spoke very low, still watching the water. "You need me to guide you, because you can't see in the dark."

This was infuriating. "Fia can show me! Tell Fia where to go!" Duncan's last word echoed eerily in the cave: *Go! Go! Go!*

Brig reared out of the water with a roar. "PLEASE, sir! Shut UP, sir! Allow the tiger to do his JOB, sir!"

Duncan clamped his mouth in a tight line. It was impossible to reason with a determined cat. Apparently there was some queen tiger on the island, who gave the orders. He just wished he knew where the tigers lived. He was getting heartily sick of the dark.

Suddenly Duncan realized that his feet were wet again. The water had risen to the knob of rock where his feet rested; and now that he paid attention, he could feel a little tugging current pushing against his ankles. The tide was coming in. They would be trapped in the cave.

Fear scooped a hollow under Duncan's breastbone, and for one frozen moment, he couldn't move. Fia, still chewing on her fish, made a small contented noise nearby. The sound released him from his trance and all at once he was in action, his mind clicking into gear and his body following. He lifted Fia up to a higher place on the rock, and then he was splashing back toward the entrance, running with knees lifted high above the water, the sound of his heart beating loud in his ears. Maybe the wooden crate was still there. Maybe he and Fia could float on it; maybe there would be air trapped near the ceiling of the cave that they could breathe.

But the water rushed in with more force as he neared the narrow cave entrance. With each succeeding wave he stood still, legs braced, hanging on to the wall as best he could against the water that raced furiously in. As the waves pulled back he splashed forward, only to stop and brace himself a moment later. The entrance was now partly filled with water, but before he reached it, he saw the crate. It was bobbing in the sea, in the inner curve of the cliffs, fifty feet away. As he watched, the crate rolled over in the surf, crashing into the unforgiving stone. He heard it crack—he watched it break apart—and then the sea, pouring through the entrance to the cave, knocked him off his feet.

Duncan was swept back into the dark cave as if by a powerful hand. He tumbled, rolled by the water and scraped along the sand, helpless as a rag doll.

"Sir! Are you all right, sir?" The tiger's muzzle was near Duncan's head, his voice barely louder than the echoing noise of the water.

Duncan struggled to his knees, spat out a mouthful of sand and grit, and sucked in air with great, wheezing gulps.

"Come along, sir, unless you prefer to swim." Brig's furry shoulder nudged Duncan onto the stone ledge. "Follow me, up and around! No time to waste!" He bent his head to the large fish he had caught and gripped it in his jaws once more.

Shaken and bruised, Duncan ran his hand along the tiger's back until he found the long, thick tail. His eyes were still adjusting to the dark; he had looked too long at the light past the entrance, and he could barely see where they were going. Half-blind, his senses dulled by the roaring of the tide in the cave, he took two steps, then a third, before his feet went out from under him.

"*OW*, SIR!" Brig yowled. "THAT WAS MY *TAIL*, SIR!"

Duncan sprawled on the slimy rock, breathing hard. He had barely managed to keep from sliding off into the pool. Below him, another wave came pushing in and smacked against the back wall of the cave with a muffled boom. If he had fallen then, he would have been dashed against the rock, just like the crate.

Brig hooked a claw in the fish he had dropped, and growled in Duncan's ear. "You must keep your footing, sir. We're going much higher up. See where Fia is?"

Higher up and farther on, two small, mismatched eyes shone in the dark. Beyond the shining eyes, Duncan could see a flaw in the wall—a natural formation of the rock like a jagged gash that went up and across the wall in a series of irregular steps. The path climbed higher than his eyes could see by the light of one thin sunbeam, and it was narrow. There would be no second chances if he slipped. And he *would* slip; there was algae on the rock as far as the waterline.

Duncan put his mouth to the tiger's ear. "It's too slick. Isn't there another way?"

Brig shook his head. "Just dig in with your claws, sir," he

said earnestly. "Didn't your mother teach you how to grip with your claws?"

Duncan shook his head. His mother hadn't taught him to use his claws, but she had taught him almost everything else. Would she ever know what had happened to him? What lies would the earl tell her when he returned?

Something fierce choked Duncan's throat. He had a sudden vision of the earl's fingers, long and graceful, patting Sylvia McKinnon's hand as he made up a story about what had happened to her son. The earl might even ask her to play her violin, to comfort them both. . . .

Duncan wiped his cheeks, wet with spray, and got to his feet. His mother would want him to be brave. She would want him to keep on trying to the end.

He fell again, but this time he landed in the pool. With great good fortune, he did not fall at the moment when the waves were rushing in but when they were sliding back. He was dragged only a little way along the bottom of the pool, although his shirt and shorts filled up with sand.

He scrambled back onto the ledge, the sand falling from his shorts as he stood. The rock beneath his feet seemed suddenly easier to stand on—gritty, not slippery—

The sand! He could use the sand!

Duncan fumbled at the buttons of his father's shirt with trembling fingers. He tied the sleeves around his waist and tied the bottom corners together to make a pouch. He watched for the next receding wave, jumped down, and feverishly scooped sand. He got back on the ledge in time to avoid the next incoming wave and gripped Brig's tail with his free hand. "Ready," he said.

It was a nightmarish journey. The rock path was broken, uneven, and Duncan had to feel his way with his feet, but he sprinkled sand before each step and didn't fall. Halfway up, the ledge widened to a broad shelf, and he sat down a moment, dully wondering how long he could go on. His hand touched the rock, and it wasn't slimy. He was above the high-tide mark, and from then on, the going was dry and much easier.

All at once, it was over. The path leveled out and turned into a wider cave. The feeble sunbeam of the sea cave was left behind, and a dim light ahead grew gradually brighter. Soon Duncan could see the colors of the tiger padding before him, and Fia's prancing white form. Now Duncan could even see something like stick figures painted on the cave wall. He didn't stop to examine them; what he saw ahead pulled him onward in a hurried, anxious rush.

Water! Clear, clean, it fell past the opening at the cave's end in a glorious scattering of mist and sunlit drops. Duncan was so eager for it that he tripped and almost fell off the ledge at the rocky door that opened onto a vast valley. He had come to the hollow interior of the island, but he had no eyes for the beautiful sight. He rolled over onto his back under the waterfall and opened his mouth wide to drink. He could feel life and energy pouring back into him, and he laughed out loud. A bush full of flowers, scarlet and gold, grew from a crack in the stone near his head, and its perfume filled the air. Beside him, Fia lapped busily with her small pink tongue from the puddles on the stone ledge.

There was a motion at the edge of his vision. But it wasn't Brig. It wasn't even one of the other tigers Brig had spoken of. It was a girl, about his size or a little taller, her dark hair in two long braids and her face pale with fright.

Duncan scrambled to his feet.

"Oh!" cried the girl. Her hands flew to her mouth, and she dropped a bundle of sticks with a clatter. Then, in a whirl of tattered skirts, she turned and ran down a slanting path like a startled deer.

Duncan looked at Brig. "Who was *that*?"

Brig cleared his throat with an apologetic rumble. "I'm sorry, sir. She should have greeted you properly. She doesn't really act the way royalty should."

"She's *royal*?" Duncan stared after the girl. "I thought you were talking about a queen *tiger* before."

"She is not a tiger, sir." Brig spoke with exaggerated patience. "Notice the lack of fur, and the placement of the ears, and how she runs on her hind legs alone. She can't even speak Cat, though I've tried to teach her often enough."

Duncan was still dazed. "But who *is* she?" he demanded again.

Brig cocked his head quizzically. "Don't you know? That's the Princess Lydia. Lydia, of Arvidia. She's the one I take orders from, see?"

CHAPTER 17

The Princess Lydia

PRINCESS LYDIA? SO SHE HADN'T BEEN LOST in the Rift after all?

The tiger said something more, but Duncan watched the slight figure of the girl as she moved rapidly down the hillside. She had tucked the center of her skirt into her waistband so that it looked as if she were wearing a pair of very baggy shorts. Her long brown legs leaped over rocks and across small, glinting streams.

Duncan looked around in wonder. The island was hollow, secret. No one looking at it from the sea could ever guess what was inside. There was a small lake or lagoon at the bottom that looked perfect for swimming, and beyond it, another waterfall, splashing down through lush green.

The island changed as he looked higher. Two-thirds of the way up the slope were blue-green pines that stood tall, like stiff arrows pointing to the sun. Still higher, the bones of the island showed through in jutting rock.

The princess had crossed the lowest part of the island, a narrow valley mostly filled with lagoon, and started up the far slope. She was smaller now, farther away, but Duncan could still follow her figure as she scrambled up a series of broad, flat ledges and hurried into a dark opening in the rock wall.

Brig's low rumble broke into Duncan's thoughts. "Here is where she painted the earl and his treacherous attack on the duke—"

Duncan turned. Brig patted the rock wall of the cave, pointing to the painted childish figures Duncan had seen before. Not all were like that, though. Whoever drew them was getting better. Now he could see that the bundle of sticks the princess had dropped were frayed and discolored at one end, as if she used them for paintbrushes.

"It's the other way around," Duncan said. "Everyone said the duke attacked the earl."

Brig tapped the wall with a shaggy paw. "*This* is not the duke."

Could Brig possibly be right? Duncan looked at the fighting figures with an irrational flutter of hope—and then the hope died. It was easy to tell which was which by their hats. A duke's hat was tall, with a pointed brim—an earl's was low and rounded. Brig's paw was tapping at the man in the duke's hat.

"You've got them mixed up," said Duncan.

Brig's rib cage huffed in and out. "Do you doubt the word of a *tiger*, sir?"

"I don't want to argue about art, Brig. I'm starving."

"Try the fish!" Fia lifted her chin from the fish Brig had dropped. The fish head bore marks of her sharp little teeth.

Duncan was not hungry enough to eat raw fish—yet. He narrowed his eyes as the princess came back out of the cave on the far side of the island. She looked as if someone had reminded her that she was royal. She was walking with dignity, her skirts free and her head high.

"I'm going down to meet her," Duncan said abruptly. "Bring the fish, Brig. And let Fia ride on your back."

They met the princess near the lagoon, where the path was bordered by sweet-smelling bushes. Bees droned in the scented air, making complicated circles around vivid red flowers. The hollow island rose about them like a leafy green funnel, but Duncan's attention was all on the girl.

Now he could see that her odd clothing was actually made of bird skins, cleverly sewn together with feathers still attached. It looked light, yet warm. Strangely, there was knitted lace at the collar and sleeves and on her skirt. And the skirt wasn't ragged after all; the holes in it were just complicated designs in the lace. He had seen old women making lace like that, sitting in the sun on the stone streets of the island of Dulle.

He gazed at the princess, mystified. How had she survived all this time? She didn't look like she was starving, and she was even running around dressed in lace, which was just plain weird, considering she had been cast away on a deserted island for—he calculated—almost seven years now.

But first things first. He lowered his head in the courtly bow his mother had taught him. On Brig's back, Fia bowed too.

"Greetings," said the princess faintly. "Brig, come."

The tiger obediently left Duncan's side and stood by the princess. She took the fish from his mouth and put it in a knotted string bag that she slung over her shoulder. Then she curled her fingers in Brig's neck fur, as if having him close gave her courage.

"You—" she began, her voice wavering like a ripple of water. She gripped Brig's fur more tightly and tried again. "You, sir, will come with me. Brig, don't let him escape."

Duncan's head snapped up. "Don't let me *escape*?"

An embarrassed growl emerged from Brig's chest. "Sorry, sir. Just tell her you're a king's man, and she'll understand."

"I'm a king's man," Duncan said at once. "Why are you treating me like a prisoner? I'm on your side."

The princess seemed to be trembling. With a visible effort, she brought her gaze up to focus on Duncan's head, just above his eyes. "You *say* you are a king's man," she said, "but

208

your head betrays you. Brig, if he sets foot off the path, attack." She turned on her heel and led the way up a narrow path through moss and ferns.

Shame rose in Duncan like a scarlet tide. His fingers moved to his forehead and felt the fringe of hair that had escaped from beneath his cap. The sea must have washed all the dye away.

No wonder the princess had treated him like a criminal. She knew whose son he was.

"Sir! I'm sorry, sir!" Brig's growl held a pleading note. "I'd explain to her, but she can't understand Cat!"

"Then don't attack me if I put a toe off the path," Duncan said irritably.

"Sorry, sir—orders." Brig stiffened his whiskers to a military angle. "Come along, if you please."

Duncan trudged up the path. After two days adrift with no food, his legs were weak. Climbing a steep slope wasn't helping.

He tried to distract himself by looking around. His first impression of a funnel had been accurate enough. Was he in the heart of an old volcano that had grown cold, or was there some other reason for the way the land sank in the middle of the island, with high cliffs all around? Whatever had caused it, the slopes led upward in a series of green and mossy terraces. Circling the top were rocky crags, jutting sharp-edged into bright sky. If he climbed to the crags, he could look out to sea. Surely a boat would come by sometime, someday? Maybe they could make a signal with smoke or paddle out on a raft. There had to be a way to get off this island and back home.

The princess, up ahead on the path, strode along like someone who had had plenty of rest and food and sleep. Duncan forced his legs to keep moving. More than anything, he wanted to know how the princess had ended up here. Clearly the history books hadn't told the whole story.

They passed a thin waterfall that splashed down a sheer rock face. Duncan was all at once ragingly thirsty again; after being without water so long, he couldn't get enough. He stepped off the path to tip his head back under the falls. Brig growled.

"Oh, come on!" cried Duncan. "I'm just getting a drink!"

The princess jumped like a frightened cat and looked back over her shoulder.

Duncan scowled up at her. Why was *she* nervous? She had a full-grown tiger to defend her! "Listen, Princess," he said, "I've been lost at sea, without food or water, for almost two days. I'm sorry you think I'm some kind of threat, but can't you at least let me get a drink? And maybe something to eat?"

Princess Lydia swallowed hard. "All right. I'm going to let you stay here, as long as you don't try to hurt Mattie or me—"

"Who's Mattie?" Duncan asked, but Princess Lydia rushed on, unheeding.

"Because I wouldn't throw even a snake back into the sea to drown. And you can help with the work—you'll have to, if you want to eat. So you can get your drink, and after that, come up to the home cave, and we'll feed you. But if you try anything—anything at all—Brig is going to eat you. You might think he's just a tiger, but he's very smart, and he understands everything I say. And he *always* obeys my commands."

Her brown eyes held his, wide with fear and blazing with defiance. She lifted her chin, and even from several yards away, Duncan could see the effort she was making to hold it steady.

I'm not like my father! Duncan wanted to shout as she turned her back and walked away. But he didn't want to make things worse. He put his head under the cool, delicious water, taking it in like a sponge. Then he took off his cap, washed the salt from his hair, and rinsed the blood from his knees where he had fallen.

Fia jumped off Brig's back, entranced by the crystal drops. She batted the falling water with her paw, turned her head sideways, and stuck out her small pink tongue.

"There's soap," Brig offered. He flicked his tail toward a small pot on a ledge. "Mattie makes it from wood ash and duck fat."

Duncan glared at him. "Oh, so now you're being nice again. Are you sure you don't want to *eat* me?"

Brig looked at him reproachfully. "I have my orders, sir."

Fia lifted her head and sniffed the air. "Mouse!" She stalked off toward a stand of waving ferns and peered between the fronds.

"Go ahead and catch it," Duncan said. "No one's going to

eat *you* if you leave the path." He was hungry enough to eat a mouse himself—his stomach was cramping again. He shook the water out of his hair and headed up to the cave.

Mattie turned out to be a very old, half-blind servant, with her lap full of knitted lace and a spindle full of tiger's-hair thread. She sat on a broad stone terrace at the mouth of the cave. Beside her was a hollowed stone laid over a fire; a savory smell of duck stew made Duncan swallow hard.

The princess came out of the cave, holding a wooden bowl and something that looked like flat bread. "This is the stranger," she said to Mattie.

"Then you must welcome him," said the old woman. "Do it properly, now, Your Highness. As I taught you."

The princess flushed. She put down the bowl and bread on a wooden slab near the fire and stood with her shoulders back. "I am the Princess Lydia. This is my trusted companion, Mattie, and my faithful tiger and guard, Brigadier. I bid you welcome to Traitor Island." She extended her hand with a graceful gesture.

Something moved within Duncan like a knife turning. Traitor Island. And the traitor had been his own father. . . .

But he must make the correct response. He knew what he should do; he had practiced it with his mother. He bent his knee and kissed the back of Princess Lydia's hand. "Your Royal Highness."

She snatched her hand back as if she had been burned.

"Well done, except for the last part," Mattie murmured. "Come closer, lad. Let me see your face. What is your name, and how did you come here?"

The old woman put her soft, wrinkled hands on Duncan's cheeks and pulled his head down. She peered closely at him with filmy eyes.

"My name is Duncan McK—" Duncan choked and didn't finish.

Mattie's gaze seemed to grow suddenly keener. She searched his face; she touched his hair; she straightened his collar. "These stitches are coming out," she said, almost to herself, and pulled at a thread. "I'll sew it up for you again—"

She stopped with a gasp. "Your Highness!" she breathed, turning the collar to show the initials that were monogrammed there. "Look at his face, his hair—does he remind you of anyone?"

The princess stood up, came closer, touched his collar. Her expression changed. "What is your name?" she whispered. "Your *whole* name?"

Duncan hesitated.

"Tell me," Princess Lydia said, low and fierce.

Duncan winced; a royal command could not be ignored. "Duncan Charles McKinnon." He hung his head. He had never said the name out loud before; he wished he didn't have to do it now.

"Oh!" cried the princess. In the next moment, she was

hugging him, hard, and then Mattie kissed his cheek, laughing and crying at the same time.

"Er . . . ," said Duncan.

Princess Lydia touched the cap in his hand. "I thought you were the *earl's* man. You have his badge on your cap."

Duncan had forgotten about the badge. "But wouldn't you be *happy* to see an earl's man? I mean, everybody said he was the one who tried to rescue you from . . . from my father, the traitor. . . ." His words faltered.

"No! No! That's not the way it happened!" cried the princess, stamping her foot. "The *earl* was the one who left us here—he drugged your father so he couldn't fight back, he tied him up and wounded him and left him for dead—"

Old Mattie looked at Duncan with her cloudy eyes, now brighter with moisture, and gripped his arms with her two gnarled hands. "The Earl of Merrick is an evil, treacherous villain," she said, and gave Duncan a little shake. "Your father was a *hero*."

"It's true," rumbled Brig. "And tigers never lie."

CHAPTER 18
Traitor Island

MATTIE DISHED UP BOWL AFTER BOWL of duck stew, until Duncan could hold no more. Then she made him a bed of dried ferns, covered it with a sack, and sent him to rest from his ordeal in the sea.

"There, now," she said. "You're feeling better, aren't you?"

Duncan thanked her with all his heart. It wasn't just the food he was grateful for. It was the kind words and the way her face wrinkled into a smile, and the small, cloudy eyes that peered at him without a hint of suspicion. She wasn't his mother, but she was motherly, and a lonely, cold corner of his heart grew a little warmer.

Princess Lydia's fear was all gone. She sat beside him and

told how his father had helped them survive, and when she had seen him for the last time.

"So my father really is dead," said Duncan.

Princess Lydia nodded soberly. "We watched him go down in the sea. Three years ago, it was."

Duncan curled up on his rustling sack, still warm from the day's sun, and shut his eyes. Three years ago, he would have been eight, almost nine. Three years ago, he had still had a father.

"He never really healed from his wound," the princess said. "At first, he was busy helping us survive. Later on, he worked hard building a boat that could take us away. But he kept falling ill with fever, and each time he recovered, he was a little weaker." The princess drew a long breath. "We tried to tell him to rest more, but he didn't listen. He said he had to get us off the island and back to the king, or die trying."

Duncan cleared his throat. "But what *happened*?"

"He died trying," said the princess simply. "He said it was our best chance if he took the boat and went for help. He made us stay here, because it was safer. And it was," she finished sadly. "He was trying to catch the Arvidian Current—he said it would take him all the way to Capital City, if he didn't run into another island first—but a black squall came up from the Rift while I was watching through the telescope and hid the boat completely."

Duncan remembered the sudden violence of a black squall. He closed his eyes.

"The boat must have flipped," Princess Lydia went on. "When the squall passed, all we could see was the bottom of the boat, and the duke clinging to it. But he was so weak. He struggled three times to get on top of it, and every time, he slipped off. Finally he couldn't even struggle. He turned his face to the island—he knew we would be watching—and he lifted his hand." The princess paused. "Then he was gone."

There was a weight on Duncan's chest that felt like the grief of the world.

The princess touched his shoulder. "I'm so sorry. If it weren't for me, he wouldn't have left the island. But he thought he had to save the heir to the throne. Brig went down through the sea cave to try to swim to him, but couldn't get there in time."

"Not your fault." Duncan's voice was unsteady. "He probably would have done the same for me."

"That's true." Princess Lydia sniffled twice. "He talked about you and your mother all the time, and he kept track of how old you would be—that is, if the earl hadn't killed you. He worried about that. See, he'd thought the earl was his friend. . . ."

Duncan turned on his bed of dried ferns to the cave wall, so no one could see his face. He felt a sudden bond with the father he didn't remember. Duncan, too, had trusted the earl. Duncan, too, had been betrayed and left to die.

Lydia's voice went on. "And your father had a trusted servant, Tammas, still on the ship. The duke hoped that

Tammas might guess at the earl's treachery and warn your mother. But there were times the duke feared the earl had already found and killed you and your mother. Those were bad times," the princess added quietly.

There was a long silence. Then came a shuffling sound, like feet moving slowly over a stone floor. "Is he asleep?" Mattie whispered.

"Almost," the princess whispered back.

Duncan was not asleep. He was thinking that he had been given back something precious, something he had thought was lost forever. His father's honor, returned to him now, seemed like a solid thing, something he could hold in his two hands. And he held not only his father's honor but the honor of the McKinnons, going far back into the past.

There would be an estate, lands, a castle. There would be portraits on the walls of his ancestors, grandparents and great-grandparents and beyond. . . .

Someday he hoped to see them all. But first he had to clear his father's name and see the Earl of Merrick get the punishment he deserved. Most important of all, he had to rescue the heir to the kingdom and bring her back to her father's court.

But to do all that, of course, he needed a boat.

Duncan slept the rest of the afternoon. It was inexpressible luxury to lie flat, and dry, and not be bobbing endlessly in briny water. He woke to the entrancing smell of dinner: roasted seagull eggs, pennycress salad, and flatbread baking on the stone hearth. He lay quietly, watching the fire from beneath half-closed eyelids, feeling lazy and still half asleep.

Mattie said something Duncan didn't quite catch as her knitting needles clicked. Fia, who had found her way to the cave, played with Mattie's ball of yarn, pouncing happily. But the princess looked glum.

"Please, Mattie, not tonight!" Lydia glanced at Duncan, who lay without moving, and lowered her voice. "Can't it wait? I don't want to do—that—in front of a stranger."

"Nonsense." Mattie dusted her hands on her skirts and rose creakily. "It's been a long time since we've had princess practice. If you ever get back to the palace, my dear, it will be full of strangers, and you will have to know how to act."

Princess Lydia pulled at her long dark braid and chewed nervously on the tip. "Please don't make me walk down the path with a basket on my head. It's embarrassing."

"Someday you'll need to know how to descend a stair with grace," Mattie said, flipping the flatbread over. "You don't want to enter your father's court looking like some out-islander who doesn't know anything, do you?"

"I don't care," muttered the princess. "And don't make me do court etiquette again, either. I know it *all*."

"Then we shall do the dances," Mattie said firmly. "They're your weak point. Duncan, kindly get up at once. I can tell you're awake by your breathing, and there's no sense lying abed when there's dancing to be done."

Princess Lydia gave a low moan and hid her face behind her hands.

"Your Royal Highness!" Mattie's voice snapped like a flag in a stiff breeze. "Is this how we act when a gentleman wishes to dance?"

"He doesn't wish to dance—do you, Duncan?" Lydia raised a hopeful face.

"Of course he does," said Mattie. "Now then, my lady, you have here a partner"—she nodded at Duncan—"and music"—she whistled a few notes—"and I shall clap the beat. If you ever do arrive at court, you must not shame yourself on the dance floor."

The princess pushed out her lower lip. "Duncan can't be my partner. He doesn't know how to dance."

Duncan suppressed a chuckle. She wouldn't get out of it that way. "I do know how to dance, actually."

Lydia glared at him. "Oh, sure, maybe you can do the Island Jig and Jump, but did you learn the *court* dances? The gavotte, the quadrille, the minuet?"

Duncan grinned. His mother had taught him every dance she knew. "And the waltz, the pavane, the contra danse, the lancers—"

"Fine," said Lydia through her teeth. "Enough."

"—the gallopade, the reel, the cross-step, the promenade—"

Mattie said, "You do need some work on your promenade, my lady."

"—and the Arvidian shuffle," Duncan finished. He felt a

sudden surge of affection for his mother, who had borne with his complaining and made him learn anyway. She had been giving him duke practice all along, and he never knew. "Come on," he said, and held out his hand. "It's actually kind of fun, with a partner."

In the next few weeks, Duncan found out how the princess and Mattie had survived on the island all this time. They worked—hard. Now that Duncan was here, he worked, too.

Every day he fetched water from the waterfall, picked greens, and carried whatever Brig caught to the cave to be plucked, gutted, cleaned, skinned, or sewn. He hauled wood, built fires, and climbed among the rocks to collect eggs from birds' nests.

But lately he had been getting some ideas of his own. He took Brig to the sea cave at high tide, carrying a flaming torch. Then he wedged the torch in a rock crevice so that it shone on the water.

"This isn't the way I fish," grumbled Brig.

"Just wait," said Duncan. Soon, tiny, transparent minnows rose to the light, darting here and there; then larger fish moved among them, five and ten inches in length.

"Those are barely a mouthful," Brig muttered, but suddenly his whiskers stiffened. A long, thick shadow passed beneath the surface of the water—over two feet in length—and then another.

Duncan grinned as Brig tensed, his paw lifted. The folk

back on the island of Dulle had talked about fishing with torches, and it worked! Brig clawed the fish, leaped in to finish his kill, and Duncan helped him drag it back onto the ledge.

The string bag that Mattie had knitted wasn't sturdy enough for a fish this size. Duncan wrapped the fish in a strong, slender vine to carry it back. He would have to make some good rope. He could do it; he'd helped the fishermen often enough at home. There was plenty of seagrass in the lagoon that he could use.

The weather had changed while they were in the sea cave. The sky was dark and purple with clouds as one more storm churned up from the Rift. Duncan walked with his head bent against the whirling wind, his eyes nearly shut to keep the grit out. By the time he and Brig crossed the valley and reached the home cave, a driving rain had soaked them through. He was glad he wasn't on the sea in this storm.

Brig shook out his fur and lay by the fire next to Fia. Mattie passed her veined hand over the huge fish with delight. "We'll smoke it, and it will keep for months!"

The kitten got up and sniffed at the fish. "I can bring food, too," she meowed, and trotted off to a dark corner of the cave. She returned a few minutes later and laid the limp body of a mouse at Mattie's feet.

"Ach, the darling kitty!" Mattie's face creased into a hundred smiling wrinkles as she rubbed Fia's small, furry head. "She's a mighty hunter!"

Fia purred, her eyes squeezed into contented slits. "Smoked fish is good," she mewed, "but raw mouse has *much* more flavor."

The smoking cave was just across the path. Lydia didn't look much like a princess of the realm as she whacked off the head of the grouper, split it down the middle, and expertly gutted it. Duncan watched, impressed, as she sliced the fish into fillets and hung them to dry on a rack made of sticks. Then she arranged small piles of wood chips and twigs, and lit them from the coals she had brought from the home fire, carried in a clod of earth.

"There," she said as the smoke spiraled up, enveloping the fish. "Mattie will have to tend the fires for days—they can never go out, but they can never get too hot, either. So we have to bring more wood for her." She looked worried. "The wood pile is getting low. We'll have to go scouting for more fallen branches. We used to have an ax, but last winter the head fell off the handle, right into the lagoon, and we could never find it again."

"How did you get those chips, then?" Duncan pointed to a pile set aside for smoking.

Lydia picked up a flattish stone, a little longer than her hand, that had flaked on one end. "Hack at wood with this, and you can get lots of chips."

Duncan reached for the stone and turned it over. One side had been flaked so it had a sharp edge, and the other side was rounded to fit in the hand. "It's a hand ax, like the ancient people used!" He turned the stone over and over in his hand. "But later on, they figured how to attach the stone to a wood handle."

"I tried to do it, but we don't have anything strong enough to tie it on," said Lydia.

"It's safer if you tie it on, but you don't have to. We can burn a hole right through the head of the handle—just big enough for the narrow end of the stone to fit, see? Then we whack the ax against some wood to shove the stone in deeper. Every time we use it, the stone gets seated more firmly in the handle."

"But how do we burn the hole without burning the whole handle—oh, wait, I know!" Lydia bounced a little. "We do it slowly, with the burning end of a narrow stick—"

"Right, and never let it catch flame—"

"Until it burns all the way through!" The princess clapped her hands. "What a clever idea!"

"Well, it's not really mine," said Duncan, grinning. "We studied ancient history at school. I did a whole unit on tool making. I remember how they made harpoons, too."

"I wish I could have gone to school," Lydia said wistfully. "I mean, for the past seven years."

"You'll go again," Duncan said, more confidently than he felt.

"But I don't want to go *now*." The princess chewed on the tip of her braid again. "I won't know anything I'm supposed to know."

"I thought Mattie was teaching you," Duncan said.

"She's just teaching me court manners. And that's another thing!" the princess blurted out. "I remember court—it was awful. I was supposed to be perfectly polite, keep my dress perfectly clean, and always say the right thing. And now that I'm older, they'll expect me to know things about government and ruling the kingdom!" She turned to him, her brown eyes anxious. "How am I supposed to rule the kingdom when I don't know *how*?"

Duncan had never thought about the duties of a king or queen—or any noble, for that matter. He had mostly thought about the privileges.

"You'll have advisers and things," he said. "Anyway, your father is still king. . . ." He trailed off, unsure of his ground. The old king had been sick for a long time. People said that he was just hanging on in the hope of seeing his daughter again.

Princess Lydia's face scrunched up in the middle. It was the look of someone trying very hard not to cry. Duncan put a few more wood chips on the smoldering fires; maybe it was more polite to pretend not to notice.

There was a muted sniffle. "I know I have a duty to be queen someday," Lydia said, her voice almost steady, "but I don't know *how*."

Duncan was at a loss for what to say. "You'll have advisers," he said again.

"But I won't know who to trust," Lydia said. "The earl taught me *that*." She curled her arms around her knees,

225

staring into the smoke. "Anyway, I'll probably never have the chance, stuck here on this island."

Duncan stirred the wood chips with a stick, thinking hard. "I don't have the skills to build a boat to get you off, like my father did."

"I wouldn't want you to build a boat anyway," Lydia said at once. "Remember what happened to your father?"

"I bet I could build a raft, though." Duncan sat up straight. "I built a little one once, at home."

"*No*," said Lydia.

"It wouldn't be as good as a boat," Duncan went on. "It would be hard to steer, too, but if I could just get to the Arvidian Current—"

"No!" said Princess Lydia again. "I forbid you. You're only going to die!"

Duncan shrugged. "I'm going to die sometime. I might as well die trying."

CHAPTER 19

Building the Raft

DUNCAN TOOK A LAST BITE of his turtle steak and chewed it thoughtfully. He glanced at Mattie, who was pulling clumps of loose, shedding fur from the tiger's chest and belly, aided by Fia. "I'll show you how to make rope tomorrow," he said to the old woman.

Mattie smiled. "That will be lovely, dear."

"You're not making rope for a boat, remember," the princess said suspiciously. "Or a raft." She poked at the fire with a long stick and raised its glowing end like a scepter. "That," she added, "is a royal command."

Duncan stared up at the night sky, pricked with thousands of stars. He could steer by the stars—he could steer all the way home. As long as he hit the Arvidian Current, he could drift—and if the wind was against him, that was exactly what he'd do. He'd lower the sail and float straight back to Capital City, or one of the populated islands that surrounded it. Before he got there, of course, he might even be picked up by a ship—farther north and east, the sea routes would be more traveled.

"I mean it," said Princess Lydia, poking savagely at the fire. "I watched your father go down in the sea. I'm not going to watch it happen to you." She picked up Fia and cuddled her as if in need of comfort.

"You could close your eyes," Duncan suggested.

Brig growled, very low. "Her Royal Highness has given you an order, sir."

Duncan stood up. "Remember, Brig, no attacking your superior officers. That's rule number one."

Lydia dropped her stick into the fire. "I'll tell Brig to stop you!" she said. "I will!"

Duncan gave her his best court bow, with a flourish. "Might I have permission to leave the royal presence?"

"Granted," snapped the princess, turning her back.

"Now, my lady," Mattie began, but Duncan was already on the path up to the ridge and he didn't hear any more.

He sat with his legs dangling, leaning back against a tall, flat stone, still warm from the day's sun. The sky arched overhead, a deep cobalt blue in the west, and the sea spread before him, dark and inky and wide as the world. He might almost have been on the stone throne on the island of Dulle.

But this time, there was no Grizel purring contentedly beside him, and no mother waiting just up the cliff road. And this time, instead of longing for adventure, he was dreading the thing he had to do.

He had not told the princess he was afraid, of course. She was worried enough already. But Duncan had not forgotten what it was like to be adrift on the open sea.

It would be easy to stay safe on the island. The princess had told him that winters were passable—the lower portion of the island was sheltered from cold winds, and there were caves with hot springs, where the air was heated and warm.

Furthermore, Princess Lydia had *ordered* him to stay here, and she had a tiger to enforce her wishes. But all of these things were just excuses. If he didn't at least try, he would know he was a coward.

A shuffling sound of feet on stone warned him that someone was climbing the path. With a rustle, the princess sat beside him and settled herself against the rock.

"I really don't want you to go," Lydia said in a low voice.

"You made that clear when you decided to give me a royal command, *Princess*." Duncan picked moodily at a scab on his elbow.

The princess sighed. "If your father couldn't do it, what makes you think you can?"

Duncan drew his legs up and crossed his arms over his knees. "I can't just stay here without doing *something* to get us back home."

"Yes, you can! That's what I've been telling you! We're happy enough here, Mattie and I. We have enough to eat, we're warm and safe, and Brig hunts for us. We keep a lookout every morning and night, and someday we'll see a ship coming our way."

"Someday," Duncan repeated incredulously. "You haven't seen a ship in seven years, Lydia. We're in a section of the sea where nobody *goes*." Except the earl, he said to himself.

"It could happen tomorrow," the princess said stubbornly.

Duncan gazed up at the stars. He could see the Huntress and the Crown, and there, just curling over the horizon, was the Cat and Kitten. The constellations moved, but he remembered what the sailing master had shown him: an imaginary line drawn from the Kitten's tail, crossed with a line from the Cat's right ear, gave a point due north that never moved. As long as he could see the stars, he could never be completely lost.

A chill breeze feathered his neck, and Duncan turned. The stars to the southwest were winking out, one by one. A storm was brewing in the Rift once more. Lydia was right; it was dangerous out there. But he felt uneasy, as if it were dangerous to stay on the island, too. And now, looking at the dark mass rising to cover the stars, Duncan suddenly was able to put his feeling into words. "It's not just about rescuing you and Mattie; it's bigger than that. Don't you see that if you don't return, the Earl of Merrick will be the next king?"

A small puff of wind blew Princess Lydia's hair across her face, and she tossed it back impatiently. "The earl isn't next in line for the throne. After the king, and then me of course, the ranks are duke, *then* earl, count, baron—oh."

"Right. There's no duke waiting to step in. So the earl will rule all of Arvidia once your father dies, and no one will try to stop him because the whole country still thinks he's a hero!"

"But my father, the king—" the princess began.

"Your father trusts him, too!" Duncan smacked his hands together. "What do you think it's going to mean for Arvidia if a traitor is trusted by the king—if a traitor will *be* the king?"

The princess did not answer. Far away, a gannet cried, and then another. The sea crashed against the cliffs below with muted thunder, and the air grew cooler still.

"That's what the earl's wanted all along," Duncan said quietly. "He tried to get rid of everyone who was between him and the throne. First you; you were the heir. Then my father; he was next in line. And then me. Now there's only *your* father to get rid of. And your father has been sick a long time."

Lydia's brow was troubled. "What are you saying? Do you think the earl has been poisoning my father?"

"I don't know. But I don't think the earl lets anything get in the way of what he wants. One way or another, he intends to be king."

Princess Lydia buried her face in her hands.

"Don't you see?" Duncan said quietly. "High rank doesn't mean just dressing up and court manners. It means we're responsible. We're supposed to keep Arvidia safe."

"You sound just like your father." Princess Lydia's voice was muffled.

"Well, good," said Duncan.

A sudden gust buffeted them where they sat, swirling around the crags. Overhead the stars were almost all gone.

"Fine." Lydia wiped her wet cheeks and tossed her braid over her shoulder. "Build your raft. But I'm helping."

The lagoon at low tide was edged with seagrass, hot in the sun. Duncan stood thigh-deep at the shallow end of the water and cut the stalks where they joined the base. When he had a load, he bundled it together and tied it on Brig's back. Then he walked with the tiger up to the home cave. Seagrass was scratchy stuff, but it made fine rope.

Duncan showed the princess and Mattie how to beat out the fibers from the dried seagrass, scrape them, and hang them to dry. Mattie's gnarled but skillful fingers quickly learned the trick of twisting strands in one direction while wrapping them around another set of strands in the opposite direction.

"There!" she said proudly as she finished her first length of cord. "That's easier than making lace. And clever, too. The twist going one direction and the wrap going the other keeps the rope from unraveling."

"That's right." Duncan reached for the cord and doubled it back on itself. "And if you want to make a thicker rope, you use double and triple cords instead of fibers, and do the same twist-and-wrap, like this."

Mattie patted Duncan's hand with her age-spotted one. "I can see well enough to do close work, like this. If you young nobles will cut the seagrass and haul it up here, I'll make the rope. You'll have all you can do to build that raft."

Young nobles! The words sang in Duncan's head as he followed Lydia down the path to the lagoon. It was still a little surprising to realize he was one of the nobles of the land; he had lived poor and hidden for so long.

Rank wouldn't matter much, though, if he couldn't get off the island. He was thinking hard as he cut the next batch of seagrass. How should he build his raft? It was important to make it light enough. He had pushed boats out to sea, and he knew how heavy they were. A raft made of whole logs would be impossible to move.

Then he noticed the kelp at the far end of the lagoon. Brownish-green, the flat, rubbery leaves grew upward and then lay across the surface of the lagoon like long gloves with narrow fingers.

He could make floats out of kelp! He and some friends had done it for fun, on the island of Dulle. If you cut off one of the leaves and stuck your hand inside the opening, you could push aside the spongy tissue and leave it hollow. Then you could blow it up like a balloon, tie it off, and use it as a swim float.

What if he made a light framework of branches, crisscrossed together, with floats underneath?

He would need to rig some kind of mast. Mattie could weave a sail, and he would need a steering oar—that would be easier to make than a rudder, and it would help with lee-way, too. Yes, it was all possible. He would have to be very careful, though, to stay on course. He could steer by the sun and stars, as long as it wasn't cloudy. But a raft was difficult to steer at the best of times.

They constructed the raft in the sea cave. When it was ready, Duncan planned to wait for high tide and then shove it off the ledge. With rope, they could let it down slowly as the tide went out; when the water level had gone down enough so that the opening to the beach could be seen, Duncan would ride the raft out with the tide.

Mattie couldn't go, of course—she was far too frail for such a journey. Lydia would have to stay on the island to take care of her. And Brig would have to stay on the island to hunt for them both.

The princess didn't agree. "Brig goes with you," she said. "Your father would have survived if Brig had been with him."

Duncan had no intention of leaving the princess and Mattie without their hunter and guard. But he would have that all out with the princess later on. First, they had a raft to build.

Summer was ending, and the days were cooler. The morning fog was still swirling around the base of the island when Duncan stepped out on the path to the crags, telescope in hand.

Fia, more leggy now, but still recognizably a kitten, swished through the grass beside the path and dropped a mouse at

Duncan's feet. She nudged the limp body with her paw until it lay neatly, its tail perfectly straight, and looked up with pride.

"Er," said Duncan. "Well done."

"It's fresh," said Fia. "I caught it especially for you."

Duncan had a sudden inspiration. "Can you catch birds, too?"

"Of course!" Fia leaped into the air to show her bird-catching prowess. "But I don't bring you the birds. They're not nearly so good as mice. Too many feathers to get stuck in your mouth. But a mouse—oh, a mouse is so tasty! So crunchy!" She laid a confiding paw on Duncan's foot. "I eat their tails last of all, as a sort of dessert. You should try it."

"Maybe someday," said Duncan, closing his eyes briefly. "But listen, Fia. Humans actually like birds *better* than mice."

"Truly?" Fia cocked her head to one side, her ears forward.

"I'm not lying. So if you would rather keep this mouse for *yourself*—"

"And bring the birds to you? Are you sure?"

"I'm absolutely sure." Duncan smiled at the earnest triangular face that was lifted to his. It was only last spring that she had failed the mouse-catching portion of her kitten examinations. Fia had learned a lot since then. Would she ever, he wondered, catch mice on the island of Dulle?

Lydia joined him on his walk up to the crags. Brig, about to leap on a quail, stopped his hunt to salute. The quail made its escape in a scurry to the undergrowth.

"Sorry," said Lydia, patting Brig between the ears as she passed. "Go! Quail!" She pointed at the scuttling bird.

Brig's expression was pained. "I can understand words of more than one syllable, Your Highness," he complained, but he turned to obey.

Lydia watched him with pride. "He understands everything I say, I think. And he's very good at following orders."

Brig growled a little over his shoulder. "Of *course* I follow orders," he grumbled. "What else would she expect of a member of the Royal Order of Gemstone Tigers?"

"Royal Order of *what*?" Duncan growled back before he could stop himself.

"Why did you growl at him?" the princess asked, frowning. "There's no need to be rude. I told you, he understands all our commands." She started up the path again.

"I wasn't being rude," Duncan muttered as he trudged after her. Should he tell the princess his secret? She was the heir to the kingdom, after all, and he was her loyal subject.

But the princess, up on the crags, seemed to have forgotten the matter. She swept the glass from north to east to south, scanning the area where they might someday see a sail.

When it was Duncan's turn, he looked to the west. The fog over the Rift was blowing away in great slow-moving swirls, the wind like a sky broom brushing the mists aside.

The water at the edge of the Rift seemed a different color—darker, more purple, with spots here and there that looked oddly turbulent. It was a treacherous place, he had no doubt. Twice now, he had seen a waterspout, a gigantic swirling funnel of water and wind moving over the sea like a searching finger. "Not much chance for a boat to cross that water," Duncan murmured.

"Your father did it." Lydia waved toward the west. "In a small boat, too. He crossed it and then he came back."

Duncan lowered the telescope. "I thought you said his boat sank."

"It did, later. But I'm talking about before, when we were still on the royal tour. You know about *that*."

"You were visiting the islands of Arvidia," said Duncan, remembering Friar Gregory's lesson in the monastery school. "A bad storm blew up out of the Rift, and you rescued two men and their tigers. Are you saying my father crossed the Rift then?"

The princess nodded. "We had to stay at anchor to repair the ship after the storm, anyway. Duke Charles said he thought he could take the miners back home to Fahr in one of the small ship's boats. Everyone thought he was crazy, but the earl encouraged him to go. I suppose the earl thought it would be an easy way to get rid of your father."

Duncan leaned forward, frowning. "I never heard that part of the story. What made my father think he could cross the Rift?"

Something large crashed through the underbrush and snuffled on the path. Brig dropped a quail at Princess Lydia's feet, and spat out a mouthful of feathers. "Bah! Birds are all the same—too much fluffery. Give me a fish or a good smooth seal any day."

"Oh, what a beautiful quail!" Lydia patted Brig between the ears. "*Good* tiger!"

Brig sighed deeply. "I wish she wouldn't patronize me. It's so undignified." He settled back on his haunches and began to clean his whiskers with his long, barbed tongue. "Oh, to answer your question," he said to Duncan, "your father knew he could cross the Rift because he had a tiger to guide him. Namely, me."

"Really?" Duncan leaned forward.

"Yes, really," said Lydia, smoothing down Brig's neck fur. "He's *such* a good tiger, aren't you, snookums?"

Brig choked on a whisker.

Duncan grinned. Poor Brig. His look of agonized pain reminded Duncan strongly of Mr. Fluffers, Betsy's cat back home, who wanted to be known as Spike. Was Betsy still calling him Fluffy Wuffy? he wondered.

But he had to find out more from Brig. And since Lydia was there, he had to make it sound as if he were asking Lydia. Duncan said, "I wonder if one of the miners guided my father across the Rift."

Lydia answered at the same time Brig growled, and Duncan had to listen to both at once, in stereo. It took him a moment to separate out that Lydia had said, "Maybe—I can't think how else he would have gotten across," and Brig had said, "Of course not, Fahrians can't sense a rock under the water any more than they can sense a jewel under the ground. It's only tigers who have stone-sense."

"Stone-sense?" said Duncan, before he could help himself.

"What?" Princess Lydia looked affronted. "It's not nonsense," she said. "And if you know so much, why are you even bothering to ask me questions?"

"Sorry," said Duncan. He put his head in his hands. "Maybe I just need to be alone for a while. All this talk about my father, you know . . ."

The princess got up at once. Duncan waited until she was well down the path before he turned to Brig and whispered, "What do you mean by stone-sense? And how did you guide my father across the Rift?"

Brig's shoulders humped in a shrug. "Animals have instincts that humans lack. Tigers happen to have a feeling for stone, and what's captured inside it. We can sense a vein of silver or gold, we know where gemstones are, and long ago we discovered that the Fahrians would dig out long, roomy caves in their search for such things. We tigers just tap the spots where they should dig, and when they've finished digging out the gems, we move into the caves. We developed a military, of course."

"Why?" Duncan asked, fascinated.

Brig sharpened his claws on the crag. "To keep mine robbers away. We want the miners to keep working for us, digging those big, beautiful caves. If they had to do their own guarding, there would be twice as many of them, and they'd get half the work done."

Duncan grinned. It was exactly like cats—to think that everything a human did was for their advantage.

"And, of course," the tiger finished, "we can sense where rocks and reefs are in the sea, even when they're underwater. We can hardly pat them with our paws, though, and the Fahrians never quite seem to understand when we try to say something like 'half a nautical mile ahead and two points off the starboard bow.' They're lovely people," he added hastily, "very fine diggers, but not one of them speaks Cat. The only human I knew who could, besides yourself, was your father."

Duncan turned sharply. "My father spoke *Cat*?"

"Yes, indeed, though with a slight accent." Brig's whiskers lifted in a fond smile. "He listened very well, though, and it was a pleasure to guide him across the Rift—he took careful notes. I believe he made a chart."

CHAPTER 20

Shadow Fight

THE RAFT WAS READY. Food and water, in kelp bags, was stowed safely and tied in place. The harpoon Duncan had whittled was slung around his body; his knife hung on a cord tied to his belt. Mattie had given the sail its last stitch, and she had even given Duncan one of her precious needles.

"Just in case the sail rips," Mattie said, winding the needle up in a roll of stout thread. She tucked it into Duncan's pocket and buttoned the pocket shut. "Do you have to go now? Can't it wait a little?"

Duncan shook his head. It was already fall; he did not want to be afloat when winter came, and he didn't want to wait until spring. "Don't worry. A raft stands up to a storm better than a boat. If a raft flips, it will still float."

He trotted across the valley and up to the sea cave. The princess was trying to lash yet another kelp bag of water on board, Brig was pressing one furry toe on the knot so that she could tie it tight, and Fia had clawed her way to the top of the mast for a better view of the action.

"I'm coming with you!" she meowed as she caught sight of Duncan, and leaped for his shoulder.

It was high tide, and the water in the sea cave was almost up to the ledge. With Brig's help, they shoved the raft off until it bobbed gently on the water.

"We'll pay out the rope as the tide goes down," Duncan said, winding the rope's end around an outcropping of rock. The raft would sink with the tide, and when the water was low enough that the raft could float out the sea entrance to the cave, he would go.

Lydia turned to Duncan, her pale face smudged and her braid half-undone. "I put on extra water for Brig. He can catch fish to eat."

Duncan paced the cave. He was keyed up, ready to go, but he had hours to wait. "Brig has to stay here," he said abruptly. "To hunt for you and Mattie."

"I can hunt," said the princess stiffly. "And fish. If you won't take Brig, then I'm coming with you."

"What? No!" Duncan stopped his pacing to stare at the princess.

"Brig is a strong swimmer," said Lydia. "He can keep you

afloat if something happens to the raft, and he can protect you."

"He's going to protect *you*," said Duncan. "You're the heir to the kingdom! I can't let you risk your life."

"But you're going to risk yours," Lydia said stubbornly. "I don't want you to be alone on the sea."

Fia meowed, twining around Duncan's legs. "Tell her that *I'll* be with you!"

Duncan paused by the cave wall. Maybe the best thing to do was change the subject. He held his torch high to peer at the figures of the duke and the earl fighting. "Listen, I've always wondered about this painting you did. See, this is supposed to be the earl, right? Stabbing my father treacherously?"

Lydia nodded.

"Well, you've got the earl wearing the duke's hat. You mixed them up."

"*You've* got it wrong. Bertram was wearing the duke's hat."

"What?" Duncan blinked at her, confused.

Princess Lydia's mouth gave a twist. "It was simple enough. Once we landed on the beach for our little ceremony—you know, the whole 'princess of the realm sets her foot on the farthest island' thing—the earl had his cook bring out glasses and his special cherry punch. It was drugged, of course," she added. "By the time we woke up, your father was tied in the sea cave, wounded and bleeding, and Bertram had taken his hat. Then the earl and Bertram staged a little shadow play, out on the tip of the rocky point, where everyone from the ship could see them. The sun was setting behind them, so even if someone had a spyglass, all they could have seen were the silhouettes."

Duncan's mouth fell open slightly. It *was* simple. Yet it had never occurred to him—or to anyone else, apparently—that it had all been faked.

"The earl and Bertram had a long time to plan it out," Lydia said bitterly. "The whole time your father was taking the miners back to Fahr, risking his life, they were plotting what they'd do if he ever came back. They thought of everything. They even dragged Mattie and me out to the rocky point so our silhouettes would show up, too. Bertram pushed Mattie and me down on the rocks, pretended to stab the earl in the back, rolled him off to the side of the point where the ship's crew couldn't see, threw me over his shoulder, and ran off."

"All with my father's tall hat on," Duncan said grimly.

"That's right. Then they brought us to the sea cave. Duke Charles was tied, but he was waking up, fighting to get out of the ropes. So Bertram stood over him and stabbed him. Your father was quiet after that." Tears stood in Princess Lydia's eyes.

Duncan felt his muscles hardening like rock; his mouth set in a bleak line. There was no heat in him, only a cold anger that reached to every part of his body.

But the princess was still talking. "Then the earl knelt beside him and whispered in his ear. I couldn't hear it all, but it was something about a secret and—" The princess hesitated. "The next part didn't make any sense."

"Just tell me anyway," said Duncan.

Lydia's face crinkled into puzzlement. "Eating cats," she said. "Maybe I heard it wrong."

Duncan sat bolt upright. "Eating *cats*?"

"I know, it's crazy!" said the princess. "But that's what it sounded like. And then the duke moved a little, and he said, like he was in a temper, 'Right. Eating cats. That's brilliant—I guess you've figured out the secret at last,' and he shut his eyes like he'd fainted. And then—and then the earl told Bertram to stab him one more time, for luck, and to take the duke's jacket and put it on. And so he did."

Princess Lydia's eyes spilled over with tears. Duncan knew he should comfort her, but he was too shaken by Lydia's story. His *father* had told the earl to eat cats? Why?

"Mattie had her sewing scissors in her pocket," the princess went on, "and when the earl bent over to tie her up, she stabbed him in the forehead. He bled all over the place," she said with satisfaction.

Duncan gave a harsh laugh. *That* was the wound in the earl's forehead that he'd kept a bandage on for seven years? A cut from an old woman's sewing scissors?

"They dragged us into the sea cave. Then they took the ship's small boats and sailed away. They left us in the cave, with the tide coming in, to drown."

Duncan glanced back at the raft. The rope that held it was

strained taut—the water level was going down. He unwound two more loops and turned back to the princess. "But you didn't drown."

Brig cut in with a growl. "I saw the shadow fight from the ship, too. But tigers, unlike humans, do not pay so much attention to hats. The man in the duke's hat didn't move like the duke or hold his sword like the duke. And so I leaped off the ship and swam to the island to find the real duke."

Lydia reached for the tiger and buried her hands in his neck fur, stroking him. "Brig saved us. Somehow he knew something was wrong. He swam to the island and bit through our ropes. Then he led us up the back wall to the ledge. Your father was still unconscious, so Brig dragged him—I don't know how he did it."

Duncan could imagine the rest, from his experience serving on a big ship. It would have taken a good deal of time for the royal ship to raise the anchor, set sail, and begin the chase— perhaps half an hour. Meantime, the sun would have set. Duncan supposed that the earl and his men had staged a pursuit for the benefit of anyone on the ship with a spyglass— Bertram in the sailboat, wearing the duke's jacket and hat, and the earl's men in the jolly boat chasing after. Once the sky went dark and the boats were impossible to see, they would have sunk the extra boat and sailed back to the ship with their tale of seeing the duke and princess go down in a whirlpool before their eyes. The earl would have been covered in blood and ready for his role as hero of the nation.

"They took my necklace of jewels," Lydia said suddenly. "But they forgot to take my ring." She lifted a chain from around her neck. On it dangled a small golden ring with a finely wrought crest stamped on its flat oval top. "That was my ring when I was seven. My father put it on my hand himself, when I set sail."

She threw the chain over Duncan's head and tucked the ring inside his shirt, a small but definite weight. "There. Show that to the king. Then he'll know that I am alive and you are telling the truth."

Duncan bent his head. "Thank you, Your Royal Highness," he said. "I'll come back for you and Mattie, I promise. And don't forget—Brig stays here."

Thigh-deep in water, on the bottom level of the sea cave, Duncan braced himself against the ebbing tide. With Fia clinging to his shoulder, he edged past an outcropping of rock sharp with barnacles and hoisted himself onto the raft. The cave smelled of seaweed and brine, and the torch in his hand cast wild, flickering shadows on the walls of stone.

Brig padded down the rough steps along the back wall and splashed through the water.

"You're not coming with me, Brig," Duncan said.

"*I'm* going, though!" Fia leaped from Duncan's shoulder to the mast and clung there with her sharp little claws. She squinted toward the seaward entrance to the cave. "I can see stars!" she meowed. "It's a clear night, sir!"

Duncan grinned. She had come a long way from the scared little kitten he had rescued from the yardarm on the earl's ship.

"Ready?" called the princess from her perch on the ledge, above.

Duncan grasped the steering oar. "Ready!" he shouted. "Cast off!"

Lydia tossed down the loose end of the mooring line, and the raft was in motion. Duncan's stomach lurched, and his heart was beating high. He was really going to do it.

There was another lurch, this time of the raft, and a snuffling sound. Duncan turned to see two large green eyes shining in the dark and two wet paws gripping the raft's stern.

"Hey!" shouted Duncan. "Go back, Brig!"

The raft moved in successive washes toward the sea entrance to the cave. Duncan gripped the steering oar and wondered if his lashings were strong enough to hold the raft together. Everything had seemed tight on the ledge, but the sea was violent and wild.

"I'll just help you over this sandbar," panted Brig, scrabbling with his hind legs.

Duncan slipped off the back end of the raft and grabbed the cleat. With his weight gone, the raft rose just enough so that he could slide it out the cave's mouth to the sea. Knee-deep in water, with hard sand underfoot, Duncan shoved hard to get the raft away from the rocks.

"Push us out, Brig!" He scrambled onto the raft, grabbed

the steering oar, and let out the sail all in an instant. Sweat fell into his eyes, and he blinked it out. Getting away from the rocks was the main thing. Even on the ebb tide, rocks were still a danger.

It wasn't until he was clear of the point that he felt the wind take hold of the sail. At last—he couldn't steer without wind. Duncan cast a quick, tense look at the rising moon, the position of the island, and nodded to himself. The wind had picked up a little, and it was behind him. A good breeze to push him toward the current.

The constellations were clear and bright. Duncan found the point that was due north and set his course from that, keeping the top of the mast in line with the stars. Then he wound the line around a cleat and relaxed slightly. He was on his way.

It was only then that he noticed that Brig was still hanging on to the stern.

"Brig! Swim back to the island!" Duncan ordered.

Brig clawed at the raft's frame and heaved himself on board. "I'm coming with you, sir."

"But—the princess and Mattie! You can't leave them alone!" Duncan protested.

"I'm here at Princess Lydia's order," Brig said, shaking the water from his furry coat. "She outranks you, sir."

CHAPTER 21

Duke's Island

THE TIGER WAS HEAVY. The raft dipped and rose on the swell with an alarming tilt, first up, then down, with water splashing over the wood every moment.

"You're sinking us!" cried Fia. She clung to the mast like a shipwrecked sailor.

"Brigadier." Duncan tried to speak calmly. "You've got to go back." He glanced nervously at the raft. It didn't seem to be sinking—yet. But it was definitely lower in the water with 300-plus pounds of tiger on it.

Brig draped himself across the raft with a sigh. "I'm sorry if I am unwelcome, sir. But I know my duty. Orders are orders. Also, tigers are excellent sailors."

"Oh, for—" Duncan bit off an exasperated word. It was

futile to argue with a cat, especially one as stubborn as Brig. He shivered in the night breeze—he was wet through—and looked over his shoulder. The island, a dark mountainous shape behind them, had dwindled surprisingly. He couldn't go back now—a raft could not steer against the wind like a boat with a keel. Duncan braced his legs against the steering oar and tipped his head back to check his course.

"Rocks, sir, off the starboard bow!"

Duncan snapped his head down in a hurry and pushed the steering oar over, but the raft was clumsy and slow to respond. The rocks, barely above the surface of the sea, were black and glinting with wet, and directly in his path. The raft was going to hit them—there was nothing he could do—

"Make way, sir!" Brig roared, shoving past. The tiger leaped for the rocks, braced his hind legs, and pushed the raft away with all his considerable weight.

It was just barely enough. The rocks slid by, looking sharp and wicked in the moon's light. Brig gave a final thrust and then jumped back onto the raft. "You want to watch out for rocks, sir," he said cheerfully. "Those low ones are nasty."

"No kidding." Duncan's voice was not entirely steady. "Thanks."

"That's my job, sir." Brig flopped down on the raft. "Next time I'll give you more warning. We should be out of the rocky zone soon, anyway."

The sail belled out, catching the moon's light in a pure curve. Duncan peered ahead through the gloom. For a moment, he thought he saw the light of a ship twinkling far ahead—a lantern hung on the stern, maybe? But just as quickly, it was gone. Perhaps it had only been a star, low on the horizon.

Slap! Something cold and clammy hit Duncan's cheek and bounced off. Near his feet, a narrow form flopped twice and slithered off into the sea. *Thump! Thump!*

Brig was up at once, growling. Fia's meow sounded like a tiny scream.

"It's only flying fish," said Duncan. He grinned as another silvery fish, its fins so elongated they acted as temporary wings, leaped from the sea and smacked into the sail. "Better catch them," he said to Brig, "if you want a snack."

"But why are they coming?" asked Fia, her eyes wide.

"They're attracted to light, same as the other fish." Duncan looked up at the sail. The gibbous moon's light, reflected off the sail, wasn't bright like a torch—but it was a large area that was certainly lighter than the surrounding darkness.

"Got one!" said Brig in triumph as he speared a fish in midair. He popped half in his mouth and lashed out with his paw at another flash of silver. "And another!" he added indistinctly, with his mouth full.

Duncan's shoulders relaxed a little. It looked as if feeding the tiger wasn't going to be a problem. But the water situation was worrying. One extra kelp bag wasn't going to be enough for a full-grown tiger.

Fortune was with them, however. The next day brought a

low shelf of clouds and a steady drizzle of rain. Duncan funneled water from the sail right into Brig's mouth. They had emptied one of the kelp bags by that time, and so Duncan filled that, too.

They were wet and uncomfortable, but that was far better than baking in the sun and being thirsty. Or so Duncan told himself all that night as he shivered in clothes that never dried out. What worried him most was the current. How could he tell whether they had found it or not? The sea was endless in all directions; there was no fixed point so Duncan could judge how fast they were moving. But the wind held steady behind them, and he tried not to fret.

On the third day, the clouds lifted, the sun came out, and everyone cheered up. Brig, who had spent much of his time napping, his bulk spread across the whole raft with his tail dipped in the water, suddenly snorted awake. "The water's too warm!"

"Oh, don't whine," said Fia. "You don't hear us complaining, do you?"

"I mean, the water's changed *temperature*," rumbled Brig, annoyed. "I have a highly sensitive tail, you know. The water was colder before."

"Maybe you just peed in it," suggested Fia. "That turns water warm, you know."

"Oh, shut up," Brig growled.

Duncan trailed his hand in the sea. "I think you're right, Brig." He beamed. "We must be in the current! The Arvidian Current is supposed to be warm!"

Brig swelled out his chest. "*I* knew that. Your father talked about it when we were crossing the Rrrrrift."

"The Rrrrrift?" said Fia, making a mewing sound that was almost a laugh.

"Tigers have their own ways of saying things," Brig said with dignity. "Just as kittens have their way. 'Oh, help, help!'" he squeaked, making his voice high and helpless sounding. "'The tiger is *sinking* us!'"

Fia muttered something about military tigers that didn't sound like a compliment, turned her back, and began to groom herself.

Duncan was so happy about the current that he almost didn't care that the two cats were bickering. But the sailing master had once told him it was important to keep a peaceful crew. Personalities rubbed up against each other on a ship—or a raft—and "better to stop trouble before it starts," the sailing master had said.

Perhaps it was time to pay some compliments. "Fia," Duncan said, "I've noticed that you've become an excellent hunter. When we get back, you are going to pass those kitten examinations with high marks!"

Fia's odd-colored eyes brightened. She began to purr.

"And Brig . . ." Duncan gazed at the tiger. "You saved my father the day the earl attacked him. You jumped off the ship when you saw something was wrong and dragged him up that slippery path in the sea cave, and Lydia and Mattie, too." He laid a hand on the tiger's shoulder. "Thank you." It seemed like an inadequate thing to say, but he hoped Brig would understand how very grateful he was.

"It was my duty, sir," said Brig, saluting.

Duncan saluted back.

"I hope you see," Brig added apologetically, "why I almost killed you the day you washed up on the beach. I saw the earl's badge on your cap, and I thought you were on his side. I hate that human. I hate everyone who works for him. When I saw that badge, I just sort of went crazy, sir."

"I understand," said Duncan. His cap was tucked away in a pocket, in case of need, but he had long ago borrowed Mattie's scissors and snipped off the earl's badge.

"We all hate him," said Fia, and she put her paw on Brig's.

Suddenly the sail flapped and the boom started to swing. Duncan adjusted the steering oar in a hurry. The wind was picking up; it made a thin whistling in his ears. They were in for a blow, if he read the signs correctly. Perhaps he should furl the sail. If he sailed under bare poles, he might avoid the wind pushing the raft out of the main current.

The storm blasted them for three cold and weary days. Duncan was glad that Brig was there, after all, for the tiger could stand a watch and brace the steering oar and growl to wake him when conditions changed.

Duncan was able to snatch a few hours of sleep with the tiger at the helm. Fia tried to do her job of lookout, but there was nothing to see except gray sea, and gray sky, and white tossing foam. Eventually she crawled into one end of an empty kelp bag and stayed there, shivering, her pointed face peering out and her whiskers whiffling in the wind.

The constant motion kept the raft creaking, the ropes alternately straining and relaxing as the sea pushed and pulled at the little craft. Duncan hoped the ropes would hold. He had been confident in his rope-making skills back on the island, but now, on the grim sea, he wasn't so sure.

Well—if it all came apart, they could hang on to the tiger. Brig would keep them afloat for as long as he could swim. If they drowned, at least they would all drown together.

The storm blew itself out at last, leaving wisps of fog trailing over the surface of the sea. Far in the distance, Duncan thought he could see a dark blot that might be an island. He could see no lights, but even an uninhabited island meant they were getting closer to Capital City.

Duncan unfurled the sail and looked over the damage. There was a tear that he could mend with Mattie's needle and thread alone, but in another spot, a whole piece had ripped free. He needed more cloth, and he had none—except the clothes he was wearing.

He pulled off his father's shirt. He still had his jacket for warmth.

Brig and Fia watched in silence as he stitched the shirt into the sail. When he was finished, he folded the point of the collar down so that the monogram could be seen, and sewed it flat. He pulled on the sheet and cleated the line. The sail filled with air, and the raft picked up speed. Above them, the duke's initials were a small bright spot in the patchwork sail.

Brig yawned widely, his fangs showing white and his tongue curling. "I can take a watch, sir," he said, and yawned again.

It was tempting. Duncan wanted nothing more than to lay his head down and sleep for days. But there had been that dark blot in the distance. It had disappeared into the gray fog and sea, but perhaps it was still ahead somewhere; he had to keep a lookout. And Brig was exhausted—he might fall asleep.

"I'll take first watch," Duncan said, shaking his head to clear it. He set the sail and lashed the steering oar. Then he leaned his head against the lashings and propped his eyelids open with his fingers. The gray light faded to black. The waves murmured alongside, rocking him gently in the cradle of the sea, and the night slid past in inky darkness.

He was dreaming. There was a moon just rising, thin like the worn edge of a coin, and the smell of salt and seaweed in his nostrils. He was damp—in a boat, perhaps? There was water sloshing somewhere—but high above, in the darkness, he saw a window, a rectangle of light.

He had not dreamed this dream for a long time. He struggled to wake, to escape the dread and longing that washed through him like a suffocating wave. Something splashed on his cheek, and he opened his eyes, but the window was still there, high and bright, surrounded by stone. It was set in a castle. . . . A corner of the high wall stood revealed, its battlements knifing against the star-sprinkled sky.

Suddenly, sharply, Duncan knew he was awake. His heart beat faster.

The raft drifted closer to the island on the flood tide. Duncan silently trimmed the sail to catch the tiny breeze that was bringing them in. It was not his home island of Dulle, he knew that much. And it could not be the island of Capital City—that would be bright with lights.

But he seemed to know it all the same. Just beyond those reeds, there would be a shallow lagoon and a stand of white birches. . . .

Brig snored lightly, his muzzle resting on his paws. Fia was curled up next to the tiger with her eyes shut.

Duncan put a hand on the steering oar and looked around him, entranced. Memory rushed in like a flood tide, and suddenly he could almost hear the whispering swirl of his mother's skirts and feel the stone floor of the castle cold and hard beneath his bare feet. His mother's hand had pulled him across the wide, sloping lawn beneath the turrets; the trees that seemed so friendly in the daytime had turned into something frightening in the dark, reaching out with long, rustling fingers. His short legs had stumbled, and then he had been picked up and carried along, bumping in his mother's arms, though he was too big to be carried anymore. The sound of surf had grown louder, and he had been lifted into something that rocked beneath him. He had gotten water in his boot. There had been a smell of tobacco.

There was a smell of tobacco now. Someone was smoking a pipe not far away.

Duncan beached the raft quietly in the sandy lagoon and let down the sail. It was almost slack water—he could see by the rim of seaweed on the sand that the tide was as high as it would go. He looped a mooring line around a slab of rock and tied it securely. He wouldn't wake the cats—they were exhausted.

The sand was firm and cool under Duncan's bare feet. He stepped up onto the wide, sloping lawn with growing excitement. The shape of things, the placement of trees, seemed as if he had always known them. Duncan tipped his head back to take in the whole castle, and the moon rinsed his face with pure light.

There was a sound like a sudden intake of breath. Duncan's hand was snatched and held in a hard, roughened grip. A man knelt before him, raising a wizened face working with emotion. "My lord duke!" said the man, and kissed Duncan's hand.

CHAPTER 22

Captured!

DUNCAN STARED AT THE MAN, BEWILDERED.

The man straightened in a hurry. "Step back into shadow where you can't be seen, sir," he muttered. He grasped Duncan's shoulder and propelled him to the birch grove at the edge of the lagoon. "How did you come here, my lord? I can't believe it!"

Duncan was shaken. He had learned to think of himself as a duke's son, but of course now that his father was dead, the title had been passed down. Duncan, Duke of Arvidia. It seemed unreal.

"Who are you?" Duncan said urgently. "How do you know me?"

"My name is Tammas, my lord." The man ducked his

head. "Tam, if you like. I served your father the duke, I served your mother the duchess, and now I serve you."

The man's smell of dried sweat, tobacco, and fish triggered a sudden pulse in Duncan's memory. "It was you!" he whispered. "When I was little! You lifted me into a boat. You told me I was a brave boy and not to cry."

Tammas ran a hand across his eyes and chuckled shakily. "It was this very spot, my lord. I brought my boat around the back side of the island and put in at the lagoon. I can still see your lady mother running across the lawn in the dark, carrying you. I often come here of an evening, to smoke a quiet pipe and remember." He smiled then—Duncan could see the bunch of his cheek in the gloom—and relit his pipe. It glowed briefly like an ember floating in the dark.

"You were the one who told me to take good care of my mother," said Duncan suddenly. "You said I would be the man of the house now."

"I might have done," said Tam. "It's likely enough. Of course, your lady mother would care for you—you were young, yet—but you're never too young to learn you have a duty in this world. A ship in harbor is safe—"

"But that's not what a ship is made for," Duncan finished with an air of discovery. "You were in my room last spring! You're the one who brought money to my mother!"

"We thought you were asleep, laddie." Tammas sucked on his pipe with a muted *ffup ffup*. "I haven't been able to do as much as I liked for you and your mother, but now and then

I've been able to sell one of the smaller treasures from Castle McKinnon and bring her the money from it."

Duncan cocked his head. "You mean you sneaked into the castle and took things?"

"You might say that. But rightfully, the castle and everything in it belonged to you and your mother—at least by my way of thinking. The housekeeper there, Mrs. Deal, she helped me. A few of the old servants stayed on, as caretakers for the king, see, and whatever they believed the duke might or might not have done, they were loyal to the duchess—and to you, my lord."

Duncan flushed in the dark. There were people in the world who had worked to help him, who had taken risks for him when he didn't even know their names.

He looked hungrily at the island through the trees. So this was where he would have grown up if it hadn't been for the earl. The castle would have been his home; he would have run through the gates to play with the village children, much as Robert, the baron's son, had played with him on the island of Dulle.

The upper window in the castle went dark. Duncan wiped his cheek with his wrist as he gazed up at the high towers. Now he understood the sense of loss and longing that had been so powerful in his dream. He would have been a duke's son. He and his mother would never have gone hungry. He would have attended the Academy as a matter of course, and no one would ever have told him he had to hide or be second-best.

"Why—" Duncan began, but his voice had an odd, strangled sound. He cleared his throat. "Why did my mother leave? Wouldn't the king let her stay?"

Tammas grunted. "When there's treason, the whole estate goes to the king; but he knew that whatever the duke had done, it wasn't your mother's fault, or yours. The king was a music lover, too, and he wanted to keep attending her concerts. So he let her keep some rooms at Castle McKinnon and a couple of servants. And the people of Duke's Island were mostly on her side. But the rest of Arvidia—well, they were angry. Their princess had been kidnapped; the heir to the throne was lost and probably dead—and all because of the duke, they believed."

"People were *angry*? That's why my mother took me away?" A vast impatience welled up in Duncan. He had lost his castle, his island, and even his true name, because his mother was afraid of—what? Getting yelled at?

"You don't understand." Tammas shot him a keen glance. "When your mother stood up to play her violin and the audience booed and walked out, it was bad enough. When the orchestra conductor came to her with tears in his eyes and said she couldn't be in the orchestra anymore, it was worse. But when it came to strangers spitting on your buggy when she took you out for a walk, and mobs sailing to the island to throw bricks at the castle doors, and letters from people threatening to kill you because they didn't want the title of duke to go to any son of your father's—well, she knew she had to take you away. You were in danger, of course. But it was more than that. She didn't want you to grow up ashamed, knowing you were hated for who you were."

Duncan was silent. He had a sudden memory of himself at five years old, running merrily along the cliffside road with his father's shirt billowing out behind him for a cape, and a stick in his hand to fight imaginary villains. How happy a childhood would he have had if he had known the villains were real, and wanted to murder him?

The castle's massive gate showed dimly in the sullen flare of torches; there were shadows on it that might have been dents. Duncan tried to imagine a mob banging on it with any weapons they had.

"Now I have a question for you, young lord." Tammas tapped his pipe against his hand and tucked it in his pocket. "What were you thinking, to run away to sea? Your mother nearly went mad with fear when she got your note in the mail!"

"My note?"

"I saw it. It said you were running away, sailing with the Earl of Merrick's ship. Your mother said it was your signature."

Duncan felt himself flush to the roots of his hair. How stupid he had been, to believe the earl had wanted his signature for a handwriting sample. "I *didn't* run away," Duncan said. "The earl tricked me into signing my name. Then he locked me in his cabin and set sail."

"Ah." Tam's tone held a sour satisfaction. "I should have known. I always suspected he was a liar, after that tale he told about your father. But how did you get away?"

"I jumped overboard. After a while I washed up on an island and built a raft. That's how I got here." Duncan hesitated. Should he tell about the princess? His hand touched the small knob under his jacket, where the ring hung about his neck. He was sure Tammas could be trusted—but on the other hand, Duncan had once been certain the earl could be trusted, too. Maybe he would just ask a few more questions first. "What did my mother do after she got the note?"

Tammas ran work-roughened fingers through his salt-crusted hair. "She knew she had to come out of hiding. She told people who she was and put on a violin concert to prove it—it was quite an event; people came from at least seven islands—and with the money from the concert, she bought clothes suitable for a duchess and booked passage on a ship to Capital City. She went straight to the king and asked for his help."

"She went straight to the *king*?" Duncan shook his head. He was used to thinking of his mother as a quiet, worried woman with stooped shoulders, an ugly green scarf, and a dread of being noticed in any way.

But all her fear had been only for him, he realized now. There had been that moment in the baron's house when he had seen her throw off her scarf, straighten her shoulders, and play the violin like a master. That must have been how she looked when she went to the king. And he had thought she lacked confidence!

Tammas went on speaking. "The king was ill, but he received her in the royal bedchamber. He told your mother that if you had run away to sea on the earl's ship, the earl would bring you back soon enough. Meantime, he asked her to play for him; music was healing, he said, and he had never held the duke's treachery against *her*."

Duncan felt his eyes narrow. "My father wasn't treacherous. It was the earl."

"Your mother wrote to me; she hoped that I would help search for you. I sailed to Capital City to meet her—my boat is small, but it's seaworthy—and found that the earl had arrived before me."

There was a tiny sound behind them. Duncan whipped his head around to see a kitten-shaped shadow stretch and yawn in the moonlight, then curl back down. Brig, a larger bulk that looked like a sailbag, stirred slightly in his sleep.

"What's that, lad?" Tammas asked sharply. "Who have you brought with you?"

"Don't worry. It's just a cat and—" Duncan cleared his throat. "Another cat. Somewhat larger." He sank down on the turf, his back to a tree. "You said the earl arrived at Capital City before you. What happened then?"

Tammas sat on the ground and stretched out his legs with a sigh. "Your mother and the king demanded to know what had happened to you. The earl was ready with his story. He told them a young boy had stowed away on his ship, giving a false name. He said the boy had complained that the work was too hard—"

"I did *not*!" said Duncan.

"And that one morning, he couldn't be found. The earl said they thought the boy must have fallen overboard in the night somehow."

"Somehow is right," Duncan muttered.

"Anyway," Tammas continued, "the earl swore up and down that he had never dreamed who you really were."

Duncan frowned. "What did my mother say? Did *she* trust the earl?"

Tammas shook his head. "She has not trusted the earl since he came back from the royal tour, saying your father had kidnapped the princess. But the earl had that whole stack of witnesses, you know," he added thoughtfully. "Your mother didn't know what to make of it. She thought that perhaps there had been a terrible misunderstanding or that Duke Charles had thought the princess was in danger from the earl somehow."

Duncan nodded slowly. "But about me . . . did she really believe I had written that note and run away? The signature was mine, but the printing wasn't."

Tammas made a sudden business of tamping out his pipe. "It was typewritten, lad. And the note had in it things only you would know. How she made you wear a cap always and told you to never come in first. How she wouldn't let you take a scholarship to the Academy. It seemed like it had to be from you, although she found it hard to believe that you would have been so heartless."

Duncan squeezed his hands together until his knuckles hurt. The boy who had complained about his life to the earl, who had signed his name to a blank sheet of paper, who had thought that his hero could do no wrong, seemed like some-one he had known a long time ago.

Tammas put his pipe in his pocket. "We can talk more of this later. Now we must make plans. You see, the earl is—"

A sudden bustle on the far side of the castle distracted Duncan. There was a glare of torchlight and the sound of men giving orders.

"Here," finished Tammas.

The torches illuminated a stone structure beyond the castle—something that looked like a pier, and a darker, pointed shadow against the starlit sky that could have been the jib boom and bowsprit of a ship. A reflection of light glimmered thinly on a forestay and edged the profile of a snarling animal: a wolf.

Duncan's shoulders contracted in a sudden chill. "Why is the earl on Duke's Island?"

Tammas found it necessary to clear his throat. "He's here to prepare the castle for your mother. The king gave every-thing back to the duchess. He said it was because of her music and to comfort her in her loss."

"Her loss?"

"She thinks you died," said Tammas bluntly.

"Oh." Duncan looked at his hands. "Where is she now?"

"She's gone back to Dulle, to get her things packed up and give one last concert. She's staying with the baron and baroness."

Duncan looked back at his raft. "Can you take me there? Quickly?"

The activity at the harbor had extended to the castle. The gates creaked open, and lanterns were lit all along the path. A small crowd of what looked like villagers waited, craning their necks toward the castle door.

Tammas leaned toward Duncan, his body as tense as a hunting dog's. "I'll take you, lad. The earl is going to sail tonight—I hear he wants to get to Dulle in time for tomorrow night's concert. But my boat is fast, too, and it's at the far end of the harbor, where it's dark. Do you need to get anything from your raft?"

"Just my cats." Duncan hesitated. "One of them's pretty big."

"I'll run and get my boat ready to sail. You get your cats and bring them to the far side of the harbor. Go behind the castle, through the trees. Stay in the shadows, and be quick, sir!"

Duncan headed back to the lagoon. Before he reached the reeds, he heard Fia meowing for him.

"I woke up, and we were on land!" The long-legged kitten pranced across the lawn, her tail like a flag. "I woke Brig up too." She stiffened, her ears alert. "Is that a mouse I smell?" She leaped toward the birch grove.

269

Duncan hurried after her. "Forget the mouse, Fia!" he hissed. "Come back!"

"What for?" Fia's eyes glowed in two different colors.

"It's dangerous here. We've got to get Brig and go."

"It doesn't *look* dangerous," Fia mewed, twisting her head around as the villagers began to cheer.

The castle doors were pulled open to the blare of a trumpet. A man in a wide-brimmed hat stood at the top of the steps, his hand upraised. He was waving, smiling. Beside him stood a bald, big-shouldered shadow.

Duncan backed away into the shadow of the trees. "*That's* what's so dangerous," he whispered to Fia. "That's the—"

"EARL OF MERRICK!" roared Brig, behind him. "I CAN SMELL HIM FROM HERE, THE TRAITOR!"

There was a sudden explosive flurry of muscle and fur as Brig streaked past, his tawny coat like striped silver in the moonlight. The crowd of villagers backed away as the tiger's roars filled the night. The earl shrank into the shadowed doorway, but the earl's men moved forward, raising their weapons, and burly sailors ran from the pier.

Duncan raced over the damp grass, legs scissoring, his callused feet hardly seeming to touch the ground.

"Come out, you black-hearted traitor of all that's royal!" Brig's snarl echoed back from the castle walls. "Come out and fight, you scum, you hound!"

Duncan had reached the edge of the frightened crowd. The tiger's tawny body was vivid in the torchlight as he reared

270

up on the flagstone path. The armed men moved closer, weapons raised. Duncan found it suddenly hard to breathe.

One tiger could probably take on several men. But a whole crowd of them? With weapons? Brig would be slaughtered.

"BRIG!" Duncan tried to put all the force of command in his growl. "NO!"

The tiger put his forepaws down. He turned his noble head toward Duncan.

There was a swift blur and swing of a long belaying pin. Then came a hollow, sickening thud as the solid brass bar hit the tiger's skull. Brig dropped where he stood.

The crowd yelled in triumph. Their noise beat upon Duncan's ears like the sound of a distant, crashing surf. In horror, he took a step back into the shadows. He could not take in what had happened; he could not think what to do next.

Suddenly two large men were on either side of him, pinning his arms to his body, turning him with a grip of iron, forcing him farther away from the circle of torchlight. Duncan twisted in their grasp and tried to shout, but a wad of cloth was stuffed in his open mouth. He had time to look up into Bertram's face for one startled instant before a sack was thrust over his head and his wrists were tied with cord. Duncan felt himself thrown over Bertram's well-muscled shoulder and then, head down and bumping against the man's back, he was carried at a trot toward a smell of fish and a sound of surf.

The crowd, noisily cheering, still intent upon the tiger, never even noticed.

CHAPTER 23

In the Cage

D UNCAN AWOKE TO UTTER DARKNESS. All around him was the sound of groaning, creaking wood, and a rushing smooth gurgle alongside. He didn't need the slant of the wooden planks beneath to tell him he was on a ship. The stink of bilgewater revealed that he was in the hold.

Ting ting . . . ting ting. The ship's bell rang four bells in the middle watch—or, for landsmen, two o'clock in the morning. The last thing he remembered was being swung off Bertram's back and banging into something hard.

Tenderly he felt above his ear, where it hurt the most, and found a lump the size of an egg with a crust of dried blood. He stretched out his hands, and his fingers brushed a wooden slat an inch thick. Next to it was another. He reached all around him and over his head. He was in a cage.

Duncan sat curled with his knees to his chin, bruised and wretched. He should have known that Brig would attack the earl on instinct. If only he had thought ahead! He should have run to the raft as soon as he knew the earl was on the island, and given Brig strict orders to stay hidden and silent. Brig would have obeyed orders, and by now they would all have been safe on Tam's boat and on their way to the island of Dulle. In a matter of hours, Duncan would have been with his mother again.

No one could see him here in the hold; he did not have to be brave for anyone. Duncan buried his face in his knees.

He was not going to clear his father's name. He was not going to return the princess to her kingdom. He was not even going to get a chance to tell his mother he was sorry, that he hadn't meant to leave her. And now he had just as good as killed Brig.

It took some time before Duncan was aware that something was breathing near him, breathing heavily.

He slid up against the bars, closer to the sound. He slipped his hand between the wooden slats; he pushed his whole arm through and touched soft, thick fur.

A small sound escaped him, as if he had suddenly been filled with something too big to contain. "Brig," he whispered. "You're alive."

The breathing went on, steady and slow.

"I'm alive, too," came a meow, and two shining spots, one amber, one gold, floated in the dark at the height of a tall kitten.

Duncan's nose prickled, and something like tears smarted behind his eyes. He opened his hands and gathered up the little cat as she sprang into his arms. He pressed his face against her furry back.

Fia twined her tail around his neck and purred. "I saw the bad men take you and Brig, and so I sneaked onto the ship when no one was looking. Wasn't I clever?"

"Very," said Duncan when he could speak, "but this is a dangerous ship for you. You've got to stay in the hold, out of sight."

Fia gave a small, impatient hiss. "Of *course* I'll stay out of sight. But I'm not staying in the hold. I'm going to find out what the earl is up to. This is the same ship we sailed in before," she informed him loftily, "and I know all the passages and spyholes."

"Fia!" Duncan protested, but the kitten was already squirming out of his hands.

Her clear, high kitten's voice came out of the darkness. "Don't worry. I'll report every few hours!"

"Report softer, will you?" came a grumbling growl. "My head is killing me, and you have a very piercing meow."

"Here's my report," said Fia importantly, some hours later. "The earl is sleeping in his cabin. He takes off his bandage at

274

night, and his forehead looks all pale and scabby. Bertram is sleeping in *his* cabin. He snorts like an old horse. The cook is in the galley baking bread, and the flab on his arms wiggles when he pounds the dough. Two sailors are on watch. One of the sailors is picking his nose. The other scratched his bottom twice and spat three times over the side." She paused. "And that's all."

Duncan wanted to laugh, but he was too worried. "That's good, Fia."

"Do you really think so?" said Fia. "It seemed kind of boring to me, so I've been doing a few cat tricks to keep things interesting."

"Cat tricks? What cat tricks? You haven't been letting anyone see you, I hope?"

"No," said Fia. "But do you know Cat Trick #8, Bringing Disgusting Gifts?"

Duncan nodded. He was familiar with the gifts that cats liked to leave where they could be found—chewed-up dead mice, for example.

"Well," Fia went on, "I've created a new one. I call it Cat Trick #8½: Leaving Hairballs Where They Are Most Likely to Be Stepped On. What do you think?"

"I think you'd better be sure you stay out of sight," Duncan said. It was bad enough to see Brig whacked on the head—he couldn't bear to have Fia end up in a pie.

Fia's meow was shrill. "But the cook slipped on my hairball and almost fell down. I'm getting revenge, see?"

An annoyed rumble came from the cage next to Duncan's. "Can you *please* meow softer? My head feels like a cracked boulder."

A sudden scraping noise made them all look up. A lantern shone far above, through two levels of deck and a large grating.

"Quiet, everyone," Duncan whispered. He watched as the squares of the grating faded from yellow lantern light to the gray of early morning. Now he was certain where they were—deep in the earl's ship, beneath the large opening used for loading cargo. He had seen something else in the brief light from the lantern, too. An iron padlock, holding a bar in place across one side of his cage.

"Can you pick a lock this big?" Duncan asked Fia quietly.

Fia perched on the crossbar and went to work with silent concentration. It was not an easy lock to open.

"I think I broke a claw," said Fia. "It's rusty."

"I'd do it, but my claws are too thick," the tiger said. "Try my cage, why don't you?"

"Wait!" said Duncan quickly. "Listen, Brig, if Fia gets your cage open, stay inside, do you hear? No attacking anyone, not yet."

A gusty sigh came from the cage next door. "Sir, what is the point of unlocking a cage if I'm not going to get out?"

Duncan had an answer ready. "This is just practice, to see if Fia can do it. We don't want to escape while we're still at sea—there's nowhere to run. Wait until the earl's ship docks."

276

"THE EARL'S SHIP?" Brig growled. "Where is he, the scum-sucking villain?"

"*Shhhhh!*" Duncan reached through the bars and grabbed a handful of fur. "Brigadier, this is an *order*. Do *not* growl, or roar, or leave your cage. Do *not* try to hunt down the earl unless I tell you to do it. Is that understood?"

There was a sulky pause. "But can't I take one little tiny bite out of him?" the tiger asked. "He's been a very *bad* earl."

"You'll get your chance," said Duncan. "Just wait for my order."

"Yes, sir," mumbled Brig. "I just hope your order comes soon, that's all. Tigers are not very good at waiting."

Boys were not very good at waiting, either, Duncan thought as the hours slowly passed. The work of the ship went on above them—he could hear voices and stamping feet, and now and then a new slant told him the ship had tacked—but no one came to check on him, or taunt him, or torture him, or any of the things Duncan had been imagining might happen on his enemy's ship.

He found out why the next time Fia came down to report.

"The earl and Bertram are arguing," she meowed. "Bertram says why not just get rid of you now, once and for all, but the earl says he wants information first. He says you can't tell him what he wants to know if you're dead."

Duncan's stomach seemed to flip within him.

"And the earl says there are too many people on board right now," Fia continued. "He's going to wait to question you until the ship docks and he sends everyone away."

"What," said Duncan, and his voice squeaked, "does he want to know?"

Fia hesitated. "He wants to know where you got Princess Lydia's ring." Duncan's hand flashed to his neck. The chain was gone, and so was the ring that had hung upon it. If his stomach had flipped before, now he felt as if it had dropped to his feet.

They must have seen it around his neck when he was put in the cage, unconscious. Now the earl knew the princess was alive—and that Duncan knew where.

No. The earl didn't know that for sure.

Duncan looked up two decks through the cargo hatch, past the grating, where daylight showed. He had a little time—how much, he didn't know—to make a plan.

He kept his voice calm with an effort. "Fia, you got Brig's cage unlocked, right? Do mine now."

The kitten worked at the rusty padlock with concentration, her small pink tongue curling out at moments of difficulty. Meantime, Duncan thought hard. He had some advantages that the earl didn't know about.

First, if they were going to Dulle—and Tammas had said so—then Duncan knew every rock of his home island, every path. He knew the baron and the fishermen and the old women who tatted lace in the sun—and he knew the cats. He would have help, lots of help, if only he could get past the earl and Bertram at the moment they docked.

Second, Fia was like a secret weapon. She had listened in on the earl's private conversations. She was unlocking Duncan's cage right now. And she could watch from a hidden place and give him a signal the moment the ship was about to dock. Docking was always a tense maneuver, with a lot to be done quickly at the last minute. Every eye would be on the task at hand—and Duncan and the tiger might be able to break free and run off the ship before anyone could stop them.

It struck Duncan that he had never fully realized what a valuable gift Grizel had given him when she taught him to speak Cat. Now, with a cat to spy for him and report back, he was going to be able to defeat even the villain of the nation—or at least have a fighting chance.

"At last!" Fia's relieved meow broke into Duncan's thoughts. He looked to see the padlock of his cage dangling open.

"Good job," he said. "You are one talented kitten."

Fia preened her whiskers and gave her tail a satisfied flick. "I bet I could pass my kitten examinations now with one paw tied behind my back!"

"Could you pass them quietly, please?" mumbled Brig. "I think I need another nap. My head still hurts."

"My head hurts, too," said Duncan, "but we can nap later. First let's go over our plans. Now, listen . . ."

Duncan woke to voices from one deck up.

"Who's going to be left on anchor watch, then?" The words floated down through the cargo hatch from the tween deck. "We're not all going off the ship at once, are we?"

"Bertram's on guard," another voice answered. "And a few are going to the manor house to announce the earl and bring back a carriage. But who cares? We're off duty! I just want to get my hands on a drink and some decent food for a change—"

"And someone friendly to dance with!" cried another.

Duncan tipped back his head. Through the bars of his cage, he could look up past the cargo hatch and see the first faint star in a far-off dusky sky, the distant crisscross of ship's rigging, and the big square sail on a yardarm in a bunt, looking like the scalloped edge of a piecrust against the sunset's pink glow.

They were still moving, but the endless rushing snore of the sea had changed to something quieter. They were in calmer waters, then—the Bay of Dulle, probably. Duncan's shoulders tightened. When the signal came, they would have to move fast.

He reached through the bars and poked Brig. "Keep your ears open. You'll hear Fia's signal before I do."

"Tigers do have excellent hearing," agreed Brig sleepily.

Boots clattered across the deck above and thumped down the ladder. Duncan gripped the bars with his hands as two sailors came near.

"So the earl's going to get a confession out of the boy,

eh?" The voice was hushed, but Duncan could hear it well enough.

"I wouldn't want to be in his shoes, not for a hundred silver barons. He'll end up in prison for tiger stealing—or worse. Hey! These padlocks are open!"

Strong callused hands snapped the locks shut. "Someone was stupid," said the first sailor, "not making sure they were shut all the way. Lucky the prisoners didn't escape. How'd you have liked it if a tiger jumped into your hammock with you, eh?"

Duncan gripped the bars; no need to panic yet, Fia could still unlock the cages. Meantime he would try something else. "I'm not a thief!" he whispered to the sailors. "I want to get a message to the king. Can you help me?"

The men's breathing was loud in the sudden stillness. "No talking to the prisoner—that's the order," said the first sailor.

"Now, lad," said the second sailor, "you're young, and the Earl of Merrick may have pity on you. Just tell him the truth about that tiger, where you got it and who you're working for, and things will go better for you in the end—"

"Hey! You down there!" The bellow came through the cargo hatch with the force of a gale. "No talking to the prisoner! Knot the line around that cage and be quick about it— unless you want your shore leave cancelled!"

Duncan tilted his head back. Two decks up, looming over the edge of the large square hole, was Bertram's unmistakable silhouette.

The deck creaked under the men's agitated feet. "Sorry, sir," called their spokesman. "Right away, sir."

A clatter of feet, high above, and the calling of orders. The yardarms creaked as sails were furled. The windlass clanked. The ship settled straight, its decks no longer at a slant. Suddenly Duncan heard a thin, high meow, repeated twice. Fia's signal.

"Should I try to bash my way out?" asked Brig worriedly. "I don't think I can—there's not enough room to get any force behind my bashing, so to speak."

The ship had grown quiet. Now and then, a distant burst of laughter or music came faintly to Duncan's ears, as if a door had been opened somewhere on the waterfront and then abruptly shut again. The sailors must have gone on their shore leave.

Duncan clenched his fists and relaxed them. "Fia!" he meowed softly. "Where are you?"

Clank. Creeeeaaak.

Duncan jerked his head up. Somewhere above him, metal was moving, scraping. What *was* that sound? If Fia were here, she would do Cat Trick #7—Perky Ears—and find out in no time. Duncan did his best to prick up his ears and listened intently.

The combination of noises was oddly familiar. It sounded like gears, pulleys, maybe a chain all working together. He knew he'd heard it before, somewhere, sometime.

His cage slid, scraped—and then it was rising. The ropes around it tightened as they took the strain. Duncan rocked sideways and then back against the corner as the cage tipped abruptly. Overhead was the dark shape of a heavy iron hook and a long linked chain above it. He could see the sharp tip against the evening sky, and slanting lines of ropes pulled tight. The cage swayed, turning gently in the air as it was raised inch by inch up through the cargo hatch.

As the cage slowly cleared the upper deck, he could see the arm of the crane that was lifting him. It was a harbor crane, mounted on the wharf with an arm that could swing over a ship to lift out cargo and then swing back to set the cargo down.

The ship was docked at a long pier, in a deep-water channel. With growing excitement, Duncan gazed through the bars of his cage at the lights lining the waterfront, the lanterns on poles—it was the island of Dulle. He was home.

But the wharf was empty of anyone who could help. Fishing boats were huddled far up on the beach, and even the harbormaster's hut was dark. And the waterfront places where the sailors were eating and drinking and dancing were too noisy for anyone to hear Duncan if he yelled.

Duncan took a deep breath and knotted his fingers around the rough bars. Where, oh where was Fia?

The long arm of the crane swung the cage across the deck, and Duncan swung dizzily with it. The gangplank passed beneath him, and now he was suspended over the dark gap of water between the ship and the massive wooden piers. He could see the man at the controls of the crane; it was Bertram. So the blurred figure standing at the railing must be the Earl of Merrick.

The cage dangled in midair, twirling slightly. Duncan twirled with it, his ears perked and ready for the slightest hint of a meow. Fia had to come. She *had* to.

He scanned the darkening waterfront. Weren't there *any* cats out there?

But no—they would have recognized the earl's ship. They would stay far away from the man who stole kittens and put them in a crate. Still, Grizel knew he had been taken away on this ship; maybe she would come. . . .

"Oh, Grizel," he murmured, filled with a sudden longing for her comforting weight in his lap, for the steady grumble of her purr. She had tried to teach him what she could, and even in his last glimpse of her she had been offering good advice. She had signaled in Cataphore everything he needed to know.

Perky Ears. Back Up. Claws Out. They were classic cat strategies for dealing with an opponent who was larger, stronger, who had you backed into a corner. Grizel had signaled danger to him with her tail and given him all the advice she could think of in Cataphore; she had known Duncan had an enemy and would need to defend himself.

And she had told him who that enemy was, he realized suddenly. Fia had told him that Grizel had spelled "watch out for eels" with her tail. But Fia had gotten the last word wrong. It had been *earl*.

The tall man at the railing lifted a long, straight hook and caught one of the ropes that was knotted around Duncan's cage. The cage stopped its lazy twirling with a jerk.

Duncan staggered slightly and glared through the bars. The Earl of Merrick watched him from the railing a few feet away, smiling with one corner of his cruel mouth.

"It's such a pleasure to see you again, my boy," said the earl, "but the little excitement with the tiger interrupted our chance to chat." He reached into his vest pocket and pulled out a shining chain that Duncan recognized. A ring dangled from it, gleaming gold.

"So," said the earl, "are you going to let me know how you got hold of Princess Lydia's ring and what you were doing with a tiger from Fahr? Or shall I tell Bertram to drop you into the sea?"

CHAPTER 24

The Rusty Lock

DUNCAN'S HEART PUNCHED INSIDE HIM like a fist. Below, water as black as tar sucked and splashed at the low-tide marks on the pier. The thought of being lowered into the sea in a *cage* filled him with horror.

The lantern on the dock cast its light upward to the ship's railing where the Earl of Merrick stood, making his face a mask with dark hollows for eyes. The slit that was his mouth opened, formed words.

"Is the princess still alive?" The earl showed his teeth in a terrifying parody of a smile. "How did you get the ring?" He gave the hook a twist, and Duncan's cage rocked a little.

Duncan swallowed down the fear that rose in his throat. He opened his eyes wide and blinked.

This was Melting Kitty Eyes—a tactic meant to confuse enemies, to make them think you were innocent and harmless. But all Duncan hoped to do was buy a little more time. If he could keep the earl at bay until Fia came up, if he could somehow get Bertram to set the cage down on the dock, if the two men could be distracted just long enough for Fia to pick the lock, then Duncan would have a chance.

At the crane's controls, Bertram moved impatiently. "Let me dunk him, sir. He's not telling you anything."

The earl's eyebrows lowered. "Start from the beginning. What happened when you jumped off my ship after your kitten?"

"Well," said Duncan, choosing his words slowly, "I washed up on an island. And there was a tiger."

"Yes? And then?" The earl's eyes glittered in the lantern light.

"I followed the tiger to where he lived, and there was the ring," Duncan said, quite truthfully. (He *had* followed the tiger to the princess, and she *had* been wearing the ring.)

"The tiger led you to the ring?" The earl's eyes narrowed. "Where was the ring, exactly?"

"In a cave," said Duncan, with sudden inspiration. It was true that the ring *had* been in a cave . . . among other places. "I think the tiger likes shiny things. The chain was there, too."

The earl sucked in his breath. "So the tiger survived somehow . . . perhaps bit the ring off her finger. Yes, yes, I suppose it's possible. The tiger must have made his way to the interior of the island somehow. I'll have to take a closer look at that island. If a tiger could live there all this time . . ."

His fingers tapped on the long metal hook, and the cage swung a little more. "The princess—did *she* survive?"

Duncan raised his eyebrows. "Everyone knows she drowned, sir," he said politely. "You said it yourself."

The earl leaned forward. "I didn't actually *see* her drown. It was a logical assumption. But you, boy—if you know anything at all about the princess, you'd better tell me now!" He spun the cage with a vicious jerk.

Duncan, whirling around like a top, saw the nightmarish face of the earl in blinks, succeeded by the harbor, the sea, and then the earl again. Wait—was that Fia? The pale blur was gone so fast he couldn't be certain.

"I can't tell you what I don't know," said Duncan loudly. "If you have more questions, why don't you set me down? I can't think while I'm dizzy."

"I have an idea," said Bertram from his place at the harbor crane's controls. He leaned out, and the lantern shone full on the brutal contours of his face. "Get rid of him now, with no more talking. It's safer."

"You always want blood, Bertram." The earl laced his elegant fingers together. "There are other ways more suitable for an earl. I have never dirtied my hands with another's blood, and I never will."

Bertram gave a coarse laugh. "But you'll give the orders for someone else to do it. Give the orders now, sir—I can take care of him in a minute!"

Meow! Meow! Meeeeeooooww!

"Bertram! Get that cat!" the earl snapped.

Bertram left the crane's controls and ran heavily from the dock up the gangplank. Duncan was spinning less quickly now, and he could see the kitten's pale fur streaking past, all too visible in the lantern light.

Meow! Meeeow! Meeeoww! Fia's voice was piercing as she tore across the deck.

"Get moving, Bertram!" the earl cried.

Duncan's nails bit into his palms. It was time for Back Up and Claws Out. "You're not much of a hero, are you?" he said. "It's not exactly *noble* to steal little kittens and squish them for dinner. Why do you do it? Do you think you're going to get furry? Grow a tail?" He was spinning very slowly now. He had time to see Fia race up the mast and out onto the yardarm just above. By the next time his cage spun around, Bertram was climbing the rigging with the slow, reluctant motions of a man doing something he didn't want to do.

"You think it's a joke?" the earl hissed. "I'm the Earl of *Merrick*, boy! I have a *kingdom* to think about! And if I have to eat cats in order to—"

The earl stopped again. Then he chuckled. It was a chilling sound.

"It doesn't matter if I tell you. You're never going to be able to tell anyone. In fact, I'll *enjoy* telling you." He leaned closer, so that his face was near the bars, and stopped the motion of the cage. "I'm learning to speak Cat," he whispered.

Duncan stared at him.

"Well, almost. It won't be long now. The more cats I eat, the quicker I'll learn to meow."

Duncan cleared his throat. *"Meow?"*

"You think it's funny, boy? You think it's impossible?" The earl's eyes narrowed. "I can assure you it's not. When I was a lad at the Academy, I knew a boy who could speak Cat. Oh, he could find out anything! People will talk in front of a cat, you know, and never think anything of it." The earl rubbed his hands together. "But he never really understood the advantage it gave him. He could have found out test questions in advance; he could have learned embarrassing things about people, things they wanted to keep private, and made them pay him money to keep the secret."

"That's cheating," said Duncan with contempt. "And blackmail, too. I thought nobles were supposed to be honorable."

The earl lifted one shoulder in a half shrug. "Honor is for people who can afford it. I was poor."

"And what's your excuse now?" said Duncan bitterly.

"Oh, there's more at stake now than just a few test questions or some pocket money. That boy, when he was grown and with the whole cat nation spying for him, could have ruled the kingdom. *I'm* going to," the earl added with a leer.

Duncan swallowed hard. He knew how well a cat could spy. What if the ability to speak Cat was in the power of someone like the earl—and if the earl were king?

Duncan cleared his throat. "Did you ask the boy to teach you to speak Cat?"

"He refused, the fool." The earl seemed to draw in on himself, a dark, hunched shadow. "But I was clever. I watched him, and I listened. One day I heard him asking his cook to make a kitty pot pie for dinner the next day. I had my suspicions. And in the end, right before he died, he told me. The secret to speaking Cat was to *eat cats*!"

Duncan's hands curled into fists. The earl was talking about Duke Charles, of course. Duncan remembered what the princess had told him about his father's last words to the earl—that eating cats was the secret—but that had seemed like sarcasm, like a bitter joke. The earl, though, in his obsessive quest for power, had taken it for truth.

Duncan wanted to punch the earl right through the bars, but that would be a momentary satisfaction at best. He forced himself to keep the conversation going. "That doesn't make sense. I eat chicken, and I don't know how to cluck."

"Well, cats are different. I don't know how it works. I just know *he* could speak their language, and believe me, there was no other reason he'd ever want to eat a cat. They're too stringy and tough. Of course, *kittens* are nice, very tasty indeed."

The earl looked up at the yardarm impatiently. "Bertram! Haven't you caught that kitten yet?"

"If you want it done faster," came the sullen answer, "then *you* come up and catch it. I said all along, get the boy out of the way first—but no, you stand there talking and send me to chase a *kitten*—"

Duncan looked up at the yardarm where Fia was sitting, glaring at Bertram with a look of deep disdain. She was meowing insults about his climbing technique.

Duncan thought of something else to keep the earl talking. "Can you understand what the cat on the yard is saying?"

Fia's insults were worth listening to. Just now she was describing Bertram's mother ("Daughter of a Corpulent Pig") and his father ("Son of a Toothless Rat") and Bertram himself ("Big Weenie with a Flabby Bottom Who Climbs Rigging Like My Aunt Sophie").

"It's not as clear as I'd like it to be," said the earl. He darted a quick look at Duncan. "I think she's saying, 'Help, help, get me down!'"

Duncan did his best to look impressed. "And can you speak Cat back to her?"

"Well . . ." The earl frowned. "I understand it better than I speak it. I don't think I've eaten enough cat yet to really solidify the language skills." He contorted his neck and issued a stream of meows.

Duncan would have laughed if he hadn't been so worried. The earl had stumbled on a few meows that were recognizable, but they were put together in a way that made no sense at all. As

292

far as he could tell, the earl had said something that could be translated as "Blobber worm grunkle, feeble go funky."

"There, you see?" The earl crossed his arms over his chest. "I told her that the big man in the rigging was going to help her get down."

"Ah," said Duncan.

"Of course, he isn't going to do any such thing. He's going to catch her and give her to the cook, and if I don't have Scrambled Kitty with Cinnamon Toast for breakfast, I'll be very surprised."

Duncan's stomach twisted with sudden loathing. He looked away, past the waterfront to the island rising beyond. The town was dotted with lamplight that glowed in a hundred window squares. A line of lanterns was moving like tiny bright ants, all converging on the baron's manor house as, even now, carriages and people on foot were starting to arrive for the concert.

One set of lights was moving swiftly away from the manor house, down the bayside road. It was a carriage, with lanterns on both sides; Duncan could trace its zigzag path with each bend of the road. He held his breath. It could be coming toward the waterfront. He needed to keep the earl talking, keep his attention, until it got here and he could yell for help.

Duncan looked at the earl and spoke deliberately. "I don't think you can speak Cat," he said. "You're just pretending."

The smile fell from the earl's face as if it had been wiped.

"And how would you know? Do *you* speak Cat?" He pushed his face close to the bars of Duncan's cage. "I heard you growl at the tiger when he was attacking. Were you trying to speak his language, by any chance?"

Duncan felt as if he were balancing on slippery rigging in a storm. "I thought it might work to growl at him. I've been experimenting with basic commands."

The earl's eyes narrowed. "And does he obey you?"

Duncan hesitated. What could he say to keep the earl interested, yet not give too much away? "Most times. I think he's been trained."

"Clever boy!" The earl's eyes lit up maliciously. "But not so clever as you think. You've brought the tiger to me at just the right time. Now, with the female in the king's zoo, I can breed up a whole squadron of military tigers. Tigers are very conscious of rank, did you know?" The earl's face contorted. "When they were on board ship, they obeyed the *duke*. They ignored *me*. But that will all be different now. Soon I'll be the highest-ranking person in all Arvidia."

"What about the king?" said Duncan, through a mouth that was suddenly dry.

"Oh, the king won't last long, I assure you. I can afford to wait."

High on the yardarm, Bertram lunged for the kitten, missed, and nearly fell. He swore several oaths Duncan had never heard before as he got his balance back again.

The earl didn't even look up. "And after I'm king, I'll go to war with the country of Fahr and rule it, too. They have all those lovely jewel mines, you know; but they think the Rift keeps them safe. Of course, it's thanks to you that I can invade, dear boy."

This was too much. "How did you work that out?" said Duncan with scorn.

The earl smiled maliciously. "You gave Bertram your house key, remember? And even your address. He picked up the sea chest, and we found your father's chart for the Rift inside. I admit, it was my oversight that allowed the sea chest with your father's things to be sent to your mother in the first place, and when she disappeared, the chest went with her. You made it easy for us to get it back, and we are so *very* grateful."

Duncan trembled with the effort to keep silent.

The earl tapped Duncan's cage with the long metal hook. "Cool in the face of danger, are you? Just like your father," he added spitefully. "Oh, in case you haven't guessed yet, your father was Charles, Duke of Arvidia. He's dead now, though. I'm looking forward to courting his widow. Don't you think I'd make her an admirable husband?"

A red haze seemed to be filling Duncan's vision—he could hardly see the earl's face. He spoke through his teeth. "She'll never marry you."

"No? What if I tell her that I've gone over the charts again, at the point where you disappeared, and that you might have been washed up on one of the many islands nearby? What if I promise to search for you and take her with me?"

Duncan could not speak. Fury washed through him in a wave. He struggled to look past the earl to the carriage on the hillside road; it would reach the waterfront soon. He thought perhaps he could hear the faint rattle of its wheels.

The earl tapped Duncan's cage with the long metal hook. "Now that the king has given her back her lands and castle, he has said that the man who marries the duchess will be duke. I'd quite like to be a duke," he said, chuckling. "And I'm looking forward to comforting your grieving mother. She'll play her violin for me every night, don't you think? If I ask nicely? I really am most terribly fond of the violin."

Suddenly Duncan became aware that Fia, high up on the yardarm, was meowing to him. She was telling him to be alert—that she would dash past Bertram, leap onto the cage, and pick the lock just as soon as the earl left the ship to attend the concert.

"Of course, if she doesn't marry me," said the earl, "no matter. Once I'm king, I can take away her castle and lands on some excuse. She'll be poorer than ever, once I'm finished with her—and you'll be just as dead as your father." The earl stepped closer, his voice bright with malice. "I was always coming in second to your precious father. He was the duke—I was just the earl. He got the academic medal, he made the winning goal, he even married the girl I wanted. But I got even at last." The earl stroked the bandage on his head with his long, thin fingers. "It's truly a pleasure to experience this moment—I only wish it could last longer—when I am taking everything away from his son."

Duncan held his breath. Close to the waterfront, a carriage was rattling, coming quickly down the hill. There was the sound of feet marching, and then flutes began to tootle and a brass horn blew. Suddenly a closely packed column of people came round the corner of a building and down the boardwalk, and they were all playing instruments. Duncan recognized the tune; he had listened to his mother's music students murder it on the piano for years. They were playing "Hero's March."

Would they see him in the cage? It was dark. If only they'd stop the music, he could yell and have a hope of being heard!

On the yardarm, the white kitten yawned as Bertram edged closer. The big man lunged for her with a sudden movement, lost his balance, and clung to the jackstay, cursing, as Fia stepped delicately just out of reach.

"Bertram!" The earl's voice cracked like a bullwhip. "Get down here! Forget the cat and get to the crane controls! People are coming!"

Bertram fumbled his slow way back across the yardarm. The earl stamped the deck in his impatience. "I'll do it myself," he muttered, striding down the gangplank to the harbor crane.

The gears made their metallic noise, and the pulleys squeaked overhead. Something white and fluffy leaped from

297

the yardarm to the top of the cage as it swayed past, and Fia tumbled through the bars and into Duncan's arms.

"Bertram climbs like an ox," she said cheerfully, "and he smells like one, too. What now?"

Duncan whispered in her ear. "As soon as that marching band gets close enough, I'm going to yell."

"I'll meow for my mother!" said Fia. "She'll be glad to hear that I could pass my kitten examinations ten times over now!"

Duncan's cage moved sideways in a series of jerks—away from the side of the ship, past the dark gap of water under the gangplank, over the dock. "Get ready, Fia," whispered Duncan. "He's going to set us down on the pier. The minute he looks away, pick the lock."

But the earl, working at the controls with hurried motions, turned the crane even farther. The crane arm stopped abruptly, and Duncan's cage swung in elliptical circles over the sucking water on the far side of the wooden pilings.

Duncan bit his lip. The ship was between him and the people on the boardwalk, and the band was still playing.

"I'm going to yell anyway," he said to Fia.

"I'll caterwaul," Fia said. "It's a very loud noise that cats make, and I've been wanting to practice."

"On three," said Duncan. "One—two—"

Clank! Clank clank clank whiiiirrrr! With a suddenness that snatched the breath from both Duncan and Fia, the pulleys spun and the cage dropped. It hit the water with a smack and a splash. The sea poured in the spaces between the bars, and the iron hook and chain fell on top and weighed it down. Duncan had one second to fill his lungs with air before his head went under and everything was cold and wet and dark.

Duncan felt the cage hit bottom. He was completely submerged. But he wasn't in the deepest channel. Surely the waves would sweep out again, giving him a chance to breathe. . . .

He could feel Fia writhing in his hands. He pushed the cat up through a gap in the bars and held her as high as he could. With the other hand, he pulled himself to the top of the cage until he could feel the bars touching his face. He couldn't hold his breath much longer. He could feel the air on his wrist—so close, just inches away—

The water rushed seaward, and suddenly he was breathing in great gasps, taking in air in a panicked rush. He stared around him, salt water dripping from his eyebrows. He had whole seconds in which he could see the earl leaving the harbor crane and walking quickly toward the boardwalk and the welcoming committee. The harbormaster stood in a bright circle of lantern light with the band playing behind him. They would never notice Duncan's dark head or the bars of the cage in the black water beyond the ship, and now the next wave was rolling in—it was over his head—

There was a rhythm to the waves as they crashed in and sucked out. Duncan had time enough to breathe in between them, but it wasn't until the third wave had come and gone that he managed to get enough air to yell.

It was a useless attempt. The sound was swallowed up in a blare of trumpets. And the shout had taken up most of his air. He would not be able to yell after every wave; he had to breathe sometime.

Obviously the earl had not wanted to give Duncan a chance to attract anyone's attention; dumping his cage into the sea had filled that requirement nicely. At least he hadn't set it down in the deep water channel. If he had done that, Duncan would have had no chance at all.

When the fourth wave came and went, Duncan caught sight of the iron hook, still attached to the ropes on the cage. Once the crowd of people went away, it would be easy enough for Bertram to raise the cage once more and lower it back onto the ship. Yes, that was what would happen. Of course it would. The earl still wanted to get more information out of Duncan about the princess. Naturally he wasn't planning to leave Duncan in the water.

But when the fifth wave washed over Duncan and back into the sea, he saw the earl getting into the carriage waiting at the end of the dock. When the sixth wave had gone, Duncan saw Bertram walking swiftly from the gangplank to the carriage as the earl beckoned to him. And when the seventh wave had passed over his head, hissing, Duncan looked toward the waterfront and saw only the blank pavement, the lonely lantern, and a blowing bit of paper that looked like sheet music.

Duncan timed his breathing and tried to think. "Can you

pick the lock underwater, Fia?" he asked when the surf rolled back.

The little cat nodded, shivering on top of the cage. "But I *hate* getting wet," she said through her clenched teeth. "I don't know how Brig stands it."

Working by feel and clinging to Duncan's hand against the push and pull of the waves, Fia held her breath and wiggled one claw in the keyhole. But this was the rusty padlock, with the stiff mechanism. It had been hard for her to open even when she had plenty of time—and plenty of air. She poked Duncan's wrist to signal that she needed to breathe.

"I can't . . . listen for . . . the click," she gasped.

"It's all right," said Duncan through chattering teeth. "Just try again." He took a deep breath and held Fia high as another wave came pouring toward him. When it receded, he sucked in air as the water streamed from his hair, his face, his neck, his shoulders—

No. Not his shoulders. The water at its lowest point was up to his neck now. The tide was coming in.

Duncan tipped his head back so he could breathe for a few extra seconds. "Hurry," he said.

"How . . . much time . . . do we have?" wheezed Fia after she had tried three more times.

Duncan calculated. He knew the bay and its tides, and at this phase of the moon, the highest point of the water would creep up an inch every two minutes or so. With every wave that came in, there would be a shorter time in which he could breathe, until at last he wouldn't be able to breathe at all.

"Seven minutes," he said when he could speak. "Maybe eight."

Fia's bedraggled face looked despairing. She sucked in another mouthful of air and poked Duncan's thumb with her claw—the signal for him to lower her to the padlock once more. She tried to unlock it again. She failed. She failed five more times.

Duncan looked up through the bars at her small anguished face, her mismatched eyes that glowed so beautifully in the dark. It wasn't going to work—he knew that now. But Fia didn't have to die.

"I'm tossing you onto the dock," he said when he could speak, not wasting any words or breath. The wave would come back all too soon, and he had to make sure Fia was safe before then. If he let her try even one more time, he might not have enough time—or air—to do it.

"No!" Fia gasped. "I won't give up!" But Duncan's arm was already through the bars and cocked to throw.

He did not say good-bye. He needed his breath. He bunched his muscles—released them in a short, explosive effort—and Fia flew in a high arc through the night air, trailing a thin, piercing *miaow*. Just for a moment, Duncan had a glimpse of the cat scrabbling for a clawhold on the wooden dock, and then the next wave rolled mercilessly in.

CHAPTER 25

Army of Cats

PANIC FILLED DUNCAN'S CHEST. It had weight and volume, like wet cement.

But he wasn't drowned yet. There were still a few waves left before the tide covered him completely; he would be able to snatch a few more breaths. There would be time enough to panic when he couldn't breathe at all.

Duncan curled his fingers around the bars above and pulled himself up until his nose pressed into the space between. His feet floated off the bottom, and he felt the cage rock slightly as the wave receded. Could he push the iron hook and chain off the top of the cage? Then it might float. . . .

Breathe. Breathe. Breathe. He found the hook with his hand, slick and cold and heavier than he had imagined, tangled in the links of chain. He had nothing to brace himself against. He pushed, but his arm was too weak.

His legs. His legs were stronger. He held on to the bars and worked one foot up through the gap. The mass of chain moved a little. If he could move it just a little more . . .

He snatched the last possible breath. He pushed with both legs, with all the force he had, and the chain slid off. He could hear the links clashing, and now their weight pulled the great iron hook, too, and the ropes lashed around the cage—

No, no, *no!* The words screamed in Duncan's mind as the cage tipped over. The waves rushed seaward, dragging it to deeper water. The iron hook and chain held it down, as firmly as any anchor. Duncan floated to the top of the cage, toward the dim, watery light from the wharf lantern. He reached up an arm through the bars. There was air on his hand; he could feel it, only inches away.

He was going to drown. This was how his father had died.

And then something large and dark blocked the lantern's glow like a fast-flying cloud. The bars above him shuddered and cracked. Everything was breaking around him; the whole cage crashed in and something had him by the collar; he was being dragged over the jagged wood and sandy bottom and then his head broke the surface at last and he breathed cool, sweet air in great shuddering gasps.

Something was licking his face with a tongue like sandpaper. Duncan rolled over to see Brig's shaggy muzzle and a pair of brightly shining, very worried eyes.

As it turned out, Fia had not wasted time meowing on the dock. She had intelligently raced back onto the ship, tumbled down three ladders to the hold, picked the lock on Brig's cage, and led him back outside where he was just in time to see Duncan's hand above the waves. Brig had launched himself at the cage, over 300 pounds of furious leaping tiger, and the wooden bars had cracked under the impact.

Duncan cuddled Fia and wheezed out his thanks. Then he threw his arms around Brig's thick neck and buried his face in the tiger's damp fur.

"Just doing my duty, sir," Brig said, but his ears flushed, and he looked ridiculously pleased. He lifted his paw in salute. "Now, with your permission, I'll secure the perimeter. It's hostile territory, so I shall use my camouflage skills. We tigers are particularly good at camouflage."

He shook the water out of his ears. Did water magnify sound? Fia's meow sounded loud, as if there were more than one cat. . . .

There *was* more than one cat. Suddenly Duncan saw furry backs and waving tails all around him. The wharf cats had begun to gather; they had heard Fia's piercing meow of alarm, then Brig's roar of fury. Now, as Duncan filled his lungs with precious air and wrung his shirt dry, Fia explained things to the ever-increasing crowd of cats.

She worked her way backward, telling how Duncan had almost drowned (but cats had rescued him), of bloody battles with shipboard rats (the cat always won), how the princess was still alive (a very large cat had saved her), and in general covered everything that had happened from a cat's point of view. When she got to the Squisher and Grinder, the cats moved restlessly, glancing at one another, and all the mother cats covered their kittens' ears.

Duncan, meantime, had been watching the lights moving on the hill. His time in the water had seemed like forever, but in reality it had probably only been a half hour since the earl and Bertram had left. The baron's manor house was lit from top to bottom; only a few lone straggling lights were still moving toward it. The concert must be about to start.

His instinct was to run straight to his mother, to just burst in and tell everyone what had happened. But he had had time to think.

It would be stupid to walk up to the front door, dripping and filthy. The baron's footmen would not let him into the manor house like that, and explanations would take time. Worse, the earl or Bertram might see him first.

Duncan knew how quickly the earl could think of a lie; he knew how quickly Bertram could bundle him out of sight. There had to be a better way.

Cats were still coming, padding through town streets, winding their way down the cliffside road. They sat around Fia in a half circle, quiet, watchful, with their ears pricked forward. Latecomers climbed trees and awnings, and Old Tom clawed his way up a thick wharf post and perched there with his shoulders hunched and his whiskers stiff, listening in perfect silence. But when Fia told about her capture and the kitnip that the Earl of Merrick had discovered and used to steal kittens, Old Tom could keep quiet no longer.

"I *told* you! I told you all!" he cried in an anguished meow. "But no one would *listen*!"

A murmuring meow swept through the ranks of cats, and then a commanding *mrreoow* rose above the rest. "All right, Tom; we're listening now."

Duncan looked for the cat who had spoken. A large marmalade cat leaped up onto the low eaves of a boatshed. He looked like the cat who had run the kitten examinations in the cemetery, so long ago.

The marmalade cat gazed calmly down at the assembled cats. "We must come to a decision about this dog of an earl. We have enough here for a quorum; I suggest we hold a cat council immediately. All in favor, meow."

A chorus of meows rose at once.

"All opposed, hiss."

The wharf was silent. Then, suddenly, a single cry rang out. "*Fia!* My baby!"

From far off, at the base of the cliffside road, a cream-colored streak came flying across the waterfront and straight through the rows of gathered cats, scattering them right and left.

"Mommy!" breathed Fia.

The cream-colored cat gave a last great spring and landed in front of Fia, her tail straight up and quivering like a feather.

"I knew it was you, I knew it!" she meowed, sniffing Fia's cheeks in a sort of ecstasy. "I could see your eyes from far off—your beautiful, beautiful eyes! I would have known you anywhere!"

Mabel butted Fia's head, rubbed along her flanks and twined their tails together, while Fia stood still in shock. "You think my eyes are beautiful?"

"Of course!" Mabel nuzzled the tender spot just behind Fia's jaw. "No other cat has such lovely eyes of two colors but my daughter!"

"But—but—" Fia stammered. "You never *said* you thought they were beautiful. I thought you were ashamed of them."

"Well, naturally, I didn't want to give you a big head." Mabel's tone was slightly acerbic. "It's never wise to pay a kitten too many compliments—they're hard enough to manage as it is. But you're way past kittenhood already—why, look at you, you're almost grown up!"

"I'm a good hunter, too," Fia said modestly. "See this scar on my ear? That's from my first rat!"

The cat council was going on, so Fia and Mabel moved to one side to exchange their news. Duncan paced around the crowd of cats—there were hundreds now—but he couldn't locate Grizel anywhere. He passed Old Tom, still perched on his post, and questioned him.

"Grizel? Old cat, a little creaky?"

Duncan nodded.

"She's been sick lately, I heard. Must be all that rich food up at the baron's house—whoa, excuse me, it's coming to a vote!"

Duncan backed up as the cats surged forward. If Grizel was at the manor house, then he knew what to do. Cats could go where humans could not, without suspicion. Robert and Betsy, the baron's children, had a cat, too, though Duncan was never sure if he should call him Mr. Fluffers or Spike.

Duncan had the beginnings of a plan now. But he didn't like the idea of going anywhere near the earl with no greater weapon than a couple of cats.

He had a tiger, of course. But all at once Duncan remembered something else that was his, by right. He ran up the long, narrow gangway to the ship, found a lantern and matches by the binnacle, and slid down the ladders to the hold. It did not take him long to find the old black sea chest and his father's sword.

Duncan stepped off the ship, sword in one hand and the swordbelt over his shoulder. Under the light of a harbor lantern, he strapped the belt around his hips and fitted the sword in the looped scabbard. The sword was too long for him, and awkward, but he felt better with it on. He practiced pulling it out, trying for one smooth motion.

Mabel had pressed back into the ranks of voting cats. Fia, off to one side, was talking to three half-grown cats who looked familiar. It took Duncan a moment to remember the names of Fia's sisters and brother: Tibby, Tabby, and Tuff.

"You actually fought *rats*?" Tibby was saying in a breathless tone. "We're only up to mice and voles."

"Did you really climb all the way up the tallest mast?" asked Tabby, her head tipped back to look up at the docked ship. "How did you get down?"

"I wish *I* could have gone to sea," said Tuff, in tones of unmistakable envy. "Some cats have all the luck."

There was a sudden chorus of meows from the cat council and another call for hisses, which was met with silence.

"Aren't you voting?" Duncan asked Fia.

"She's not of voting age yet," said Tabby. "None of us are. Look, they've decided!"

The marmalade cat held up a paw for quiet. "We are unanimous, then. Backs up, claws out, and send the kittens home. Onward to the Big House!"

The cats milled about, breaking ranks and then re-forming into lines.

"And the Big House means . . . ?" said Duncan.

Tibby flicked her ears toward the baron's manor house, festive with lights. "Up there. That's where the earl went, they say."

Duncan was taken aback. He had not expected a whole army of cats to come with him. "Has anybody seen the tiger?"

"You mean that very *big* cat?" came a meow from the crowd.

Something moved amid the trees, and the shape of a large, tawny tiger appeared where Duncan would have sworn there was only leaf-dappled shadow.

"Just practicing my camouflage skills, sir," said Brig.

Mabel wound her way through the crowd to her children. "Tibby, Tabby, and Tuff, you must go to the monastery at once. The rest of us are going after the earl, and that is not a job for young cats."

The three cats looked sulky. Their ears flattened slightly. "What about Fia?" said Tibby. "She's the same age as we are."

"Fia has been on her own for a long time now," said their mother. "She's had to grow up faster."

"It's not *fair*!" hissed Tabby. "She hasn't even passed her kitten examinations!"

CHAPTER 26

The Young Duke

Mice squeaked the alarm; chipmunks scampered for their burrows. A red fox, out for a night of hunting, stepped back in surprise as a long line of cats rippled in single file up the hillside path.

Behind them was the glimmering sea; above them was the crescent moon. But the cats kept their eyes on the great manor house halfway up the hill and padded steadily forward, eyes glowing in the dark.

Duncan trudged alongside the line of cats, stumbling on rocks he couldn't see. His ankle twisted beneath him, and he grunted in pain.

Brig bulked large next to him, his voice a comforting

rumble. "Hold on to me, sir. You can't expect to see in the dark; you're not a cat."

"I've noticed that." Duncan twined his fingers into Brig's neck fur and limped on at a slower pace.

The baron's house loomed larger, ablaze with light in every window square. Somewhere behind those windows was his mother. Somewhere in that house was the earl. Duncan had to find one and keep out of sight of the other. He had to warn his mother—in fact, he should warn everyone! He should tell every single person on the island the truth about the earl, and the princess, and his father. But would they believe his word against the earl's?

The adults would think he was confused or was making it up to get attention. His mother might believe that the earl was a dangerous traitor, but no one else would—not right away, not when they were used to thinking of him as a hero. Duncan wouldn't have believed it himself, a few months ago.

A lone owl glided silently overhead, blocking the crescent moon for a single heartbeat. The line of cats, their backs rising and falling, looked like one long, furry animal—far too large to be an owl's prey.

Duncan stumbled again. He was very tired. If only he had proof of the earl's treachery! He had the feeling there was something he had missed, something in the story of the earl and his father that didn't fit.

"Brig?" he said.

"Right here, sir."

"You know, the earl and his men are up there in that lighted house."

Brig's hackles rose beneath Duncan's hand. "I'll be ready for them," the tiger growled.

"This time," Duncan said firmly, "you're going to control yourself. Wait for my orders. Do you hear?"

"Yes, sir," rumbled the tiger, hanging his head.

"And now tell me again what happened the day the earl betrayed my father. Tell me every detail—don't leave anything out."

The great arched doors of the manor house were shut. Torches blazed in iron cressets on either side, flaring yellow against the sooty stone. Overhead, drifting down from the crenellated tower, Duncan could hear the click of dice and the low laughter of men. The baron's guards must be up on the battlements, keeping watch for incoming ships or any danger. Duncan had a feeling they weren't expecting a cat invasion. Even if they were, they couldn't have seen the cats in the dark, not unless a cat happened to look up at the precise moment a guard looked down in its direction. Cats' eyes gleamed in the dark only when you looked right at them.

The cats had taken up positions in a ring around the manor house. Silent, eyes glowing in the dark, they sat without moving. Only the occasional tail flick showed that they were alive.

What were their plans?

Well, it was their business. He had to make plans himself. But now, looking at the great iron-studded doors, his heart failed him. What was he going to do—just go up and knock? The earl might have men stationed inside the doors.

"Brig," Duncan whispered, "do you see Fia? I need her."

Brig was not listening. The sheep that normally grazed the wide green lawn had taken one look at the tiger and, bleating, had scattered and then bunched together in a far corner by a stone wall. Brig was watching them with great interest.

"They look easy to catch," he rumbled under his breath. "But doesn't all that fluff get stuck in your teeth?"

"Leave them alone, Brig." Duncan scanned the circle of glowing cats' eyes for a mismatched set, and saw Fia at last. "All right, Brig, remember—no attacking anyone unless I order it."

The tiger gazed earnestly in the direction of the bunched sheep. A small line of drool glistened at the corner of his mouth.

"Brig!" Duncan whispered sharply.

"Sir?" Brig turned his head away from the sheep with an obvious effort.

"You *can't* go after someone else's sheep—especially the baron's. He'd turn you into a tigerskin rug in no time."

Brig sighed. "Understood, sir." He looked at the sheep with obvious regret. "But sooner or later, I *would* like some dinner."

The sword made it awkward to climb. Duncan struggled up the familiar footholds; he had not eaten for a long time, and his near drowning in the cage, followed by the steep climb up the hill, had exhausted him. Arms trembling with fatigue, he heaved himself up onto the second-story ledge and bumped the drainpipe with a rattle. Fia, tucked in his shirt, gave a protesting meow.

He sidled along the ledge to Robert's window and levered the window up with his toes. "Stay quiet," he warned Fia, and ducked into Robert's room.

He crossed the floor carefully, sliding his feet forward in case he needed to kick clothes out of the way. Robert had never kept his room very tidy. But the floor was clear. Of course—Robert must be away at the Academy.

Duncan inched the door open and peered out. The long hallway was deserted.

Betsy's bedroom was two doors down. She was probably at the concert, but just in case. . . . He tapped at her door and opened it a crack. Something extremely fluffy butted it farther open and slipped past his legs.

"Hey!" Duncan's whisper was urgent. "Mr. Fluffers!"

The smoke-colored Persian was halfway down the hall already. "Spike is the preferred name," he said coldly, and then he turned. "I know you! You're the one who turned out to be a duke's son and sent a letter saying you were running away to sea. You made your mother weep, sir."

"I didn't run away; I was kidnapped!" Duncan said hotly. "And the earl tricked me into signing my name. I didn't know he would write a fake letter and send it."

Spike crooked his tail at the tip as he considered this information. "The cat council was furious about that earl. They suspected him of stealing a crate full of kittens, but the humans still think he's a big hero."

"He's not," said Duncan briefly.

"He's a kitten squisher!" Fia mewed.

Spike's ears flattened, and a low hiss escaped him.

"He's a traitor to the king, too," Duncan added, "and he just tried to murder me. I'm going to tell everyone at the concert the truth about him right now."

Spike tapped his claws against the polished wooden floor. "May I suggest—may I *strongly* suggest—that you change your clothes? Robert's room is just down the hall; I am sure you can find something in his closet that isn't damp, torn, or smelling of seaweed."

Duncan glanced down at his clothes. It was true that he looked bad and smelled worse.

"In fact," Spike meowed, "I suggest that you put on Robert's braided jacket with the gold buttons and sash."

Duncan blinked. "What for?"

"Remember that you are the young duke," Spike said. "You should look like one, especially when meeting the enemy. A cat looks more formidable if he fluffs out his fur, my lord."

Resplendent in gold buttons, sash, and sword, Duncan moved silently along the passage, followed by two cats. Fia was busy meowing all the news to Spike, but Duncan had other things on his mind. He had to get Brig into the house, but the back door would be crowded with servants.

Three corridors and one side stair later, Duncan slipped into the small garden room, breathing hard. It had large windows, he knew, and was seldom used.

"What are we doing here?" meowed Fia.

Duncan pushed open the window shutters and stuck his head out into the night. Across the lawn he could see small pinpoints of light, all in a line—the cats' eyes, gleaming in the dark. But there were no larger, higher gleaming eyes. Maybe Brig was on the other side of the house. Duncan fervently hoped Brig was not chasing sheep.

Could the tiger leap through the window? It was at least six feet off the ground.

Duncan unwound the gold sash from Robert's jacket. "Fia, go find Brig for me."

Fia poked her head over the sill. "That's a long way down."

"Hook your claws into the sash, and I'll lower you. When you find Brig, bring him back to this window and tell him to jump in. He can follow my scent to where I am. Oh, and, Fia?"

The kitten, swinging from the sash, looked up, her mismatched eyes glowing orange and gold.

"You'd better say those are my orders."

Duncan crouched beneath the final curve of the grand staircase and peered past the newel post. This was a place where he and Robert had hidden many times while playing bandits, and though a little small for him now, it still served. Spike was on the other side of the carved fretwork panels and curled up in front of the stairs, his ears alert.

The entrance hall was a vast, echoing space, with flagstone floor and high timbered ceiling. From his position, Duncan could see the massive front door, its oaken slabs studded with iron. Two of the baron's footmen stood stiffly at either side. Near them, two of the earl's sailors leaned against the wall, their arms folded. Each had a cutlass in his belt.

Through a small side door, narrow stone steps curved up and around, ending (Duncan knew) in the tower where the baron's men kept watch over land and sea. On the other side, the wide entrance hall opened into the ballroom. The brown velvet curtains drawn across the opening were not quite closed.

A sound of clapping died down. There was a waiting silence. The first notes of a piano accompaniment came tinkling through the gap in the curtain. And then the clear, pure notes of a violin rose like larks singing.

The hair on Duncan's neck lifted. What *was* it about his mother's playing? It was haunting, somehow, sweet and sad and fierce all at once, and it felt like a cord being pulled inside his chest. As he listened, Duncan found himself remembering blue sky and wind in white sails, hot sand and a golden tiger's rough breath, and he shivered.

The earl's men moved closer to the velvet curtain as if they couldn't help themselves, their heads cocked to listen. The violin gave a last, high, shimmering note that fell into silence like snow drifting into a still gray pond. For the space of three heartbeats, there was no sound at all, and then came a roaring applause that the velvet curtain seemed hardly to muffle at all. The earl's sailors glanced at one another sheepishly, then pushed through the curtain into the ballroom.

Boots clattered on the tower stairs. A young baron's guard, his hair falling in his eyes, ran down two steps at a time. He skidded on the flagstones, saluted the guards at the door, and muttered something Duncan couldn't hear.

Duncan's fingers curled tightly into his palms. Had the tower guard seen a tiger?

The heavy front door creaked open as the guards stepped out onto the portico. A waft of cool night air swirled in and ruffled the hair along Spike's back.

Duncan put his mouth to an opening in the carved fretwork panel; his meow to Spike was hardly louder than a breath. "Go find out what's going on."

Spike strolled across the flagstone floor. He nosed at a corner near the door as if smelling for a mouse, but his ears swiveled toward the guards talking outside.

Duncan told himself that Brig was very good at camouflage. He told himself that if someone had spotted a tiger, there would have been more noise and commotion.

The Persian cat drifted back across the entrance hall, his smoky fur almost the same color as the flagstones. He paused by the newel post and meowed his report just loud enough for Duncan to hear. "One of the tower guards sighted a ship coming in, signaling something or the other. He's sending a carriage down to the wharf to meet it."

"A ship?" whispered Duncan, relieved. "I thought they might have seen Brig! Did you hear anything else?"

Spike scraped his claws across the gray stone floor. "I did notice a slight disturbance among the sheep."

Outside the open door, the guard and footmen were talking beneath the flaring torchlight. A faint sound of panicked bleating came from somewhere in the dark.

Duncan's heart sank. He had been so sure that Brig would obey orders, no matter what.

Off in the ballroom, the piano began a lively island dance. Duncan recognized the tune at once: "Red-Haired Boy." His mother had hummed it when she taught him the steps to the Arvidian reel. She had bubbled with laughter when his feet had gotten tangled, and he had made the same mistake three times over just to hear her laugh again.

But now the violin joined the piano with long, low, quivering tones, like the cry of a seabird at dusk. An undercurrent of sadness washed through the lighthearted tune, turning it into something broken and alone.

Duncan clenched his fists. Of course his mother was grieving. According to Tammas, the Earl of Merrick had told her that her son was dead. And that lying, murdering kitten-squisher of an earl was probably in the front row right now, clapping and smiling and planning the lies that would persuade the duchess to marry him and make him a duke—and soon enough, a king.

A wave of fury surged in Duncan, tinting his vision red and thrumming in his ears. The guards were still outside as he strode across the flagstones to the velvet curtains. He would do it without Brig. He had to. He put his face to the gap and looked into the ballroom.

The crowd was quiet, entranced, every eye on the slender figure on the dais who was playing her violin as if she were drowning and music alone was air and light.

Duncan hesitated, his hands on the soft velvet. His whole life, his mother had trained him to avoid notice and attention. Now he had to interrupt a concert, stand in front of hundreds of people, and accuse the most powerful man in Arvidia next to the king himself.

It would have been so much better with a tiger.

The ballroom was alight with candles, their glow reflected and magnified by hanging chandeliers with hundreds of glass prisms. The edges of the ballroom were shadowed, lined with figures in dark jackets—earl's men, wearing the sailors' navy blue. No one was paying any attention to Duncan yet. A meek voice in his head told him it was not too late to back out. Near his ankles, Spike gave a small cough.

He set his teeth grimly and started forward. But before his foot quite left the floor, something jerked at his hip. His heart gave a violent bound.

"Sorry I bumped your sword, sir," rumbled Brig. "It sticks out kind of far, doesn't it?"

Duncan gripped Brig's shaggy head, speechless.

"I told him and *told* him to come!" shrilled Fia, leaping around Duncan's ankles, "but he said the orders had to come direct from you!"

Brig lifted his chin with dignity. "With respect, sir, the chain of command was *not* clearly defined."

Duncan's heart settled to a rapid, forceful beat. "It doesn't matter—don't worry about it." He breathed deeply, expanding his chest as far as he could. He wove his fingers into Brig's neck fur and set his eyes on the aisle that stretched out before him.

They moved forward, quickly and steadily—the boy, the tiger, an extra-fluffy cat, and a kitten. At first no one seemed to notice. Then row by row, as if touched by a moving wave, heads turned, shoulders shifted, mouths opened in shock. Duncan could feel the crowd's collective gaze on his skin, and their murmur pushed at him like audible hands. Some of the people were half standing now. There was a sudden movement of men along the side walls.

"Steady," Duncan murmured to Brig.

Someone large moved in on Duncan from his left. At the same time, a golden cat with brown-tipped ears trotted stiffly down the center aisle.

"Grizel!" gasped Duncan.

"Cat Trick #17!" Grizel meowed sharply. "Now, Fia!"

There was a stumble and a crash somewhere behind him. A part of Duncan's brain rummaged around in his memory. Of course—#17 was Getting in the Way. He wanted to laugh, but his mouth felt stiff. His mother was still playing, her eyes closed, oblivious to everything but the music.

A footman came up from behind and reached for Duncan's elbow. "Sir!" he hissed. "Remove yourself at once! I have called the guards down to deal with the tiger!"

"Let me go!" Duncan tried to pull his arm free without success.

"Spike!" hissed Grizel. "Together, now—Cat Trick #24!"

The cats, golden and smoky, launched themselves at the footman below his knees in a coordinated assault. The man gave a yip of pain and released his grip on Duncan's arm.

Duncan grinned. Cat Trick #24 had to be Surprise Ankle Attack—or was it Rapid Toe Pounce? Either way, it had worked perfectly. But now another footman approached, holding an umbrella like a club, and sailors from the side wall were headed their way. Spike meowed a loud warning.

The cat's piercing cry reached to the front row; Robert's sister, Betsy, leaped up from her chair and came running back. "Bad Mr. Fluffers!" she hissed, and then skidded to a halt, her mouth hanging open.

Duncan put a hand on her shoulder. "Don't worry, Betsy— the tiger's trained."

Betsy's eyes were as wide open as her mouth. "But the earl said you were lost at sea!"

"The earl's a liar," Duncan said. "And he squishes *kittens*."

Betsy's eyes narrowed. Her mouth snapped shut. She made an imperious gesture to the room at large and said, "Leave my friend alone. *And* his tiger."

"But, Lady Betsy," began the first footman. Betsy glared at him, and he took a step back.

In a stately manner, with chins lifted high, Duncan and Betsy walked down the center aisle with the tiger between them. Spike, Grizel, and Fia brought up the rear, their tails waving like flags in a stiff breeze.

Duncan's mother, standing above the crowd on the dais and fully absorbed in her music, lifted her head at last. The violin's clear melody faltered, trailed away. There was a tiny clatter as the bow dropped to the floor. Someone reached forward and caught the violin before it fell.

"Duncan." The sound was hardly more than a whisper. Lady Sylvia stood motionless, her eyes wide and dark in a face gone suddenly pale.

Duncan took three great strides, leaped up the steps of the dais, and threw his arms around her. "Mother," he said, burying his face in her shoulder. He took a deep breath of her scent; for one short moment, he felt like a small child once more. Then he leaned back and looked her in the eyes. "I didn't run away."

Color was beginning to flood back into his mother's face. "But the note?" she whispered. "The signed note?"

"I didn't write it. He tricked me into signing my name, and then he locked me in and took me away."

"He?" his mother demanded. "Who?"

Duncan turned. "Him," he said, pointing to the man whose face had turned an unhealthy shade of gray beneath its bandage. He raised his voice. "The Earl of Merrick!"

Brig growled.

CHAPTER 27

Cat Justice

THE ROOM HUSHED. Duncan could hear the tick of a clock somewhere, and the quiet scrape of a chair.

The Baron of Dulle was a bulky man, with a nose that tended to be large and a face that tended to be red. He moved hastily, and his chair tipped over with a crash. "Come, my boy. You're overwrought—you've had some difficult experiences. You'll feel better after a good night's sleep." His bluff, good-humored face looked anxiously from Duncan to the tiger.

"No, Daddy, listen to him," Betsy begged.

"Taking advice from little girls now, are you, Baron?" The earl got to his feet with a forced-sounding chuckle. "We're sensible men, you and I—we have no time to listen to the wild imaginings of a couple of children. Allow my men to handle the tiger, if you will—it escaped from my ship, and the boy doesn't realize how dangerous it is."

Brig growled, low in his chest. "I'm dangerous to *you*, chum."

The earl took a step back. Bertram was half out of his chair, and the baron looked from the tiger to Duncan, startled.

"Don't worry, sir, this is a trained tiger," said Duncan quickly. "And I'm not making anything up. The earl kidnapped me, and then once we were far out to sea, he left me to drown!"

Duncan's mother made a small sound. He glanced at her quickly and saw that she had a hand over her mouth.

The earl shook his head as if deeply sad. "My dear boy, you must have hit your head when you fell off my ship. You've been through a terrible time, and your thinking is muddled! I'm delighted to see you're alive, though."

"You *liar*," Duncan said through his teeth. "You just tried to *murder* me. You left me to drown in a cage at the wharf—"

"Wait, now, which is it?" The earl cocked his head to one side. "First you said I left you to drown in the middle of the sea, and now you say I tried to drown you at the wharf. Which one, lad? You seem terribly confused."

"It was both, and you know it!"

"Now, don't get excited," said the earl in a soothing tone. "Come, my boy, you need rest. We'll get you to bed—we'll call in the best doctors to see if they can find a cure. Don't worry," he added, turning to Duncan's mother, "I've seen cases like this recover before, with care. A blow to the head is a terrible thing."

Brig moved restlessly under Duncan's restraining hand. "I'd like to give *him* a blow to the head," he rumbled.

The cats were all meowing at once. Duncan caught Spike's "don't let him play you like a mouse," and Fia's frantic "tell about the *kitten squishing*!" But it was Grizel's meow that steadied him: "A cat does not give up, Duncan—a cat changes tactics. Try a new line of attack."

Duncan took in a breath and pitched his voice so that it could be heard in every corner of the room. "You are all used to thinking of the Earl of Merrick as a hero. But I am here to tell you that he's a traitor. He tried to kill the princess! He tried to kill my father!"

There was a rippling murmur from the crowd; heads were shaken, lips were pursed. Someone laughed.

The earl turned so that he faced both Duncan and the crowd. "Of course the lad prefers to believe that I am the traitor. We understand, my boy. It's hard to accept such a terrible truth about your very own fath—"

"It's *not* the truth!" Duncan flung his head back as he stared at his mortal enemy. "He wasn't a traitor, he wasn't a liar, he wasn't a murderer—you were! And I have proof!"

A mumbling mutter rose from the crowd, sounding like a swarm of angry bees. A few loud-voiced comments came clear: "But the earl had a whole shipful of witnesses!" "We're glad you're alive, Duncan, but you're talking nonsense!" "The young duke is as deluded as his father was!"

Duncan flushed hotly. This wasn't going well.

"Tell how the princess is still alive," urged Fia, at Duncan's feet.

"He can't," snapped Spike. "Not until the king knows."

"Otherwise the dirty hound might go back to the island and finish the job," growled Brig.

"Remember," said Grizel, "you are the young duke. Act with dignity, like a cat. Breathe in and out calmly, without ruffling the whiskers."

Duncan nodded. His heart was pounding so violently that it seemed it might burst out of his chest, but he stepped up onto the dais and raised his hand to quiet the crowd. "I know this is hard to believe. It took me a long time to believe it, too. But everything those witnesses thought they saw was a fake—nothing but a staged shadow play, acted out against the sunset."

"This is nonsense!" roared the earl. "Don't listen to him!"

Suddenly there came three high, piercing notes, played with power on the violin by someone who knew how to get attention with music. Everyone fell silent as the duchess lowered her violin.

"Go ahead, son," she said, her eyes like dark pools. "Speak so everyone can hear."

Duncan filled his lungs and spoke loudly. "The witnesses

thought they saw my father stabbing the earl treacherously and throwing the princess to the ground," he said. "But it was just the earl, wearing my father's tall hat. My father was tied up out of sight the whole time—"

The earl gave a high, scornful laugh. "He told you this himself, I suppose," he said. "What, do you want us to believe that your father spoke to you from the dead?"

An ache, sudden and unexpected, filled Duncan's chest at the words. "I spoke to someone who was tied up with him. She told me everything."

"She?" The earl's face went a pasty white beneath the yellowed bandage.

"Yes, *she*!" Duncan flung off all caution. "You know who I'm talking about, don't you? And she told me you got that cut on your forehead from an old lady's sewing scissors!"

Someone in the crowd tittered. The earl looked sharply over the assembly, and his mouth thinned. "Come, Baron," he said, "this is neither the time nor the place to listen to a delusional boy. Let Bertram take him away to a quiet room to rest."

Bertram took a step toward Duncan, but Brig snarled.

"That's a dangerous beast!" shouted the earl. "Men! Capture the tiger!"

The earl's men moved closer. There was a panicked scrambling in the first few rows as people tried to get out of the way.

"Sir!" Duncan cried to the baron. "Don't let him do it— the tiger won't hurt anyone unless I give the order!"

The earl showed his teeth in a terrifying smile. "Let me remind you, Baron, that I outrank you."

"Let me remind you, Earl, that someone else here out-ranks *you*—and you are a guest in my home," the baron snapped. "Stay back, everyone!"

He stepped up to stand beside Duncan and spoke low. "You don't have armed men behind you, and I may not be able to hold him off for long. You say the tiger is trained?"

Duncan nodded, his heart in his throat. "He won't hurt anyone unless they try to hurt me."

Duncan's mother promptly put her hand on the tiger's back and stroked his fur. "Good tiger," she whispered.

Brig's chest rumbled with something that sounded like a very powerful purr.

The baron raised his voice as Bertram edged closer. "You say you have proof of your accusations, Duncan. What proof?"

The earl cried, "Proof? What further proof do you need than this?" He pulled off his yellowed bandage and pointed to his forehead. "This is the mark of a traitor's sword!"

The scar, jagged and white, was a good two inches long. Duncan felt a moment's flash of respect for old Mattie—he hadn't known that sewing scissors could do that much damage. And then something else occurred to him. Something, he realized with growing excitement, that he should have thought of long ago.

"So you say my father attacked you," Duncan said loudly.

"And then, you say, he sailed away? With his sword still covered in your blood, I suppose?"

"Dripping with it," snapped the earl.

Bertram moved a step closer. "Boss," he whispered.

The earl ignored him and raised his voice to the crowd like a storyteller. "The duke sailed away with the princess. My men and I took the other boat and went after him, but we were too late. He sailed into a whirlpool, and it sucked them down right before our eyes."

"It sucked them down?" Duncan repeated. "Princess, duke, sword, and all?"

"That's what I said, you stupid boy!"

Duncan reached for the hilt of his father's sword and pulled it out across his body with one strong motion. "*This* sword?" he said, holding it high.

The insignia on the pommel winked in the light. The Baron of Dulle leaned close to peer at it, frowning. The stamp of *McK* under a crown, inside a double square, showed up clearly, and even the three thin lines on either side shone in the candlelight, made brilliant by the chandelier overhead.

Duncan raised his voice so that it echoed from the rafters. "If the Duke of Arvidia sailed away with the princess, never to be seen again," he said clearly, "and he took his sword with him, dripping with your blood—how is it, then, that I found my father's sword on your ship, together with his slashed and bloody jacket?"

The earl's mouth opened and shut, like the mouth of a fish.

Duncan's mother gripped the tiger's fur so tightly that he whimpered.

"Maybe the jacket floated," Bertram muttered.

The baron's face had been growing redder by the moment. Purple veins stuck out on his neck. "And did the sword float, too?" he demanded, glaring at the earl. "Or is there something else you're not telling us?"

Bertram was at the earl's elbow. "Let's get away now—we can deal with this later—"

"Brig, keep them here," ordered Duncan.

"Yes, sir!" The tiger stepped forward, snarling.

The earl and Bertram froze in place. Suddenly there was a commotion in the back of the ballroom, and a man strode forward.

He was not dressed for an evening concert. In fact, he wore the same salt-stained clothes that he had on the last time Duncan had seen him.

"Tammas!" Duncan cried, and Duncan's mother gasped.

Tammas, sturdy, sun-browned, smelling of fish and tobacco, stumped up to the baron and stood squarely before him. "I don't know what lies you have been told, my lord baron," he said, "but I sailed over from Duke's Island just to keep the young duke safe from *him*!" He glared at the Earl of Merrick. "The earl knew who Duncan was—how could he not? Just look at the boy—he's the image of his father! But still he sent his men to capture the boy and make him a prisoner in the earl's ship. I saw it all from a distance."

"But," the earl sputtered, "his tiger was trying to attack me!"

"Any sensible tiger would." Tammas lifted his voice. "In any case, I'm a loyal subject of the true Duke of Arvidia, and there he stands!" He threw out an arm to point to Duncan. "If anyone wants to threaten him, they'll have to go through me first."

"And me," rumbled Brig.

But now there was another interruption, and this one came with the blare of a trumpet at the door and the sound of shouting. A man rushed in, breathing hard, and made his way through the frightened crowd to the baron and baroness.

"My lord—my lady," the man gasped, holding his side. "A ship—just in—"

"That's one of our guards," Betsy whispered to Duncan.

"Well? Speak up, man!" said the baron.

"My lord—the king is dead!"

Candle flames burned with a soft hiss in a room gone so silent and still it seemed that everyone had forgotten to breathe. Then the Baron of Dulle straightened his shoulders and stepped forward, commanding the room.

"The king is dead!" the baron roared, and his words echoed from the walls. He turned to face Duncan. "Long live the king!"

The baron bowed low. With a whisper of moving cloth, the whole assembly bowed, too.

There was a moment of shock so great that it felt as if the earth had shifted beneath Duncan's feet.

His eyes didn't seem to be working in the usual way. The crowded room had melted into a sort of burnished haze. Here and there, individual faces stood out, sharp and clear and etched forever in his mind, their expressions an odd mix of sorrow, excitement, and awe. Even his own mother was kneeling to him.

Strangely, the Earl of Merrick was whispering in Betsy's ear.

The wind outside had picked up. It sifted through half-open windows so that the curtains billowed in great curving waves, like sails. Somewhere a candle guttered out with a little spurt. And then the crowd was on its feet and the hall was alive with cheering, shouting, and it was all for him.

Duncan stood perfectly still, his hand rooted in Brig's neck fur. He could feel the tiger's warmth and living muscle against his thigh, the slight pressure as Brig's flanks moved in and out with the tiger's breathing. Grizel was meowing something at him, her mouth open, but he couldn't hear her over the noise.

His initial bewilderment was turning to realization. He was not used to thinking of himself as a duke, but of course he had been one ever since his father had died. And a duke was of higher rank than an earl. As far as everyone knew, Duncan was next in line for the throne.

Betsy moved at the corner of his vision, her face

frightened. She came close to his ear. "The earl told me to say that you'd better talk to him and give him what he wants, or he'll tell," she whispered. "What will he tell?"

Duncan raised his head to see the Earl of Merrick smile crookedly as he pulled something from his vest pocket. It swung gently on its chain, catching the light with a gleam of gold. Princess Lydia's ring.

In a flash, Duncan understood. The earl had guessed that the princess was still alive. But he thought that Duncan wanted to keep on being king, to keep the crown for himself. So the earl was threatening to tell about the princess, unless Duncan gave him—what? Castles, land, money, a royal pardon for his crimes?

The earl thought Duncan was just as wicked as himself. Duncan could not repress a shudder.

The Earl of Merrick's smile grew a little broader. He gave Duncan the ghost of a wink and tucked the ring back in his pocket.

Duncan's temper rose and foamed like a cresting wave. The only reason he hadn't told about the princess yet was because he was protecting her—he didn't want the earl to find out before the king.

But the king was dead. He, Duncan, was king now; everyone had to obey his orders. The blood mounted to his head, thundering in his ears.

"Don't do anything in anger!" Grizel meowed beside him. "A cat is cautious!"

Duncan ignored her. He was going to deal with the earl once and for all.

"Princess Lydia is *alive*!" Duncan said, his voice ringing out. "I found her on the island where the Earl of Merrick left her to die. We must sail there at once, and Bertram and the earl must be put in chains!"

There was a sudden explosive movement near the front of the ballroom. Bertram was on his feet, wielding his chair like a weapon. The earl himself rocketed over the potted palm and along the side aisle before anyone could react.

GGGRRRROOOOAAAAHHH!!! Brig's outraged roar filled the ballroom as he leaped after the fleeing men.

"Seize them! Seize them!" the baron shouted, but the guests in the ballroom parted down the middle as the tiger came charging through. Duncan saw their shocked faces like so many painted dolls as he tore after Brig. Behind him he heard the thud of feet as the baron and half the room followed.

Someone threw a chair at the fleeing men, but it hit Brig instead. Then the tiger's claws caught in the swinging velvet curtain. Worst of all, the baron's guards, called down from the tower, were confused and thought the tiger was attacking.

"*Aarrrgh!*" roared Brig, and he gave a mighty twist to avoid a flailing sword. He came down hard, skidding on his claws.

"NO!" cried the baron. "Not the tiger—get the *earl*!"

But the earl and Bertram had already escaped. Duncan

ran through the great front door, his heart thudding. If the earl got to his ship—if he set out for Traitor Island—

But the earl and Bertram had not gotten away. They stood on the sheep-bitten grass surrounded by a ring of cats, seven circles deep, with more coming all the time. The cats' eyes glowed like small colored coals in the night.

"Go away! Bad kitties!" the earl cried. Bertram aimed a violent kick at the cat who was nearest.

The cat avoided his feet easily, while cats behind dashed to claw at Bertram's legs. Seven more leaped on the earl's back, biting his ears, raking his neck, and meowing insults in his ears. In an instant, at least thirty cats had fastened themselves to the two men, all howling in concert.

Grizel padded up and peered through Duncan's legs. "A fine performance of Cat Trick #48. The best I've ever heard!"

"I don't remember #48," Duncan said.

"Repeated Insistent Yowling, of course," said Grizel. "If it's done correctly, it can drive a human nearly mad."

"They're down," said Betsy, who had pushed in next to Duncan. "No, they're up again—"

"That won't last long," said Tammas, chuckling as the earl and Bertram staggered in circles, trying to shake off cats as they went. Now and then, a cat went flying, but it would land lightly on its feet and another cat jumped up to take its place.

"The cats are substituting for each other," Duncan said, climbing onto the balustrade for a better view. "It's like they're playing some sort of cat team sport. There's always a fresh one ready to come in."

"I'm playing too!" roared Brig. He bounded joyfully across the lawn and into the fray. With one heavy blow of his paw, both Bertram and the earl were knocked on their backs. The other cats promptly pounced on top in a yowling, smothering pile of fur and claws and lashing tails.

One of the baron's men stepped forward. "Shall we put them in chains, my lord?"

The baron snorted with laughter. "Yes, if you can get them out from under the cats. I don't know what the earl did to make them angry, but they're doing an excellent job of punishing him for it." He wiped his eyes, still laughing. "Cat justice! I love it!"

The baron's guards reached into the writhing, furry mass and snagged two feebly kicking legs. With a clank and a snap, shackles were attached to their ankles, and the earl and Bertram were hauled to their feet. They clung to the guards, their faces pale as they shrank from the mob of hissing cats.

Duncan jumped down from the balustrade and flung his arms around Brig's thick, soft neck. "Good work, Brigadier. You came just in the nick of time."

"Thank you, sir," rumbled Brig plaintively. "May I please have a sheep *now*?"

CHAPTER 28

Kittens' Revenge

THEY SAILED FOR CAPITAL CITY AT DAWN. When they landed, an emergency session of the Arvidian Council was called at the palace. And before nightfall, Duncan was sworn in as King and Protector of the Realm.

"But I'm not really the king," he said.

"You are," said his mother, "until we find the princess alive and well."

Mr. Corbie, the old sailing master, had been called to the palace and was deep in consultation with Tammas. They spread out the charts on a vast table in the royal library and began to plot a course.

"I've sighted that island," said the sailing master, "from a distance. But Tammas has anchored there, and he knows the currents and reefs. I'll want him along to help."

Duncan said, "I can help, too."

His mother straightened abruptly. "You won't be going."

"You must stay here, in the palace," said the baron. "Arvidia can't lose another king, not so soon."

Duncan glared at them. It was the same old thing; someone was always trying to keep him safe. He opened his mouth to argue, but Grizel meowed at him from the window seat where she lay curled in the last golden rays of the setting sun.

Duncan stalked to the library window, his hands jammed in his pockets.

"Remember your training," Grizel meowed softly. "A cat never argues, nor does it plead. A cat considers the facts calmly and then decides. A king should do the same."

Duncan gazed out the window for a long moment. Below him, Capital City lay spread out like a patchwork quilt, and in the harbor was a ship at anchor. Beyond that was the blue-green sea, stretching to the horizon. Somewhere, out there, the princess and old Mattie were waiting for him.

Duncan turned with dignity and heard Grizel give an approving sniff.

"I promised I'd go back for them," he said. "And I'm the only one who knows how to get to the interior of the island. You need me to come along."

"It would be most helpful," the sailing master admitted.

Duncan's mother clasped her hands together. "I can't let you go again! You only just returned to me!"

"You can sail with us." Duncan smiled at his mother. "And I'll appoint the Baron of Dulle to be my regent. He can stay here and rule until we bring the princess back—to be queen."

Duncan climbed high on the ship's rigging and turned his spyglass on the far horizon. By the sailing master's calculations, they should have sighted Traitor Island two days ago. But even Tammas admitted that sailing was not an exact science . . . and they were on the far edge of the known world, where currents collided and winds were violent.

Duncan looked down at the deck a moment to rest his eyes and frowned slightly as he caught sight of Brig. The tiger was another worry.

Brig hadn't been himself since the day they sailed from Capital City. He picked at his food with a disinterested claw, stared glumly into space, and sighed a great deal; even obeying orders didn't seem to give him much satisfaction, and he refused to say what was wrong. Duncan let out his breath in an exasperated puff. Whatever was bothering the tiger, it seemed clear that he wanted to work it out on his own.

Meanwhile, Duncan was glad to be sailing again. Tammas was teaching him how to use a sextant and take the altitude of the sun. Duncan liked learning how to find his way on the trackless sea. One of these days, he was going to be an excellent navigator, Tammas said.

If only he could find Traitor Island! Duncan put the glass to his eye again and scanned the far, thin line where blue sky met bluer sea.

The breeze had freshened and was growing stronger. Duncan clung with his legs and gave a brief wave to his mother, who had just come on deck. He was starting to get used to this new, laughing mother who let the wind whip her hair and never wore a scarf at all, much less an ugly green one.

She answered every question he asked about his father now, as fully as possible. And she had explained about the grave on the hilltop cemetery, too.

"I saw a tombstone with the initials CDM," she had said, "and I told you they were your father's initials. Naturally you thought that meant the grave was his, and I let you believe it. There was so little I could tell you; I wanted to let you have something, however small. And I wasn't lying—the initials *were* his."

Duncan blinked. Then he rubbed his eyes and looked again. "LAND!" he bellowed. "TRAITOR ISLAND!"

∞

They had had weeks on the return trip for Lydia to get used to the idea of being an orphan—and a queen. Mattie had found the trunk of new clothes that had been brought for Lydia, and she'd promptly begun to sew, altering them to fit. And there were daily sessions with the duchess on everything from court etiquette to affairs of state. So on the evening when the ship sailed into the Capital City harbor with signal flags flying, Lydia put on her new royal garments, listened to her twenty-one-gun salute with calm composure, and walked down the gangplank to the sound of trumpets as if she had been hearing them all her life.

Brig disappeared somewhere into the twilight the minute they docked. Duncan was just as happy to let him go. The tiger had been moody the entire trip, and Duncan was tired of asking him what was wrong.

That night, Duncan slept in a huge chamber at the palace, on a vast feather bed with a swansdown pillow—and the feeling that his room was rocking beneath him. He almost felt as if he were still on the sea, he had been afloat for so long.

Early the next morning, Duncan swung his leg idly from a broad marble windowsill and stroked Grizel as she purred beside him. He gazed at the spacious landing, the Persian carpets, and the wide, sweeping staircase descending below, and wondered when Lydia was going to wake up. They had a plan to visit the palace dungeon.

The baron had told them that he'd transferred the earl and Bertram from the jail at Dulle to the more secure dungeon in the palace. "Some of the island cats seemed to want to come too," the baron had added, chuckling, "so I let 'em. I'll tell you this—cats on a ship, or in a jail, make for fewer rats!"

Duncan fidgeted. He wanted to see for himself that the Earl of Merrick was locked up securely, but if Lydia didn't hurry up, there would be no time. She was going to be crowned today.

There was a click of claws on the marble floor behind him, and a tiger's apologetic cough. "Sir?"

Duncan raised an eyebrow. Brig's moody expression was gone, and in its place was a look of high delight. Yet his tail was held low—something Duncan had hardly ever seen. In cat language, it meant the cat was unsure or needed a favor.

"What is it, Brig?"

The inside of Brig's ears turned pink. "Might I take a leave from active duty, sir? For a few days . . . or weeks . . . or maybe more? I want to go on a nice, long—er—"

Duncan waited.

"Honeymoon," the tiger said in a small voice.

Duncan choked. Something horribly like a hoot seemed caught in his throat, and he strained a cheek muscle trying not to grin.

Brig cleared his throat. "You may remember," he said, "that the Fahrian miners left *two* tigers with the royal ship, as a gift to the king. I was one. The other tiger was a young female, barely more than a cub. Anyway, the earl brought her to the king, who put her in the zoo here in Capital City. Betsy took me there to visit, before we set sail for Traitor Island."

"Aha!" said Duncan.

Grizel's purr stopped. She lifted her head alertly.

Brig's ears turned pink right down to his scalp. "Well, that tiger is older now. She has a really lovely pattern of stripes, quite fetching, and such perky ears—"

Grizel made a rasping noise that sounded like a snort, suddenly smothered.

Duncan gave up the battle to keep from grinning. "What's her name?"

Brig's furry face took on a besotted look. "Bertha," he said tenderly. "Isn't that the most beautiful name you've ever heard? Berrrrrtha," he murmured, stretching out on the parquet floor. He closed his eyes, as if in some happy dream.

"A name meant to be purred," said Duncan, gazing at the tiger fondly.

"She doesn't like the zoo," Brig said earnestly. "I finally got up the nerve this morning to ask her to be my mate. And she said *yes*! So I was wondering, would you let us live on Duke's Island, in the forest? The wild is a much better place for a tiger than a zoo. And Bertha thinks it would be a much better place to raise the cubs." He smiled foolishly.

Duncan chuckled. "Sure, you and Bertha can live in the forest on my island—"

"Oh, sir!" Brig reared back in an excess of joy. "I'll tell her right away!"

"On one condition," Duncan added. "Promise to stay away from my sheep—if I ever get any, that is."

A door squeaked somewhere down the hall, and Lydia dashed out with one shoe in her hand. "Hurry! I barely escaped. Get out of sight, or they'll catch us!"

"Who?" Duncan held Lydia's arm as she hopped into her second shoe.

"Servants!" Lydia hissed. "They want to do everything for me! It's making me crazy!"

They ran on tiptoes along the echoing hall and turned a maze of corners, followed (more slowly) by Grizel. "Right, left, right, right," Lydia whispered, keeping track of the turns. "I studied a map of the castle. I'm pretty sure this is where we go down."

They had come to a narrow staircase of stone, rough-hewn and with no handrail, that curled down and around a central tower. One hundred and fifty-three steps down, they stopped at a wooden panel in the tower wall and slid it open.

Spike was there, curled up on an inner ledge. "Visiting hours are—oh, hello! It's you!"

Duncan raised an eyebrow. The cats had things awfully organized if they had set up visiting hours for the dungeon. He stuck his head over the ledge and looked down.

Twenty feet below was a small, stone-walled room with two benches, two buckets, and two men sitting hunched. A pungent smell rose up, and Duncan could guess at the contents of one of the buckets, at least. A bit of crisscrossed iron showed where the barred door must be, and a torch on the wall filled the dungeon cell with flickering light and shadow.

The earl looked up. His expression, forbidding in the wavering light, turned wicked. "Come to gloat, have you?" he shouted up at Duncan.

Lydia pressed up against Duncan's side and peered down as well.

The earl gave a great start. "Who are you?" he demanded.

"I am the Princess Lydia, whom you betrayed!" Her voice carried down the echoing tower, clear and cold and regal.

There was a strangled sound from below.

"She's the *queen* now," Duncan shouted down.

The earl laughed, a harsh noise almost like a sob. "You're a bigger fool than your father, you stupid boy."

Duncan frowned. "What do you mean?"

"You could have been *king*. . . ." The earl's voice drifted up like smoke, dark and oily. "But now you're only second-best."

Something glistened briefly in midair, like a short burst of falling golden rain.

"Nooooooooo! Not *again*!" The two men ducked and covered their heads, moving as far down their benches as their chains would allow.

Duncan looked up. Wooden beams crossed the tower above him, going from wall to wall in a pattern like the spokes of a wheel, and on the beams were . . .

"*Kittens?*" said Duncan in disbelief.

Spike meowed, "Why not? They're practicing their balancing skills. Of course," he added, his whiskers twitching, "they're not all litter-trained yet. They're still very young, you know."

"Litter-trained?" Duncan mouthed.

"You'd call it potty-trained, I believe." Spike turned aside to cough into his paw. "It seems to cause some inconvenience to the gentlemen below. However, what they did to kittens was far worse."

Duncan had to agree. The earl *had* done far worse, and not just to kittens, either. He gazed out along the wooden beam and saw Fia's bright, mismatched eyes staring back. He waved.

"So," Duncan said to Lydia, "what are you going to do with the earl and Bertram? Leave them here forever?"

Fia leaped down from the beam to sit on the ledge beside Spike. "She could cut off their heads!"

"Or have them clawed to death," Spike meowed. "We cats would be glad to oblige. Or we could feed them a diet of hairballs until they exploded."

Lydia pulled her head out of the dungeon tower. "I think I'll just put them on the chain gang and have them break rocks the rest of their lives."

"If they break rocks into gravel, you could use it for kitty litter," Spike said.

"I know some cats who could use it," Fia said darkly.

Duncan snorted with laughter. "Kitty litter—that's perfect!" he meowed without thinking.

Lydia turned, her eyes brightly attentive. Her hand went to her pocket, and there was a sound of crinkling paper.

Duncan stopped meowing. He had forgotten to be careful in front of Lydia.

"Go on," she said. "Talk to the cats. I know you can."

"Er—what?" Duncan hoped he looked mystified. He carefully shut the sliding panel to the dungeon tower.

Lydia pulled a folded piece of paper out of her pocket. "The baron gave this to me last night—he found it among my father's papers. It was in a sealed envelope, addressed to me. My father wrote it just before he died."

Duncan moved beneath a flaring torch in a wall cresset, and read:

> My Dear Lydia,
> If you are reading this, you have been found at long last.
> How I wish I could give you a father's last embrace and
> the counsel you will need to rule wisely as queen! I can,
> however, tell you a secret that only I know. I pass it on to
> you in the hope that there is still one person in this land
> who can speak Cat.

Duncan sagged against the stone wall.

Grizel padded down the steps, curling her tail like a question mark.

"You're the one, aren't you?" Lydia took a step closer. "You're the one who can speak Cat."

Duncan looked at Grizel. She had made him promise not to tell, ever.

Grizel's whiskers cupped forward. "Read it aloud," she meowed.

Duncan read.

> A cat can go everywhere and hear everything. Someone
> who can speak Cat, therefore, is a valuable adviser to a
> ruler who wishes to know the truth—and I had such an
> adviser, in Duke Charles of Arvidia.

Duncan slid down to sit on the narrow steps, and Grizel leaped up to his shoulder, looking down at the letter.

*Now, I know you may think the duke is a traitor, yet I think
there may have been some terrible misunderstanding. I can
hardly believe that my old friend would change so much.*

Duncan blinked. For some reason, his eyes were filling.
He brushed the back of his hand across his eyes and read on.

*Be that as it may, long ago, Duke Charles promised he
would make sure his son was instructed in Cat, so that
someday the boy could be your adviser, as Duke Charles
was mine.*

*The boy has disappeared. But if he is found, ask him
if he has this skill, for it will help you greatly as you try
to discover the heart and mind of your people.*

Duncan let the letter fall to his lap.

"I always sort of wondered." Lydia faltered. "I mean, you
meowed and growled, and Brig obeyed you right away—but it
seemed so crazy."

"Go ahead," meowed Grizel. "You can tell her."

"But—" Duncan was meowing now, too. "You always told
me the reason you taught me Cat was because you felt sorry
for me when my father died."

"I did feel sorry for you." Grizel slipped down onto his lap
and looked up into his face. "But your father also asked me to
teach you when the time was right."

Duncan still felt dazed. "Who taught *him*, though? You?"

"Of course not. I'm not that old," said Grizel. "But I knew

the granddaughter of the cat who taught him. And the great-great-grandson of the cat who taught *his* father."

"You mean this has been going on for three dukes in a row?"

"Longer than that," said Grizel, looking pleased with herself. "I admit, the first cat who began it did it for her own amusement. But ever since then, it's been a duty we cats take very seriously. Haven't you ever wondered why the insignia for the Duke of Arvidia looks like a cat?"

"It does?" said Duncan.

Grizel used her claw to scratch lightly on the stone. "See this square with the two triangles on top?"

"That's a crown."

"No, it's a cat. See, the triangles are the ears."

Duncan bent over the drawing. Of course! And the lines at the side weren't rays of light, but—

"Whiskers," said Grizel, drawing them in. "You see? It's the Sign of the Cat."

"With the letters *McK* to show that the McKinnons are the Cat-Speakers," Duncan finished. It was all starting to fit. But there was one thing more that bothered him. "Did you ever hear about my father serving a dish called . . ." He hesitated.

"Kitty pie? Cataroni and cheese?" Grizel chuckled in the half-coughing, half-hissing way that cats express amusement. "Charming idea of your father's. He had his cook make special dishes when the cats came in with their reports. A little incentive, you might say."

Duncan looked at her, horrified.

"Those little pastry ears!" Grizel purred, squeezing her eyes shut. "That braided pastry tail wound around the outside of the pie . . . so delicately crunchy! And the cataroni and cheese was very good indeed, very slippery in the mouth."

Duncan felt as if his voice were coming from far away. "But what was *in* the pies?"

Grizel lifted her shoulders in a shrug. "Fish, bird, mouse—mouse was my favorite."

Duncan breathed again. Of course! The earl had misunderstood. He had thought the dishes were made *of* cats, not *for* cats. The earl had misunderstood a lot of things. But Duncan had not answered Lydia yet.

"Yes," he said to Queen Lydia. "I can speak Cat."

It was late at night in the palace. The crowning ceremony was over. Duncan shrugged off his velvet coronation robe with the ermine collar, set his gold coronet on a dressing table, and sent his servant to bed.

He was tired, but he could not sleep. The day had been packed full—first the visit to the dungeon, then the crowning, then the coronation dinner and dance—and he couldn't slow his mind enough to rest. He paced his room, pausing by the table that held his coronet. It was a smaller crown than the queen's, and it had only one jewel.

Duncan turned abruptly away. He padded softly across the marble hall to the landing and the window that looked out over the city. Someone had left newspapers on the window seat. The moon was so bright that he could pick out the head-lines: "Earl of Merrick's No Hero!" and "Queen Safe, Thanks to Bold Young Duke!"

He pushed aside the papers and sat down. Capital City spread beneath him, etched in silvery light. Far down the hill lay the wharf, with its tall ships floating quietly, sails furled; he had arrived on one of them yesterday. High on the hill was the cathedral, where today a queen had been crowned to the peal of bells and a crowd's roaring acclaim. And off in the distance was the Academy, where he would enroll tomorrow.

What did he have left to wish for?

To come in first, the earl's voice seemed to whisper in his ear. *To be king.*

Duncan felt something twist inside, as if a coiled snake had suddenly lifted its head. Was it true? Was that what he had secretly wanted, all along?

"Can't sleep?" Mattie's gentle voice interrupted his thoughts. Her slippers shuffled along the marble floor, and her candle spread a soft glow on the wall.

Duncan jumped up. "Please, sit down," he said, clearing the papers away. His eye caught the bold type below the fold: "Wild Tiger Stripes—Hot New Style for Fall," and "Stop! Don't Eat That Sausage (It May Be Someone's Pet)."

Mattie clasped her gnarled hands in her lap, and moon-light traced the fine network of wrinkles in her cheeks. "We old folks are often wakeful. But what's keeping a young man like you up at night?"

Duncan did not answer. He was wondering why he didn't mind coming in second, this time.

"Do you miss Traitor Island?" he asked abruptly.

"Oh, yes," Mattie said, raising her cloudy eyes. "But I'll see it again, I'm sure."

"How will you get there?"

"You'll take me," she said, and a crinkling smile spread over her face. She pulled a square of lace out of her pocket and held it up to the moonlight. "Because I'm going to Fahr."

Duncan didn't know what to say. Was the old lady losing her wits?

Mattie chuckled as if she knew what was on his mind. "I may not have told you," she said, "but when your father, Duke Charles, said he would take the miners back across the Rift to their land, I gave him a bit of lace for luck. To tuck in his pocket, you see?"

Duncan nodded, still confused.

"When he returned, he had a necklace of small jewels. Lydia told you about it, I think."

Duncan nodded again. Was this going anywhere?

Mattie leaned forward, her cloudy eyes suddenly bright. "The miners had never seen anything like my lace! No one in Fahr knows how to knit!"

"That's nice," said Duncan, "but I still don't get—"

"They traded a *jeweled necklace* for that square of lace! And they said that if your father ever came back, he should bring all the lace he could, because they could sell it in their country."

Duncan was dumbfounded.

"Now, on the ship you showed us that chart of your father's. You said the earl had planned to use it to rob the Fahrians of their jewels. Why shouldn't we use the chart to trade with them, instead of stealing and going to war? The Rift is still dangerous, but in the summer months, with a good crew and a sailing master . . ."

Grizel came padding down the hall with the slowness of an old cat, but her ears were alert.

"Well, it's been a lovely chat," said Mattie, getting up with an effort. "Remember, there are lots of old women like me who make lace."

Duncan stared after the elderly figure limping down the hall with growing excitement. That was it! That was *exactly* what he wanted to do! He had always wanted to explore, to find new places, and—well, of course school had to come first. But why shouldn't he do what Mattie suggested? Maybe his mother wouldn't let him cross the Rift when he was this young. But every summer he could sail with Tammas. Every year he would learn more and grow older. There *would* come a time when he could cross the Rift, with a tiger to help sense the rocks and dangerous shoals. There would come a time when he could lead an expedition to the country of Fahr and give the old women of Arvidia a chance to earn a decent living and bring back jewels in trade.

Grizel butted her head against Duncan's leg, and he picked her up and held her in his lap. In the distance the Academy dome shone pale against the darker trees, and its spire pierced the moon. Suddenly Duncan felt light, as light as seafoam on a high, curling wave.

Who said he wanted to be king? That had never been his dream. He didn't want to be stuck in a palace, making judgments and having meetings and wearing heavy robes that itched.

And he had never expected to come in first *all* the time. No one could do that. The thing he had really wanted was to stop pretending to be less than he was.

Grizel purred under his hand, and Duncan stroked her head, smiling. He didn't need to plan the rest of his life out this minute. He was going to the Academy tomorrow. He would line his room with books, and he would hang his father's sword on the wall. That was enough glory for now.

"I'm looking forward to fencing with Robert," Duncan told Grizel.

The cat twisted her neck to look back at him. "I hope you're not going to lose on purpose next time."

Duncan grinned. "Never again," he said.

Acknowledgments

THE AUTHOR WISHES TO ACKNOWLEDGE THE following, with a grateful heart:

Drue Heinz, for the Hawthornden Castle Fellowship—a precious month in which to write with no distractions whatsoever, in an atmosphere of "peace and decent ease."

Kathleen Coskran, for weeks of splendid hospitality at the Malmo Art Colony.

Lisa Bullard, for lending me her very thick cat book and answering questions for three solid hours on all things feline.

Stephen Barbara, agent of agents, who listened to the story at its earliest stage and said, "I like the tiger."

Laura Amy Schlitz, friend of friends, who sent me her best cat books and all her knowledge of Murphy and Susannah, cats extraordinaire.

Swati Avasthi, Heather Bouwman, Stephanie Watson, and Anne Ursu, who gave critiques that exceeded all prior standards of excellence for any writers' group heretofore known.

Christy Ottaviano, who loved the book, bought the book, edited the book, and patiently shepherded the book as it jumped through the many hoops of publishing.

And Bill, as always.

GOFISH

QUESTIONS FOR THE AUTHOR

LYNNE JONELL

What did you want to be when you grew up?
A writer, an artist, a singer, an actor, a brain surgeon, a pilot, and a superhero. Oh, and a missionary, during my holy periods (admittedly somewhat short).

When did you realize you wanted to be a writer?
I got the first real inklings in third grade. But I was sure one day in sixth grade, when I read the last page of *A Wrinkle in Time.* That's when I knew that what I wanted most of all was to write books like that, for kids just like me.

What's your first childhood memory?
Being tossed in a blanket by my big brother and sister. The heart-stopping swoop and drop—and laughing out loud in the middle of it, delight and terror mixed!

What's your most embarrassing childhood memory?

The day Rick Johnson caught me crawling on my stomach at the local park with a stick. Rick started to laugh and accused me of playing army. I was too embarrassed to tell him I was a Dakota scout, about to save my tribe from the warring Apaches.

As a young person, who did you look up to most?

My dad. He was my first hero and still is.

What was your worst subject in school?

Math. It took me a long time to get over my habit of counting on my fingers. (Actually, I may not quite be over it yet.)

What was your first job?

Taking out the wastepaper baskets (when I was a kid). First job when I was a teen was working the Christmas rush at a store called LaBelle's. Two weeks of horror, as I recall, trying to look busy dusting useless objects on glass shelves, and a break room full of cigarette smoke.

How did you celebrate publishing your first book?

I can't even remember, can you believe it? I'm brain-dead, I tell you! Brain-dead! But it probably involved wine and song. And a fabulous meal with someone I loved.

But I can tell you how I celebrated when I got an offer for a second and third book together: I bought a little sailboat and hit the water!

Where do you write your books?

Wherever I can. I start in my office at home, and when that fails, I go to the kitchen or dining room. Pretty soon, I'm out on the patio (if it's warm enough) or at a coffee shop (if it's cold). I've written in airport terminals and at resorts and on planes and in hotels, on notebooks and computers and paper napkins. Basically, if one place doesn't work, I try another until something clicks.

Where do you find inspiration for your writing?

Also wherever I can!

What sparked your inspiration for *The Sign of the Cat*?

A book, for me, usually starts with an image, and sometimes another fragment—perhaps a personality, or a situation, or a single plot point. Most of the time I don't know where these things come from. Sometimes, much later on, I figure it out—but at the time I'm writing the book, I'm traveling without a map or compass.

In the case of *The Sign of the Cat*, very early on I knew it would be about a boy who could speak Cat, and whose father had disappeared under mysterious circumstances. I also had a vivid mental image of that same boy leaping off a ship to save a kitten who had been thrown overboard. I saw the boy clinging to a crate while his ship sailed away, and I saw a man on deck, watching.

There was enough interest and power in those images to sustain me for the whole book. Writing then became a process of uncovering what had happened to the boy before that moment, and what was going to happen after.

If you could have a superpower, what would it be?
I have always wished I could fly.

What is your favorite part of this adventure and why?
I think it's that same scene when Duncan is in the sea, bobbing up and down with only Fia for company, and he watches in disbelief as the ship sails away and disappears from sight. For one thing, this is a scene that appeared to me very early on, when I was just toying with the whole idea of the book. And for another, it's a powerful moment. Here's Duncan, who has just been betrayed and abandoned by someone he trusted—and where does he go from there? How does he gather the strength and courage to hang on and not give up?

Who is your favorite character?
I love all my characters, but I have a particular fondness for Brig. I knew there would be a tiger, but I didn't know anything about him. So when it came time to write his first scene, I paused to ask myself some questions. What was his name? What was he like? The tiger's name came immediately, as if it had been waiting all along: "Brig." I thought that was interesting—I had never heard of such a name before—and wondered if it was short for something. "Brigadier," came the answer immediately. And I thought—ah! He's a military tiger! At that point, Brig really just walked onstage and began to speak, and I simply wrote it down. I hardly had to think.

Not all characters come to me like that, but when they do, it's very special!

You did the artwork in this book. Was it fun to render the characters as you imagined them? Did some characteristics change when going from how you dreamed them up in written form to when you drew them? How so? What is your favorite piece?

I loved doing the artwork for this book. The characters and situations were coming alive under my pencil in a different way than they had in the text, and that was a rich experience. I wouldn't say the characters really changed when I drew them—it was more that, in drawing them, I realized them more fully. I knew what they looked like in my head, and I drew until what I saw on paper felt right to me.

And I can't choose one favorite piece; sorry! But I can say that, while the pictures showing dangerous settings and scary things were exciting to draw, I am especially proud of the close-ups of the living characters. I loved infusing their personalities into the drawings.

When you finish a book, who reads it first?

My husband, Bill, is my first reader. He's a good one, too!

Are you a morning person or a night owl?

I am a night owl, nighthawk, nightjar, night crawler . . . my eyes don't really focus until about three in the afternoon. And then I sometimes work all night, to the dismay of my dear first reader.

What's your idea of the best meal ever?

Oh, wow. So many delicious thoughts suddenly flooded my brain that it's paralyzed. Let's see. It would have to involve a green salad that absolutely sings in the mouth—let's say it has red onions, a little prosciutto, maybe gorgonzola cheese, a light fruity vinaigrette . . . then a soup, something with clams and lobster maybe? And—oh, a lovely little pasta dish with an absolutely decadent sauce, butter and cream and wine to start, with some tantalizing spice that I can't quite name. And a very good wine, and maybe some thinly sliced marinated beef that is paired with some lovely, big, fat mushrooms and a few roasted potatoes, crispy on the outside and steaming and tender inside . . . mmmm. And then some cheese and fruit. . . . And, of course, something fabulously chocolate, with raspberries and cream and coffee. And—why not? I think a little champagne!

Which do you like better: cats or dogs?
Oh, cats, no question. They're independent, mysterious, and they have dignity. They don't drool, sniff in embarrassing places, or smell like wet dog.

What do you value most in your friends?
Loyalty, kindness, humor, and a noble heart.

Where do you go for peace and quiet?
My house is actually pretty quiet most of the time. But my favorite spot would be up high, among rocks and a few trees, with the scent of pine and a long view.

What makes you laugh out loud?
Almost everything. I am easily amused. I often laugh at what I write, especially when it's about rabbits.

What's your favorite song?
That changes constantly. But I have to say I love old jazz standards, like "God Bless the Child" and "The Nearness of You."

Who is your favorite fictional character?
David, from *North to Freedom* by Anne Holm.

What are you most afraid of?
Failing to do what I was meant to do with my life.

What time of the year do you like best?
Fall, no question. September is the loveliest month of the year, for me. Warm, glowing, golden, and fleeting.

What is your favorite TV show?
I actually don't have a regular show that I watch. But I used to love *Batman* when I was a kid. *Biff! Bam!! Pow!!!*

If you could travel in time, where would you go?
To the future. I'd like to see how my kids turn out in the end.

What's the best advice you have ever received about writing?
That revision is what separates the women from the girls, the men from the boys, the sheep from the goats. And to not write at all if you don't *have* to . . . but if you do have to, then don't give up until you get it right.

What do you want readers to remember about your books?
The sheer joy and delight of being swept away into another reality and out of their own. . . .

What would you do if you ever stopped writing?
I imagine at that point I really would be brain-dead. I can't really imagine it.

What do you like best about yourself?
That I'm honest.

What is your worst habit?
Checking e-mail a gazillion times a day.

What do you consider to be your greatest accomplishment?
Not quitting when things got tough—whether in writing, marriage, parenting, or any other sphere.

What do you wish you could do better?
I would really love to have a photographic memory. I hate to forget names, and I do it all the time! Plus, it would make memorizing music so much easier.

What would your readers be most surprised to learn about you?
I'm not all that funny in real life. I just think I am.

Emmy is a good girl. The rat is no good at all. Then Emmy does something bad—she frees the rat from its cage. Thus begins a series of strange misadventures.

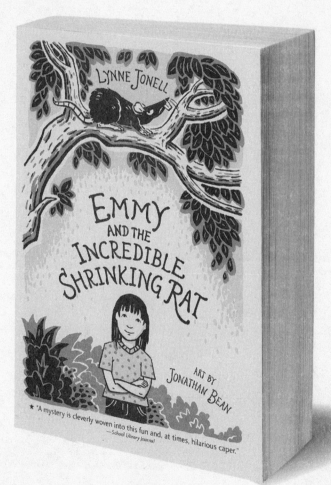

LYNNE JONELL

EMMY
AND THE
INCREDIBLE
SHRINKING RAT

ART BY
JONATHAN BEAN

★ "A mystery is cleverly woven into this fun and, at times, hilarious caper."
—*School Library Journal*

Read on for an excerpt.

EMMY WAS A GOOD GIRL. At least she tried very hard to be good.

She did her homework without being told. She ate all her vegetables, even the slimy ones. And she never talked back to her nanny, Miss Barmy, although it was almost impossible to keep quiet, some days.

Of course no one can keep this kind of thing up forever. But Miss Barmy had told Emmy that if she were a good girl, her parents would probably want to see her more often; and so Emmy kept on bravely trying.

So far it hadn't helped. Emmy's parents went on one vacation after another—to Paris, to Salamanca, to the Isle of Bugaloo—and hardly ever seemed to come home, or even to miss her at all.

"If you did better in school, I'm sure they would be pleased," said Miss Barmy, admiring her polished fingernails.

This was unjust. "My last report card was all As," Emmy said sturdily, remembering how hard she had worked for them.

"But not a single A+, dear." Miss Barmy smiled sweetly, checking her lipstick in a pocket mirror. "And how are your ballet lessons coming? Are you getting any less clumsy?"

Emmy's shoulders slumped. She had tripped just last week.

"Really, Emmaline, your parents might pay attention to you, if you ever did anything worth paying attention *to*. Why don't you bring home some more ribbons and trophies?"

"I have a whole shelfful," Emmy said faintly.

"You'll just have to try a little harder, dear. Fill *two* shelves."

So Emmy did. Not that anyone noticed.

Still, Miss Barmy said that good girls didn't care too much about being noticed—so Emmy tried not to care.

She really was a little *too* good.

Which is why she liked to sit by the Rat.

The Rat was not good at all.

When the children at Grayson Lake Elementary reached in to feed him, he snapped at their fingers. When they had a little trouble with fractions, he sneered. And he often made cutting remarks in a low voice when the teacher was just out of earshot.

Emmy was the only one who heard him. And even she wondered sometimes if she was just imagining things.

DON'T MISS THESE CLASSIC ADVENTURE STORIES FROM LYNNE JONELL!

★ "This exciting ta[l] with just a touch of fan[tasy] and humor, is a winne[r]" —*School Library Jour[nal]* starred review

THE EMMY AND THE RAT SERIES

★ "A mystery is cleverly woven into this fun and, at times, hilarious caper. . . . [A] delightful read." —*School Library Journal* on *Emmy and the Incredible Shrinking Rat*, starred review